T0099566

COLLISION OF CENTURIES

Also by John J. Le Beau

Collision of Evil

Collision of Lies

COLLISION OF CENTURIES

A Franz Waldbaer Novel

JOHN J. LE BEAU

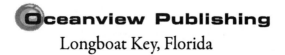
Oceanview Publishing
Longboat Key, Florida

Copyright © 2015 by John J. Le Beau

FIRST EDITION

All rights reserved. No part of this book may be reproduced in any form or by any electronic or mechanical means, including information storage and retrieval systems, without permission in writing from the publisher, except by a reviewer who may quote brief passages in a review.

This book is a work of fiction. Names, characters, businesses, organizations, places, and incidents either are the products of the author's imagination or are used fictitiously. Any resemblance to actual events, businesses, locales, or persons, living or dead, is entirely coincidental.

ISBN: 978-1-60809-162-1

Published in the United States of America by Oceanview Publishing
Longboat Key, Florida

www.oceanviewpub.com

10 9 8 7 6 5 4 3 2 1

PRINTED IN THE UNITED STATES OF AMERICA

FOREWORD

This book is a work of fiction. Nonetheless, the novel is based upon historical accounts of a communicable disease that struck Europe with savage force in the years 1348 through 1350. This disease that hit the center of the western world eventually acquired the title of the bubonic plague, but was most commonly known, and feared, as the Black Death.

The plague that ravaged Europe was virtually unstoppable, having traveled by ship from Asia to Italy, and it is reputed to have killed one out of four people living in Europe at the time; other accounts claim that the death toll was closer to one out of three. In the wake of the plague, society as it had existed up to that time changed. Family lines were entirely wiped out by the plague, a type of social engineering as tragic as it was unintended.

After wrecking the human population for three years and killing cleric as well as commoner, and noble as well as peasant, the plague retreated and took its place as a historical curiosity, but it did not entirely disappear. The plague exists today and is found in rodents and their constant companions, rat fleas, Xenopsylla cheopis, which live off of the blood of their hosts. At the present time the plague is found in the United States, and in parts of Asia and Africa, especially on the island of Madagascar. The plague today is responsive to antibiotics which are frequently—though by no means always—effective.

This novel has many coauthors, if one includes all of the people who contributed their knowledge and informed views and considered speculation. Dr. Kenneth Duncan of Scotland, Father Dr. John Sawicki of Duquesne University and Dr. Peter Forster at Penn State University number among these, as does the late and greatly lamented Nick Pratt, of the George C. Marshall Center for Security Studies in Garmisch, Germany. Dr. John Braithwaite, who divides his time between Germany and Great Britain, was invaluable with his trenchant commentaries and viciously humorous critiques.

For their firm editorial guidance and unerring insistence on logic and common sense, the affectionate contributions of Gerlinde Le Beau, my wife, and Angelika Le Beau, my daughter, were absolutely indispensable.

The author is infinitely grateful to all of these people for their unswerving support.

COLLISION OF CENTURIES

PROLOGUE

The insect was small, about one fourteenth of an inch in length, it was a lusterless dull black in color, and it fed quietly and serenely on a diet of blood. It lived on blood, and died without it.

The insect, unseen in most cases by the human eye, was known to the biologist as Xenopsylla cheopis, but the great majority of men simply called it a rat flea. The flea took up residence on a rodent, a rat usually, and feasted on its blood. But the fleas carried a disease, though they themselves were vectors, and not made sick by the contagion they transmitted.

The rats which carried the fleas moved, from time to time, close to man and were by and large unnoticed by the human population. The fleas, nestled in the fetid fur of the rats, took that opportunity to leave their rodent host by leaping onto the skin of men, where they resided silently. Devouring blood from Homo sapiens by inflicting a covert and painless bite, the flea loosened the mass of disease lodged in its stomach, regurgitating it into the bite wound.

Those who were bitten by such a flea, although they did not know it, became quickly infected and inescapably ill. Bacteria coursed through the veins of the human system and spread inexorably to the lymph nodes. In a few days' time, great gouts of blood would form under the skin, appearing black on the arms, chest, and groin of the massively pain-ridden victim. The extremities of those unlucky men and women would begin to fester and rot with necrosis, the fingers and toes transforming jet black. Death was frequently by hemorrhage.

The fleas, having feasted adequately on their host, moved on to seek a temporary home, and additional liquid food, on other human beings.

CHAPTER ONE

SCHLOSS WINTERLOCH, BAVARIA, GERMANY

He moved without haste down the familiar arched corridor, the sconce lamps bathing the ancient passage in subdued light. He would have to report what he had so recently discovered, and he was troubled by the implications and the cascade of consequences it would bring. As he strode the length of the broad arched hallway, its stone surface uneven and buckled with accumulated age, he considered what exactly he should say to the owner of the estate.

A slight noise issued from behind him, as sibilant and stealthy as a whisper. He began to turn to determine the source of the sound, his thick blond eyebrows forming crescents of curiosity. There was a rush of air and a sudden, shattering burst of cosmic pain, searing in intensity and as cutting as a razor. The pain exploded like a blinding, frenzied convulsion inside his brain. His eyes instantly narrowed in reaction and his features contorted in a disfiguring wince. He saw the venerable, arching walls fall away in front of him, the age-darkened ceiling appearing for a second in his line of vision and then vanishing from sight as he fell. And then his eyes began to darken, capable of taking in only the ancient expanse of the gray stone floor upon which he now lay.

The surface of the stone felt cool against his cheek. The pain seemed to lose its sharpness and transformed into a throbbing dullness, but remorselessly expanded its grip until it encompassed his entire head. The light began to drain from his vision and the number of floor stones he could discern diminished one by one as his vision began to fade. He was aware, though distantly, that his sight was rapidly giving way to an unsummoned shadow and his last thought was a surprised comprehension that death was at its core darkness, pure and unalloyed.

* * *

Autumn, that season brilliant and breathtakingly colorful in many regions, was here muted and subdued in its dominion. Mornings were embraced by damp tendrils of mist, while afternoons witnessed the ascendancy of long, silent shadows, and a suffocating darkness reigned at evening, the reflected light of the moon and the stars obscured by a thick and clutching tapestry of branches that stretched upward to the sky, like open hands warding off a blow. The few remaining, desiccated leaves of oak trees scratched discordant notes in the occasional breeze, whispering of the inexorable approach of a hard winter.

The imposing, somber edifice of the castle consisted of equal amounts of quarried stone, roughhewn timber, and ancient memories. Erected in the 12th century, the massive, imposing walls had partly fallen to ruin by the 21st, and large fragments of stone which had tumbled to earth generations removed were now covered with moss and lush fern so that they seemed to have always been part of the landscape. The landscape itself surrounded the medieval structure like a coarse shawl. The ground was untamed, dark stands of fir trees and narrow, shaded mounds and dales contributing to an atmosphere predominated by shadow. An artist from the Romantic Age would have captured the scene in dark hues of intensely brooding black, earthy brown and deep, subdued green.

Dampness prevailed over the castle and its environs, the terrain dank and the stone walls slick with a wet residue reminiscent of perspiration. Even on the infrequent sunny days, the place engendered the illusion of half-light, as if some unspoken dark secret actively resisted illumination.

The reality was that the venerable castle, like others of its time and era, had not been built as a welcoming structure to enchant the eye of the wary traveler, but as a fortress designed to shut out a hostile world of enemies, real and suspected, actual and potential. The structure had been designed to withstand a determined assault and frustrate the attacker. It had been constructed, massive stone upon stone, to convey an impression of impregnability to the observer, be they casual passerby or someone of malignant intent. The towers and crenellated walls were solid meters thick, their surface smooth and affording little purchase. Windows, called arrowslits, were small, grudging architectural details meant only to afford the castle inhabitants a sufficient tactical view of the surrounding terrain and provide space for the deployment of crossbows and other weapons.

The main castle gate was a high sally port intended in its day to permit the entrance and egress of mounted, armed knights, sitting heavy on their foaming chargers with the crushing weight of worked, black armor. The gate itself was fabricated of thick, brute slabs of timber cut centuries ago from the nearby forest by cursing, lashed peasants and subsequently reinforced with broad bands of metal, now long turned to rust. As a governing rule that endured for centuries, the gate was closed firmly shut, opened only to permit the castle occupant warily out or the invited guardedly in.

For all of the wear of the weather and the ravages of countless winters, the castle remained inhabitable and, indeed, inhabited. Where candlelight once flickered through portals as an uncertain sentinel against such dangers as might be concealed in darkness, electric lamps now reigned. But the castle was still unremittingly cold, its chill corridors and high-ceilinged chambers pleasant enough in the summer months but a horror in winter, that long and jealous season.

There had been, of course, no central heating when the castle had risen from its cocoon of scaffolding, and none had been installed in the centuries since. The destructive work and the funding that would have been required made such a venture chimerical. Large, ornate fireplaces were employed to ward off freezing temperatures, but in truth, afforded only spots of warmth. In more recent times, electric heaters had been deployed, but the underlying chill in the air and the occasional involuntary shiver of the castle dweller still prevailed.

The fortress, after all, was not situated in pleasant Tuscany, washed with the golden benediction of the Italian sun. Bavaria in the northern Alps provided a less happy clime, although dramatic, in terms of natural surroundings. The bulk of the castle afforded no view other than that of the clutching, claustrophobic pines of the encroaching forest, but the flagstone top of the castle's high main tower provided a panoramic display—on a clear day—of the Tyrolean Alps in the distance. The castle keep, as it was known, peered over the alpine mountain tops. Some of the jagged peaks were over nine thousand feet high and formed a graceful chain of summits that lined the horizon. The light-gray dolomite slopes were located many miles away from the castle and the intervening distance gave them a faded-blue and gauzy, surreal appearance, as if they were perhaps an optical illusion. Still, they were really there, fixed on the landscape, providing some relief from the closeness of the castle and its earnest surroundings.

Even though many of the original castle rooms and chambers had been locked up or sealed in over the generations, there was more than sufficient space for the modest rank of current tenants, much reduced in number from the 12th century. In those distant days the castle had served as the refuge and residence of a Bavarian graf or count, who had carved a place for himself in the region with sword and dagger and stubborn resolve, and booty brought from distant battlefields.

Heinrich Graf Stefan von Winterloch had seemingly stamped the fortress out of the ground, occupying it even in the nearly twenty years of its construction. Although reliable records from those times were limited, available accounts suggested that the Count came from a line of mercenaries, originally from the flatlands of Franconia, who had slashed and hacked their way to status and wealth in the interminable struggles that had laid waste to vast swaths of central Europe at the time. The limited documentation indicated that Heinrich von Winterloch was disposed neither to humor nor compassion.

Although careful not to overtly breach the prevailing mores of the times, he evidenced little of what would have been termed Christian virtue. Nor did he care a whit for the world of intellect and inquiry. Unknown to him, those enduring traits would eventually propel the patchwork of Europe into something other than a festering conglomerate of petty, warring, homicidal fiefdoms whose vision extended only to the conquest or ruin of the neighboring village.

The severity of Graf Heinrich's personality seemed to be carried on his visage, if the cracked and paraffin-clouded oil portrait in the Great Hall of the castle was at all reliable. The artist, anonymous to the ages, had with slashing strokes captured the pallid and angular features of the portrayed nobleman with an arresting realism unusual for the time. Dark, hooded eyes gazed suspiciously down from the oversized painting, as if assessing the qualities and weaknesses of others in the cavernous room. The full lower lip appeared firm and betrayed no hint of a smile. An aquiline nose that might have implied stately demeanor was flawed, veering slightly to the left and riven by a deep scar at the bridge; the result, it was said, of a Swedish sword blow. But that tale could as well have been apocryphal, no one knew with certitude.

The saturnine man with shoulder-length, straw-colored hair, captured by the artist's brush and imprisoned in a heavy gilded frame had presence, and gravitas as well. Still, something about the combination of facial features spoke not only of inveterate harshness and pitiless iron discipline, but as well of incipient dissolution and characteristics purposely concealed.

Count Heinrich's castle had remained the seat of the von Winterloch family over decades and centuries up to the present time. This was why his severe countenance still presided in the

Great Hall. The Count himself had gone to rot in 1121, carried away to some other place gagging, moaning, and vomiting in an unappetizing fit of blood, feces, and sweat brought on by the Pest, or plague, known as the Black Death, to this part of Upper Bavaria. Even the old count's uncompromising, flinty, and acidic demeanor proved no match for the rapid progress of a disease which put a third of Europe in early graves with no regard for their standing; peasant and knight, pauper and noble, cleric and apostate.

The plague, its lethality eventually expended, moved on to other regions, and the two of the count's six children that survived him became the next masters of Winterloch Castle, or, as it was called in native German, Schloss Winterloch.

The old count was buried in his polished and impressive ceremonial armor beneath an elaborately carved Italian sandstone, emblazoned with his escutcheon—depicting a bear, which existed in Bavaria at the time, and a lion rampant, which never did, improbably holding aloft a broadsword clutched in their collective paws. This great, ornate dead weight of cold stone was placed beneath the altar of the small chapel within the castle walls, and over time forgotten.

And so the sturdy, slowly aging walls of the vast forest keep housed one generation of von Winterloch after another, the counts and countesses as well as assorted mistresses, paramours, and companions. It was the fortress itself that provided permanency. But floods, storms, disease, and a variety of wars exacted their toll, and as many of the counts met a violent end as died quietly in their oversized beds.

Over time, the company of courtiers serving the count lost its utility as technological developments ended the need for on-premises tailors, smithies, carpenters, bakers, and other tradesmen resident in the estate. Changes in society too, eventually ended the requirement for ladies-in-waiting, ranks of servants with their own hierarchy and platoons of watchmen, once proud warriors reduced over time to the embarrassing and useless spectacle of ceremonial guards. These professions simply faded away.

The current owner of the castle retained the von Winterloch name but made do with a retinue of employees that in the 21st century had dwindled to only seven in number, including a gardener aged over eighty. This situation demonstrated the truth of the unremarkable but perceptive phrase that "things change."

Rheinhold Graf von Winterloch, it was said by his friends, who were few, and by his detractors, who were more substantial in number, had much in common with his antecedent, the baleful Heinrich. There was a certain physical resemblance. At seventy-plus years, Rheinhold faced the world with a look of permanent contempt that was as empty of warmth as the stone floor of the Great Hall on a February night.

Like his ancestor, Rheinhold had an aquiline nose, but absent the slash mark of a nameless Swedish swordsman. The portrait of Heinrich, the first castle resident, depicted him in shining black Italian armor, handsomely set off with traces and filigrees of gold at the joints and breastplate. Centuries later, the heir to the fortress dressed rather more indifferently. Black remained the preferred color, present in the form of rich cashmere sweaters and rustic-cut faux Bavarian hunter's jackets tailored in Munich.

In addition to some shared physical similarity, Rheinhold held some of the temperamental features of the long dead Heinrich. This list of traits: easy to anger, quick to take offense, dismissive of the accomplishments of others, prideful of familial deeds not of his own doing. The living von Winterloch was on a regular basis fond of wine and cognac, and he dined well but moderately. He was tall and spare of frame, with a spine unbent by decades.

On most evenings, whether spent entirely solitarily, or after guests had departed in a flurry of theatrical and insincere kisses and embraces, the count would pour himself a large, deep snifter of deep amber Asbach brandy and wander into the cavernous Great Hall, his footfall of Italian leather resonating against the smooth surface of ancient stone. There he would stare up for long minutes at the stern countenance of Heinrich, captured in an antique oil portrait, brush his fingers slowly through thick white hair and savor his drink in delicate sips before raising the Czech crystal glass to the somber painting. "The same blood, after all," he would sometimes say to himself in a gruff voice. "The same blood, after all."

* * *

Blood was less the problem than the lack of it. At least, that is how the scene initially appeared to Franz Waldbaer, the Bavarian police Kommissar standing on the damp stones of the ancient fortress this day. Waldbaer felt himself vaguely unhappy and tried to analyze the cause of his discontent.

There was the weather, for one thing. Mid-November in the Alps was hardly the optimal month; the air heavy with moisture and the sky leaden and low. Trees were stripped of leaves and appeared spectral, like ranks of stationary wraiths. But it was not just the weather. He sighed, felt a brief pain at the small of his back, attributed it to the insinuating ravages of age, and sighed again. Every year, he realized, he burrowed deeper into his fifties, and this thought alone depressed him. He resolved, as often before, to sweep the thought away, and not to think about age, or for that matter, the process of aging.

Still, something vaguely indefinable about the surroundings did not please him. The castle itself struck him as a depressed place, a sullen and stolid mound of stones. Not all castles affected him this way. Castle Schloss Ambras near Innsbruck and Mad King Ludwig's Neuschwanstein he found architecturally pleasant enough, and there were many others set along the rolling landscape of the Rhein that were equally palatable. But Schloss Winterloch lacked grace and flair. The walls, built for defense against enemies long vanished, were the triumph of function over appearance. The fortress was more the creation of the dour engineer than the creative architect.

The centuries had also done their work, Waldbaer considered. There was the scent and trace of decay about the whole place, of slow ruin retarded in the castle but still not arrested.

There was little joy to be had in that. And in addition, there was the owner of the stone fortress to be considered. The old count was not someone of his personal acquaintance, but the nobleman's reputation was very negative, and Waldbaer had long ago learned that reputations are most often earned for a valid reason.

The detective knew that an introduction to the count on this day would be as certain as the eventual onset of evening, and there was the matter immediately at hand, the corpse lying splayed less than two meters in front of him.

The inanimate form had been discovered early in the morning by the castle employee charged with keeping the structure clean and dust-free, a thick-waisted, middle-aged woman named Frau Anna Marie Mayerhof. The woman had immediately woken the count and breathlessly reported the event. The count, in turn, had gone to see for himself and had subsequently called the police. The police had, in turn, reached Waldbaer, who had been up until that moment happily in route to Munich to attend a conference on human trafficking in Europe sponsored by Interpol. He had been contemplating a stop at the Löwenbräukeller beer hall when the call reached him.

Now, two hours after the discovery of the corpse, Franz Waldbaer stood in a broad ground-floor corridor of Schloss Winterloch as four policemen and a medical doctor in disposable plastic gloves fussed about the space in the manner required by a death of uncertain provenance. Count Rheinhold had yet to make his appearance, but a taciturn Frau Mayerhof was there at the detective's side, her sausage fingers clasped together. The information she had been able to provide to the Kommisar was so far unilluminating.

Waldbaer exhaled a breath and was not surprised to see it hover in the air before him. He longed to return to the heated seat of his Volkswagen Passat and to the classical music that the CD player offered. Those modest pleasures would have to wait a while.

"Frau Mayerhof," he began, "just so I am certain, let me ask you to repeat for me the circumstances that led to your discovery of the body. Please take your time." Waldbaer rubbed a hand across his eyes and the bridge of his nose in an subconscious gesture of weariness.

The stout woman nodded, the movement made somewhat odd by her bulk, as if her square head sat directly on her shoulders without benefit of an intervening neck. "*Ja, Herr Kommissar,* it's exactly as I said before. I was performing my usual morning routine, the way I've done it nearly every single day for the last twelve years. Proper sequence is important when you're responsible for the upkeep of an estate of this size. You have to be quite organized and take care of things in a certain order. Sequencing is very important. So, the first thing I do in the morning, after a cup of coffee in the kitchen, is make a tour of the public rooms to see if anything special requires attention."

"Special attention?" the detective queried, glancing at the woman from baggy eyes. He had not slept well lately; his back was giving him problems. He wondered if he should consult a physician.

"Yes, special attention, that's right. Like seeing if anything has been spilled the night before. Sometimes there are guests for cocktails or dinner, and God knows, something has been spilled and not noticed; it's my job to take care of it. Or perhaps something has been broken. That doesn't happen often, but I assure you, it does happen now and then. High winds snapped a branch right through a window once a few years ago, and there were glass shards all around on the floor. Or a nail just giving way and a picture in a heavy frame falling from the wall. That's happened too, and more often than once, mind you, and it can destroy a painting. Things like that don't happen every day. That's what I mean by special. *Ja?*" The woman raised thick eyebrows to query whether the detective had taken her point.

Waldbaer nodded comprehension and swayed a bit on the balls of his feet, feeling the spot where an incipient hole was working its way into the sole of one shoe. "Thank you, Frau Mayerhof. That is most helpful. Everything is clear to me now. Please, continue your narrative."

The woman nodded with a look of benign self-contentment, her tightly pulled bun of gray hair reflecting the surgically bright light now emanating from the crime scene lamp that had just been placed by one of the policemen. "Of course, Kommissar. Well, I was making my morning rounds, as I say, to assess what needed to be done. I always carry a duster with me, to touch up things as I go, wherever it might be needed. Anyway, I had been through the east side of the castle and everything was in order in the gathering room, the old carpenter's quarters, the art gallery, and the smaller rooms. There was nothing out of the ordinary anywhere."

The detective nodded and Frau Mayerhof continued, "So, I exited that part of the castle through what's called The Watchman's Door, and crossed the courtyard. I surprised a fox there that had wandered in from the woods, and he darted away in a hurry. I don't like seeing them here; a lot of them are diseased these days with rabies. I checked to see if he had gotten into any garbage or left a mess, but there was nothing to be seen. Well, after that, I re-entered the castle on the opposite side of the courtyard and continued my inspection. I dusted some of the paintings in the main hallway—the old oil of a wild boar hunt, for one. The silver-gilded frame is ornate, a real dust trap."

Frau Mayerhof paused for a moment, her dark eyes occupied with thought. "After that, I surveyed the Great Hall and then went to the Hall of Banners, as it's called, which the count sometimes uses to host his cocktail gatherings. But it didn't appear to have been used last night and everything was perfectly clean. I left those rooms and came down this corridor and past the entrance to the basement on my way to the entrance hall and the front gate. The light is poor here, especially in the early morning, and then I saw this strange shape," she raised a beefy hand and pointed to the nearby corpse.

"I wasn't exactly sure what it was at first. I thought for a moment that it was a big dog sleeping there. That didn't make me at all happy, not only because dogs are terribly filthy in their habits and always leave traces around, but because the count does not keep his pair of dogs within these walls, which would mean that the canine had somehow just gotten in here. Anyway, as I moved a bit closer and could focus my eyes better to the light, I saw that it wasn't a dog at all, it was poor Andreas. I don't know why, I suppose it was the way the body was spread out, but I could tell immediately that he was dead. A heart attack, I thought; that takes so many these days, and Andreas had been out of shape for many years. But then I saw, well, what you see there, Herr Kommissar."

Waldbaer nodded. The head of the blond-haired man was damaged in the back, a small, uneven splotch of burgundy-colored blood having matted and stained the straw-hued hair.

Waldbaer nodded. "Thank you, Frau Mayerhof, thank you for your account, it will be most helpful."

He studied the body and concluded that the woman was right; the man collapsed on the worn fieldstone floor was out of shape. The corpse was overweight with a large belly straining against the buttons of a taut, faded-blue denim shirt, and there was a general flabbiness in the arms and at the chin. This judgment did nothing to lighten the detective's mood, as he had concluded that he himself was in no better shape than the recently deceased. Waldbaer much wanted to return to his trimmer form of a decade ago, but detested mindless exercise almost as much as he despised dieting. He forced the intruding thought aside and turned his attention again to the woman still at his side.

"Now, Frau Mayerhof, suppose you tell me everything you know about this Andreas here. Just tell me what you know and don't worry about what's relevant. We'll get the records on him quickly, but I'd like to hear whatever you can tell me."

The woman buried her head turtle-like a degree deeper into her shapeless floral-patterned dress of lavender and crossed her fleshy forearms in front of her. She pursed her lips and took a moment to consider her words.

"*Ja.* Andreas was responsible for the physical upkeep of the castle. Not cleaning, that is for me to do, as I said, but real upkeep. For one thing, if there is repair work to be done, Andreas is responsible for it. If the work required is too much for him, he is supposed to find the right person or firm to contract with, by arrangement, of course, with Count von Winterloch.

"I can give you some examples, Kommissar. Andreas performed minor repair work on window frames, cracks in the wall, fixed leaking pipes, that sort of thing. He was always looking for signs of problems, and in this old place, you don't have to look far. Stains on the ceiling that could mean a water problem, or a hole in the roof. Andreas would go around testing for loose stones in the parapet, cracked mortar, rotting timbers, all sorts of things. Repairs that require scaffolding or that have to do with plumbing, well, he knew who to get to do that, and he watched their work like a falcon watches a field mouse. I suppose he knew this whole place, every corner and stairwell, like no one else did, even the count. Andreas knew every nook and cranny of the place. And now he's gone. Kommissar, if you don't mind my asking, that blood on Andreas' head, did he maybe fall and crack his skull?"

Waldbaer noted that his hands felt unpleasantly cold, and he jammed them into the pockets of his worn, forest-green corduroy trousers for warmth. "I'm afraid it's too early for us to know, Frau Mayerhof, far too early yet. What was Andreas' full name, by the way? And how long had he been employed here?"

The woman laughed softly. "Oh, Andreas has been here forever or nearly forever, it seems. He preceded me, and I've been wandering these halls for over twelve years. I would think he's been here over twenty years, perhaps almost thirty. Count Rheinhold will know more exactly when you talk to him, and there have to be employment records somewhere. Andreas has been at the castle a long, long time, he grew old in this job. I remember when he was much younger."

Waldbaer reflected that he knew more than he cared to

about growing old. He sighed involuntarily. "And what is Andreas' full name?"

"Pichler. Andreas Pichler. It's an old, established family in these parts, and the name is fairly common around here, even today. There have been Pichlers in this Bavarian village for centuries. Andreas wasn't a loud or gregarious sort of man, was even a bit sparing with words you could say, but a lot of people knew him. I expect that the funeral service will be well attended. It certainly won't be an empty church for his requiem Mass."

Waldbaer thanked the earnest woman and ushered her from the corridor with a litany of accolades for her helpful attitude. She trundled off with a brisk nod of the head and not the shadow of a smile to lighten her plain features.

The detective swept a hand through his thick hair. "So, gentlemen, what do we have so far?" Waldbaer addressed his comment to no one in particular.

A lanky policeman with a receding chin, clothed in a loose-fitting green uniform jacket and white, visored cap was the first to answer. He left the group of his compatriots and sauntered toward the detective. "Well, sir, we found this fellow's wallet in his trouser pocket. His driver's license gives his name as what the woman said just now. Andreas Augustus Pichler. He was fifty-nine years old, though I guess his blond hair makes him look a bit younger. When we arrived here the old gardener—he's in the kitchen right now having coffee—provided the same name. They all knew each other up here. The gardener said that Pichler usually arrived here early to start his day; around five a.m. or so. The other help arrives two or three hours later, so I imagine Pichler was the first one of the employees to be on site this morning."

Waldbaer slowly circled the body and the little clutch of officials busy with it. "All right, that's a start, if not much of one. Has anyone spoken to Count von Winterloch yet? As a matter of fact, has anybody even seen him?"

The gangly policeman was the first to reluctantly reply. "No, sir. He seems to be upstairs somewhere in his private rooms; that's what the woman told us before you arrived. She said the count was not in a very good mood because of all this, and that he'll be down to see us once he gets a bit more composed."

Waldbaer smiled wearily and closed his eyes and rubbed a hand against his forehead. "Composed? Now there's a wonderful word, isn't it, really wonderful. Sergeant, I want you to go find one of the people who work here and have them go and advise Count von Winterloch that I require his presence right here in ten minutes. Whether the count is composed or not is of no concern to me. I need to talk to him, and I don't much care whether he's happy or unhappy. *Alles klar?*"

The police sergeant grinned through nicotine-dulled teeth and made a casual saluting motion, pleased to be reassured that the hereditary Teutonic nobility would receive no special privileges from the detective in charge. Positioning his peaked cap at a more rakish angle and the visor over his eyes, he headed off to find one of the employees to serve as courier to the castle's master.

Waldbaer began a more attentive inspection of the body of Andreas Pichler, sprawled so inelegantly before him. He studied the features first and wondered again as he had many times in the past at how death robs a face of animation and expression. Death makes man a cipher, Waldbaer thought, mute and unable to communicate with those subtle gestures of muscle and flesh that relay so much in life. Pichler's empty visage was that way now, drained of life, presenting no clue of how the man had looked some hours ago. Had he usually carried a pleasant expression, or a severe one? Did he present an initial impression of intelligence or limited mental ability? Did his comportment suggest grace or coarseness? The cooling corpse of Pichler would provide no commentary. Such judgments would now depend on the impressions of others who had known him. Still, Waldbaer had been trained to extract whatever information he could from the dead.

There were the hands for one thing. They were not hands that would have easily danced on an ivory keyboard, teasing out

the delightful rush of notes from a Mozart sonata. No, these were
hands more at home with a hammer or saw, axe or shovel. There
was nothing debased about that, he reminded himself even as
the tinkle of a Mozart tune tumbled pleasantly though his head.
The hands were strong, the fingers straight and blunt and doubtless suited to a variety of tasks useful for a tradesman. They were
scratched and a bit rough, from what Waldbaer could see, but
there were no marks to suggest a recent life-and-death struggle.
Pichler's torso and broad shoulders carried hints of a man who
had once been of powerful natural build but who had run to fat
over the years. The neck was laid bare above the shirt collar and,
this too, was free of injury while betraying an excess of flesh.

Waldbaer returned to the slack facial features, stepping
closer to the body and bending slowly at the knees. The blank
eyes and the mouth were open and a swath of thick, if lusterless,
blond hair cascaded over a broad Bavarian forehead. A pencil-
thin trace of dark blood was evident, running from one nostril
over the lower lip, its progress ending at the chin. Waldbaer
noted that aside from this and the gash of thick scarlet at the
back of the head, there seemed to be no blood. Moving his
eyes away from the corpse and down the corridor, the detective
failed to see any evidence of a blood trail or a struggle nearby.
Standing erect again, Waldbaer's knees made a cracking sound,
and he wondered what it meant. Nothing positive, he imagined.
He moved a few steps further and consulted Pichler's rough
and oil-stained, laced leather working boots. The soles were
wet. Perhaps of interest, perhaps not. All in all, Pichler was not
providing him with much of use.

Waldbaer turned his attention to the silent, balding figure in
an un-pressed, dark charcoal suit and dark burgundy cravat who
was scribbling into a small notebook and wearing a frown, standing near the field lamp's illumination. He knew the funereally-at-
tired medical practitioner vaguely from a few past encounters but
could not readily attach a name. No matter, Waldbaer decided, he
would use the physician's title.

"*Herr Doktor,* is there perhaps anything of interest that you can tell me so early in the game?"

The man looked up from his task with an uncertain expression that indicated surprise. He shook his head emphatically from side to side. "No, Herr Kommissar, not yet by any means. Anyway, that's not the way I like to conduct my business. First impressions can be wrong after all, and I don't want people going off and doing wild things based on suppositions. When we get him properly looked at," he tipped his jet-black ballpoint pen at the body, "then I'll put together my report with supporting documentation, and that's what you'll see on your desk as soon as it's finished."

Waldbaer experienced some difficulty in deciding whether the doctor's abrupt way was offensive or not. He decided to let it pass as professionalism. "*Danke sehr, Herr Doktor.* I most certainly look forward to reading it. But you can clarify one item now that interests me. Approximately when did this man die? Can you perhaps give me your best estimate?"

The balding man brushed a hand through invisible strands of hair and nodded. "*Ja,* I suppose I can. Judging from the temperature of the body, I would say that he died about ten or eleven hours ago. More or less. But again, I would wait for my full report."

"Of course, I just want a general sense of things. It seems, Doctor, that would mean that Herr Pichler died early in the morning, considerably before sunrise."

The doctor fixed Waldbaer with steely gray eyes. "That is correct. He died about five in the morning, perhaps even a bit earlier. I'll have further details after I've assembled all of the information."

"Permit me one more question, if you please, Doctor. From what you can see, is this a case of murder or was the death caused by some sort of accident?"

The doctor moved his hands to the pockets of his suit and took a moment to organize his thoughts. "This is off the record, of course, Kommissar. It would appear to me that this death was caused by foul play. I can tell you now that this man was struck from behind by a sharp instrument, a bladed instrument most probably, driven with significant motive force into the cranium. The weapon was something like a knife, even more likely a sword, though I hesitate to say it. The blow cracked the skull like an eggshell. I imagine that the victim was dead within seconds caused by severe trauma to the brain. Yes, in my view this is almost certainly murder, but, again, you will have to wait till tomorrow morning until I can confirm that."

Waldbaer moved his head in a quick up-and-down motion, muttered a perfunctory word of thanks, and considered the information.

"So, someone has asked to speak with me, and here I am." The gravel voice did not exude happiness. The unhappy tone belonged to a smoking man, Waldbaer knew, as he turned to the source. A tall, silver-haired man wearing a black Norwegian sweater with two bright red stripes at chest level stood with hands on his hips in the corridor behind the detective. An imperious pose under the circumstances, Waldbaer thought.

"You are Rheinhold von Winterloch, owner of this estate?" Waldbaer asked. He had decided to purposely omit the honorific title of count, not out of any pettiness but to begin to establish who was in charge in matters of violence and death.

The count paused for a moment, assessing his interlocutor. "Yes, I am Count von Winterloch, quite so. And you would be?"

The detective walked a few steps closer to the castle owner. "Kommissar Waldbaer. *Grüss Gott*," he said, employing the ancient and still common Bavarian greeting. He extended a hand and the count shook it with a limp lack of enthusiasm.

"Yes. As you might well imagine, I have some questions for you concerning what we have here."

"Well, perhaps you can tell me. What in fact do we have here?" von Winterloch intoned, a hint of what might be a smirk working its way across his features.

Best to nip that flippancy in the bud right now, Waldbaer thought.

"What we have here, Count von Winterloch, is a corpse, as I am sure you can see and as you have certainly been aware of since earlier this morning. We might have a natural, if unexpected, death or we might have something much more sinister, it's too early to tell. What we need are as many facts as possible. We can conduct our business here or, if you would find it less distracting, we can adjourn to my office at the police station." The comment had, as Waldbaer hoped, the desired sobering effect on the lean aristocrat.

"No, no, Herr Kommissar, here is just fine, there's no need to take you away from your investigation. I don't know that I can be of much help regarding Pichler, but if you have any questions..."

Better, Waldbaer concluded. The count had called the dead man by his last name, suggesting, perhaps in a studied way, the difference in station between the two.

"To start with, how well did you know Herr Andreas Pichler, and for how long?"

The count relaxed his frame and moved his hands from his hips into his side pockets with a casual motion as he stared up at the arched stone ceiling, considering. "How well did I know him? I suppose as well as an employer generally knows an employee. Obviously, we have nothing at all socially in common; we had nothing at all to do with each other beyond the castle grounds. I do not, for example, have the faintest idea where he lives, or lived, other than in the village somewhere."

The count's face appeared to soften a degree. "I liked him well enough in his way, though, I might add. Pichler was a completely honest worker, as far as I could tell, and very capable in the tasks he did around here, innovative even. He didn't drink on the job or anything of that sort and always went about his assigned duties properly and promptly. That's not always the case with the younger generation, but Pichler's age group knew what hardship was and it helped form character, if you want my view."

The count paused and lifted his head toward the ceiling, considering. "He was a hard worker, certainly, even put his back out for a few weeks once repairing an interior wall on his own. Pichler didn't say much, which is a trait I can well appreciate. If there was something that should interest me, he would let me know, but he didn't try to strike up banter just for the sake of it. I understand from some passing remarks of his that he spent his evening hours sometimes at the Adlerstube in the village, at least for a beer or two. I'm afraid that I can't add to that as far as his time away from the job is concerned. As I say, a solid employee insofar as I can judge, which is why he was kept on all these years."

Waldbaer studied the count's highly polished, tasseled black loafers; Italian, he judged, and hand sewn, almost feminine in elegance. "I see. And how long was he actually kept on?" The detective let his voice assume a slightly increased degree of warmth.

"*Ja.* Well, Herr Kommissar, the household tax files will certainly have that precise information, and you should feel free to consult them in my study in the other wing of the castle. But, if my memory serves, Pichler has been here since his youth—I would guess for the last forty years. Yes, that would seem about right. My father hired him. When he was going around looking for work as a teenager, he had learned something about carpentry and structural repairs, which met our requirements here. The building was erected in stages over time but all of it is old, Herr Kommissar, and something always needs fixing, always. Pichler usually knew what to do, and when not, he knew where to get the best experts for the right price. That is not an inconsiderable talent."

"No, certainly not," Waldbaer allowed. "Tell me, what was Herr Pichler working on at the time of his death?"

Count von Winterloch furrowed his brow and narrowed his pale eyes in concentration. "He was always performing more than a single task at a time; that is called multitasking these days. His main activity of late was fortifying the cellar spaces beneath the castle; the wine cellar and the large unused areas beneath where we are standing. The castle is a cavernous place. The problem is, the terrain here is wet and even after all these centuries, the castle is still settling. This causes structural stress. Pichler was good at detecting the early signs, and sometimes the problem can be postponed for a decade or so with some spot repair work—a new timber here, a reinforcing iron band there, sealing cracks on a pillar somewhere. He had been taking care of that kind of thing recently, and I told him to keep at it. There are lots of spaces that we don't use anymore, and it would be easy to miss some developing structural problem."

Winterloch paused before continuing. "Pichler was our watchman in that regard, you could say. He knew this place as well as I do, perhaps more intimately, and I was born here. I wouldn't be astounded if he were on his way to, or back from, the cellar when he died. Tell me, do you think his heart gave out?"

Waldbaer had an aversion to questions from interrogation subjects, but knew that they were a common enough manifestation of human curiosity. "Herr Pichler's heart certainly gave out, but what caused it to give out is a matter of some conjecture." The count nodded in a puzzled way and Waldbaer decided to push a bit further. "Did you not notice on your initial inspection of the body, Count von Winterloch, that there is what appears to be a wound at the back of Herr Pichler's head? With the accumulation of some blood? If not, you might want to take a look now."

The count sighed and focused his eyes directly on Waldbaer and ignored Pichler's corpse. "I did notice the blood this morning. I don't know what it means though. I mean, he might have fallen hard on the stone floor and rolled if he had, say, a heart attack or a stroke or an aneurysm. Are you suggesting that he was struck from behind?"

Waldbaer shook his head. "I suggest nothing. I just wanted to clarify whether you noticed the blood and the head wound earlier. It could be anything, from what we know at this stage.

Natural causes, or assault, both are equally possible, though I am inclined to think that the blood is from a wound, and not a casual injury. Tell me, Count von Winterloch, who was here in the castle this morning?"

If the count was at all shaken, he betrayed no trace of it. "Frau Mayerhof found the body while doing her rounds, but I expect you already know that. And then she came to get me upstairs in my quarters; I was obviously here. And the gardener Sepp may have been here at that hour, I can't swear to it though. He's around here somewhere by this time, and you can clarify the details with him. There are others who work here, but most of them show up a bit later. I can assure you, Kommissar, none of the people who work here would have done anything violent to Pichler, or, for that matter, to anyone else. I can read people well enough to pass judgment."

"Thank you for your viewpoint." Waldbaer told the tall, frowning, black-clad man in front of him. "You saw nothing out of the ordinary this morning, I suppose, nothing particular stands out in your mind?"

The older man snorted, moving his head upwards in an almost equestrian gesture. "No, no. I saw nothing out of the ordinary except one of my longest-serving employees dead on the floor of my own home. Perhaps that distracted me from noting whether there was anything else unusual. There was no sign of an intruder or thief, if that's what you're trying to get at. Of course, I haven't made an inspection of the estate. I expect that your people will be doing that at any rate, whether I like it or not."

Waldbaer realized that the count was returning to his initial stance of distant superiority. "Yes, we will be looking into things here in some detail. I expect that you have activities to occupy you, Count, and I won't detain you any longer. You are free to go—for now. I may need to summon you to clarify some things, but please, feel free to go about conducting your business until further notice."

Just right, Waldbaer thought. Use of the word "summon"

established again who was in charge and von Winterloch would understand that he had just been granted the privilege of taking his leave. Entirely courteous but surely not lost on someone as status-conscious as the reigning master of the house of Winterloch. Waldbaer decided that he did not yet detest the count, merely found him unappetizing. There would be sufficient opportunity to reassess this initial judgment later.

Waldbaer watched as the imperious nobleman, descendent of a long line of noblemen, made a formal nod of farewell, turned on his well-soled heels and walked off, back ramrod straight. His footfalls reverberated off of the stone corridor as he disappeared from view.

Waldbaer turned again to the gangly uniformed police officer who was now simply standing next to the corpse, apparently having exhausted his repertoire of death scene duties. "Sergeant, I'm going to head back to my office and get the formal paperwork started, at least the items that I can take care of before we ascertain the precise cause of death. Take one of your colleagues and give the ground floor a general inspection, including all of the basement, the courtyards, and the outbuildings. I know it's too large an area for a detailed look but check for any obvious signs of disturbance, intrusion, or anything that looks like blood. Look for a bladed weapon as well, though I doubt you'll find it. After I get the medical report tomorrow morning, I'll be back up here. In the meantime, you can ring my cell phone if you find anything. Oh, and tell the cleaning woman that nothing is to be cleaned for the moment, or even dusted, until I say so. Give me a full list of employees and the usual supporting data. We'll check to see if any of them have a criminal record, just to be safe. Is everything clear?"

The policeman nodded assent.

Waldbaer set off down the long corridor, the shadows gathering around him as he moved away from the intrusive glare of the police lantern. The corridor debouched onto a set of broad, marble steps and into a large, representational entrance hall through which Waldbaer had passed earlier in the morning. Glancing up above the massively oversized door, he noted the von Winterloch Wappen, or escutcheon, centered above it, carved into the stone.

He could not suppress a wry smile at the images on the shield. What was it about the mighty that made them take on beasts as their symbols? Man, granted reason to compensate for a variety of corporeal weaknesses, was enchanted, beguiled perhaps, by the raw strength of wild beasts. And so the distant predecessors of the current, annoying count had decided to grace the familial symbol with a bear and a stylized lion. It was, in its way, childlike, an adolescent excess. No chance of a sheep or a turtle serving here. They lacked the required ferocity. This meant, in the end, that the von Winterloch clan equated nobility with unreasoning, animalistic strength. They were pleased to represent themselves allegorically to the world with fanged jaws and taloned paws. The von Winterloch menagerie was portrayed in aggressive posture. It was all a bit mad, Waldbaer concluded, but then, the conceits of men were surely endless.

Waldbaer stepped out into the damp air, his Volkswagen on the parking apron. Murder always requires at least two participants, the victim and the perpetrator. The murderer was the primary subject of law enforcement attentions, for the obvious reasons, and the victim played a distant secondary role. Still, this did not mean that the dead had nothing to say. The dead had been entirely alive until robbed of that state by an act of violence, a breathtaking affront to human nature. But the murder victim left a record of his life in the memories and recollections of others.

Sometimes, knowledge of the victim and the victim's habits and associations assisted the authorities in identifying the murderer. At other times, especially when the victim was a loner or person of solitary inclination, this was not the case. Still, Waldbaer had throughout his career made it a personal requirement to try to learn something of the victim, to reconstruct the deceased from the testimonies of the living, to give back to the dead, in a sense, flesh and blood and sentience. Such a procedure was, he believed,

an absolute necessity if an investigation were to proceed with humanity and dignity.

Von Winterloch had commented that Pichler sometimes
passed his leisure hours at a public house, the Adlerstube, located
in the village. Given the modest size of the village, there should
only be two or three drinking establishments and the pub should
not be hard to locate. Waldbaer decided to drive there for a look
before heading back to his office in Gamsdorf, about thirty minutes distant. It would, at least, get him away from the disagreeable
castle.

CHAPTER TWO

The woman was in agony, undoubtedly dying, and she knew it. Olivia Razanakoto had first felt poorly five days ago; her joints ached, as did her stomach and head, and she felt unaccountably listless. The next day her head had exploded with lacerating pain and she had seen with alarm the first of the buboes on her neck and on her breast. By the time she had stumbled several kilometers down dirt roads to a clinic in Toliara, she had been infected three days, collapsing in front of the faded Red Cross which was painted on a piece of wood attached to a rusting metal pole of the ramshackle whitewashed hospital. Olivia had been placed on a bed by the male nurses and kept hydrated and given antibiotics every few hours.

Her doctor was a white man with blond hair who told her that he was from Germany. He was young and looked like an apparition in a white smock with high cheekbones and pale-blue eyes. The doctor seemed reserved, and he did not smile. A twenty-year old black Madagascar resident named Jean was always by his side to take care of translation and handle simple medical tasks. Olivia had asked him what was wrong with her, what was causing the tormenting pain.

Jean looked kindly at her as if she were a small child, although she was a woman of thirty. "Doctor says that you have the plague. You got it from a flea bite some days ago. People don't think about it, but fleas are everywhere. A flea bit you and put plague in your blood. Doctor is treating it."

Olivia wet her lips and considered what Jean had said. "Do I have the plague bad, I mean really bad? Am I going to get better?"

Jean did not answer but stared at a calendar taped above her bed, as if he could find an answer there. "You have the plague, Doctor says. It is in your lungs now because you have had it a while. But he is treating it with antibiotics. Doctor knows best about these things. You are in very good hands."

Olivia knew that there was something Jean was not saying. "I think you have had other people get this disease from fleas and come to this hospital, no? Tell me, did they live?"

Jean smiled at her, revealing perfectly white teeth, and reached out a hand to stroke her shining black hair. "We have had other plague victims come to the hospital over the years, yes," he said. "Some of them live, and they get better and then they go back home. You are worried but you are in Doctor's hands now, and he knows what to do. All I want you to do is try to rest."

Olivia heard his words, gently spoken but meant to conceal the truth, and knew that he was pronouncing a death sentence. She would not be going home, and she would not leave this bed. She was drugged against the pain and was taking antibiotics but, she knew, it would do no good. The plague would simply carry her away. She closed her eyes, turned her head to one side, and calmly waited to die.

* * *

In a separate room of the clinic a few yards away the blond doctor was feeling content. Quietly and calmly, he adjusted the table microscope and pulled the Oriental rat flea fully into focus. The insect had three legs on each side and moved them spastically. An excellent find, the blond man mused, he would add it immediately to his collection. Of course, for the woman who had been bitten, it was far too late to devise a cure. But that was immaterial. He had taken the flea from her leg and had discovered the bite mark above the ankle. Her symptoms were severe, the plague had invaded her lymph nodes and lungs. Both her hands and feet were necrotic. She was festered with buboes, some about to burst. At this stage nothing could be done. But saving her life was not his concern.

His concern, his mission, was to acquire a collection of Oriental rat fleas, all of which were vectors of the plague. The fleas, in the cycle of nature, became infected with the plague when biting rodents that carried the disease. From that point on, the fleas carried the plague but did not succumb to it. The plague bacteria existed in miniscule amounts within the fleas, which then passed the disease on to humans that they bit. The sanitary and hygienic conditions in Madagascar were terrible, meaning that the rat fleas survived, while many humans did not.

Later on, the doctor mused, using the colony of fleas, he would mutate the bacteria they carried and make it impervious to antibiotics such as those he had administered to the woman. If she had gotten to the hospital soon after becoming infected, the treatment with antibiotics would probably have saved her. But he was going to reengineer the plague to make it resistant to antibiotics. The common treatment and cure of the plague would no longer be effective.

His work in Madagascar was nearing its end. He was tired of the place. He loathed the endemic poverty and primitive culture that held the island in its underdeveloped thrall. But for all that, his collection of rat fleas, ripe with their reservoirs of plague, had made it a most fascinating experience. He would take his collection with him and spend some rather intense time tinkering with the plague to make it antibiotic resistant. He would do this in the pleasant surroundings of Florida, in the United States.

CHAPTER THREE

There was nothing remarkable about the establishment, Waldbaer judged, as he swung his forest-green Volkswagen sedan into the small, birch tree-lined parking lot of the Adlerstube. It was one of a thousand Upper Bavarian bars and restaurants presenting a rustic façade and friendly ambience, whether authentic or feigned.

The building was a solid square with thick stucco walls painted an unimaginative white and carved wooden balconies protruding from under a firm roof. A fading fresco near the entrance portrayed the figure of Saint Martin on horseback, clad in the martial accoutrements of a Roman legionary and rending his fine red cloak with a short sword.

Kneeling at the horse's hooves in the painting was a gray-bearded beggar, portrayed as tubercularly thin and garbed in rags. The saint, with halo, was caught in the pose of preparing to pass half of his cape to the indigent. Saint Martin was a popular figure in this part of southern Germany, and the image was widely familiar. Waldbaer wondered whether the proprietors of the Adlerstube were subtly suggesting through their choice of artistic theme that their establishment was a font of largesse, a trough of altruism.

As he entered through the heavy oak door with faded veneer, Waldbaer glanced up and took in the painted metal sign with the word ADLERSTUBE and the eponymous bird of prey, a hook-beaked eagle. Held firmly in its talons was a shield portraying the cowled head of a bearded monk, the symbol of the Paulaner brewery in Munich. The detective pushed the heavy door open, groaning slightly himself in accompaniment to the noise from the dry hinges.

The broad, cool room was nearly empty, not unexpected in view of the early hour. Two elderly women, both spindly figures in dark dresses, huddled over cups of steaming tea at a corner table. They were deep in half-whispered conversation.

Glancing around the room past several empty tables, Waldbaer's gaze encountered the figure of a man sitting alone immersed in the broadsheet folds of the *Süddeutsche Zeitung* newspaper, a half-empty glass of wheat beer close to hand on the tabletop. The reader appeared to be about sixty, give or take a few years. He had the telltale look of the bored retiree, but Waldbaer's first stop would be to speak to an Adlerstube employee. One of these was readily available cleaning glasses behind the oaken bar.

"*Grüss Gott*," Waldbaer intoned as he approached the young woman clad in a starched white blouse and black skirt, a burgundy apron cinched tight about her narrow waist. The blond-haired woman was perhaps twenty-five, too young to be the Adlerstube owner or manager. The waitress glanced up at the greeting, her thin eyebrows raised. Waldbaer took in the narrow face with pleasant, symmetrical features. The nose perhaps slightly broad above full lips and a delicate chin.

The woman smiled with an array of straight, bright teeth, and Waldbaer knew immediately that had he been closer to twenty-five than his present uninvited and unwanted decrepitude, he would have been inclined to flirt with her. She was pretty, and her eyes and demeanor hinted at humor and intelligence. Judge not, Waldbaer heard a voice whisper in his head, lest you too be judged. He brushed the injunction aside and settled into his professional mode.

"*Ja*, and what might I get for you, *mein Herr*?" the young woman inquired in a pleasant voice.

"A coffee, black, please. And a few words as accompaniment."

The detective produced his laminated police identification card for inspection. The young woman was clearly surprised, but she nodded and pointed to a nearby table where they might converse.

Once seated at a round table, his unsweetened cup of coffee before him, Waldbaer opened the conversation. "My name is Kommissar Franz Waldbaer from Gamsdorf. There has been an unexpected death at Castle Winterloch, not far from here. I'm trying to sort out a few facts and thought I might start my inquiries here."

The girl clasped her hands together on the tabletop and widened her eyes in alarm. "A death at the castle? Do you mean a murder?"

Waldbaer gave a weary smile and waved a hand in a dismissive gesture. "Oh, it's far too early to reach that conclusion, I'm afraid. At this point, I'm dealing with an unexpected death, the cause of which isn't yet clear. Forgive me for not having asked earlier, but your name is?"

The young woman returned the smile with a hint of distraction and leaned forward over the table. "I'm Wilhelma Beck, Herr Kommissar. Around here everybody calls me Helmi. I've been a waitress here for the last three-and-a-half years. May I ask who has died, or can't you say yet?"

Waldbaer took a sip of coffee from the ceramic mug and swallowed, savoring its richness. "I can tell you, Frau Beck. The deceased is Herr Andreas Pichler. He has no known relatives, according to police information. It would seem that he died sometime during the last several hours. I've been told that he came here occasionally. Do you perhaps know him?"

The woman nodded vigorously, her eyes wide and blond hair shimmering with the movement. "Not Andreas! *Um Himmels Willen!* Almost everyone around this village knows Andreas. He came to the Adlerstube quite a lot. I imagine I served Andreas a couple of times a week, unless he was on vacation or something."

"And when exactly was the last time you saw Herr Pichler, do you recall, Frau Beck?"

The woman unclasped her well-scrubbed, manicured hands, arranged them into small fists and placed them under her chin. "Yes, not long ago at all. Today is Thursday. Andreas was in here for a while, about an hour, I suppose, on Tuesday evening. I'm certain of that. He seemed entirely fine then as far as I noticed."

Waldbaer nodded. "Nothing in his demeanor seemed unusual, as far as you could tell?"

Frau Beck shook her head sideways, eyes briefly closed. "*Nein.* He seemed no different than he usually did, not at all."

Waldbaer looked up with a sympathetic countenance into clear blue eyes that registered no guile. "You raise an interesting point. How did Herr Pichler usually seem when he visited the Adlerstube? What was he like?"

Frau Beck's young brow furrowed in thought, and she gazed over Waldbaer's shoulder to the window beyond. "What was Andreas like? Well, he wasn't ever a problem, that's for sure. He wasn't loud or obnoxious, even after a couple of beers. I can't say that about every customer. Andreas had a sense of humor, though, and people liked his company, as far as I can tell. He was always polite, too, and he always left a tip. He was a bit lonely, I think, but I quite liked him."

Waldbaer extracted a pen and folded piece of paper from the pocket of his jacket and scribbled a brief note. "Frau Beck, how often did Herr Pichler show up here?"

"Andreas was a regular customer. I'd guess that he was here for an hour or two about three times a week, after his work was done at the castle. You are correct about him not having relatives. He didn't have family and never married so I suppose he had no reason to go directly from work at the castle to an empty apartment, with only a television for company. He knew the other regular customers here. The Adlerstube was a place where he felt comfortable and could relax. It's very hard to think that he won't be coming through that door again. Poor Andreas."

The detective arranged the pen and papers on the tabletop and steepled his hands. "Yes. Tell me, did Herr Pichler talk much about his work at the castle? Was he inclined to explain his duties there and perhaps his interaction with his employer or the other employees?"

Frau Beck arched her eyebrows mischievously and offered Waldbaer a broad smile. A natural coquette, the Kommissar thought, not unkindly. The woman spoke with a tinkle of laughter in her voice for the first time. "Herr Kommissar, what you want to know is whether Andreas was a gossip, right? Did he suggest rumors or spread dirt about the count and some of the others up there, *nicht wahr?* No, he didn't. Sometimes he would mention some project he was working on—mortaring some part of the outer wall or trying to find the source of water damage somewhere. The last few months he'd been laboring in the castle cellar. He mentioned how cold and damp it was and how it was a labyrinth of forgotten spaces."

The blond girl reflected for a moment, then spoke again. "But he didn't make any remarks about Count von Winterloch or castle guests. Andreas just wasn't that way. Everyone in the village knows about the count anyway, but Andreas was always circumspect—a smart policy as I gather that he wanted to retain his job. Andreas could probably have won some free beer from the other regulars if he regaled them with gossip from the castle, but he had more character than that. Andreas was not mean spirited, and he never attacked anyone personally."

Waldbaer smiled, nodded, and finished his coffee. "I understand, Frau Beck. Thank you for providing a helpful portrait of Herr Pichler. You may see me back in here at some point, depending on how the investigation develops."

Frau Beck stood as the detective rose from his chair and smoothed her skirt at the waist. "I hope that Andreas wasn't murdered. He was a decent fellow. God knows, he didn't deserve to be killed."

Waldbaer looked the young woman in the eyes with a gaze

less weary than it had been a moment before. "In my experience, most people don't deserve to be murdered, Frau Beck. Whatever transgressions they might have committed in life, they have generally earned a better end than murder. That is, I suppose, why murder is a capital crime in every country and in every culture." He bowed from the waist in the traditional Bavarian manner and exited the cool and well-scrubbed spaces of the Adlerstube.

GAMSDORF, BAVARIA

Waldbaer entered the familiar confines of his Polizeiamt office the next morning and immediately noted the blue folder placed at the center of his desktop. He allowed himself a smile; the autopsy report had been sent forward by the doctor, as promised. He stared at it for a moment and decided to fetch a cup of coffee first as a necessary prelude to a thorough examination of the information on Andreas Pichler's demise. Moments later, a steaming cup of Tchibos' Classic Crown securely in hand, the detective settled himself in the battered leather desk chair and flipped open the file.

He did not consult the starkly lit, graphic photographs of the autopsied deceased. He regarded these as necessary but morbid artifacts of police inquiry best ignored without compelling cause. He flipped through the pages rapidly until he came to the sheet marked Cause of Death. He closed the folder after a few minutes' reading, pushed it aside, and stared at a topographical map of Bavaria occupying the opposite wall. Andreas Pichler had been felled by a sword blow administered from behind. The sword strike had cracked Pichler's skull with a single blow and entered his brain.

"So then, it begins," he murmured. Waldbaer drained his strong coffee in a long swallow, fished the car keys from his pocket, and exited the spartan police spaces he had so recently entered. "In the unlikely event that anybody wants to know or cares to know, you can tell them I'm at Schloss Winterloch; I expect that

I'll be there a while," he advised the desk sergeant on duty with characteristic gruffness.

SCHLOSS WINTERLOCH

Thirty minutes later Waldbaer's Volkswagen was parked on the damp cobblestone of the parking apron in front of the fortress. As Waldbaer exited the vehicle he saw the approaching shape of the count lurching toward him, his spare frame cloaked in a dark-green, waxed hunting jacket. Two large burgundy hounds, German pointers, tripped about von Winterloch's booted feet with a series of snorts and yelps. The detective saw that the count carried a wooden walking stick, its silver crest carved into the shape of a lion. Waldbaer dismissed this accouterment as a base affectation, silently adding it to the inventory of the count's sins.

"I was walking a constitutional in the woods when I saw your car approaching," von Winterloch intoned without preamble. "I had expected that your work here, and the disturbance it entails, was concluded. It appears I was wrong. Pichler's body is gone, it was removed yesterday, so why are you back?" The count halted a few feet from Waldbaer, placed the walking stick in front of him and clasped both his leather-gloved hands over it with a commanding gesture. The dogs went immediately to sitting positions, emitting a duet of low growls.

The detective fairly growled himself. "A short answer to that question, Graf Winterloch, would be that I am here because I choose to be. That is the sole reason I require. Consider it a prerogative of Kommissars."

Waldbaer paused and inhaled the damp, cloying air. "But," he continued, "As it transpires, I have a particular reason for my return that I'm sure you will understand. The autopsy results establish beyond any doubt that Herr Pichler did not die from either a heart attack or an accidental fall. Herr Pichler was struck from behind with a bladed instrument. Perhaps a sword, bizarrely enough. He was hit with significant force, so much force that the blade cracked Pichler's skull at the sagittal suture and entered the brain. He died instantaneously. Additionally, it appears that your employee was murdered within your walls. The castle, your castle, is the scene of the crime."

Von Winterloch stared at the detective, but Waldbaer detected a trace of uncertainty in the cold blue eyes. For a moment neither man spoke and the only sound was the baritone background of the hounds' unease.

"I find that hard to believe, Kommissar," the count said. "Who the hell would want to kill Andreas Pichler, for God's sake? Why? He had nothing valuable to speak of. And why would they kill him here in my castle? I could better understand if someone had wanted to kill me; that would at least make sense. Unlike Pichler, I have a fair bit of money, and social standing, which means I probably have accumulated a few enemies over the years. Murdering Pichler—that would be utterly senseless." The count shook his head vigorously from side to side, reminding Waldbaer of a trout trying to free itself from an angler's hook.

An obstinate and self-absorbed man, Waldbaer thought, adding these characteristics to his mental inventory of the count's negative traits. He felt an incremental increase in his dislike for the frowning, white-haired nobleman. Waldbaer looked past von Winterloch toward the brooding, gray edifice of the castle. "Pichler's murder might be senseless, as you say, Count, but it is an established fact. As for the motive, that is for me and my associates to uncover. As you can imagine, we will be required to spend more time at your estate. I expect that this is not to your liking, but this is hardly a matter of choice."

Von Winterloch looked severely unhappy. "You are exactly right, Kommissar. I don't like it one damned bit. I value my privacy intensely, as is my right. I hope you and your underlings will be as quick as you can with this investigatory intrusion."

Waldbaer smiled glacially, eyes still regarding the mass of castle stone behind the count. "We will be finished, when we are finished. But believe me, I don't intend to spend a second longer up here in this mausoleum than I have to."

Sensing palpable tension between the two men, the hounds rose nervously, their growled disapproval intensifying. Waldbaer regarded the animals with unconcealed distaste. "You had better keep those dogs in check, Count. If one of them even tries to bite a policeman, I assure you, I will have them shot."

Von Winterloch's eyes widened and he snorted with disdain. Turning on his hand-crafted heels, he marched off toward the castle, the duo of hounds bounding about the polished English boots.

As von Winterloch's disciplined, ramrod-straight form disappeared through the main portal, Waldbaer heard the distinctive crackle of tires against gravel. Turning his head, he noted the arrival of a green-and-white Audi sedan, the word Polizei emblazoned in large silver letters across the hood. Good, he thought with a burst of satisfaction, let's waste no time demonstrating for von Winterloch exactly who is in charge.

The lanky policeman in need of a haircut pulled himself from the vehicle, stretched, and provided the Kommissar the courtesy of a sloppy salute. Waldbaer recognized him from the initial police team that had busied itself about Pichler's corpse. He recalled that the policeman's name was Braun.

"*Guten Morgen, Herr Kommissar.*" The policeman's greeting suggested contentment, a feeling not shared by Waldbaer at the moment.

"Exactly how good the morning will be remains to be seen, Braun." Waldbaer swept his arm at the expanse of Winterloch estate. "Tell me, what do you see over there?"

The police officer shrugged his narrow shoulders and shot Waldbaer a quizzical look. "I see a castle. It's a hell of a big building. It's an old Bavarian castle from the Middle Ages. I imagine, in those days, that it was built for defense against marauders and enemy armies. The place is meant to keep people out, not to invite them in."

Waldbaer nodded almost imperceptibly. "You are looking at it with a tourist's eyes, Braun. If you look at that crumbling heap of stone with a policeman's eyes you will see a murder scene. A dauntingly large murder scene, full of unexamined spaces, yes. Locked somewhere behind those thick, damp, rotting walls is the answer to who murdered Andreas Pichler. I insist on getting that answer. I also insist on getting the identity of the killer as soon as possible so that we can leave this splendid fever swamp behind. We get to work now, Braun. I want every room in that museum of a building dusted for fingerprints and I want a thorough search for the sword that slammed into the back of Pichler's cranium. You aren't alone, are you?"

The officer shook his. "No, I'm just an advance. Three other officers will get here shortly. We know what to do, Kommissar, but that's one hell of a big building to examine. God knows how big the cellar space is."

"That's unfortunately true. But it will be examined. Every hall, every archway, every closet, every bit of stone floor. I'll be doing my own poking around in there too. *Alles klar,* Braun?"

Braun nodded his unhappy comprehension and reached into the pocket of his leather jacket for a cigarette. Unsympathetic to the disconsolate look of his subordinate, Waldbaer strode toward the gray granite structure on worn rubber soles of Asian rather than Italian provenance.

The floor space where Pichler had been discovered was not hard to locate. The spot was bordered by crime scene tape and the police lamp illuminating the place was still there. Waldbaer turned the lamp on with an audible click that resonated down the long corridor, jammed his cold hands into the pockets of his wool jacket, and stared at the silent stones. What do I not see, he asked himself. He considered his inquiry and provided an initial answer.

There is no suggestion of struggle, for one thing. A large, dark oil painting of an elk hanging on one wall had not been disturbed. Some feet away, an antique chest held a candelabra and this too seemed undisturbed. No trace of blood was discernible along the hallway either. It was possible that at the time he was struck down, Pichler had been running from his assailant in a vain attempt at evasion, but there was nothing evident to indicate this. The manner in which the corpse had come to rest on the castle floor suggested to Waldbaer that Pichler had not known he was being stalked. Had the killer betrayed no sound of his approach? Waldbaer lifted a foot and let it fall again onto the stone. The sound reverberated along the walls of the corridor. The detective nodded to himself. Yes, of course, he thought, a thin smile working across his face as he strode off toward the kitchen.

Minutes later he was seated at an oval oak table across from the rotund form of Frau Mayerhof, the cleaning woman. She poured them each a cup of Earl Gray tea and the steam rose between them like an alpine mist.

"Do you happen to recall, Frau Mayerhof, if Herr Pichler was at all hard of hearing?"

The solid woman considered, jutting out her full lower lip in concentration and brushing a strand of graying hair back into place. "I must have spoken with Andreas thousands of times over the years. He certainly never mentioned a hearing loss of any kind. He didn't wear a hearing aid, that much I can say for sure. Still, I have to say that over the last few years, now that you mention it, he didn't always seem to hear me at first. Sometimes, when I entered a room behind him and said something, he didn't react. I recall that I had to repeat his name three times some weeks ago before he looked up from his repair work. I didn't think too much of it. Herr Kommissar, his hearing must have deteriorated over time; with age, I suppose. Why do you ask?"

"Oh, just trying to put a picture together," the detective said after savoring a sip of the unsweetened tea. "It is often the little things that tell us how an event took place. A murder investigation assembles the little things, gathers them together like a squirrel gathering acorns. It is much like that. Thank you very much, Frau Mayerhof, you have been most helpful indeed." He left her sitting there with a cup of tea, content with his answer, if no wiser for it.

As Waldbaer exited the kitchen his cell phone emitted its familiar series of electronic notes, arranged to mimic Mozart. He fished it from his jacket pocket and flipped up the thin plastic lid. He recognized the voice of Police Officer Braun. "What is it, Braun?"

"I think we might have found something of interest, Kommissar. We're in the cellar. It's a real maze down here, and easy to lose your way. I'm dispatching one of the other officers to meet you in the Hall of Banners and guide you to us. He'll be there in a couple of minutes."

Waldbaer grumbled agreement and set off through the array of capacious rooms to meet his escort.

The object they stared at in the harsh arc of a police heavy-duty flashlight was a human bone. Of this, Waldbaer had no doubt. He had been sufficiently exposed to crime and forensics to recognize this partial remnant of a once-living person. Waldbaer could also see that the long, beveled piece was very old; its surface had a dark patina and a trace of blackened tissue, apparently human skin, visible on the bone. A humerus bone, he noted, from the upper arm, and undamaged. It was a curious find.

"We haven't moved it," Braun explained, "it was lying right there where you see it, Kommissar. God knows how it got there or how long it's been there."

Waldbaer rubbed a hand against his chin, his eyes narrowing. "And where, exactly, is here, anyway?"

Braun shifted his spindly form a degree and shrugged. "Hard to say, other than that we're deep in the cellar. There's no electricity in here, and it looks like there never has been. We don't have blueprints or a map, but it hardly appears well traveled." The policeman let the lamp play fleetingly around the chamber. It was large, the rough-hewn and damp-stained stone walls interrupted only by two arched doors of black wood, the one Waldbaer and his escort had arrived through, and another, further away.

Waldbaer felt a shiver pass through his body and buttoned his loden jacket. It was cold and there was a vague, unpleasant mustiness to the air. He glanced over at Braun and the other police officer. "This bone might have nothing to do with Pichler's murder. In fact, it's hard to see how it could be connected. God knows, this Schloss is a labyrinth and probably full of animal tunnels and cracks in the foundation. It could be that one of the count's hunting dogs or a marder or something dragged the bone in here from a cemetery nearby. Still, we have to check it out as best we can. Call back to the station and get a photographer out here. When he's finished, bring that thing over to the coroner. He can probably tell us how old the bone is."

The two policemen nodded in unison. Braun unbuttoned a pocket on his black leather service jacket and pulled out a mobile phone. Waldbaer signaled him to stop. "Did you go through that other door and see where it leads?"

Braun frowned and shook his head. "No, Kommissar. This chamber is as far as I've proceeded. I started at the stairs you came down, and I've been going from empty room to empty room, checking out the scene as you instructed. So far none of the doors have been locked, but we've had to shoulder a few of them open. A lot of them look like they haven't been used in ages and some of them are warped and have rusty hinges. I haven't yet tried that one, though." He indicated the far door with a wag of his long chin.

"Let's see where this leads," Waldbaer sighed, unhappy with the cloying dampness and the imperfect illumination of the flashlight. With annoyance, he imagined the Italian-loafered count Winterloch seated in one of the plush, antique chairs in the Great Hall, sipping a brandy and leafing through some obscure leather-bound volume. The trio moved to the black door, their shoes crackling against stray pieces of mortar, their progress stirring silent swirls of protest in the dust.

Braun worked the rusting, primitively-cast door handle. The door issued a protesting sound but did not open. After a quick exchange of glances, Braun and the other police officer extended their arms and pushed together at the resisting slab of wood. The door fell open slowly, its bottom scrapping out an objection along the floor.

The flashlight beam played out in front of the three men, illuminating a world of gray, a dust-blanketed stone floor and rude concrete walls from which, here and there, a block of granite protruded. Moving on, the circle of light forced the darkness away from a long, heavy-beamed table supporting a disorderly and neglected collection of pewter and clay beer steins and mugs, some intact, others in shards. The collection was shrouded in a gauze of cobwebs and appeared very old.

On the margins of the visible space Waldbaer detected something else. "Move the flashlight to the left," he said. The arc of light responded and the detective emitted a satisfied grunt. There was a channel visible in the expanse of dust and detritus. "Well, well, someone has been through here recently. The dust is heavier here than in the other rooms we've passed through, and so the passage is more apparent." He stared more closely at the path of disturbance. "It doesn't look like there are any footprints visible, but we'll have to check that with flood lamps later. We might get lucky."

Braun shook his head in agreement. "You think maybe Herr Pichler was down here?"

"Could be," Waldbaer replied. "Pichler was supposedly conducting repair work of some sort in the cellar, among other tasks. Now, where does this track of prints lead?"

Braun urged the beam of light further along the floor, following the spoor. It ended several yards away, at the threshold of another door. The policeman snickered. "Just more of the same."

"Not exactly," Waldbaer grumbled. "Focus the light directly on the door."

The illumination revealed not a simple wooden door like the others but an arched object made of metal, apparently bronze, its surface elaborately worked with filigree depicting vines, leaves, and flowers. At the center of the creation a lion and bear faced each other. Waldbaer recognized the Winterloch escutcheon, the familial Wappen. Below the bas-relief symbol a large keyhole was visible.

"Try the door," Waldbaer ordered, and Braun's partner moved to the bronze door and pulled a heavy ring handle. It did not move. "This one's locked," the policeman murmured.

"No matter. Now things are getting a bit more interesting," Waldbaer said. "We'll see if any of the staff has a key. These footprints lead to that door, and I expect they continue on the other side. Maybe it was Pichler who wandered through here, maybe it was his killer, maybe both. Let's go back up. Braun, call for some assistance and have them send the police photographer. Have them bring some battery lamps. I want to clear this up." Careful to avoid disturbing the chain of foot markings in the sea of dust, the three men retraced their way to the staircase and the welcome warmth of the quarters above.

CHAPTER FOUR

He had been sitting in silence for quite a long time, gazing in immense satisfaction at the object before him. It was all-consuming, he thought, to contemplate the object's seductive beauty and venerability. The curved, black iron surface of the piece reflected the light thrown by the ceiling lamp above the mahogany table on which the object lay.

Delicate lines and images of burnished gold against the jet-black metal surface captured and reflected the light with even more intensity. Exquisite artistry, the man concluded, nodding his head appreciatively. The artist who had crafted the metal piece was unknown to the ages; his name had vanished into obscurity long ago. But his handiwork remained, its luster and beauty undiminished by time.

Time, the man considered, his eyes momentarily closing. Long centuries had passed, great bundles of years had marched by, since the shining metal object had been commissioned and completed. It had been hidden away, of course, for most of that time. But precisely for that reason, the piece had been perfectly preserved and survived for so long unravaged by wars, revolution, fire, famine, and flood. There was no pitting of the silky smooth metal surface, no trace of rust or corrosion, nor any dent or abrasion to mar the artist's craftsmanship. The worked metal looked exactly as it must have looked on the very day of its completion.

Reaching out a hand reverentially, the man touched the metal, his fingertips feeling the coolness of the metal surface. He smiled in contentment. There was an additional object yet to be examined. Something of equal beauty to be venerated for its aesthetic symmetry and high level of exquisite craftsmanship. Its long form rested on the shining mahogany table as well, concealed by layered wrappings of cotton and burlap, bound together by twine. No need to rush. This object, as well, had waited unseen and unappreciated for hundreds of years. There was sufficient time to anticipate it, to savor it, and he would do so without haste.

CHAPTER FIVE

SCHLOSS WINTERLOCH

Waldbaer stood on the parking apron in front of the castle's main sally port and frowned as Braun reported to him, one hand cinched in his belt and the other by his side.

"None of the staff has a key, Kommissar, and I asked everyone. Most of them say they've never been to the basement, at least not as far into its spaces as we've gone. No reason for them to go down there, they say. The cellar spaces were Pichler's to deal with, apparently. He probably had a key to that door, but God knows where it is."

Waldbaer rubbed a hand over his forehead and down to the bridge of his nose. He felt the first stirrings of a headache and blamed the dampness, the castle, and the homicide case itself. "Did you talk to the count about the key?"

The gaunt policeman looked down at the pebbled driveway and grimaced. "No, not to the count. I figured he wasn't likely to deal with little details like the keys to cellar doors. Count von Winterloch is the type of person who would expect his people to take care of those things and not bother him with it."

Waldbaer expressed no censure, the policeman's reasoning was sound and Braun had been instructed only to talk to the staff, not the master of the house.

"All right, then. I'll talk to the count myself. Have him meet me in the Great Hall in a few minutes. You can tell him I have a few questions for him. If he whines or throws a tantrum, feel free to note that the alternate, and indeed preferred, location for a chat is my office at the police station."

Braun straightened his posture and a smile lanced across his thin features. An opportunity to toss a bit of dust in the face of nobility was something to be relished. He tossed off a casual salute and strode away.

Waldbaer furrowed his brow and enveloped his hands in the pockets of his jacket. It was the second day of the investigation, and he had come up with very little. He exhaled and was surprised to see tendrils of mist where his breath met the dank air. He did not like the castle and did not much like the castle owner. He tried to push this personal prejudice aside and concentrate on the case itself.

For one thing, there was Pichler. He seemed to be a typical handyman. He was circumspect and did not speak badly of his employer; that was prudent in a small town. Pichler had been doing routine work at the time of the murder, this too had been established. But exactly what type of routine work? Waldbaer made a note to himself to ask the count. At any rate, Pichler had been killed, and the killer probably covertly assaulted him from behind, the crime made easier due to Pichler's hearing loss. And Pichler had died in the very early hours of the morning, perhaps around five a.m., and had been found dead some time later by Frau Mayerhof.

Waldbaer scraped a shoe along the stone floor. The question remained: who had killed Pichler. And why? What motivation was there? Hatred, and revenge, and theft were, of course, the trifecta. Theft could probably be ruled out. Pichler's wallet had two hundred euros in it, untouched. Waldbaer would find out, and quickly, with precision. Buttoning his jacket against the dampness, he marched off to see the count.

Waldbaer entered the Great Hall through an oversized door. Count von Winterloch was imperiously present. Chin thrust high, and arms crossed at his chest, Winterloch seemed posed for a portrait artist.

"You doubtless don't realize it, but I have several things to do, all of them quite important. What is it now? Why do I suffer another interruption?"

Waldbaer glared at von Winterloch, noticing that the count was dressed in an elaborate and undoubtedly expensive, faux peasant shirt with deer-horn buttons. "Well, have it your way. It will, sadly, be rather more of an interruption than you anticipate. You'll have the opportunity to answer my questions, all of them, at the police station. In the sublime hospitality of our interrogation room. One of the policemen will take you there."

Waldbaer watched with satisfaction as a dark red, nearly purple, flush crept up from von Winterloch's neck and illuminated his cheeks. "This is an affront."

The detective raised his eyebrows and shoulders at the same time and dropped them. "Whatever. But I anticipate that the monastic surroundings of the police interrogation room will perhaps see to it that you provide the answers that I require. I have items of investigation which take priority at the moment. I'll meet you somewhat later. The policemen will now escort you to the station." He strode off, suppressing a wicked smile, feeling von Winterloch's eyes on him like drawn daggers. Waldbaer felt his mood lift, as it had not lifted all day.

CHAPTER SIX

He unwrapped the pliant burlap carefully, gently urging the folds of fabric apart. They fell away, revealing a burnished object of shining black, with dramatic traces and flourishes of gold.

"Yes, it is a remarkable find," the man breathed.

He lifted the heavy piece of armor gingerly, as if afraid that it would break apart in his hands, but the ancient weight was cold and solid. Just below the ceremonial gardbrace at the shoulder, at the center of the breastplate, the images of two beasts pawed the imaginary air menacingly, their torsos raised solemnly. A bear, its formidable, toothed mouth open, and a lion rampant, its large paws surmounted by talons. The man lifted a hand and stroked the metal, coming to rest on the lion's mane where the light's reflection shone most intently. More impressive than the primitively rendered bear, it was the lion that commanded respect.

"Worth a fortune, an absolute fortune," the man whispered. With a reverential motion, he replaced the heavy breastplate in the folds of burlap.

He also regarded for several moments the gold pommel, grip and cross guard of the ancient sword, propped against a wall. The gold was inset with precious stones, predominantly diamonds. The hand guard merged with a steel blade that was nearly four feet long, and bore the inscription "Behold, I Am Death" emblazoned down its length.

Dr. Stefan Hofgartner, an art history graduate of the Fine

Arts Academy of Munich, was pleased and hugged his arms around his chest in satisfaction. The theft, from the planning stage to execution, had been most successful. But the planning had been exceedingly intricate, and the time taken to extract the objects from the von Winterloch crypt considerable.

Hofgartner shrugged and brushed a hand through thick hair that was lusterless blond, running to gray. Planning to steal something took longer than the physical act of stealing. Without his active intervention, the metal objects would have remained, conceivably forever, cloaking the bones of the long-dead and long-forgotten Count Heinrich von Winterloch. Hofgartner smoothed a tuft of hair back in place and considered for a moment how it had been.

* * *

Hofgartner had discovered the von Winterloch grave quite by accident. An article in the *Münchner Merker* had included a feature on the Winterloch castle outside of Gamsdorf and had mentioned that the ancient crypt of Heinrich lay in the private chapel which was attached to the castle. Aside from Heinrich, the castle these days was the home of the as yet undeceased Count Rheinhold von Winterloch. The article had mentioned, in passing, that the grave of the long-interred Count Heinrich had been undisturbed since 1121.

Hofgartner had read the article with professional interest. He had ascertained that the castle was isolated by several miles from any village and occupied rural, forested grounds far removed from prying eyes. With the help of night vision goggles and infrared cameras, he had located and observed the chapel, which fortunately was a considerable distance from the residential rooms of the fortress.

Parking a rented Audi sedan over a mile away from the Winterloch estate, he had bided his time and spent a week full of nights wedged against a thick pine tree covered with moss, in the perennially damp evening mist of the forest. Finally, around eight on a Friday evening, he observed the count's dark-blue Mercedes leave the castle, presumably to go to a dinner or some other hours-long social affair. No sooner had the headlights of the car disappeared from sight than Hofgartner had bounded through the trees, eyes fixed on the fortress. Using the tools of the burglar's trade as well as wearing a pair of night vision goggles, he carefully split a lock on a door in the castle wall, and, impervious to its protesting squeal, entered the compound.

The chapel was a typically Roman architectural structure and, Hofgartner discovered, was mercifully unlocked, saving him much time and effort. He entered the church and felt its cold, stagnant air, and in a matter of seconds had found the crypt of Heinrich. It was located to the right of the main aisle, an enormous carved mass of worn and age-discolored marble set directly in the floor. At the side of the crypt on the stone floor, Hofgartner discovered a hatch of deeply veneered worn wood.

He knew that this was a portal which must descend to the sarcophagus containing the bones—and the armor—of Heinrich. With effort, he pried the doorway open, and the space below revealed a ladder descending some thirty feet. Hofgartner tested the ladder, gingerly at first, and found that it could easily take his weight. He climbed down carefully in the event that a rung was broken, but found the ladder still intact. A minute later, Hofgartner placed his feet on solid ground and turned to the crypt. He removed his night vision goggles, placed them in a pocket of his vest, and flicked on a flashlight.

Hofgartner saw that the richly carved stone of the sarcophagus was marble. Moving closer, he read the word identifying the grave's only resident: Heinrich. Drawing on a pair of black leather gloves, Hofgartner brushed his hand over the top of the sarcophagus, finding it was made of limestone. He judged that it would take two people to move the object. He photographed the lid in close-up focus and took several shots of the marble siding. There was nothing left to do.

Hofgartner grabbed the sides of the ladder and made his way up through the wooden hatch in the chapel floor. For a few moments his heart raced as the hatch refused to fall into place, its form wedged on the church floor tiles. Finally, he managed to push the wooden door shut, but was distressed by its resistant growl of protest. He would have to instruct the break-in team that he selected to find another way out of the castle.

Wiping his clothes clean of dust, Hofgartner conducted a final survey of the chapel. He photographed the crypt from every angle and took several other interior shots of the chapel for perspective. Not one to linger without cause, he exited the church the way he had entered, leaving not a trace behind him.

The reconnaissance completed, he had taken his time before selecting the individuals to conduct the actual grave-robbing. He had chosen well. Karl Ortner, an established criminal with a record of success, and another petty criminal from Munich, had agreed to his terms. Hofgartner rose and poured himself a cognac from the nineteenth century bar. All would be well. He sipped it, scratching at a spot between his neck and shoulder. It must have been a damned mosquito, he concluded.

He determined that the next step toward making a profit from the robbery would be to assemble a list of clients. In this, he needed to exercise caution. He took a pad of paper from the polished surface of a nearby desk and, with reflection, scribbled down a handful of names. The list would be a short one, and consist of the rapacious, the wealthy, and the inherently introverted. Hofgartner smiled. Clients for stolen, precious medieval objects were much the same archetype as those who paid vast sums for purloined art. Six names would do, a short list was more secure under the circumstances. It was essential that, whether the prospective customers bought the objects or not, they could be trusted to keep their mouths shut. There was work to do. Hofgartner seated himself at the desk, sighed with a mix of resignation and con-

tentment, and picked up the leather-bound booklet that contained the private phone numbers of potential buyers across
Europe. He scratched again at his neck; the itch continued to
annoy. Damned mosquitoes.

CHAPTER SEVEN

GAMSDORF POLICE STATION

Waldbaer sat at the metal table with folded hands. He had chosen the austere surroundings of the police interrogation room solely to discomfit and annoy the count. A large lamp hung overhead, emitting a low but distinct electrical hum along with its intrusive, shadow-banishing illumination. It suited the situation perfectly. Winterloch sat opposite the detective, his face wrapped in a scowl, his hands clasped together, white at the knuckles.

"I would like to get some answers to a number of questions. I thought perhaps that this task could be best accomplished here. It is an environment that will focus the mind." Waldbaer regarded the count with unblinking eyes.

"I take it that I am under arrest?" the count asked in a gruff voice.

"No. You are not under arrest."

"Then I want to leave, and I want to leave now. I'm not comfortable here. I will answer your queries in my residence."

"You may not leave. I have summoned you here, and that is within my legal authority. You may recall that I did not want this interrogation to happen, but you apparently did. You had your chance, Count, and I do not have infinite patience. You may leave once I am satisfied I have answers to my questions. It's as simple as that. Shall we begin, Count?"

The count glowered and said nothing.

"When did you last see Andreas Pichler alive?"

Winterloch hesitated before spitting out an answer. "On

the day before he died, for less than five minutes. Nothing of the slightest consequence was said."

"If the conversation is of consequence or not, Count, I will be the judge. What was discussed?"

Winterloch swept one hand dismissively across the table. "Nothing important, and nothing remotely related to his death. I happened to see Pichler entering the castle while I was on the way out, rather early in the morning. As I say, it was an exchange of no real importance. He told me that he had been in the cellar, checking the structural foundations, and he was a bit worried about something he'd seen. He said he'd give me a full report in a day or two. That was it, aside from the usual courtesies."

Waldbaer steepled his hands together, reflecting for a moment. "What was Pichler actually doing in the cellar? And where in the basement was he exactly?"

Winterloch shrugged. "To answer your first question, Pichler was doing things that a handyman does, I suppose. I gather that he was ascertaining what damage water, as well as time, had done to the original structure. The basement is not impervious to the elements. Pichler had located some pillars, or a portion of the original building, that needed repair or, at least, would need repair over the next few years. As to where in the basement he was, I haven't the faintest clue."

Waldbaer stared unblinkingly at the count. "Did Pichler say, specifically, what he had found, or what damage would need to be repaired?"

A smirk crossed the count's face. "Naturally not, he knew I didn't have much interest or time for such things. Such repair work is invariably tied up with cost. If the cost of any proposed repairs would be significantly beyond Pichler's normal expense account, he would bring it to my attention, for my personal approval. The castle does, by the way, have insurance, though that is purchased at a considerable fee."

"Yes, I see. But Pichler did not discuss this with you? That strikes me as odd."

Winterloch's eyes narrowed. "No, it's not odd at all. I trusted Pichler, and I am not interested in the mundane details of whether sandstone needs to be replaced or what kind of steel braces need to be emplaced on granite pillars. I'm sure it was something like that. It doesn't interest me in the least. Anyway, Pichler indicated that he would need to talk with me in a day or two. He seemed a bit worried and hesitant. It could be that he discovered that some item of repair was more expensive than it originally seemed. I assume that you can believe me, Waldbaer, when I say that unexpected costs can be a major headache."

Waldbaer regarded the count with hard brown eyes, and shrugged. "The cost of major repair can surely be staggering. But I want to know one thing: did Pichler ever say, ever make mention, of it being the cost of repair work that was worrying him? Or is that simply your assumption? What did Pichler say, can you recall?"

Winterloch snorted. "I can hardly be expected to recall what every employee has said to me, in their own words, in living color. But, for what it's worth, Pichler didn't quite say that it was the repair work that worried him. Just that he was worried. I presumed that repair of the cellar was the source of his distraction, but that's all."

Waldbaer stared off into the distance and mumbled, as if to himself. "A presumption? Pichler might have been worried about other things. Perhaps about something that he discovered, something he stumbled upon. But what could that be? Do you have any ideas, Count?"

"I can't think of a thing, no. Nothing of note is down there in the cellar spaces, nothing valuable, at least. There is some antique furniture and tapestries that are very old. But that stuff is large; nobody is likely to abscond with it. And I've told you, the people in my employment I trust completely, without exception. Theft is not to be considered."

Waldbaer nodded. "You mentioned that you have seven employees here. Do any of them live in the castle?"

Winterloch sneered. "Not everyone wants to live where they work, Kommissar. Even in a castle as full of history as mine. Sepp, the old gardener, resides there, but he is well over eighty. He has a single room near the kitchen; formerly for the cook, but the days when one kept a cook around are gone. Sepp, by the way, is a bit addled with age. Frankly, he has never been overburdened by intellect, but he knows the grounds and is able to choose the flowers wisely. He will probably die in his room near the kitchen. He has been a loyal worker for many years, and I will permit it. In addition to him, there is Markus Zimmerman. Zimmerman is a young man, about thirty-five, and handles bookkeeping matters. He asked to stay in the castle, due to the expense of renting an apartment. For better or for worse, I permitted it for a while. I expect that he'll find an apartment in a few months' time. He has some rooms above the main hall."

Waldbaer studied Winterloch's face, searching for any trace of deception. "Other than yourself and the gardener and the bookkeeper, then, the castle is home to no one. Very well. Are there any regular visitors to this place? Do you have friends or acquaintances whose presence here would be routine?"

Winterloch assumed a look of repose and folded his hands, one into the other. "Let me think. There were no visitors the morning of Pichler's death. The postman shows up Monday through Friday, but I don't even know his name. Tobias Steiner, a fellow I know, dropped by to chat a few days ago. And the local mayor, anxious and fretting about the next election, was also here around the same time."

"Who exactly is this Tobias Steiner?"

"He is, I guess you would say, a good acquaintance, nothing more than that. He's in his thirties, he's educated, and has traveled to Africa, among other places. We have a shared interest in African art, and he drops by every now and then. Sometimes I invite him to stay for dinner because he's such a good conversationalist."

Waldbaer thought for a moment. "Good. I will probably be talking to him. Now, to return to Pichler, he apparently had been working in the cellar spaces recently. What is down there in the basement, exactly? And where do the corridors lead?"

Winterloch shook his head, as if he were a teacher whose time was being driveled away by a dull schoolboy. "What is down there is nothing. Just a vast amount of space, divided into dozens of halls and corridors. The cellar spaces comprise the foundations of the fortress, as they do in all castles. The spaces are quite extensive, you yourself have seen it. That labyrinth of rooms is twelve to twenty feet in height, and the entire castle is cellared. Not to mention the chapel and the old cookery, all of these buildings are connected through the cellar."

"The chapel?" Waldbaer gave the count a quizzical look.

Winterloch flashed a brief smile, devoid of any humor. "Quite right. It contains the bones, or more probably the dust, of my ancestor, Count Heinrich von Winterloch. He built this edifice and is buried in the chapel. He died in one of the outbreaks of the plague that swept over Europe. The plague killed about a third of the population on the continent. A heroic war record and noble blood were of no defense against it. The "Black Death" as they called it.

Waldbaer interrupted. "As I recall, the ordinary blood of ordinary men paid most of the toll, Count. Bishops and the nobility died too, of course. The plague killed without exception, peasant and serf, captains and kings. It changed the way society developed. But I digress. So, then, you can add nothing at all to what may have been bothering Pichler?"

"I expect not. May I leave you to consider the infinite array of possibilities?" Winterloch paused and swept a hand through his white hair, looking directly at the detective. "Kommissar, I have things to do, and I want to go home."

Waldbaer took his time to answer and considered whether there was a percentage in continuing to annoy the count, but he concluded that his point had been adequately made. "You may leave, I permit it. But, Count, I will call on you again. I want Pichler's set of keys, for one thing. We will be in and out of the castle, and I do not know for how long. The castle is the scene of a murder, and I intend to find the murderer. You will find that I am sadly ill-humored when anything or anyone distracts me from that goal. Do you understand me?"

"Perfectly, Kommissar. I will be at my residence if you require further assistance. I will have my servant deliver the keys."

When they parted, Waldbaer felt somewhat satisfied, but was not content. The castle, and its tubercular cellar spaces, beckoned him.

CHAPTER EIGHT

MUNICH, CAPITAL OF BAVARIA

Karl Ortner swilled beer from his foaming glass of Löwenbräu, decorated with the eponymous logo of the brewery. The beer hall in the early evening was noisy, and nearly every table was filled with loud and boisterous tourists or local patrons. Ortner sneered as he brushed a hand through his thinning, jet black hair and unzipped his nylon jacket. He didn't give a toss about the customers, or for that matter, about the noise level at Löwenbräu on the Nymphenburgerstrasse, a prosperous shopping street of Munich. He raised his hand and signaled to a passing ponytailed waitress. "Get me another one," he slurred.

Ortner had money, more than enough to purchase as much beer as he wanted. He had, in fact, five thousand euros, in denominations of one hundred euro notes, stuffed into the pockets of his trousers and jacket. There was more secreted away in the kitchen drawers of his rented apartment. A total of fifty thousand euros in cash. Indulging another long sip of amber-colored beer, Ortner smiled in contentment. He had been paid the money for successfully breaking into a crypt and delivering the antique contents to his employer. Still, he had the annoyance of a persistent headache which had been with him since that morning, and it dampened his mood. He had tossed down two aspirin earlier in the day to rid himself of the pain and two more tablets later, but the headache's gnawing, voracious insistence would not vanish.

A shadow loomed over the white tablecloth in front of him, turning the ivory surface to gray. "You called, Karl, and I came over. Here I am, the very man. Are you having dinner, by the way?" The gruff voice belonged to a massive hulk of a man whose form seemed to spill out of his clothes. His long gray hair was pulled tautly over his skull and arranged in a ponytail which cascaded over the collar of his unbuttoned black wool suit in greasy strands.

"No. I'm only drinking tonight, but feel free to order anything you want, Uwe, it's on me." Ortner pointed to an empty wooden chair, and the man lowered his bulk onto it with a grunt. The man looked at Ortner with porcine, ebony eyes that seemed to have no pupils. He squinted at Ortner from a bloated, heavily reddened, pockmarked face. "No, I'll pass on dinner. What's up, Karl? You didn't call me because you like my company."

True enough, Ortner thought to himself, while manufacturing a smile. "Listen, Uwe, do I have a deal for you. I like you, and I wanted to give you first shot at it."

The man rubbed a rough hand against his beefy visage and sighed. "Cut the crap, Karl. I assume you've got your paws on something that I can unload in my antique store. What is it, and how much does it cost?"

Karl Ortner winced, but once again feigned a smile. "I'm going to tell you that, Uwe. I've got something special here. Really special. And I know that it's real, because I retrieved it myself."

"Okay, whatever. Are you going to show me?"

Ortner nodded. "You bet I am." Without ceremony he inserted a hand deep into his trouser pocket and removed a small object, swathed in a folded strip of newspaper.

"You've spared no expense on the wrapping, I see," Uwe remarked.

Ortner shrugged. "It's what lies within that counts. Just open it."

Uwe hesitated then reached across the table to where Ortner had deposited the parcel next to his beer. He unwrapped the folds of paper and removed the item.

Uwe looked puzzled as he gently moved about the minute piece of gold in his hands. "What is it? Is it a ring?"

Ortner's face brightened and he reached for his beer. "It's a ring all right. And it's pure gold, I think from an Italian gold-smith. Just take a look at how intricate the artwork is."

"Yeah. Well, Karl, it's just a ring as far as I can see. I already have lots of rings in the antique shop, too damned many, and most of them have accumulated a lot of dust. I don't need another one."

Ortner shook his head, as if disappointed with the intransi-gence of a small child. "No, Uwe. It's not just a ring, and it's noth-ing like an engagement ring or wedding ring or any of that crap. It has history, lots of history, and centuries of history. It belonged to a count in the Middle Ages, and it was on his hand when he was buried. Look at the symbols: at its center you'll see a sword, a medieval broadsword. And there are two little figures at the sides, a lion and a bear."

Uwe looked at the piece and traced a thick finger along the ring. The finger and a dirty nail stopped under an impression in the ring. "What's this?"

Ortner smiled and nodded, but rubbed a hand across his temple; his headache was not receding. "That's an initial. It's a W. I shouldn't say this but I'll share it with you, Uwe. The 'W' stands for Winterloch, if you really want to know. That would be Count Von Winterloch. He was a knight and a member of the nobility. Don't breathe a word of that to anyone, Uwe. It could put me in a most unpleasant situation."

"Really? Satisfy my curiosity. Tell me, Karl, how did you get this damn ring?"

Ortner pressed his hands against the glass of beer, then de-cided to take another long swallow. "Well, Uwe, I stole it, to be absolutely frank with you. I took it right from Winterloch's desic-cated hand, what there was left of it. I guess you could say that I robbed the crypt. I stripped the corpse, you might say."

Uwe raised his dark-brown eyes from examining the ring. "You robbed the crypt of this count? You must have entirely lost your mind. Are you fucking crazy?"

Ortner snickered, hands twined around his beer glass. "Uwe, as the British commandos say, 'who dares, wins'. I had a few tough moments getting that ring off, I'll admit, but I can vouch for the authenticity of that piece of gold you're holding. It's real, and it's from the Middle Ages. And, as you well know, unlike the Roman Empire, there aren't many rings around from that period."

Uwe grunted. "Let's say just for argument's sake that I'm interested. How much do you want for this piece?"

Ortner sat back in his chair and pursed his lips. "Well, let me ask you, how much do you think it's worth? I mean, think of it, this ring was probably worn in countless battles centuries ago during the religious wars when everybody was a Catholic or Protestant. And, at the time the count carved out his estate here in Bavaria, that ring was a sign of authority."

Uwe placed the ring back in the disheveled folds of newspaper. "All right. I'll make you an offer. I take the ring with me, right now, for four thousand euros, period. In cash."

Ortner blanched. A thin smile traced its way across his features. "Now, Uwe, one thing you need to understand—"

The larger man hunched over the table and a vein stood out in the middle of his forehead. "No, Karl, you need to understand that my offer is final. I don't barter. Four thousand in cash. I have that amount on me. I'll pay you four thousand for the ring and not a cent more. You can take it or leave it; no bitching and no whining. If you robbed the crypt, hurray for you. If you didn't, well, let's just say that you always did tell a good story. But the fact is that I have to unload whatever I buy to discriminating, paying customers, and I have to take my chances if the police are nosing around. Anyway, I'm willing to bet that no one else will give you four thousand euros in crisp five hundred euro notes for this, shall we say, little piece of history. But it's your call, Karl."

Ortner's smile faded, and there was a distracting, insistent throbbing deep inside of his forehead. Aspirin was having no effect; the pain was distracting him.

"Uwe, I can't really argue with you, and I won't argue with

you; I invited you here because you're a business man. The ring is a steal for four thousand, and I mean that. Look, I'm not whining, but I hope you know who your friends are. Four thousand euros in cash it is. After all, what are friends for?"

Ortner watched the red face with narrow dark eyes and a stubble of beard nod. "Okay," Uwe mumbled with breath that was sour. He removed a stack of notes from his jacket, counted off eight, and slid them across the table. The transaction accomplished, Uwe slicked his hair hard to his skull. He wrapped the ring within its folds of newspaper and carefully placed it in the depths of his trouser pocket. "Pleasure doing business with you, Karl," he said, raising one hand in a mock salute, and then drifted off into the noise and the growing mass of customers in the Löwenbräu beer hall.

Ortner sighed, feeling not at all happy. Four thousand euros was less of a sum than he had envisioned, considerably less. Still, he couldn't complain and it was all profit. The ring was only one of four pieces that he had taken from the crypt, and from the black-skinned, rotting skeleton of Heinrich von Winterloch. After all, he reasoned, having a little cash on the side, without the knowledge of Doktor Hofgartner, was only fair. It was he who had taken all of the risks. He had even had to kill a handyman who had stumbled upon his work; the sword that he had stolen had come in handy. In addition, he had to settle accounts with his so-called partner in the theft; it would have made no sense to let him live. And besides, he was entitled to a little free-market profit in addition to Hofgartner's handsome payment.

The severe throbbing in his brain refused to subside. He could almost hear it, a slow, persistent pounding that incrementally increased. It was as if someone were beating a hammer on the inside of his skull. Ortner decided that if the pain was present tomorrow, he would have to consult a doctor. He pulled twenty euros from his pocket and left it on the table, underneath his beer glass. He needed to get home and go to bed. His chair scraped against the stone floor as he rose, and he made his way with a grimace through the din of diners and laughing tourists.

As he approached the twin doors exiting to the crowded Munich street, he scratched at his wrist, plagued by a burning sensation. Looking down, he gasped. An expanse of his skin, larger than a quarter, had turned dark, almost black. The dark blemish was at the sleeve of his jacket and seemed to move when his fingers touched it. Dear God, Ortner thought, what in the hell is this? What caused it? With a low groan he determined to get some sleep and deal with it in the morning. Ortner felt exhausted, and hoped that morning would bring some relief.

CHAPTER NINE

SCHLOSS WINTERLOCH

The morning fog, thick and choking, issued from the forests around the castle like the specters of the long dead. But it was the recently dead that occupied Franz Waldbaer's thoughts at the moment. Andreas Pichler had been in the realm of the deceased for three days, and the police had nothing substantive in hand on the identity of the murderer. Nothing at all. It was this simple fact which was responsible for the frown pulling down like gravity on Waldbaer's features. The detective stood before the aged stone of the castle, at the enormous entrance door, replete with a bronze lion's head. There was also, at the side of the door, a buzzer, a tool of innovative modernity which Waldbaer used to seek entrance.

The oversize door opened a moment later, accompanied by a protesting creak, and the detective was confronted by an ample-bellied bald man in his late sixties, with a sympathetic face, whom Waldbaer recognized as one of the count's staff. "Good morning, sir," the man said.

"*Guten Morgen*," Waldbaer replied, with unintended gruffness. "I'm Franz Waldbaer, *Kommissar der Polizei*. I'll be checking on the Pichler murder today. By the way, some policemen will be following shortly. They're part of the investigation, and I require their presence." Waldbaer waited for some objection, but there was none.

"Of course, sir," the man intoned, "I take it you know where you are going. If I can get you a refreshment of some sort, or if you need me in any way, please just say the word."

Waldbaer, stunned by the courtesy, was nearly without words. He wondered if von Winterloch had primed his staff to be inordinately respectful. He decided to ignore this suspicion. "No, no, I won't be requiring anything, except the key to a door in the basement. The uniformed police had it the other day."

"I have it here, sir," the man said, producing a long polished mortice key. "Will there be anything else, sir?"

Waldbaer stared at the key in his hand. "No, no. I know my way to the cellar spaces."

The detective made his way to the Great Hall and into the Hall of Banners with its array of flags and beyond, to the black painted door that led to the cellar. Descending the stairs, he noted that the must of the damp fortress was gradually replaced by the smell of cold soil and moldering decay, as the stairs took him deeper into the earth. He had switched on the lights at the entrance door, and the tempered illumination cascaded in a yellow beam over his shoulders. Eventually, the stairs came to an end, and Waldbaer made his way by memory, until the dust in the seldom-used rooms revealed the footprints he and his police escort had made the other day. He came to the elaborate door with the carved Wappen of the Winterlochs, the family coat of arms. The solid wood of the door was surmounted with a mortice key shield.

Waldbaer looked at the enormous key in his hand and felt its heft. The key appeared to be of iron, with traces of rust, and was perhaps a hundred years old, perhaps two hundred. It had a long shaft and a relatively small bit at the end. The detective inserted it into the mortise lock in the door, and felt the key plate issue a resonating click. He grinned with the momentary satisfaction of a child. Inclining an arm against the dormant weight of the door, he pushed it open. He located the battery-powered lamp left at the door the day before by his police escort and clicked it on.

The darkness fell away. The cavernous room, now bathed in illumination, was buttressed by four stone pillars. The shapes of the columns were crudely cut, and Waldbaer realized that this was typical for cellar spaces, which would not have been expected to host visitors. But there was something else in the room as well.

A large, rectangular structure, running from ceiling to floor, and its size embraced the entire center of the hall. Made of stone blocks and mortar, it appeared as old as the castle itself, if the walls of the vast room were any indication. Waldbaer sighed and expelled a mist of breath. "Damn the cold," he muttered, and walked to the nearest wall that formed the stone rectangle. Light bathed the stone and banished the shadows. Waldbaer studied the stone and traced a hand against an impression on the wall.

"Ah, yes," Waldbaer said to himself. He had noticed the new mortar yesterday. His hand continued to trace the line of mortar about five feet, until it stopped. The new mortar then jutted up at a perpendicular angle for about five feet. Waldbaer stepped back a few feet and put it all in perspective. "Well, well," he breathed. The bond of un-aged mortar formed its own rectangle, mimicking the solid structure itself.

The silence of the cellar was broken by a loud report as a piece of masonry crumbled into dust behind him.

Swinging around, and ripping his Glock firearm from its leather holster, Waldbaer found himself aiming the piece at the lifted eyebrows and shocked face of Braun, the policeman.

"*Verdammt*, Braun, don't you know to announce yourself?"

The policeman nodded, visibly relieved. "I'm sorry, I guess I wasn't thinking. Trust me, it won't happen again." Waldbaer returned the weapon to his holster, feeling its form nestle back into the familiar space.

Waldbaer pointed toward the stone wall. "Braun, what do you see here? Tell me what it is."

Braun adjusted his eyes, glanced, and nodded, running his service cap up above his forehead. "It looks like someone has been at work. Pichler maybe? That wall has been reinforced with new mortar. It's a deeper gray than the rest of the wall, like it's still moist."

Waldbaer's face lightened with a sardonic smile. "You are

partly right, Braun. It is new mortar and it's not completely dry yet. But the wall has not been reinforced. I think it has been replaced, an exchange of new mortar for old. This rectangle of stone at the center of the vault is most unusual. I suspect that Count Winterloch could be of assistance. Fetch him for me, if you don't mind."

Ten minutes later Waldbaer was staring at the scowling countenance of von Winterloch. "Count, I need to know where we are with some precision. What lies above?"

Winterloch raised his head for a moment, looking like a hound sniffing the wind. "We are directly below the chapel, or the castle church. I came through here decades and decades ago, as a child. As it was described to me, this elongated structure you see before you is the crypt of Heinrich Graf Stefan von Winterloch. His remains, or what's left of them, are behind those stones. Heinrich was, incidentally, only the first in a long line of Winterloch soldiers. The Winterlochs fought the Turks in the seventeenth century and the Franco-Prussian war saw the service of a colonel. The First World War had a brigadier general, and the Second World War, his son, also as a general. My grandfather fought the French at Messines in 1918, and my father commanded a Wehrmacht regiment through 1945, on the Eastern Front. Service, you see, was a point of honor for the Winterlochs."

"I see. And you did your required service in the Bundeswehr, I presume?" Waldbaer knew the answer to his question, and kept a smirk off his face, but waited for the reaction. The count's features colored violent red.

"No. I was studying in Berlin. At that time during the cold war, residents of Berlin were exempted from military service. Had the political realities been different, I certainly would have served."

"Of course," Waldbaer let his response linger. He knew, and he wanted Winterloch to know, that the count was, as the Americans would say, a draft dodger. It was enough.

"Let's return to the matter at hand, your predecessor Heinrich. I have to tell you, I am going to have to intrude on the crypt, and, as you say, his bones. I suspect someone has done that already, to speak frankly. You can object, of course, but then I will get a warrant to do the search." Waldbaer shrugged his shoulders. "It is entirely your choice."

Winterloch looked resigned. He placed his hands in his pockets and stood straight. "You say somebody has intruded on the crypt already. What do you mean by that?"

Waldbaer ran a hand roughly through his hair. "*Ja.* Look closely, Count. Do you see where the old, original concrete ends? I am willing to bet that someone, over a couple of nights, removed the stones, and tore down the edifice. The same person, more than likely, then replaced the old, destroyed mortar with new mortar. It's a pretty simple task, with the right tools. I also surmise that the perpetrator was looking for something. Can you enlighten me on what some person might have been looking for?"

"Perhaps Pichler was doing some construction work? This is the oldest part of the castle, after all. Perhaps he was doing structural repair work of some sort and failed to mention it to me."

"Yes, perhaps it was Pichler. But I want to see what is inside that vault." Waldbaer's tone radiated self-confidence. "Will I require a court order? It is all the same to me."

Winterloch held out his hands in a sign of seeming resignation. "Do what you will. But, Kommissar, please remember that this is the grave of a Graf and knight, the final resting place of a courageous von Winterloch."

"I will give him all the respect that is due the dead," Waldbaer said.

BENEATH THE SCHLOSS WINTERLOCH CASTLE

A battery of police lamps transformed the place of shadows that was the cellar room of the castle into a surgical amphitheater, creating a sea of illumination. After dusting the wall of the vault for fingerprints, two police employees with hydraulic power drills were brought in to do their work. Two policemen stood by, observing.

Waldbaer stood with hands thrust into the pockets of his loden jacket as a steady drum of noise echoed through the chamber. At his side, Winterloch stood beside him, arms crossed defensively against his chest, his frown having deepened into a disapproving grimace. Grit and stone flew around the two drillers in a billowing, gray cloud.

"They will be through the wall in a minute," Waldbaer shouted above the din.

"And they will pay, of course, to have the wall restored to its original condition," Winterloch barked in reply. The detective decided to let the remark go unanawered.

With a warning groan, a stone as large as a man's torso smashed to the ground, carrying a torrent of debris in in its wake. The two drillers silenced their instruments and stepped aside. "It's open. You can get through now, Kommissar, but watch your step," one of them yelled.

Waldbaer shuffled forward to the crypt, his ears ringing, taking in the scent of centuries of dead air and vestigial traces of decay. The vault displayed a large hole that was perhaps three feet in height, its bottom rimming only inches off the floor.

One of the drillers spoke up. "The concrete wasn't old, Kommissar, and we followed its trace pretty well, I think. Do you need a hand getting in there?" Waldbaer took the remark as an affront. "I'll bloody well manage on my own, I'm a police officer, dammit," he grumbled. Expelling a grunt, he bent down on his knees, which issued a cracking sound, and pulled himself through the opening. He swore, feeling the annoyance of concrete pebbles that insinuated themselves against his corduroy trousers. Once through the entrance provided by the drills, he stood and surveyed the scene. Subdued light, hazed by the dust, filtered through the chamber. The room was bare, except for the outline of crosses that ornamented a dozen or so thin pillars supporting the room at intervals. But there was more.

A massive sarcophagus of white marble, its condition and color barely sullied by the intervening centuries, was at the center of the space, its weight supported by the granite floor. Intrigued, Waldbaer moved closer, his eyes taking in every detail. A shout startled him.

"Waldbaer, I want to come in, and I want to come in now. This is the tomb of my relative, of my blood. I demand to see it." The voice was Winterloch's.

Waldbaer turned shaking his head, and replied. "Not yet, Count. This is a police investigation, and I am a trained investigator. When I have seen what there is to see, you will be allowed in. I anticipate that you have a few minutes yet to wait." A truculent sound eased through the yawning hole behind him, but Waldbaer ignored it.

His gaze arrested on the striking iconography facing him, emblazoned on the stone of the sarcophagus. A carved series of knights, some on horseback and some standing, were realistically displayed. Their dedication to things martial was attested to not only by their armor, but by their accoutrements. Their mailed and gauntleted hands grasped broadswords, medieval maces, fiercely long lances, and wind-tossed banners. The multitude of armed men seemed to gesture, or point, to a figure that was leading the column. Squinting, Waldbaer made out a bearded knight mounted on a stern charger waving a sword forward, toward infinity. The commanding figure of the knight, Waldbaer surmised, was none other than Heinrich, whose crypt this was.

Moving a degree closer, Waldbaer estimated that the sarcophagus came to chest level, and the lid covering it appeared to be of limestone, not of marble. The top of the device was emblazoned with an impressive carved image as well. The artist who had carved Heinreich's full-size image on the stone had portrayed the ancient and long-forgotten count at rest, doubtless appearing much as he had in life. At one corner of the coffin lid, Waldbaer noted, was the familiar Wappen of the lion rampant and the fierce bear.

Underneath this signet was the knight brought nearly to life in repose, eyes closed as if in pleasant and temporary sleep, attired in the manner of his profession, hands intertwined in repose. The bas-relief portrait was life-size, permitting Waldbaer to take in the details of how a medieval knight outfitted himself. The visored salet, or helmet, was placed in the count's left hand. The arms were protected by studded gauntlets; rising almost to the elbow, and the legs and thighs were afforded the protection of the cuisse and greave. Waldbaer recalled the names of the pieces from his avid study of combatant knights and the Middle Ages in high school. At the center of the carved image was the placard, or breastplate, which displayed the Christian cross at the center.

Waldbaer's examination of the image faltered. A wedge of darkness intruded. Moving a hand across the cold stone, Waldbaer saw that the lid had not been hermetically sealed. "Well, well," he breathed, "a sure sign that someone has been mucking about down here." Removing a thin flashlight from his jacket pocket, he focused the narrow beam through the crevice.

A hail of debris falling to the stone floor startled him. He turned to see that Winterloch had struggled through the recently excavated hole in the masonry, despite Waldbaer's admonition.

"I said not now, and I meant it," Waldbaer ordered.

The count's voice was firm. "You are forgetting that this is a von Winterloch crypt, and has been for centuries. And I demand to know what's going on here. This is my bloody property. Here rest the remains of my ancestor. I could demand that you get a search warrant."

Even through the haze and the uncertain glow of his flashlight, Waldbaer could see that the count was flushed, and his deep-set eyes illuminated by anger. He decided not to press the point, not least because getting a search warrant would take hours.

"All right, Count, have it your way. If you'd care to come over here and stand by my side, you can see for yourself what has been done."

Winterloch's gaze settled on the sarcophagus. "This is my ancestor's grave," he murmured.

"Yes, the very one," Waldbaer replied. Winterloch approached, saying nothing. The detective heard his breathing, and guessed that it was a moment of emotion for the seventy year old. He returned his gaze to the limestone lid.

"I found the lid partially opened, it was as you see it. This grave has been tampered with, I think relatively recently. What lies within are the remains of your distant antecedent. You can avert your gaze if you'd prefer, but I'm afraid I have to move the lid to get a better view."

Winterloch shook his head. "No. I have seen the dead before, Kommissar, it will not trouble me. Do what you must."

"You can help. This lid is made of stone. We have to put our shoulders into it and just push it aside." But first, put these on." Waldbaer pulled from his jacket pocket a pair of thin blue rubber gloves and then another, passing a pair to the Count.

Von Winterloch held the gloves in his hand and looked at them with narrowed eyes. "What are these for?"

"They are just a precaution. I always bring gloves to a crime scene." The detective inserted his hands into the gloves and flexed his fingers. "Put them on. The gloves will protect the stone lid from any trace of your DNA. The last thing I want to do is to contaminate this crypt."

Von Winterloch shrugged, and drew the gloves on. "All right, whenever you're ready," he said.

Without further discussion, the two men gripped the stone lid and forced it slowly and protestingly aside, the motion accompanied by the loud, grating sound of stone upon stone.

The limestone lid was now about halfway off of the sarcophagus. Waldbaer arched his back and felt a brief spasm of pain. The flashlight beam flickered back and forth and then came to rest on something other than skeletal remains or a mound of dust. Revealed in the imperfect illumination was an emaciated face, which bore a long scar on the forehead that stretched to the bridge of the nose, surrounded by unshorn, twisted strands of hair, cascading to the shoulders. It was the visage of someone long dead, but was still fully recognizable as a human face.

"My dear God," Winterloch exclaimed.

The eye sockets were bare to the bone, it was true, but the forehead, cheeks, and mouth, although darkened and discolored with age, were undamaged by the ravages of time. The features, taken together, seemed fixed in a grimace. The neck was desiccated but intact, and disappeared into the collar of a mail suit. The mail suit was sunken, presumably long ago as the organs lost their integrity, but it still enclosed the body in its cold metal embrace.

"Something is missing, don't you think?" Waldbaer said.

Winterloch raised his eyebrows in surprise. "Yes. I see that some of the armor is gone. It's decayed centuries ago, probably."

"No. The gauntlets, as you can see, are on the arms. There's no sign of decay that I can see, none at all. But the placard, or armored vest, is gone. It hasn't decayed, because there would be a residue of accumulated rust, yet nothing is to be seen. And there is something else unusual." Waldbaer lowered the flashlight beam to the corpse's waist. The hands were enclosed in metal gloves, but the fingers were articulated. The hands, one under the other, were curved into a grasp.

"I suspect that he was buried with his sword. Or is his sword on display elsewhere in the castle?"

Winterloch swept his hand away in a dismissive gesture. "No, the sword is not in the castle, the ancient texts insist that it has always rested with its owner from the day he was buried. We have very few artifacts from Heinrich's era. According to the legends, at any rate, his sword would have been buried with him. It should be here."

"Well, it isn't," Waldbaer said. "The hands are formed as if holding the pommel. That, I imagine, is how it was for centuries. Until someone violated this tomb and took both the sword and the armored vest, and possibly some other pieces as well. If the perpetrator was one man acting alone, he probably couldn't take all of the armor with him, because of the weight and the inconvenience of transporting a full suit of armor. So he settled for the most valuable pieces."

Winterloch eased a hand through his mane of white hair. "It doesn't make sense, Kommissar. He couldn't have gotten out of here without being seen."

"Oh, but he could, and he did," Waldbaer said with a cold smile. "He deposited a small leathered bone on his way out, not far from here. It must have been torn off Heinrich's body with the pieces of armor and fallen unnoticed on the floor. I surmise that he scaled the wall at night, or very early in the morning, and entered the chapel. Is the chapel kept locked?"

"No. It didn't seem necessary."

"Right, there you have it. He got in through the chapel, located the crypt, and he entered it. He climbed down, opened this sarcophagus, took what he could carry, and left, also aided by darkness."

Winterloch was adamant. "It makes no sense, Kommissar. None at all. He would have been detected."

Waldbaer turned toward the count, eying him skeptically. "Really? Does the castle have a security system, such as motion detectors, video cameras, heat sensors, that sort of thing?"

Winterloch hesitated. "No, but there are always people about," he mumbled.

"Not at three or four in the morning, I reckon. You will forgive my speculating, but for a crime like this, it didn't happen all at once. There would have been a week or more of observation. The man who robbed this crypt would have watched the lights go off in the castle at night. He made his approach stealthily. He had tools that were mostly silent implements. He egressed through the castle, bet on it. And, just possibly, someone stumbled upon him. That someone would have been Andreas Pichler. Who had his skull broken by the thief."

Winterloch nodded, seemingly entranced by the corpse of his relative. "One thing is not clear to me. Is it clear to you? The body of Heinrich is in incredibly good condition. It is, in fact, amazing that the body has not disintegrated to dust after all this time. I am at a loss to explain it."

Waldbaer returned his gaze to the remarkably intact Heinrich, the scourge of his day and generation. "I fear that I am not the right person to ask. But for what it's worth, and based on what I know, I would say that conditions in the sarcophagus were exactly right to preserve the body in a mummified state. It will decompose in time, I expect, as the covering lid has been left ajar. Oxygen will do its work." The detective said no more, but he too could not help but wonder about the remains of the long-dead and mordantly grimacing knight.

CHAPTER TEN

DORFRAM COUNTRYSIDE

The call came at mid-morning and caused Waldbaer to grab his car keys, leaving his cup of coffee at the police station percolator, where it steamed unnoticed and gradually cooled to room temperature. The detective, deprived of his usual morning libation, reached for a cigarette from the rumpled packet inside his jacket pocket. He had aimed to quit, a pledge to himself that had lasted over a week. But today, it seemed, was not a day when things went according to plan.

Waldbaer stood in silence, less than two miles from Schloss Winterloch, savoring the taste of the tobacco as he inhaled its smoke into his lungs. Braun stood next to him and consulted a pad of paper as he spoke. The uniformed policeman sported a black leather jacket and visored cap pulled down over his eyes.

"He was found by a thirty-year-old female jogger this morning, a little before seven. It looks like the dead man was buried in a shallow grave, hastily dug. It was covered with some earth and leaves, but apparently some fox or other animal got to it."

Waldbaer's eyes regarded the corpse. The body had been pulled from the morass of dark-brown earth and tawny dank leaves and now lay beside the narrow gully which had concealed its presence for some days. There were what appeared to be bite marks on the man's cheek. The eyes were closed and there was a smear of dirt along the mouth. The dead man had thick, matted hair and a trimmed beard, closely shaven.

Waldbaer noticed the hands. The fingers were torn and fleck-ed with dried blood. He noticed as well the wound which almost certainly was the cause of death. The head was nearly severed from the body by a deep slash which covered half the neck. A quantity of blood had issued from the wound, soaking the dead man's shirt and jacket in its wake. It was not an attractive sight.

"Any idea who this victim is?" Waldbaer waited for an answer.

"Yes," the policeman replied. "The driver's license appears au-thentic. I've already called the information in to the police station for confirmation." It was Braun who handed the laminated paper over to Waldbaer without comment. Waldbaer's vision was not what it once was, and he squinted to bring the document into fo-cus while tossing the cigarette away.

A healthier version of the dead man stared at him from the color photograph. The subject stared at the camera sullenly, his mouth curved in a frown. Waldbaer glanced at the text. The man's name was given as Roland Dietrich. His birthdate made him twenty-seven, and he had been born in Munich.

Waldbaer handed the license back to the policeman. "All right. Tell me, what else do we know about Herr Dietrich?"

Braun pushed his police cap further up on his head. "We have some background on him; it came in a few minutes ago. Ac-cording to the Munich police files, Roland Dietrich has a crimi-nal record going back ten years. It's the usual stuff for a loser. As-sault while intoxicated. Possession of an unauthorized switchblade knife. Possession of an illegal substance. And maybe this next bit is interesting. He was found guilty on three charges of breaking and entering and two charges of grand theft involving an automo-bile in the past few years. He only served six months' time, that's all. But what he was doing up here in the woods of Upper Bavaria, I have no idea."

"Allow me to speculate, Braun. Roland Dietrich did not come here to take in the scenery or to breathe in the purifying mountain air. This location is not even two miles from the Win-terloch castle. I wager that Dietrich was hired to take part in the break-in at the castle and the grave robbery as a kind of assistant. They needed two men for that job, not one."

Braun looked at Waldbaer quizzically. "Kommissar, what makes you think they needed two men?"

"Because of the crypt. To move the lid of the sarcophagus two men were needed. You may recall that I required the help of Winterloch to move that sandstone slab. It's dead weight and it takes considerable force to push it any distance. Even with Winterloch's help, it was an effort. Tell me Braun, what do you make of Dietrich's hands?"

Braun looked puzzled and scratched at his cheek. "It sort of looks like he was in a fight."

"Yes, indeed he was. It was a fight with a sarcophagus. He scraped his fingers raw and bloody on the stone. I'm willing to bet that the blood from the lid will match the blood on his hand."

Waldbaer stared at the corpse, considering. "Look at the wound. It would appear that Dietrich was struck by a sword blow and it nearly severed his head. Allow me to speculate further. Dietrich was killed so that there would be one less potential witness to the crime. And one less person who would have to be paid for participating in it. But Dietrich's partner in the grave robbery was too stupid to determine if Dietrich had any identification documents with him, which he did. Gross stupidity, Braun, is relatively easy to exploit. Have our colleagues put all of the criminal record information on Dietrich on my desk, including any known associates. I'm sure Dietrich was involved in the break-in at the castle. For my part, I'm going back to the police station." Waldbaer began the trek to his car and felt weary, though the day was just beginning. He reached absently for his pack of cigarettes.

MUNICH

Karl Ortner awoke to the world slowly, and felt as if he had been crucified to his bed. Every incremental motion of his limbs brought a burst of pain and he groaned, only partly understanding the state he was in. The sheets were wet with sweat, and cold, and heavy against his skin. With half-hooded eyes, Ortner stared down at his wrist and saw that the blemish had not gone away, but had increased in size during the night. It was now about three inches long and expanded over most of his wrist.

"Oh, God, what in the hell is this," he groaned, conscious of the fact that he should see a doctor. But it seemed impossible to rise from the cold dampness of the bed, never mind to engage in the infinity of motions that constituted getting dressed. Just thinking of rising from the dank bundle of sheets exhausted him. A swath of sweat cascaded from his forehead to his eyes. He whimpered, unsure of what to do.

He did not even have a doctor, had never needed one until now. The continuous, overwhelming pain at every motion threatened to rob him of focus. He closed his eyes and forced himself to think clearly. He recalled that there was a doctor's office four blocks away, not too far from the U-Bahn station, he had seen the plaque on the door. If he could get there, Ortner reasoned, the doctor would see him, and would make him better. But how was he to get there? Struggling to think clearly, Ortner decided that he could call a taxi, walking the five blocks was completely out of the question. To do this, he would have to rest and gain a degree of strength. His apartment was on the fourth floor, and there was no elevator. Yes, rest first, for an hour or two, perhaps longer. After all, he told himself, as a flow of mucous exited his nostril, he was only sick, it wasn't as if he were about to die.

CHAPTER ELEVEN

GAMSDORF

Waldbaer sat at his desk in the Gamsdorf police station, hands folded under his chin, his belt digging into his abdomen. A young, fresh-faced policeman in a pressed and spotless uniform of beige shirt and brown, utilitarian trousers was reading from a sheet of paper.

"What's the name again?" Waldbaer asked, somewhat gruffly. It was early morning, not his favorite time of day.

The policeman repeated the information. "Karl Ernst Ortner. There were partial fingerprints from his left hand on the lid of the coffin at Schloss Winterloch. It's a perfect match. And Ortner was arrested along with Dietrich for a breaking-and-entering crime committed in Munich some years ago."

Waldbaer's eyes studied the young policeman with the interest a falcon displays for a field mouse. "I think I can picture it. Ortner probably wore gloves most of the time. He stupidly took them off to get a better purchase on the lid before pushing it aside. He didn't think anyone would detect his grave-robbing theft, so he didn't really care. Too bad for him, *nicht wahr*? What does our beloved Herr Ortner have for a criminal record, if I may ask?"

The policeman glanced down the page. "Breaking and entering is apparently Ortner's thing. And the theft of an Athenian Greek vase and rare Egyptian antiquities from a Munich gallery. During that arrest he was additionally sentenced for possession of an unregistered firearm, a Sauer semi-automatic. He did three years in Stadlheim prison for that one."

"They should have kept him there," Waldbaer grumbled. "When was he released?"

"Eighteen months ago."

"That's very nice; we have a commendable and highly efficient justice system. Well, it fits, doesn't it? Herr Ortner is, after all, an otherwise unemployable and only moderately successful thief. Is there a photograph?"

The policeman smiled and passed the sheet of paper to Waldbaer. A color photo displayed the image of a sneering, sunken-cheeked Ortner.

Waldbaer brushed a finger across the thinning hair and dark-brown eyes. "His looks suggest a limited intellect. He's far too stupid to have planned this on his own. Ortner was contracted for his services by someone more intelligent. By whom, I wonder?" The detective sat for a moment, immersed in thought. He handed the piece of paper back to the policeman. "All right then. Do the following for me: contact the Munich police headquarters. Tell them we want to apprehend one of their lambs for grand theft and suspicion of murder. Tell them I'll go to Munich personally, with their permission, of course."

The policeman nodded and scribbled a note. "Is there anything else?"

Waldbaer rubbed his eyes wearily. "Yes. Tell them I'll drive to Munich in a couple of hours. I'll have all of the necessary paperwork with me. And you might remind them that Ortner is likely to be armed and he may be dangerous. You can tell them that Ortner doesn't appear to be the brightest bulb in the box, so he's probably stupid enough to be violent. You can tell them that he will almost certainly resist arrest, because he's wanted for two murders."

CHAPTER TWELVE

Pain, constant and intense, coursed down his nerve endings and racked his entire body, leaving him without relief. Karl Ortner stood on the street before his red-brick apartment building and watched the world through hooded, half closed eyes. He was conscious of a tremor in his right leg, but found that he could do nothing to stop it. His breathing was shallow; for the last hour or two breathing deeply had become epic in its discomfort. Where, he wondered, was the bloody taxi he had called?

Just then, his eyes detected motion as a pale-beige Mercedes with its blinker engaged pulled off the main road and came to a halt in front of him. The driver, Ortner saw, had dark-green sunglasses and a shaved head.

"You called for a cab, right," the face with sunglasses said through an open window.

Without answering, Ortner fumbled with the passenger door and collapsed into the back seat. "Take me to the doctor's office at the intersection of Kreisner and Ebbert streets. And make it goddamn quick." Ortner felt a trace of warmth oozing onto his chin and wondered if he had drooled.

The face with sunglasses registered shock. "Jesus Christ, your mouth is bleeding."

Perplexed, Ortner touched a hand to his face and was stunned to see it coated with thick, scarlet blood that oozed down his fingers into his palm. "Get me to the fucking doctor, now, get this piece of shit moving," he groaned. Ortner felt a sudden and massive cramp in his abdomen, and became incontinent, gushing a stream of fluid and feces with a groan.

"Oh Christ, that's it, get out of my car right now. You're going to wreck the damn leather seats," the driver yelled.

Rage swept over Ortner. "Okay, you miserable, rotten fuck, you want me out of the car, do you?" With a tremor-ridden, discolored hand, Ortner pulled a Heckler & Koch semi-automatic from where it rested beneath his jacket, flicked off the safety, and fired four rounds through the back of the driver's seat in rapid succession. The bullets tore through the leather seating and into the driver's torso. The bald man moaned loudly, his head bucked backward and his sunglasses pitched to the floor. Ortner saw that the man's eyes, rapidly losing focus as they lost life, were blue. "Fuck you, too," he yelled, coughing up bloody sputum, as he clambered from the taxi.

* * *

An Audi green-and-white police car engaged its right signal blinker and pulled out from the torrent of traffic on the main thoroughfare. The policeman driving the vehicle was overweight, a fact not lost on Waldbaer. It was true, Waldbaer averred, that he himself had put on, perhaps, an undesired five or ten or even fifteen pounds. But the man in the driver's seat next to him denoted sad decline. The driver's face, lost in a multiplicity of chins, was testimony to the local Munich taste for beer, pretzels, and sausage.

The Bavarian squad car came to a stop directly behind a Mercedes taxi and the Munich policeman spoke up. "This is Ortner's address, it's a working-class apartment building; he appears to be living on the fourth floor." As Waldbaer unbuckled his seatbelt, four muffled reports rang out from the Mercedes. "Gunshots, draw your weapon," the detective snapped, bolting out of the police car passenger door with his weapon in hand.

As he bent his knees and stood in a crouch on the sidewalk, Waldbaer fixed his gaze on the taxi. The rear door of the vehicle swung open, and the frame of a person emerged. It was Ortner,

Waldbaer instantly recognized the features from the photo. Ortner stumbled, seemed to lose his balance, and swayed on his feet
like a drunken man. He held a handgun in his grasp and appeared
to be bleeding from the mouth.

"Drop the gun, Ortner," Waldbaer barked out, falling to one
knee. "This is the police and you're under arrest."

Pallid and dripping sweat, Ortner grimaced, a rictus creas-
ing his face. "You shit-eater, you're all just police shit-eaters" he
yelled, and hauled the weapon swervingly toward Waldbaer. He
fired a round that went wild and high, the resonance echoing off
of the nearby buildings. He groaned and steadied the barrel with
both hands and fired a second round which missed its target, but
threatened to hit pedestrians walking down the street.

Waldbaer grasped his pistol with both hands. Flicking off the
safety in an instantaneous motion, he aimed with both hands and
fired. Once, twice.

The rounds impacted at the center mass, as Waldbaer had
been taught at the police firing range long ago. The first bullet entered the stomach, and the second slammed into the chest,
two inches below the heart. The gun flew with force from Ortner's hand, and he released a deep moan, spitting flecks of blood.
He fell to his knees and fixed Waldbaer with a blank stare before
pitching backwards. Ortner was splayed half on the sidewalk,
half on a narrow strip of grass, in a second. Waldbaer's heart was
hammering out a beat, and his arms were shaking. He stood erect
slowly. His right knee hurt.

The other police officer, the driver of their vehicle, was on
Waldbaer's left, weapon also drawn and aimed at Ortner's prostrate form. "Are you okay over there," the policeman shouted.

"*Ja*, I'm all right. I'm much better than he is." Holding the
pistol in front of him, Waldbaer approached the sprawled form of
Ortner. As he approached the body, he hesitated. Something in
the tableaux of death was wrong.

Ortner's thinning hair was plastered to his forehead, as if
he had just come out of a shower. A thick, viscous coat of blood

emanated from the mouth, covered the entire chin, and soaked the front of Ortner's white shirt. Waldbaer doubted that this hemorrhage of blood had been caused by the impact of his two rounds.

The overweight policeman had made his way to the Mercedes taxi. He touched the wrist of the driver's crumpled body, feeling for a pulse. "The driver's dead. He's been shot, it looks like several times. I'll call for an ambulance."

Waldbaer said nothing, focusing on the dead man lying before him. Ortner's eyes were open and blank, with the unseeing stare of the dead. His skin was severely lacerated on the neck and hands, as if by constant scratching. Waldbaer wondered if it was a reaction to illicit drugs. But there was more. A large, uneven spot, purplish-black in appearance, protruded from Ortner's wrist. Impulsively, Waldbaer touched it with his Glock. The anomaly seemed to move as if alive and then burst. A sudden stench, fiercely putrid to its core, forced Waldbaer to gag. He steeled himself, with effort, against throwing up.

Minutes later, the sound of ambulances reverberated off of the façades of the apartment buildings along the street. Waldbaer noticed that a crowd of curious onlookers was building, and approaching slowly, like modern connoisseurs of death.

Waldbaer addressed them, his tone gruff. "All right, everybody, there's nothing to see here. Nothing you really want to see, anyway. Clear a path for the ambulances." Hesitantly, still mesmerized by sudden death, the crowd pulled away. Troubled by the stench and the state of Ortner's corpse, Waldbaer wondered what it meant. There was one word he did not like to consider, that indeed he feared, although it was only a distant possibility, he reflected. The word was *contagion*.

CHAPTER THIRTEEN

The morgue, tiled to the ceiling in rows of antiseptic white blocks, contained the overpowering trace of ammonia. Death in the city of Munich was an inevitable daily occurrence, and any questionable death ended up here, in the yawning, impersonal spaces of the central police station morgue. Waldbaer was seated on a bench of the morgue corridor, arms crossed over his chest.

Karl Ortner was located somewhere behind him, his remains concealed behind a stainless steel door. Waldbaer had declined the well-intentioned invitation to attend the autopsy and had insisted that the doctor and assistants get on with their work. He had sat in the corridor on a folding chair. With a glance at his wristwatch, Waldbaer saw that they had been with the corpse for the better part of an hour.

The steel door creaked open, scraping the floor, and then banged shut. The detective saw a middle-aged man with crew-cut black hair and a frame that was appropriately cadaverous, step out of the autopsy room. Blue eyes studied Waldbaer from behind thick glasses in a metal frame.

"Doctor?" Waldbaer inquired.

The man, clothed in light blue surgical clothes, nodded his head. "Yes, I'm Dr. Mayerling," he said.

"Dr. Mayerling," Waldbaer began, "I know that Ortner died from the two rounds that hit him. I fired them. But I noticed he looked sick when I examined his body. He looked like he had been deathly ill. He was a pool of sweat, and I presume you've seen the stream of blood issuing from his mouth and caked on his chin. Was that a reaction to drugs or something?"

Mayerling glanced at the floor and nodded, adjusting his glasses. "No. There are no drugs traceable in his system, except an excessive amount of aspirin in his stomach."

"What is it then?"

The doctor exhaled and looked at the detective as if inspecting him. "Ortner was terminally infected with a disease, he wasn't a drug addict. Had he not been shot, he probably would have died from the infection, at least unless he had received the appropriate antibiotics. The disease had reached a stage where it apparently caused Ortner tremendous pain. He had lacerated himself from scratching his skin with his fingernails. You may have well detected the marks. And there were other signs of his affliction as well."

Waldbaer narrowed his eyes. "What do you mean exactly? That mark on his wrist?"

Mayerling nodded. "Precisely, I'm glad you noticed. It is a bubo. That is, it's an accumulation of pus and blood trapped beneath the skin. It's something that isn't seen much these days. Ortner had a number of buboes; you perhaps only saw the one on his wrist. He had another extending from an armpit and yet another on the back of his neck, just beneath the collar line of his shirt. At the time of death, he was bleeding from the mouth as a result of the disease attacking his internal organs. I would estimate that his eyes probably couldn't focus well at that stage. Under normal circumstances, if he hadn't been shot, I estimate that he would have died within about twelve hours."

Waldbaer raised his eyebrows. "Dead in twelve hours? When do you suppose he contacted this disease?"

Mayerling closed his eyes and rubbed the base of his nose before answering. "That's hard to say. Ortner's body shows the terminal stage of Yersinia pestis. Textbooks say Yersinia pestis will kill a person within about five or six days. That is, if he doesn't get access to antibiotics in the meantime, within about twenty-four hours. Antibiotics are very effective against this infection."

"I defer to you. But how the hell would he get this disease?

Yersinia pestis is a zoonotic disease. It exists in fleas. They pass it to rats or directly to humans. The fact is, this infection is notoriously deadly if people contract it. By the way, what kind of profession did Ortner have?"

Waldbaer's features creased with a weary smile. "What profession? Ortner was a trained and experienced thief. He majored in antiquities."

"God knows where he picked it up then. This sort of thing isn't a European problem these days, far from it. Cases of infection are basically an African problem; there's a fairly severe outbreak every year or so. From what I understand, and you might want to talk to an expert about this, the disease can be spread through an infected flea or even by coughing."

Waldbaer looked puzzled. "How communicable is this disease anyway?"

"Very." Mayerling shoved his hands into his surgical gown. "When the disease reaches the lungs, and the victim coughs, it spreads to whomever is within a few feet of him. It is highly contagious. I'd be willing to bet that Ortner picked up the disease from a flea, or some sort of biting insect. Anyway, we've got to inform a number of health organizations about this, that's what the assistant doctor is doing right now, by the way. The bad news is that this probably isn't the only case of the infection that we are going to see. The good news, on the other hand, is that antibiotics kill the infection very efficiently."

Waldbaer looked at the doctor and decided that the humorless man was a professional. "Antibiotics or no antibiotics aren't my department, I'm afraid. But you said that Ortner had buboes, I remember that I ruptured one of them and nearly passed out from the stench. But buboes, where have I heard that before?"

Mayerling shrugged. "I would guess that you probably heard it in grammar school or at university, Kommissar. The vernacular expression for this disease is the plague. It scourged Europe, including Germany, during the eleventh and fourteenth centuries causing enormous fatalities. It wiped out the population of entire cities and killed maybe a third of Europe's inhabitants. It's believed that it was carried by infected rodents which prospered in the unsanitary living conditions that existed at the time. The buboes appeared black on the skin of victims. That led to the plague being called the Black Death. That, alas, is the history of the disease."

"History is not my concern, Dr. Mayerling. With the exception of the history that we are making. And I fear that you are right. Before this is over, Karl Ortner, I suspect, will not be the only victim."

GAMSDORF

Evening had set in quietly and slowly, as if by stealth, and the landscape outside Zum Alten Post had taken on the darkness without protest, bathed in a full moon and the pinpricks of light from a thousand stars. Franz Waldbaer took a foaming swig of Spaten beer from its mug and then placed the glass on its coaster, swiping a hand across his lips. Seated across from him at the *stammtisch*, or permanently reserved table, were Sabine Reiner, a russet-haired and radiant Austrian policewoman, a Kommissarin, from Innsbruck. She had made Waldbaer's acquaintance, and a bit more, on a previous case involving murder and illicit international transactions. Dr. Hans Lechner, a white-haired retired general practitioner in his seventies was present, too, rotating a glass of beer in his hands as if clinically inspecting it.

Sabine Reiner seemed to take in the casual interaction between paying customers and the permanently scowling, overweight waitress of the establishment. It was not, she thought, the manner employed in Innsbruck to endear customers to a restaurant.

The doctor had chosen bright red suspenders to secure his trousers to his plump frame, obviating the need for the discomfiture of a leather belt. One suspender was held in a casual grip by its owner, the other hand cosseted his half-full glass of beer.

Waldbaer placed both hands around his beer glass and the woman smiled at the not unfamiliar gesture. At least, since their work together on the Somalian centrifuge case, Waldbaer had put his hands around Sabine as well. And he had invited her to the restaurant this evening, along with Dr. Lechner. If a trio did not exactly make an intimate dinner, she was willing to consider it a date. Besides, the drive from Innsbruck, Austria to Gamsdorf, Germany had taken less than an hour.

"From what you say, Franz, there's a lot, a hell of a lot, to be concerned about with this case of the plague, and that's my professional opinion," Dr. Lechner offered. "After all, these days little is known about the plague in Europe or the United States."

"True, Hans, very true. But at the moment I'm prompted to wonder only about the provenance of the disease. Let me repeat what I know one more time. Count Heinrich von Winterloch lived in the fourteenth century. He apparently was a soldier, maybe a soldier of fortune, a Söldner. He contracted the plague— the Black Death—when it swept through Central Europe like the wind off the Alps. As with most victims inflicted with the disease, it killed him. He was buried by his relatives and friends, who were frightened that they themselves might contract the disease. Some of them probably did."

The doctor interjected a question. "And Heinrich was buried as a soldier and a nobleman, in full ceremonial armor, you say?"

"That's right. Heinrich was buried, I gather, in the best armor available at the time, apparently Italian in manufacture, though that's just word of mouth, passed down from generation to generation of the Winterloch family. Anyway, his corpse was supposedly clothed in the armor, encased in it, the story goes, and his dead hands gripped the very broadsword that he had fought with."

"An intriguing story, if only a story," Sabine said, lifting her wine glass to her lips.

"Whatever," Waldbaer replied with a grin. "Now, fast forward to the twenty-first century. Somehow, word gets out of Heinrich's death and the suit of armor. The chapel at Winterloch castle is identified as the warrior-count's last resting place in a newspaper article, I am advised. Somebody devises a plan to get into the chapel by stealth, locate and break into the crypt, and rob the grave. Karl Ortner, far too stupid a Cretan to have planned anything that intricate, was hired to perform the illegal act and run the risks, I might add. Ortner gets into the chapel, at night, while the world slumbers, and breaks into the crypt, and the grave itself."

The doctor nodded, his eyes alert.

Waldbaer paused, and took a long sip of his beer, savoring its tartness. "For Ortner, so far, so good. He finds the corpse of Heinrich, but is simply too dumb to ask himself why the body is so well-preserved. Or, maybe, he was perhaps rushing to commit theft and leave the castle, and didn't notice the state of the corpse. He took the most valuable pieces of armor off the corpse and the broadsword. On his way out, Ortner was surprised to run into Andreas Pichler, a handyman at the castle, and kills him, almost certainly with a blow from the sword that he has taken from the hands of the dead Heinrich. He exits the castle through a front door, makes for the nearby forest and his parked car. Ortner, I might add, has an assistant who helped him break into the crypt. Ortner decides to kill him, too, and buries him in a shallow grave. This happens during the early morning hours under cover of darkness."

"Yes, I see." The doctor slouched forward in the chair, placing both hands on the table in front of him. "Let me put the events in order. Ortner escapes the scene of the robbery successfully in the wee hours of the morning. You investigate the murder of Andreas Pichler. But partial fingerprints link Ortner to the scene of the crime. You go to Munich to arrest him for the murder of Pichler, and I suppose for having engaged in grave robbery. Ortner resists arrest, he shoots and is shot—by you—and he is brought to the Munich morgue. The autopsy confirms that Ortner, in addition to being shot, had a terminal phase of the plague. You want to know where he contracted it. Right?"

Waldbaer eased back in his chair. "Yes. But, Hans, my question is precisely this: did he get the plague from the corpse of Heinrich somehow? Is it possible for the plague to...I don't know, lie dormant for centuries? And if not, where did Ortner contract the disease?"

Saying nothing for the moment, Lechner considered his response. "You need an expert on the plague I expect, Franz; I'm just a general practitioner, after all. But I'll speculate a bit. One, Ortner contracted the infection somewhere, that's clear. The plague didn't just develop out of thin air, the usual culprits are fleas or rats. Two, we know that Ortner plundered the grave and came into direct contact with the corpse, a victim of the Black Death. Three, all of these centuries later, any traces of the plague should have vanished entirely. That seems clear. The plague is a bacterium, and it too would die, no question about it."

Lechner's hand drummed the table in front of him. "But there are some interesting anomalies. For example, the mummified corpse of Heinrich. From what you say, it is extraordinarily well preserved. In most circumstances, it should have decayed to bone long ago, or perhaps to dust. There would be skeletal remains, nothing more."

Waldbaer traced a finger around the rim of his beer glass. "Yes. The skin is discolored, certainly, but it is largely intact, at least it was when I saw it."

"That doesn't sound like the corpse of a man who's been dead hundreds of years," Sabine said.

Lechner nodded his agreement. "And it leaves open the question of why the body didn't degenerate for centuries. Decomposition is the course of nature. For some, it would constitute a miracle, but I suspect that Heinrich was not a model for 'Lives of the Saints'. Something scientifically definable retarded the corruption of the tissue. Something, perhaps, that has to do with temperature where the body was buried. I would consult an expert, and examine conditions in the crypt further, and conditions in the sarcophagus."

"Examine the conditions for what exactly, Hans?" Waldbaer asked.

"Well, for dormancy. You know, 'dormant' means slowing things down. Take the cicada, an insect. They are common in parts of the United States, for example in Virginia. Cicadas live most of their lives underground, and emerge to the surface every seventeen years, to live aboveground. During most of their lives underground, the cicadas are basically dormant. That's why the cicadas enjoy such a long life. Now, seventeen years is not a century, to be sure. But let's speculate that an insect, a different type of insect, could live in dormancy, and at some point reproduce. If this occurred generation after generation, century after century, it's theoretically possible that such an insect—infected with the plague—could transmit the disease that its ancestors carried centuries ago. Of course, I'm just speculating. Do you see where I'm going?"

Waldbaer gave the doctor a quizzical look and frowned. "No, not really. I'm afraid I don't follow you."

Lechner smiled. "Fleas, Franz, fleas. It was really the fleas that were to blame for spreading the plague during the Middle Ages, partly due to the appalling hygiene prevailing at the time. The fleas infected the rodents, rats mainly, and then they infected humans. Ortner may have been bitten by a flea that had been in the crypt since the Middle Ages, and contracted the disease. He wasn't aware that these days simple antibiotics could have treated it."

Waldbaer reached for his glass of Spaten beer, turning it in his hands. "I know, I know, I've heard that before. Antibiotics could have prevented the bubonic plague."

The doctor shook his head. "No. Not prevented. The initial bubonic plague existed at a time long before antibiotics were even invented. But today, the plague isn't much of a problem, except in underdeveloped, remote third-world areas. Anyway, somebody should check for bugs at the crypt in the castle, that's my advice. Oh, and by the way Franz, you had better get a medical checkup to make sure that you haven't been infected yourself. You seem fine; it's just an appropriate precaution."

Waldbaer stared at the doctor and felt a sudden chill. "You have a good point. Just as a precaution, of course."

Sabine must have suspected that he was scared as she reached out a hand and placed it atop his. "Franz, you aren't sick. It really is a precaution, nothing more."

Waldbaer grabbed her proffered hand and slid his fingers between hers. "I'm not worried at all," he said without conviction.

CHAPTER FOURTEEN

Stefan Hofgartner adjusted his silk foulard tie and poured himself a steaming cup of Dallmayr coffee, filling the delicate porcelain vessel to the rim. He added brown sugar, dispensed from an antique silver spoon, which he placed gently on the saucer. He smiled at his companion with diffident courtesy. His graying hair was cut short and a wisp of it hung over his forehead. Taking a sip of his coffee, Hofgartner held the cup in both hands. "Truly excellent coffee, isn't it? This comes from Ethiopia and is exclusively imported to a firm in Munich."

The balding man in his late seventies seated across from him at Hofgartner's English breakfast table spoke with a French-accented German. "Yes, well, it is quite pleasant indeed." The man cleared his throat, signaling a change in the topic. "Doktor Hofgartner, if I might just return to the purpose of my trip to Bavaria, it was in fact to see the materials you have for sale. I was just thinking that now would be an excellent opportunity to inspect them."

Lingering over a sip of coffee, savoring it, Hofgartner smiled again, in a show of courtesy. "Of course. There is nothing wrong with the present time. Nothing at all. Let us, then, get down to business. If you would be so kind as to follow me, I will show you what I've acquired."

Hofgartner buttoned his blazer and led the way to a long, deeply varnished mahogany table in the adjoining room, situated beneath a dark nineteenth-century oil painting of the snow-capped Zugspitze mountain peak in Garmisch, as seen from the shores of the Eibsee Lake. He pointed to the objects, and his silver cufflinks caught and reflected a glint of sun from a nearby window. The armored vest and ancient broadsword were carefully arranged for display on generous swaths of white silk.

Hofgartner's guest stood momentarily wordless and transfixed before the sight. The gleaming, ornately worked breastplate competed for attention with the flawless, shining metal sword. Insets of precious stone were carefully fitted into the gold pommel of the grip. The guest reached out a hand, and then hesitated, unsure of what was permitted him.

"Please, go ahead, touch it, hold it if you'd like. It's quite all right, examine it thoroughly, it deserves to be touched." Hofgartner's voice was sympathetic and soothing.

The guest traced a hand reverently down the gardbrace of the armored vest, touching the gold filigree. "It's extraordinary; it's stunningly beautiful," he mumbled, as if to himself.

"Isn't it?" Hofgartner brushed a strand of stray hair from his forehead. "And you may now count yourself among the very few men of special tastes to have seen it. In the present century, at any rate."

The guest turned toward Hofgartner. He raised an eyebrow in an arch. "The armored vest appears to be, I surmise, from the twelfth century. What do you know of the history of these pieces?"

Hofgartner lowered his gaze to the floor and laughed with a sound reminiscent of tinkling crystal and smiled engagingly. "I can tell you the history of these pieces in detail, with an educated guess here and there. Would you like to hear it?"

"Yes, indeed I would."

Hofgartner raised his head toward the high ceiling and massaged his chin with a manicured hand. "Well, to start with, the ownership of the breastplate and sword are Bavarian. The armor was made for a warrior count, commissioned by a Graf who was an important personage at the time. An Italian artist was commissioned to do the work, but his identity has sadly vanished. It is known, however, that the armor and the sword are products of the 1100s. The armor was intended to be ceremonial, and was worn to celebrate various events, including Easter and Christmas. The lines on the armor are done in pure gold; it is quite real. You will note the Wappen at the center of the breastplate."

The gentleman did so, traced it with his hand and nodded.

Hofgartner enjoyed playing the host and smiled. "That is gold as well. And if I may say so, it is exquisite."

The guest touched the device gently. "It is a bear, I believe, facing a dragon."

Hofgartner held out a hand and smiled. "Almost, but not quite. It is a bear prepared to attack, and a stylized lion rampant. Lions, on the whole, had not been much seen here in Europe, and so artistic imagination played a role in their creation. The lion does seem a bit dragon-like, now that you mention it. The bear and the lion are, in fact, part of the traditional family crest. They are both symbols of stability and strength, qualities the von Winterlochs valued."

The guest pursed his lips, and his eyes became more hooded. "Tell me, is the family still living today? You mentioned that the armor was made for a count."

"You have arrived at a most delicate topic," Hofgartner said. "I will confide in you, but I must ask for absolute confidentiality in this matter."

"Yes. It is understood. Whatever you tell me I will treat as a secret. I assure you, I always treat the topic of medieval antiquities and my purchases with complete discretion."

Hofgartner nodded. "Very well. To answer your first question, the family is very much alive. They are the von Winterlochs and they make their home in Upper Bavaria, in Dorfram, not too far from here. The count—whose armor this is—was known as Count Heinrich von Winterloch. There are several accounts of his military exploits available. The current count, I fear, is some-thing of a misanthrope named Rheinhold von Winterloch. He is not widely loved. He is the last of the line, I believe, he doesn't have any children. Now, you are probably wondering about the provenance of these acquisitions."

The man said nothing, studied Hofgartner and waited.

"I'm embarrassed to say that these goods were acquired, shall we say, by a most unusual means. In a word, sir, they were pur-loined."

"You mean stolen. Or, if I may be unashamedly direct, they were robbed."

Hofgartner grimaced, as if offended, but managed a weak smile. "As you say, the artifacts were stolen then. I, for one, do not believe that objects of art should be buried, taken away from the world for all eternity. These antiquities were meant to be seen. I prefer to see the act that I engaged in as rescuing precious pieces of history that had been sadly committed to the ground. Unjustly committed to the ground, to be sure. I don't know if you are a religious man, it is certainly not my concern, but the term of the trade for what I engaged in is grave robbing, regarded by true believers as an immoral act. To be horribly pedestrian about it, we accessed the grave of Count Heinrich in the castle chapel and took the items you see before you. I am being frank with you because your dedication—both to history and to art—is so well known. I felt that I could confide in you without reservation and take a man of your evident sophistication into my confidence."

Hofgartner's guest blushed at the compliment. I have hooked the trout, Hofgartner smiled to himself.

The balding man pursed his hands before him. "To respond to your query, Doktor Hofgartner, I am, to be blunt, a religious man, but I leave the judgment of the activity of others to God. Life is simpler that way. Judging people is not my concern. And you are right to take me into your confidence. I certainly won't reveal your secret. You will have no worries with me. And now, if

I may be so bold, we can cut to the chase. I have seen the objects that you propose to sell and they are magnificent. How much are you asking for the breastplate and broadsword?"

Hofgartner tightened his lips. "You must understand that I have expenses to cover. Breaking into the grave was not easy, and not without risk. I also had associates that I have had to pay; there are unavoidable costs."

"How much?" the guest said, through a smile.

"The quality of the armor has much to do with the price," Hofgartner continued. "The escutcheon is real gold and it was applied by a craftsman. I'm afraid that I cannot part with the breastplate for less than half a million euros. The broadsword, which as you can see is in breathtakingly excellent condition, is half a million as well. I know that must seem like an extraordinary amount, an enormous amount, but there it is. Getting these artifacts, believe me, was not without great cost. I'm sure you understand my terms."

The guest crossed his arms and cupped an elbow in each hand. "You're right, Doktor Hofgartner, half a million is an absolutely enormous sum of money, and a million for the set of antiques is rather breathtaking. But I will not argue with you over the price that you have set. That is not my style, I do not like haggling. After all, what you offer here is a relic, and as you say, a piece of history, the evidence of a vanished past." The man turned and looked long and greedily at the breastplate and sword. "I will confess to you that I am a rather voracious collector of medieval artifacts. These pieces would not be the first that I have purchased. Still, it is the price alone that gives me pause."

It was Hofgartner's turn to say nothing.

The older man continued. "I thank you for the opportunity to view the objects. It was well worth the trip to Bavaria, even at this rather depressing time of year. I will definitely consider the fixed price and make up my mind in the next day or two. I'll call you directly within twenty-four hours with my decision."

Hofgartner shook his head. "Better to send me an email

from a neutral address, if you don't mind. In this business, security is a real consideration. The police are everywhere these days." Suddenly and unexpectedly, Hofgartner coughed wetly, mumbled an apology, and immediately coughed again.

The guest smiled. "*Gesundheit*, and of course, I will send an appropriate email, in view of your concerns. In the meantime, I would appreciate it if you show these pieces to no one else."

Hofgartner nodded. "Of course. Thank you for your time, Monsieur Rouchford," Hofgartner said before coughing again and offering a mumbled apology. The host escorted him to the front door of his dwelling, keeping the polite tone of the conversation alive with small talk. As the potential client slipped into the seat of his rented, metallic black Audi sedan and drove off, Hofgartner contemplated how it had gone.

As well as can be expected, he mused. He was asking an enormously steep price, and any man, no matter how wealthy, would want to think about parting with such a mass of cash. A weak smile creased Hofgartner's face. He was confident; he was certain that he would make the sale. And, at any rate, if the old gentleman declined to make the purchase, there were other collectors, equally rich and equally obsessed with collecting medieval artifacts illegally. Hofgartner had a list; it was only a matter of time before he located the right buyer. He paused to scratch at a sudden pain in his chest. He had felt oddly out of sorts for the past few days, and his eyes were watering. A quick nap in bed, perhaps for an hour he decided, would surely not be a bad idea.

CHAPTER FIFTEEN

Waldbaer felt unaccountably good, felt rather like smiling, and did. A quick visit to the police clinic had confirmed that he suffered no trace of bubonic plague, and was free of the disease.

"If an infected person doesn't cough or sneeze or spit his blood on you, it's hard to catch the disease," Waldbaer's doctor told him. Less happily, the doctor also said, "You're in your fifties and getting older, Kommissar, and you need to watch your weight. I recommend less beer and fewer pretzels. And a less sedentary lifestyle would help. Go for a brisk walk of a mile or two in the evening, or go swimming four times a week, that's my suggestion." Waldbaer felt irritated. He had put on a pound or two, but the demands of the job made it impossible to take long walks like a mindless deer in the woods, never mind the evident insanity of swimming every other day. And three or four half-liter beers and a plate of snack food in the evening helped him to wind down. The doctor had made his comment as an aside, Waldbaer concluded, and he decided to file the unwelcome recommendation away, and tossed it into the cerebral dustbin.

There were many other things to think about at present, and now Waldbaer focused on them. There was the matter of who had murdered Pichler. That, at least, seemed to be resolved. Pichler was murdered by Ortner. The petty criminal had stolen a sword and some armor from the Winterloch grave, and had used the sword as a weapon of convenience to cave in Pichler's skull.

That just led to another question. Ortner was a mere instrument, far too stupid to have dreamed up the robbery of artifacts from a medieval grave on his own. But what master did he serve? Waldbaer did not know. It would perhaps be possible to trace Ortner's path to the master thief, even with Ortner dead. Just as possibly, Waldbaer considered, his nemesis might never be uncovered. This thought did much to dampen the detective's mood. The man who profited from the crime, Waldbaer knew, might get away with it. Waldbaer's train of thought was shattered by the musical notes of Mozart emanating from his cell phone. Yanking it from his pocket, he grumbled out his name.

"This is Dr. Mayerling. Kommissar, I have a bit of information for you."

Waldbaer furrowed his brow. "On Ortner's autopsy? Our connection is good, Doctor, can we discuss it on the phone?"

There was a moment of hesitation on the line. "It is about the autopsy, yes. Some new information has surfaced. I think it would be more than worthwhile for you to get this from me personally."

Waldbaer agreed, made the arrangements, and felt disconcertingly troubled. His good mood, so full a few minutes ago, had disappeared.

* * *

"You will recall that we sent out a notice on the bubonic plague death to hospitals throughout Europe and to the European Center for Disease Control in Stockholm. That is required procedure, Kommissar. This morning, we received notification of a second death from the plague. If you want my personal view, they're related." Dr. Mayerling seemed to weigh every word before it was spoken.

Waldbaer did not much like halting speech and did his best to move the conversation along. "Why do you think the two deaths are related?"

"Because of their proximity, for one thing. Ortner died here in Munich and the other victim died in Augsburg. Less than sixty kilometers separate the two cities."

Waldbaer nodded uncertainly. "Is there anything else, Doctor?"

"Yes, there is. Victim number two, in Augsburg, died about twenty-four hours ago. Unlike Ortner, the man did get professional medical assistance. He was admitted to the main hospital in Augsburg and they diagnosed him as having the plague. He was given streptomycin, an antibiotic which has a history of success with plague victims." Mayerling paused.

"And?" Waldbaer queried.

"And the antibiotic failed to cure him. It usually works. But he developed buboes in the lymph glands, he was bleeding internally, and it killed him."

Waldbaer felt a shiver. "You mean he drowned in his own blood."

"In a manner of speaking, yes, Kommissar. There are other antibiotics, such as gentamicin, but streptomycin should have worked. Nothing, I'm afraid, could be done for him."

Neither man spoke for a moment until Waldbaer broke the silence. "What is the reason that you are telling me this, Doctor?"

"I'm telling you this because it may change the calculus of the disease, Kommissar. This particular emergence of the 'Black Death', if you want to call it that, seems very resistant to or even immune to antibiotics. The Augsburg case is testimony to that. A person contracts the disease somehow, somewhere, and about four days later is dead, treatment or no treatment."

Waldbaer eyed the doctor closely, like an owl observing a mouse. "Meaning what exactly?"

"Meaning that we could have a problem on our hands, and I mean a really big problem. It's a known and troubling fact that antibiotics have had a decreasing effect on infectious diseases for years. With the Yersinia pestis bacteria, that means that even with treatment, even with the victims hospitalized, the death rate will climb. Antibiotics appear basically ineffective."

"How high will the death rate climb?" Waldbaer interjected.

Mayerling ran a hand through his patch of dark hair. "It's hard to know. We only have two men who were infected with the bacillus and they are both dead. One had no medical treatment, the other did. What concerns me, Kommissar, is that this disease could spread dramatically and exponentially. And what we thought could handle the problem, maybe cannot, our treatment may amount to nothing."

"All right, Doctor, let's say ten people get infected. They all go to the hospital and they are all given antibiotics. How many will survive?"

Dr. Mayerling shook his head and frowned. "There's no way of knowing. In 1348, the plague was probably killing four out of five people who were infected. Four out of five! Unless this outbreak of plague is nipped in the bud, we could be talking hundreds of potential victims, maybe thousands. I don't want to sound melodramatic, but the facts are leading us in that direction. I have to notify God knows how many organizations internationally now about the possibility of a bubonic plague epidemic here in Germany."

The detective stood as motionless as a statue. "Doctor, I'm not telling you how to conduct your business. But it surely will not be helpful if this causes a general panic. A people in panic can do crazy things.'"

"And a people who aren't informed about the presence of a deadly disease can die. They may die anyway. That's what worries me."

Waldbaer relented. "And it worries me no less. I am not insensitive, but I can sense the opportunity for chaos and violence, Doctor. At any rate, I anticipate that I'll be seeing you or your colleagues at the probable source of this pestilence, and that's the von Winterloch crypt."

CHAPTER SIXTEEN

The morning broke with a radiance that displayed the Alps rising above the terrain, a distant, mountainous vision that beckoned like the gates of heaven. Even the solemn forests and tubercular swamps around Castle Winterloch were washed by the sunlight, the perennial mists and choking fog temporarily in decline. Crenellated towers and the castle keep itself seemed to lose centuries of age, the heavy stone blocks happily reflecting the sunlight.

Surveying the scene, Waldbaer found little to like, and much to disdain. The castle fortress he regarded as a vast heap of stone, its form oppressive and primitive. The sunlight did little to extirpate the structure's brooding presence. Nor, for that matter, did the sunlight illuminate the personality of the castle's present inhabitant, the arrogant von Winterloch. Waldbaer sighed in resignation, knowing that he could surrender his interest in the castle only when the shadowy figure who stood behind the theft had been apprehended.

A man exited the sally port that led to the Hall of Banners and walked across the lawn toward Waldbaer. Washed in sunlight, the tall, thin frame of Dr. Mayerling did not appear to be smiling at the fortuitous turn in the weather. Behold a sublime realist, Waldbaer concluded.

"Good morning, Doctor. Did your inspection of the crypt on this bright and shining day result in any conclusions?"

Dr. Mayerling glanced upward at the sun, winced, and inspected Waldbaer through his thick glasses. "Well, Kommissar, I was able to make some interesting observations just now. For one thing, what you said about the body of Heinrich is correct. The corpse is, in fact, mummified, a fascinating occurrence, and rare. It seems to me that must have been caused by the circumstances of the burial. Basically, once the stone lid was placed on the sarcophagus, it more or less stopped the ingress of oxygen. Add to that the location of the grave. It is a constant temperature, and it is uncommonly cold. That would slow down the normal process of decay severely."

"Yes, and I suppose it explains why the armor is in such excellent condition, it is essentially unflawed. And I presume that is the case with the pieces of armor that were stolen as well. But, Doctor, what does the gravesite tell you about the plague?"

Mayerling removed his glasses and rubbed at his eyes. "I have taken samples from around the crypt and from the sarcophagus itself. Some sediment, scrapings from the wall, and pieces of apparent debris that were proximate to the body of Heinrich. They'll be sent immediately to the central lab in Berlin that handles this sort of thing. We'll see if there is any contamination in a day, two days at most. Oh, and one other thing. I've arranged for all of the staff to have a physical examination to ensure that they are not carrying the plague. It's important that we control the spread of the disease any way that we can. But you'll be surprised to hear that one of the residents objected to taking an exam."

Waldbaer closed his eyes and stifled a sigh. "Let me guess. It is the esteemed Count Rheinhold von Winterloch, no? He is decidedly prickly at the best of times. You needn't trouble yourself further, Doctor. I will explain that taking an examination is in this case an order, not a request. Trust me, I will make him understand."

* * *

The count's voice was adamant. "I will under no circumstances allow a physical examination to be performed on me. At least, not by some incompetent oaf of a doctor who is reporting the results to a damned federal center. It's a matter of privacy, something I value. You can see that I'm fine, Kommissar, so let's dispense with the medical nonsense. I obviously don't have the plague." Von Winterloch's features framed in a red face were set in a habitual frown, as he stood in a damp corridor of the castle.

Waldbaer felt a headache beginning to take hold and rubbed a hand against his forehead. "You know, Count, your misapprehension is so severe that I have to wonder whether it's intentional. Your privacy will surely be respected, you may rely on it. The physicians merely report the results to a center in Berlin for coordination purposes. I'd think you would be grateful for a medical exam, and I don't mind telling you that I've had one. I'm fine, in case you were wondering."

Winterloch's face did not lose its florid color, accentuated by his white hair. "I'm fine too, perfectly fit, I can assure you."

"I believe you, for what it's worth. This is a pro forma exercise, and it has to get done. All of the staff here are taking the examination, and you are the only person objecting. I am not Father Confessor, but I have to wonder, is there something that you aren't telling me?"

Winterloch spit out his reply. "Certainly not. I have nothing to hide, not from the police, and not from doctors. If you insist, I will take this ridiculous medical examination but only under protest. This is just a load of bureaucratic crap."

Waldbaer's voice was clipped. "Good. I do insist. I'll have the doctors schedule your physical. It's a simple matter."

The older man's face seemed to lose some of its color. "The police have done nothing to help me, absolutely nothing. You have a murder to solve. You haven't done that. And I have an impudent theft to deal with. I want the broadsword returned, just as I want the armor. When these things are found, they will be returned to the grave of Heinrich, where they belong."

Waldbaer happily found that his headache was receding. He buttoned his jacket and prepared to leave. "The murderer, I believe, is quite dead. But the man, or woman, who arranged for the theft, the one who planned it, is still at large. But I have a sense that we may be able to identify him."

Winterloch looked puzzled and spoke warily. "Why in the world do you think you can identify him? He's an anonymous bastard, so far."

Waldbaer's face creased with a weary smile. "I have a feeling, call it intuitive, that the culprit is a specialist in the Middle Ages. He may have a history of collecting antiques, or of buying and selling them. Any fact that you can add to that picture would be helpful."

"I know of no such person."

"Well then, Count, I fear that the despised police, and perhaps a despised Kommissar, represent your last hope." Then Waldbaer began his stroll down the corridor, toward the reigning embrace of sunlight outside.

CHAPTER SEVENTEEN

He had slept fitfully, and awoke at dawn feeling unaccountably exhausted. The sheets of Etienne Rouchford's bed were moist with spent sweat. He rose slowly, and the pain in his sides and down his spine seemed to rebuke him for the effort. His physical complaints and malaise felt like past encounters he had experienced with the flu, and at seventy-five, he did not take such illnesses lightly.

The light that was seeping into the world at six in the morning was predominately gray, and the monochromatic hue that washed in through the thick curtains colored the furniture in the hotel room in half-light and perfectly matched his mood. The picture window of his spacious room opened onto the lake below, and the water, a metallic black also suited his mood. Struggling with effort to a sitting position on the bed, the man suppressed a groan as his head felt painfully constricted, as if squeezed by some invisible vice. He forced himself to his feet with a burst of effort.

His chest hurt with a low, deep throbbing. He raised a hand and unbuttoned his pajama shirt and scratched there, underneath the collarbone. The flesh did not feel firm, and he glanced down.

"Jesus Christ," he exclaimed with a start, eyes bulging. A bubble of pustulating black, as large as a boxer's fist, had appeared, seemingly out of nowhere, overnight. He moved his hand and touched the growth and felt it move like partially coagulated jelly under his fingers; a burst of searing pain accompanied the probe. Feeling faint, he reached for the hotel phone located on a table next to the bed. He punched the number for the main reception desk and waited, breathing hard and moaning while it rang. A male voice, oddly distant, spoke from the other end. "Tegernsee Hotel. How may I be of assistance?"

"This is Monsieur Rouchford in room 402. I am not at all well. Get me a doctor, and get him immediately."

GAMSDORF

The call came at mid-morning and interrupted Waldbaer midway through a chocolate croissant. Sitting at his desk, the detective grimaced and gulped down a remnant of the breakfast pastry as the familiar tone of *Eine kleine Nachtmusik* filled the confines of his office at the Gamsdorf police station. "Waldbaer," he snarled into the sleek form of the mobile phone.

"Dr. Mayerling here. We seem to have a third case of plague, and not very far from you. The victim is named Etienne Rouchford."

Waldbaer rubbed a piece of offending pastry off his front teeth. "Is he alive or dead?"

"He's alive. But barely, from what I understand. He's being kept at the emergency clinic in Traunstein. It occurred to me that you might want to talk to him, Kommissar. The medical authorities have taken all of the information that they require, but you may have your own additional inquiries."

Waldbaer focused on a map of Upper Bavaria fixed to the opposite wall of his office. He located Traunstein easily, a town of twenty-thousand inhabitants.

"I do have some questions. I hope he's well enough to answer them."

There was an instant's hesitation before Mayerling answered, "I'd get there as quickly as possible, if I were you. Herr Rouchford is apparently in a bad way. The doctors aren't sure he'll survive. By the way, do you speak French?"

"A little, what vestiges I remember from Gymnasium. Why do you ask?"

"Because Rouchford is a French citizen from Grenoble, I'm told. That's all I know. I leave the investigation, after all, to you."

"The vicissitudes of investigative work are my sorry lot in life, Doctor. I'll let you know what I find out in Traunstein, if it's relevant." Waldbaer flicked off the phone, and eased his frame up from his desk.

Opening his office door, he grumbled at the uniformed sergeant nursing a cardboard cup of coffee. "Get me anything and everything we have on a Herr Etienne Rouchford, date of birth unknown, place of birth somewhere in France. Send the information to me as an SMS as soon as you have it. I'll be in Traunstein." With that, Waldbaer reached for his jacket, and was gone.

TRAUNSTEIN

Traunstein lay much as it had since the sixth century, quietly nestled in hilly ground on the banks of the shallow river Traun that gradually transformed into the alpine vastness. The clinic, located on the outskirts, was a modern, four-story glass-and-steel interruption of the pine forests that swept upwards toward the mountain peaks. Waldbaer had parked his Volkswagen and stared for a moment at the large and imposing medical edifice, studying it. "Utter trash," he muttered to himself, musing that the structure was an unfortunate reminder that contemporary architects had invented no style that surpassed the beauty of the Ionic or Corinthian. The man-made world, it seemed, was a long paean to stainless steel and tinted glass.

Waldbaer's first cup of coffee, hot but without taste, was with the Bavarian doctor who was in charge of the internal medicine department. The doctor had short-cut, thin brown hair turning to gray, and the athletic frame of a runner. He bore the Prussian-sounding name of Heinrich Schmitz. Waldbaer sat in an uncomfortable folding chair in the doctor's brightly lit office, legs splayed in frayed corduroy trousers.

"It's like this," the doctor was saying, "When he checked in here, Herr Rouchford was already in a severely infected state. He is in marked decline, and I doubt that he will survive this episode, although we're doing our best for him. I estimate that his chances are less than fifty percent. At the very least, it appears that we are going to have to amputate his hands. He has begun to vomit blood and has an infection in his lungs."

Waldbaer winced as he asked, "Why would you amputate his hands?"

"You'll see for yourself, I'm afraid. His hands are rotting away, to be blunt. There's nothing else we can do. He's conscious now, but I don't know how long that will last. He's under very strong painkillers."

"When can I talk to Herr Rouchford? Is he in surgery?"

"No. He's in the isolation ward. You can don a hazardous material suit and talk to him. Twenty minutes is the absolute longest that I can allow. He speaks German and English, by the way, so you don't have to rely on your French. I can take you to his room right now, if you wish."

"Thank you. There's just one thing, Doctor. Herr Rouchford apparently received the disease from somewhere, he didn't just contract it out of the blue. Where did he get it, and how?"

Schmitz placed both hands deep in the pockets of his medical smock. "That's difficult to say. Rouchford is not being entirely cooperative about where he's been in the last seventy-four hours. As to how he acquired the plague, I would say that a flea bit him, I discovered a tiny bite mark on his left thigh. The incubation period for the plague is between two days and six days."

Waldbaer eyed the doctor without blinking. "So, the transmission of the plague is dependent upon contact with infected fleas?"

Schmitz hesitated. "Well, Kommissar, it's a bit complicated, but fleas aren't the sole carriers of the plague. Rats can carry infected fleas, or a canine, in certain circumstances. A person can carry it too. If an infected person coughs, droplets from the cough can be highly virulent. So, if Rouchford wasn't bitten by an infected flea, he could have been coughed on or spit on by an infected person. But Rouchford has no recollection of something like that occurring, or says he doesn't. Again, in my view, Rouchford is not being completely candid."

"Perhaps it is within my powers to persuade a dying man to come clean, Doctor. Tell me, have antibiotics been part of his treatment?"

"Yes, but Rouchford came to us fairly late, he had already been infected more than twenty-four hours, beyond the period when antibiotics are most effective. He has been treated with doses of streptomycin, but that has sadly had no effect."

Waldbaer gave a weary smile. "Thank you, Doctor. Well, then, let's see if Monsieur Rouchford chooses to answer our questions on his recent past."

The ward of isolation rooms occupied a small wing in the hospital and was lit with high-powered, overhead lamps and smelled of regular encounters with ammonia. Neither the lighting nor the odor pleased Waldbaer, who didn't like hospitals in the first place.

Waldbaer had donned the hazmat suit in bad humor, his temperament not lightened by the added humiliation of having a smiling young nurse help him into it. "I can do this myself," he had grumbled at his cheerful assistant. Suitably adorned in blue fabric, the detective was permitted to enter the room alone.

Etienne Rouchford was awake, his eyes hooded from lack of sleep or the medication, but, Waldbaer sensed, from fear as well. The air smelled fetid, a cloying putrid hint of the rancid, which even the institutionalized ammonia could not subdue. Rouchford's face was alabaster white, blue veins in his cheeks and across his prominent nose marking him with the appearance of a very sick man. His hands, slick with ointment, had severely bent fingers and cracked flesh and were fully, appallingly black. A transparent, plastic breathing device was wedged into his nose, and an intravenous drip was taped to one arm. Waldbaer noted a bubo below the shoulder, a pustulating black sack of blood and fluid that threatened to break.

Go slowly, the man looks to be dying, Waldbaer counseled himself.

"*Bonjour, Monsieur Rouchford, comment allez-vous?*" Waldbaer began in an even tone.

A pair of yellowed eyes focused wetly on the detective and a weak smile crossed his whitewashed face. The man sucked in a gulp of air before speaking. "*Guten Tag, mein Herr,*" he replied, signaling that he preferred to speak German. Rouchford summoned up a grimace that mimicked a smile. "I've had better days. Are you perhaps a physician, a specialist of some sort?"

Waldbaer found a folding chair next to the wall and pulled it to the bedside, sitting down. He pursed his lips a moment before answering. "Sadly, I am not. No, I am not of the medical profession. I am, to be honest, a Kommissar of police, and I am conducting an investigation into a murder and a robbery. I have some questions. Of course, you may not choose to answer and, in your condition, I would have to respect that. But let me add that under the present circumstances, I believe honest answers would do you no harm."

The eyes opened fully, revealing alarm. "You mean, because I am going to die?"

Waldbaer sat ramrod straight in the chair and folded his hands. "No, I didn't mean that at all. As I have said, I am not a doctor, and must leave a prognosis to them. It is my hope, surely, that you survive this infection and return to full health. I meant to say that as far as any criminal accusation is concerned, you are not, as the saying goes, 'a subject of interest.' You are also a French citizen and that passport formality affords you an additional protection. I trust that much is clear?"

Rouchford opened his mouth to take in another prodigious gulp of air, but his eyes remained on Waldbaer. "Yes, Kommissar, it is clear. You expect me, perhaps, to sing like a canary because death is likely to take me? Is that it? Well, it could be that I believe in immortality, no? In fact, I do sense that death is near but it is not the end. I am a Catholic, I will have you know."

Waldbaer leaned forward, and his chair gave a metallic creak of protest. "I confess that I am a Catholic too, Herr Rouchford, at least I was baptized one. Perhaps both of us are creatures of a certain age and a certain time. But I think that, as a Catholic, I would be inclined to tell all, and perhaps to tell the unvarnished truth. I am not a priest, not a father confessor, just a simple policeman. It would seem that your disease is linked to a crime that someone else committed. Other innocent people, like you, are likely to contract this disease unless we can locate the man who committed the crime. To be entirely honest, even that is a long shot. For what it's worth, if you could answer a few questions I expect that you would...rest easier."

Rouchford turned his head a degree on the hospital pillow and grimaced. He closed his eyes. "What is it that you want to know, Kommissar?"

"I want to know if you were with anyone who was trying to sell you medieval artifacts. I am very interested in obtaining the name of this person. This individual, probably unknown to you, sponsored a break-in to a private residence, a castle, and obtained the artifacts by robbing a grave, by violating a last resting place. He stole the items, or caused them to be stolen. He took into his possession at least an ancient broadsword and an armored ceremonial vest. An innocent man was killed during the robbery, murdered. A petty criminal was also murdered. Tell me, did you meet anyone who offered to sell you these antique goods for money?"

Rouchford twitched, but Waldbaer could not tell if it was an involuntary spasm or a reaction to direct questioning. Rouchford's voice was low, and Waldbaer strained to listen. "Kommissar, humor me, if you will, and answer a question of my own first. Then I will answer yours. Does this man know that he is spreading this disease?"

"No. At least, I do not think that he does."

Rouchford nodded, satisfied. "All right. I was contacted by a man who deals in antiquities. He is an expert in the Middle

Ages. He is known to acquire exquisite pieces from that epoch. Of course, the details of his sales must be handled discreetly."

"Yes, of course. The sale of antiquities has to be handled discreetly, Monsieur Rouchford, because the goods he deals in are stolen."

Rouchford opened his eyes and seemed to focus on the wall behind Waldbaer. "That is not my concern. In most cases, I don't know the history or the circumstances of the acquisition, and it is often best not to ask. But I will admit, I knew the history of this sword and the breastplate, worked in gold. I know that they were taken from the von Winterloch estate and date back to the twelfth century. Can you imagine it, Kommissar? The objects are nearly priceless, they are exquisite."

"Yes, I have no reason to doubt it. And now, will you tell me the name of this dealer?"

Rouchford turned his stare to the detective. "Ah, you are anxious for his name, no? All right, the dealer's name is Stefan Hofgartner. That is, Doktor Stefan Hofgartner. He is a German."

"And he is a master thief and a sordid robber of crypts. Where did you meet this Hofgartner, and when?"

"I met him at his villa although I have dealt indirectly with him for years and know the quality of his work. His villa is an impressive house located in the countryide near the town of Traunstein. He had the objects there for me to view privately. The sword was magnificent, and the breastplate was of shining black metal and worked with gold. An enviable find, I must say. He invited me there to a quiet exhibition three days ago."

"You said that the items were exquisite. Did you purchase them?"

Rouchford managed a wan smile. "No. It is a very great pity, but I did not. I intended first to organize the funds required to close the deal. The sword and the breastplate cost a million euro. It would have taken a couple of days, but then I was struck by this terrible disease. Too late." As he spoke, a trickle of bright blood was visible on Rouchford's teeth. Alarmed, Waldbaer looked about the room for a buzzer to alert the medical staff.

"Don't be alarmed, Kommissar. It is all part of Yersenia pestis and what it does to the human body, I am afraid. That's what the doctors tell me. There is lots of blood, lots of blood, and it finds a way to pour out of me, like a bottle of good red wine that's been spilled. But there is not much time left, I fear. So please tell me, do you intend to find Doktor Hofgartner?"

"I will find him, and I intend to arrest him. At least, that is my preference. I want you to think back to the time of your meeting three days ago. Was Hofgartner visibly sick in any way?"

Rouchford raised his eyebrows with effort. "No. He was not sick. But, as you mention it, he did have a nasty cough."

"A cough?"

"Yes. It was persistent. I recall that he coughed, it was a distressingly wet sound, as if something had gotten into his lungs and taken up residence there. I do not know if the disease can be spread that way. I also handled the artifacts, and of course they seemed clean of any patina. The blade of the broadsword looked as if it were newly minted, although, of course, it was very old. I could even read the script that had been emblazoned on it. The writing was in German."

Waldbaer's face betrayed a reluctant smile. "Oh? And what did the Winterloch blade have written on it?"

"It struck me as most unusual. And given my present situation, it seems infinitely ironic. The pommel, grip, and cross guard are finished in gold. But written on the blade was this: 'Behold, I am Death'. Perhaps it is poetry, perhaps a curse. Perhaps it is indeed true."

Rouchford's eyes suddenly displayed a look of incomprehension. A severe spasm shook his body, arching his spine, and his blackened hands curled into gripped fists grasping the bedsheet. He gasped for air, and the sound became a low moan. The trickle of blood from between his teeth at once became an explosive torrent. As the mass of red liquid turned to black against the white of his gown, the bubo on his arm suppurated as well, unleashing a great gout of pus and viscous blood onto the tile floor. A powerful stench filled the room, and Rouchford groaned with strident force.

Waldbaer stood, knocking his chair to the floor behind him with an angry clang of metal. He grabbed the red buzzer that hovered over Rouchford's bedframe and pressed down with force. Rouchford continued to gasp for air, as if he were drowning, his eyes bulging. A moment later, the door to the room burst open and a nurse in an isolation suit rushed in, signaling to Waldbaer with a flailing arm that he needed to leave. Waldbaer complied without a word, and as he reached the anteroom to the isolation chamber, made way for an earnest-looking Doctor Schmitz with a hypodermic needle at the ready. The door slammed shut, leaving Waldbaer to remove his mask on his own.

A moment later the door creaked open, and the doctor who had just entered Rouchford's room emerged. "I'm afraid that Rouchford is dead," he announced.

Shaken, Waldbaer only nodded. He remembered the words that Rouchford had seen engraved on the blade of the broadsword. "Behold, I am Death."

CHAPTER EIGHTEEN

Death was very much on Waldbaer's mind, as he slouched in his leather chair at the Gamsdorf police station afterhours, as the sun descended on an early November evening, robbing the town at an early hour of natural light and the mirth of color. He considered the events since the murder of Andreas Pichler and had scribed these on a sheet of paper marked Schloss Winterloch. Rubbing a hand over his eyes to ward off weariness, he contemplated the script that he had scrawled.

Andreas Pichler—most probably killed by Karl Ortner— with a sword. No sign of plague.

Roland Dietrich—small-time criminal from Munich, probably assisting Ortner. Killed by Ortner after the robbery. No sign of plague.

Karl Ortner—identified through fingerprints and criminal record: Ortner shot some days later. Infected with terminal late-stage plague.

Waldbaer nodded to himself and read the line penciled below it.

Herr Rouchford: wealthy Frenchman hospitalized for plague at Traunstein. Did not know Ortner. Identified Doktor Stefan Hofgartner as individual selling illicit medieval goods for one million euro. Rouchford died of plague.

Waldbaer placed the paper on his desk, drummed the fingers of one hand on it, and considered. Hofgartner had been identified, but had escaped arrest. The presumed master thief had left an empty villa outside of Traunstein in disarray and gone to ground. The objects from von Winterloch's tomb were gone as well, seemingly vanished into the earth.

Bathed in the soft yellow glow of his bronze desk lamp, the detective considered how and where Hofgartner might be hiding. Hofgartner had a car, but had probably ditched it in a long-term parking garage as the police would know the registration. Hofgartner would also avoid using credit cards. At any rate, Waldbaer knew, Hofgartner in all likelihood had more than enough cash with him, and might even acquire another vehicle. On the other hand, he was on the run, a development the antiquities dealer had not anticipated. Hofgartner's plans had unraveled, at least for the moment. And what about that wet cough Rouchford had described?

Waldbaer sank back into the comforting plushness of his chair to consider. He hoped that Hofgartner had not built an alternate personality, a workable alias. If he had done so, tracking him would become infinitely more difficult, even if Interpol was asked for assistance. But, Waldbaer reasoned, all men are only men and sooner or later they make mistakes. Hofgartner had now clearly emerged as the key figure in the investigation.

Still, Waldbaer was uneasy, and he shifted in his chair, ignoring its squeak of protest. Was there something, anything, that he failed to see, an element that he did not grasp?

A familiar strain of Mozart's *Eine kleine Nachtmusik* erupted from a pocket inside his jacket and startled him for a moment. He reached in and pushed a button on the cell phone and the symphonic, vibrating device went silent.

"Kommissar Waldbaer here," he muttered into the diminutive form of plastic.

"Yes, good evening Kommissar," a low and measured masculine voice said. "This is Dr. Magnus Nilsson calling from the European Center for Disease Control in Stockholm, Sweden. You're probably wondering why I'm calling, yes?" The voice spoke in English and sounded warm and avuncular.

Waldbaer, who disliked telephone conversations in any language, was guarded in his reply. "I presume, Doctor, that you will enlighten me about the purpose of this call. Now would be a good time."

He heard a muffled laugh. "Well, to be brief, I'm informed that you have been working on a case that interests both of our organizations. You have been directly involved, if I understand things properly, with Yersinia pestis. The interests of the European Center for Disease Control—ECDC—should be rather obvious."

"I'm only familiar with the center from what I've read in the newspapers. I assume you're looking at the plague as a health issue."

"That's correct, Kommissar. We're interested in current health risks and the potential for future risks in a Europe without borders. The plague, to put it mildly, has us all on edge. Only a few people appear to have been infected so far, thank God, but our concern is that thousands, even hundreds of thousands, of people could become infected."

Waldbaer sighed. "That concerns me as well. But I think that you need to speak to one of the physicians who have treated the disease, they are much more informed than I, and they speak your language. I can give you their names."

The voice from Stockholm drew in a breath. "If you don't mind my saying so, the ECDC will be in touch with them through the usual established channels. But it's you that I want to talk to. This center is a large organization, and I have a rather special task. I deal with predicting disease futures and the risks a disease poses to the general population. That is, I draw up the models of how an infectious disease can be expected to progress. It is exacting work, and I can use all the help that I can get."

Nilsson continued without interruption. "Let me get to the point, Kommissar. I would like you to fly to Stockholm immediately for an exchange of information with me. Ask me anything you want, and I'll answer it. That may prove useful to your investigation. In turn, I have a number of questions I would dearly like to bounce off of you. By the way, the government of the Federal Republic of Germany has agreed to our request. I expect you'll be notified through channels shortly. And we've even taken the liberty of booking a flight for you to Stockholm on our coin. If you don't strenuously object, I'll even buy you a salmon dinner in an excellent restaurant."

Waldbaer could not restrain a grin. "All right, Doctor, that's more like it. The salmon dinner won the day, hands down. My understanding is that Atlantic fish is best accompanied by a dry pilsner beer. And my intuition tells me that there are some details about this case that you prefer not to mention on a public phone."

There was silence for a moment on the telephone, before Nilsson responded. "I would advise you to trust your intuition, Kommissar, trust your intuition."

CHAPTER NINETEEN

STOCKHOLM, SWEDEN

Waldbaer gazed through the double glass window at his side as the Airbus began its long descent into Stockholm Arlanda Airport. He was wedged into economy-class seating with an overweight, florid featured and snoring German businessman at his shoulder, spilling over the seat into Waldbaer's space. Yet another testimony for his unshakeable preference to travel in cars, unaccompanied.

The plane banked to the right, dipped a wing, and began its final descent. Waldbaer saw what appeared to be an infinity of dark pine forest, stretching out in all directions. The Swedish terrain struck him as monotonous, as flat as a farmer's field. Already Waldbaer missed the craggy vastness of the Alps with its roaring streams. The fir trees came into focus more sharply, as the plane lined up with a still distant asphalt runway. Stockholm was not in sight. Waldbaer had been advised that the city was about an hour's taxi ride from Arlanda. He wondered again what role the European Center for Disease Control had, or thought it had, in a case of Bavarian homicide. He counseled himself that he would know soon enough. The Airbus deployed its landing wheels with a hum of metallic efficiency, and Waldbaer took a glance at the majestic, solemn trees, and then closed his eyes and laced his hands together, as he had always done on landing in an aircraft.

Waldbaer paid the Swedish taxi his fee at the conclusion of his ride into Stockholm, and grudgingly included a ten-krona tip, an amount that he suspected was too generous.

"Kommissar Waldbaer, unless I am grossly mistaken?"

The detective turned to see a tall man of athletic build with gold-framed glasses and cropped gray hair smiling at him.

"Dr. Nilsson?"

The tall man came closer and shook hands, his smile not disappearing. "Yes, that's me. I'm not too comfortable with formality, Kommissar, please call me Magnus."

"I don't object," Waldbaer said. He did not offer to employ his first name, believing that his title gave him the edge in authority. "I'm anxious to hear what you have to say, Magnus. And I can add a detail or two about this Yersinia pestis case myself."

Nilsson's smile had evaporated but was replaced by an attitude of reserved politeness. "Good. There is someone else we will be discussing this with. I believe that you know him."

Waldbaer was caught off guard. "Really? Someone I know in Stockholm?"

Without answering, Magnus Nilsson nodded and extended an arm toward the red brick building surmounted by a bell tower.

The pine-veneer door to the doctor's office swung open without a sound and Waldbaer entered, Nilsson behind him. Seated in a metal-and-black plastic chair was another figure, hands clasped behind his head in a casual stance. The man laughed and rose to his feet, grasping Waldbaer by the shoulders, shaking his hand with a firm grip.

"Hirter! Well, I'll be damned!" Waldbaer exclaimed, instantly wondering what involved the operational division of the Central Intelligence Agency in a murder case.

Hirter, broad shouldered, tall, and sporting the lean and healthy look of a runner, regarded Waldbaer. "Well, Kommissar, you look fairly fit for a man of your advanced years. It's encouraging to see that you don't seem to have gained too much weight. It's damned good to see you again."

Waldbaer feigned a look of irritation. "I'm precisely as fit as I have to be, Hirter. The extra weight that I unhappily carry is commensurate with the weight of my office. And, for what it's worth, it's good to see you again, after our time together on the terrorism case in Munich, and chasing a ship full of nuclear centrifuges halfway around the world onboard the *Condor Fury*."

Nilsson's voice intruded on the familiarity of the conversation. "May I invite you both to sit down? There's coffee on the table, and we have a great deal to discuss."

The three men sat in casual coordination, and Waldbaer noted unhappily that his knees cracked in protest. "Hirter, it's you who are stationed in Washington, far away. You've traveled far to get here. May I ask why?"

Hirter nodded his head, his dark hair waving slightly, picking up the glint of the sun shining brightly through the trees outside. "You're right, Kommissar, as pleased as I am to see you. As I've already told Dr. Nilsson, this trip is very important to the CIA, for reasons that I'll make clear in a minute. Dr. Nilsson and a few other ECDC officials know that I'm a clandestine service officer, as do the appropriate officials of the Swedish government. No one else is aware that I'm affiliated with an intelligence organization, so we're being circumspect about my presence here."

Waldbaer leaned forward and placed his hands on his knees and spoke through a smile. "That explains who knows that you are with the CIA, Hirter, but it doesn't explain why the CIA sent you here in the first place."

Nilsson spoke up, his voice calm and reserved. "Gentlemen, I think I can add a little to the picture at this point. Kommissar Waldbaer, you are aware that the ECDC was some days ago contacted by medical personnel in Germany, in Munich to be exact, with a report of a case of Yersinia pestis, commonly called the plague. The plague victim was shot to death for reasons not relevant to the medical history of the case, but he would have died of the disease anyway, according to the doctors. We received notification of two more deaths soon thereafter, in Augsburg and Traunstein. Just hours ago we received word that two more people—one of them a child of twelve—are hospitalized in Bavaria and have tested positive for the plague. When the ECDC was advised of the first case of plague in Germany, we notified medical facilities throughout Europe to be alert to its presence. So far, not a single hospital outside Germany has reported back. Our feeling is that, up to the present time, Germany is the sole locus of the disease. We have an outbreak of the plague in Germany, gentlemen, and if that's not enough, this strain of the disease seems impervious to antibiotics."

"I didn't know about today's cases," Waldbaer said. "I was on board a plane this morning and I haven't received an update. I've been advised that the plague seems resistant to antibiotics. But if we add up the cases of people who have been exposed to the plague, living and dead, we now get a total of five. That means that this outbreak is—more or less—contained at present, doesn't it?"

Nilsson removed his glasses and addressed Waldbaer. "Yes and no. It is contained at the moment, that's true, but only for the moment. But the real concern, Kommissar, is that this particular strain of the plague seems to be highly infectious. It can be spread, the ECDC believes, by a simple cough or a sneeze. That's called pneumonic plague. Think about that for a moment. You see the problem, don't you? Today we have five cases, yes. Tomorrow we could have fifty, and by the weekend five hundred. But there's more to the story, isn't there, Mr. Hirter?"

Hirter's face was expressionless and betrayed no emotion, the mask of the professional, thought Waldbaer. "Okay. Let me cut to the chase. The reason that the CIA is so concerned, and the reason that the agency quietly and quickly sent me here, is that this plague strain appears to be resistant to antibiotics, which have worked in controlling the disease for years. That's a real game changer. The Office of Disease Control in Atlanta—ODC— alerted the CIA to the danger, with the proviso that this plague seems to have been engineered to successfully resist attempts to deal with it. So, I don't hesitate to say that it appears that we're dealing with an intentional malefactor, that is, a person who is using the plague as a weapon, as well as the disease."

Waldbaer raised his arms and put his hands in the air in a cautionary gesture. "Wait, slow down, I'm a bit confused. This plague is ancient, as far as I know, and it somehow became deadly and dangerous again in modern times. I don't quite comprehend all this because my education is in criminology and not medicine, but my understanding is that this is essentially the same disease that swept through Europe in 1348, and earlier. The Black Death is a very old disease, not a new one. Am I wrong, or am I right?"

Nilsson looked at his two guests with raised eyebrows. "You are wrong in some important respects, Kommissar. This plague is not the same strain that afflicted Europe centuries ago, not by any means. It is related to it, yes, but it is certainly not the same. Our tests make it clear that this Yersinia pestis came from Madagascar."

"Madagascar? You mean the island off the coast of Africa?"

Nilsson nodded. "That's correct. It's not well known that Madagascar has had well over a hundred deaths annually due to the plague. You just don't hear about it because the information is not considered newsworthy in the western world. The plague bacteria now found in Europe is related to that found in Madagascar, our tests make that incontrovertible. And by the way, this particular strain didn't exist seven hundred years ago, it's contemporary. The plague organism in Madagascar killed inhabitants there in 2014 and 2015, and it's still there today."

Waldbaer closed his eyes and rubbed at his temples. "You know, it's perversely funny, isn't it? I had intended to tell you that the origin of this outbreak of the Black Death was the crypt of Count Heinrich von Winterloch. He died of the disease in 1121. I had thought, until now, that the plague went dormant, that it existed in von Winterloch's grave since the twelfth century. The dead count's body was unnaturally preserved, due, I imagine, to the temperature of the grave and the lack of oxygen in the sarcophagus. I thought that this helped explain why the plague survived in the crypt for so long. Are you telling me that is wrong? This has a direct impact on an ongoing murder investigation."

Nilsson and Hirter exchanged glances, and, with a nod from

Hirter, Nilsson answered again. "Kommissar, the state of the dead count's body has nothing to do with it. It's an anomaly, a rare occurrence. Bodies are occasionally well preserved for a variety of accidental reasons. But it's simply not possible that the plague somehow went dormant and survived in that crypt over the centuries, to be reanimated today."

Waldbaer crossed his arms in front of his chest. "Why isn't it possible? Could you explain?"

Nilsson steepled his hands and regarded Waldbaer. "It's like the graveyard for plague victims discovered in London a few years ago. The skeletons were of twenty people who had died from the Black Death, but the plague had disappeared completely from their bones. It proved perfectly safe to remove the skeletons without anyone becoming infected. It's precisely the same in this case. But that doesn't mean that the crypt is unimportant."

Nilsson elaborated as Waldbaer hunched forward in his chair. "Some fleas containing the bacteria certainly could have been placed in the crypt and could have claimed the first victim— the grave robber. But let me say again that this plague came from Madagascar, nowhere else. It came from Oriental rat fleas which are themselves immune to infection. The rat flea can flourish in the European environment so long as it's fairly humid. Maybe Mr. Hirter would like to add something."

Hirter's frame was tensed, as if he were if ready to spring at an assailant. "Right. Whoever is behind this has a solid knowledge of pneumonic plague as well as the training necessary to re-engineer Yersinia pestis to make it resistant to antibiotics. Look, there's history to this. The CIA has been worried, extremely worried, about this sort of thing since the era when the Soviet Union existed. As recently as the 1980s, the Russians conducted extensive work in weaponizing disease, including the plague, and the CIA discovered it."

"I don't follow you. Meaning what exactly?" Waldbaer prodded.

"Meaning that the Soviet military fully expected to be able

to launch and win a war against the West by sickening or killing divisions of NATO soldiers with a mutated swine flu, bird flu, or the plague," Hirter said. "The Soviet Union experimented with communicable disease as a weapon and had established several top secret laboratories for that purpose. Scores of Soviet scientists were trained and dedicated to weaponizing disease. Fortunately, as you well know, Kommissar, it never came to a shooting war. The Berlin Wall fell, and the Soviet Union collapsed before any weaponized disease could ever be used. But there was more than enough bad news. The Soviet scientists who were schooled in having expertise in swine flu and the plague were now unemployed and out of money. The fact that weapons containing disease hadn't been used in an armed conflict didn't mean that they couldn't be used. The Russian scientists certainly had developed the knowledge."

"Are you suggesting, Hirter," Waldbaer asked, "that a rogue Russian medical expert or scientist is somehow behind the deaths in Bavaria?"

"I don't know, but maybe. Or maybe a Russian passed on his knowledge to someone else. At the end of the day, the fact is the preparation of genetically modified plague is not the work of some unskilled, crazy person. It takes exceptional skill to work with the plague and not get killed yourself."

Waldbaer nodded to Hirter. "All right, I've got that. A skilled scientist is required, not a crazy person. What else?"

Hirter stood, smoothed his wool trousers, and walked to the window where the sunlight illuminated the autumnal landscape. "A laboratory is necessary; it has to exist somewhere and it has to be equipped with research hardware. If a government is involved in a biological weapons program, they'll use a state-of-the-art building, or buildings, and keep it secret. If you want to get depressed, think for a moment of North Korea. It has literally thousands of buildings capable of housing a laboratory. On the other hand, if this modified plague is the creation of just one man or one woman, he or she will need to create a laboratory somewhere

and stock it with the medical devices capable of genetic engineering. It's very expensive to do, but you could make a lab in an
apartment, or simply rent space in a warehouse. The CIA experts
tell me that a lab of this nature doesn't have to be large."

Waldbaer shook his head. "Well! That will certainly help
with the investigation. Look for a lab, either a large lab, or a small
one. And it either belongs to a government or a clever madman.
That will get me far, Hirter."

Waldbaer looked exceedingly tired. "Gentlemen, one thing is
certain. A Dr. Hofgartner appears to be spreading the plague in
Bavaria. He is a known dealer in antiquities, mostly stolen antiquities. Hofgartner was clever enough to plan the robbery of medieval armor from the grave of a medieval knight, a victim of the
Black Death that swept through Europe. He may also be the individual we want to get our hands on, the man who created this
killing machine of a disease. Either way, it is my intention to get
him."

Nilsson studied Waldbaer with a dry smile. "That is, I'm
afraid, a police matter, Kommissar, and I have no competence
to comment on it. But speaking for the ECDC, we are going to
be putting out a public health warning for the state of Bavaria.
The German Ministry of Health is already aware of this. The an-
nouncement will be made tomorrow morning, as there is no time
to lose with a hazard like this. The health warning is required by
European Union legislation and won't make your job any harder, I
hope."

"And it won't make it any easier, I'd wager. But it's all right. I
understand that the police are just one player in what has become
a public health case. I intend to concentrate on apprehending Dr.
Hofgartner, that's my job."

Hirter joined the conversation again. "The CIA has sort of
stumbled into a supporting role in this matter. Our fear is that
this plague will continue until we identify exactly who is responsible. If you want my view, the culprit probably isn't this Hofgartner. It doesn't make sense that he'd introduce a reengineered form

of the plague to the Winterloch crypt. Hell, if he's a grave robber, he would likely be the first victim. I wager that the perpetrator is a highly educated individual, maybe socially a loner, with a severe personality disorder. That's the type of man or woman that I'd focus on. But, after all, I'm a case officer, not a detective."

Waldbaer hesitated as his features creased with a smile. "Well, one thing is certain. Whatever his role, I have a suspicion that Hofgartner is probably infected with the disease by now, and I imagine that the ECDC as well as the police want to stop him."

Nilsson nodded in silent agreement.

"I'm not saying that Hofgartner is the key to this case," Waldbaer said, "by no means, but he is damned important. I believe that if we get Hofgartner, we can stop the spread of the plague."

Nilsson sat ramrod straight in his chair and raised a cautionary hand. "Yes, by all means, try to find and detain Hofgartner, Kommissar. But I agree with Mr. Hirter. He is not likely to be the man we are looking for. Whether he's a Russian scientist or not, I don't know, but Hirter is right, the person responsible for this has a superior education and probably a personality that marks him as peculiar. And as for ending the plague, that depends on our success in identifying who is responsible. If the plague is now pneumatic, it is highly contagious and we can expect the number of infected individuals to skyrocket exponentially. I want you to consider for a moment that hundreds of people a day, conceivably thousands of people, could be hospitalized."

"I know, I know," Waldbaer said with a deep frown. "I don't want that situation either, and let's hope to hell it doesn't come to that. I fly back to Munich tonight at seven, and the very last thing I hope to see are bodies lining the corridors of hospitals or stacked to the ceiling. If we get Hofgartner, we've made progress. He'll be interrogated, and we'll get to the bottom of the story. If he doesn't know who reengineered the plague, then we'll broaden our search to the medical profession and the scientific community. I'll keep you advised of developments, Dr. Nilsson. And, Hirter, I've got your phone number."

Nilsson exuded a contented smile, while Hirter laughed. "Don't worry, Kommissar, if you can't reach me, I can surely reach you."

"That is as I feared, Hirter. I'll be in touch."

"By the way," Hirter said with a smile, "I have some shopping errands to take care of in Stockholm for my girlfriend, and they involve buying outrageously priced smoked salmon in ornate boxes. After I take care of that, I'll be out at the airport, too, to catch my return flight to D.C. If you've got time to chat, I'd like to buy us both a Lapin Kulta beer at the airport lounge."

Waldbaer lifted his chin and narrowed his eyes. "If I understand properly that you are buying, Hirter, then I most certainly stand ready to please you."

* * *

The intense November sunlight had faded early, and by four in the afternoon, all was darkness. The airport stood out as a vast oasis of electric light surrounded by rows of stately pines which stood like silent sentries of approaching winter.

Hirter's shopping bag of smoked salmon was placed on the bar, his tall glass of pilsner beer held lightly by the stem. Waldbaer sat beside him at a corner of the bar, his loden business jacket on, his tie loosened, both hands cosseting a long, fluted beer glass.

"If as you say, Hirter, there is an individual with a medical or a scientific background behind this, I am quite clueless. No one remotely of that background has surfaced in this case."

Hirter swirled the beer in his glass and watched it foam before taking a sip, and then regarded Waldbaer. "I've got a little secret that I want to share with you." A flicker of a smile traced its way across Hirter's face.

"A secret, I see. Is that why we are here, ostensibly having a beer at your expense and chatting about old times?"

"Yes, that would be correct."

"Indeed. And I take it that you lack permission from your

superiors to include Dr. Nilsson and his colleagues at the Swedish ECDC in the little circle of those who are aware of this secret?"

"That would also be correct."

"Splendid, Hirter, truly splendid. But I know the rules of the game, and I grudgingly accept them. Well, don't tease me. What do you have to say?"

Hirter hunched his athletic frame over the polished wooden bar. "The reason that I couldn't reveal this to the ECDC is that it's potentially part of an ongoing investigation and not relevant to the health concerns of the case. As a policeman, you can understand that. The initial information came from the Miami Metropolitan Police Department. Operating on a tip, the narcotics squad of the police raided a former slaughterhouse, an abattoir, in a part of town called Hialeah. Upon entering, they did find a quantity of cocaine, but they also uncovered much more."

Waldbaer drummed his fingers on the bar and eyed the effervescence of his pilsner. "Do continue, Hirter."

"The police found that the slaughterhouse was equipped as a lab, but not as a narcotics lab for the production of illicit drugs like cocaine or heroin. Eventually, the police contacted the FBI and the FBI contacted the CIA to see if we could make any sense of it. We could, all right. Among the equipment the CIA identified was gear designed for bacteriological tests, microscopes, and lots of other exotic scientific equipment. Because the premises had been a butcher shop, it had been tiled from floor to the ceiling, perfectly ideal for working with infectious disease. Trace elements of bacteria were found. The bacterium was Yersinia pestis."

Waldbaer ceased drumming his fingers and pursed his lips. "Did the Miami police find and arrest the owner of the lab?"

"No." Hirter shook his head. "There was unfortunately no one to arrest. The owner had finished the work that he had started in the slaughterhouse-turned-laboratory, and then he had left the state of Florida, and probably the country. But as luck would have it, there was a whiteboard in the lab and, although it had been swept clean, my CIA colleagues wisely decided to try to analyze it. Although most of the notes on bacterial testing that they recovered were written in English, some were in a foreign language."

"Hirter, forgive me, but how certain is the CIA that these scribblings were in another language? After all, you said that the board had been wiped clean."

Hirter nodded. "Yes. Much of what was written on the whiteboard will never be recovered despite the Agency's best efforts, it's true. But fragments of foreign words did come up, including *Die Pest*, which, as you know, means the plague, and *Die Orientalischer Rattenfloh*; the Oriental rat flea. And the word *Gefärhrlich*, which to my mind means dangerous."

"That's thin gruel and speculative," muttered Waldbaer.

"No, rather robust gruel, I would say, Kommissar. Most of the notes on the white board were written in English, which as far as I'm aware is the medical language of choice. Only a few words were written in German. They are common words, precisely the kind of words that a German speaker would scribe in his native language. To my mind, and to the CIA analysts as well, this means the chances are high that our suspect comes from Germany or possibly Austria or perhaps Switzerland."

"Or maybe from Luxembourg. Let's say for the sake of argument that you are correct, Hirter. Why do you suppose that our German left Florida in the first place? Did he sense the police were interested in him?"

Hirter took a sip of beer through the crown of foam. "Not at all. He left because he was finished with what he set out to do. He had gotten samples of Yersinia pestis somewhere, in Madagascar according to ECDC, and I think he had genetically reengineered these samples in Florida. He had done what he wanted to do and had altered his sample of the plague. When he left Florida, I think it's a safe bet that he flew to Germany."

"Hirter, do you have any idea how many German citizens visit Florida for the sun and the sand and that wretched American beer?" Waldbaer exhibited a weary smile. "It's a vacation spot. Winter, you may recall, is very long in Germany, a good six months. The Germans go to Florida for the weather, for the beaches, and to see Disney World and frolic with the Little Mermaid. I can tell you that half of the policemen working in Gamsdorf go to Florida for vacation."

Hirter shook his head. "This individual didn't go to Florida for a vacationer's view of the beaches and palm trees, Kommissar, I think we can forget that. He came to Florida with the plague samples that he collected in Africa. Why Florida? That's simple. Because it has loads of medical facilities, medical specialty centers, and research facilities. Ordering the equipment for reengineering bacteria wouldn't have raised an eyebrow in Florida. He stayed in Miami until he had manipulated the plague's resistance to antibiotics. When that task was finished, he took the plague with him, concealed in special packaging in his luggage, I imagine, and flew to the country where he intended to use it. My colleagues at CIA believe that country is Germany. It's just a guess at this stage, but I believe it too."

"You are concealing information, Hirter," Waldbaer said, fixing his friend with his gaze. "You have a name for the individual who rented the slaughterhouse, don't you?"

Hirter flashed a smile. "Yes, I do. The rental records show that the space was paid for by a man named Christian Slatner, ostensibly born in Chicago. The name, as you might guess, is fake. That's another thing you can do in Florida with relative ease, buy a false identity with cash. Money will accomplish lots of things in an underworld that defines itself by dealing in illegal narcotics. Money will buy you a switchblade knife or an Uzi submachine gun or, as in this case, a perfect alias. Slatner, by the way, is a German name, and could have been used to cover a German accent."

Waldbaer reached into the pocket of his jacket and scrawled the name onto a pad of paper with his ball point pen. "It is probably pointless, Hirter, but I will trace the name when I get back to Gamsdorf. And, for what it's worth, I will keep in mind all that you said."

"That's fair enough, Kommissar. Here, let me give you a little gift that might be useful." Hirter produced a small ebony mobile phone and passed the glossy piece of plastic to the detective. "It's a cell phone and it's encrypted, courtesy of the CIA. If it's all right with you, I'll call you on it if I develop any relevant information on the Slatner case. You can call me as well. My number shows up automatically when you turn on the phone."

Waldbaer looked at the device, devoid of a brand name, and placed it in his jacket pocket. "Very nice of you and your always thoughtful and kind CIA brethren. Am I correct to assume that they don't want prying ears to hear us discussing the Slatner case?"

"You might say that. It's a small precaution, but I expect that it's one you can live with. As I've said, I'll get in touch with you if I receive any further information. You should feel free to do the same."

Waldbaer reached for his beer glass and examined the still-foaming contents. "Oh, I will, Hirter, I most certainly will."

CHAPTER TWENTY

CHIEMSEE LAKE, BAVARIA

He drove the Mercedes sedan into the pebbled parking lot that was separated by a field of waving, tall grass from the shores of the lake, and heard the small pebbles giving way to his tires. He turned off the baritone noise of the diesel engine and exited the vehicle, locking the car from a few feet away with the electronic key and hearing the dull sound of the door tabs falling into place. There was a slight chill in the air blown in off the water, a reminder that the month was November, and he buttoned his dark blue business suit and adjusted the collar of his shirt to stay warm.

There were only a few people underway, the jostling hordes of tourists having vanished with the gradual regress of summer. Anyone who bothered to look at the solitary man would have noticed that, aside from a white shirt and the muted blue of his tailored flannel suit, he wore no tie. His face, underneath the close-cropped, graying hair, was cut granitic and angular, and mottled now in traces of angry scarlet that had not felt a razor for four days.

Stefan Hofgartner did not pay the occasional passerby the slightest heed and walked past the worn wooden ticketing house with its shuttered windows to the pier which jutted out over the gray, wind-driven waves of Chiemsee Lake. Hofgartner was not well, and his progress was marked by dizziness and a distant, constant buzzing in his ears. He had first heard about his illness on the radio, and read about it in more detail in the *Süddeutsche Zeitung* and online.

He had the plague, the same disease that spread like brush fire in the Middle Ages. The newspaper had been remarkably correct about the symptoms of the disease. Buboes had grown out of nowhere in his armpits and groin and throbbed painfully. They were black and slick with repelling viscous secretions. Blood was everywhere; he bled routinely from the nose and from his putrefying gums. He knew that he smelled rancid and could not abide the stench of his own breath.

Hofgartner's shuffling gait stopped at the end of the pier. He stared for a moment at the windswept water and, with a squint, turned his face skyward. Funereal clouds had turned its vastness a brooding black as well, at least morose if not malevolent. He hacked out a cough and the winds caught flecks of black and scarlet and carried them away.

Not without irony, Hofgartner reflected that everything in his life had fallen completely apart in a matter of days. It was ironic how quickly things came tumbling down. He had carefully arranged the robbery of the grave of a long-dead noble and acquired a magnificently worked broadsword and a gold-embossed armored vest of breathtaking quality. He was set to make a fortune off of those trophies, which were immensely valuable to collectors. He had even located a likely buyer, Monsieur Rouchford, who was known to be vastly wealthy and who was apparently willing to make the purchase. But then, with staggering suddenness Rouchford had died of the plague, gagging, spewing blood, and vomiting bile. This, too, he had heard on the radio.

Hofgartner giggled in a low tone to himself as he recalled the radio and television reports of Rouchford's demise and the public health warnings about the plague. Concerned people were checking themselves into hospitals in a panic. Well, if they had the plague, the so-called Black Death from the Middle Ages, they might check themselves into a clinic all right, but they would most certainly be carried out. Antibiotics, he understood, were of no use in stopping the relentless and savage progress of the disease.

Hofgartner felt a burst of pain in his mouth and placed a

hand to his lips and saw that it was smeared with blood, which oozed like oil between his fingers. He gave a low moan. Life was seeping out of him bit by bit. Life itself, destiny and fortune, is nothing more than a roll of the dice, no more certain than a card game.

He was certain that Rouchford had spoken to the police and he had fled from his magnificent villa in Traunstein and taken up residence in a cheap tourist hotel near Prien, on the shores of the lake. He had five thousand euros in cash and that had served him for a while, but he knew, only a while. He did not have an alternate identity with supporting documents, because that sort of thing had always struck him as unnecessary for a man in his position.

Well, I guess you never know, he told himself, and began to laugh uproariously at the irony of it. Another explosively deep cough racked through him and shook his entire frame. The cough brought up from somewhere deep within a thick stew of steaming mucous and black blood which exploded from his mouth, the issue as thick as tar. It covered his shirt and stained his suit, and Hofgartner was vaguely aware that the viscous liquid was sinking into his skin. He felt humiliated by the abject surrender of his body to the disease. It is more than time, he thought.

A tremulous hand sank into the space underneath his tailored suit coat and Hofgartner produced a Heckler & Koch semi-automatic pistol, its dull, cold metal surface as dark as the sky overhead.

Without a whimper he took a deep breath, expelled it, and placed the barrel of the gun in his mouth, making sure that the barrel was directed toward his brain. He tasted metal as he flicked off the trigger guard. His eyes once again took in the waves and the silhouette of a tree-lined island in the distance. The island, he remembered, was home to a centuries-old palace built for Ludwig the Mad, the crazed king of the Bavarians. Hofgartner reflected that all men were perhaps crazy now and again. Some of them, like the scowling king Ludwig, gradually succumbed to a lifelong bout of madness. Better to end things now and go out with a modicum of dignity, he concluded. Hofgartner closed his eyes, inhaled one more deep breath, held it, and pulled the trigger in one smooth movement. The loud, echoing report of the pistol startled the gulls on the waves near the pier, and sent them into frantic, though temporary, flight.

CHAPTER TWENTY-ONE

Waldbaer stood in the dark by the shining blue Mercedes, corralled by a taut strand of police tape. The blue lights of half a dozen police cars flickered silently in the early evening air, like sentinels of death. Hofgartner's remains had been zipped into a plastic bag and removed for autopsy, and the pistol, the barrel matted with blood and brain tissue, placed in a sealed container for analysis by the forensic team.

The car was locked. Waldbaer held a steaming Styrofoam cup of coffee in his gloved hands and considered the scene. The Mercedes belonged to Hofgartner, the identifying documentation had been in his wallet. It is a fine car, Waldbaer thought, mildly annoyed at having a Volkswagen key in his pocket. He glanced around and saw two policemen in black leather bomber jackets in conversation a few yards away.

"When you gentlemen have solved all the world's problems, perhaps you could pry open the trunk."

One of the policemen, who looked to be in his late twenties, smiled. "No need for that, Kommissar. We have the keys. They were in Hofgartner's pocket."

"That's superb work, really excellent; I should write you up for a commendation. Now, presuming you're ready, open the damned trunk," Waldbaer growled into his coffee cup.

The policeman gulped and saluted and climbed into the Mercedes and seconds later the trunk rose slowly open to the autumn air. Waldbaer moved closer and placed himself squarely beside it. A tire was visible as was a small red fire extinguisher. Next to the cylindered extinguisher was a long and bulky swath of burlap, the shape tied tightly with two thick strings.

"Well, what do we have here?" Waldbaer grumbled.

Waldbaer dug in the pocket of his loden coat for a small, red Swiss army knife, flicking open a miniature blade. Severing the strings, he took hold of the coarse burlap and separated the folds gently. The long broadsword with its embossed pommel and grip, and long blade caught his attention first, and then his eyes took in the gently curved, gold-lined armored vest by its side, reflecting the diffused evening light. The gold pommel of the sword glittered, as did the equally resplendent lion and bear menagerie, standing face to face on their haunches, separated only by a broad gold W at the center of the ceremonial armored vest.

Waldbaer stared at the pieces a moment and signaled to the impossibly young policeman with a motion of his chin. "Listen well, I don't enjoy repeating myself. Have the boys at the station send in two men in hazmat suits. Tell them to take this sword and vest to Dr. Mayerling at Munich police headquarters, and to do it immediately. Take a police cruiser to Munich and don't spare the lights and siren. I'll call ahead and have Mayerling test that stuff for the presence or absence of plague."

The policeman blanched. "Plague? The plague is really contagious, I heard about it on a news show on television. It scared the hell out of me. People who get the disease are dropping like flies, and it doesn't seem like the hospitals are able to do anything for them. In fact, I wonder if we should even be close to those objects without more protection. Don't you think that we should have some specialists deal with the situation, Kommissar?"

Waldbaer stared at the policeman and let the familiar pull of irritation take hold of his features. "You know, you could be right. After all, why take a chance? Get the sergeant to order a medical test for you. The owner of the car certainly had the plague, and come to think of it, the infection caused him to blow his brains out.

I'm certain that it's fine that you sat exactly where he had been sitting, but still, you never know..."

The policeman's face lost all color. Waldbaer was happily satisfied. He clapped the policeman's shoulder.

"Look, you'll be all right. If Hofgartner had been alive and coughed on you, or spit on you, that might be another matter, but we have only a corpse. Just go and see a doctor as a precaution; you'll feel better for having done it. That is, after you get the artifacts to Dr. Mayerling. *Alles klar?*"

The policeman nodded, wide eyed, and wordlessly moved away. Waldbaer walked off to the edge of the parking lot where the marsh grass rose to five feet and more. He stood alone, put the coffee to his lips, and wondered long and silently about the type of man that would unleash pestilence indiscriminately, unaware and unconcerned about whom the victims might be. Hofgartner was the perpetrator of the grave robbery, true, but he was also the victim of the plague. Hirter had been correct after all, Hofgartner was not the key figure involved in unleashing the plague.

The pseudonym mentioned by Hirter came quickly to mind. Christian Slatner. The name that Waldbaer had dismissed. "Yes," Waldbaer muttered to himself, arriving suddenly at an answer.

GAMSDORF POLICE STATION

"Gentlemen, it's like this. We're up against a man who is as embittered as he is lethal, and, I admit, I initially failed to see it." Waldbaer leaned backwards, bracing himself on his solid, scarred desk and looked at his two-person audience. They sat on an Ikea couch, Braun in his police uniform slouched against the office wall, and Dr. Mayerling straight and attentive, hands clasped in front of him.

"We have a name, though it is admittedly of limited utility. Christian Slatner. It is an alias, and we know that, but it's all we have at the moment. What do we know about the man who uses the name Slatner? Nothing, nothing at all, or nearly nothing. But we can speculate about him, based upon what Slatner has done. In my view, this says legions about Slatner."

Mayerling and Braun watched him, neither one saying a word.

Waldbaer crossed his thick arms on his chest. "To begin with, Slatner, or whatever his true name is, has an advanced education in medical science, or in laboratory research. He may have had— and I admit to stretching here—contact with a Russian scientist who was formerly employed in his country's biological weaponization programs in the final years of the Soviet Union. At any rate, Slatner became interested, I would say obsessed, in infectious diseases. Somehow, he focused on the plague, probably because it was such an appalling human catastrophe centuries ago and because it still exists today."

Not expecting a response, Waldbaer continued after a short pause. "I am informed that the disease Slatner has worked with has its origins in Africa, on the island of Madagascar, to be precise. He took the samples from his medical research, and, using a self-made laboratory in a former slaughterhouse in Florida, he biologically reengineered the plague. It must have cost quite a bit of money, so we can assume Slatner had access to generous funds. He was in Florida for six months, and I gather that is how long it took him to do the engineering to his satisfaction. Then, he took the reengineered plague with him on a flight back to—presumably—Germany."

Waldbaer looked to see if his diminutive audience was following him. They were. "So, Slatner is here, probably hiding somewhere in Bavaria, because all of the victims of plague have contracted the disease in this region. But precisely what type of person is he?"

Waldbaer again paused for a response, got none, and continued. "He has an enormous ego. He is probably a solipsist—a person for whom all other people are regarded as inferior and unworthy. In his day-to-day dealings, Slatner is, in my estimation, a good conversationalist and can be amusing in a cynical kind of way. For all of that, he is deadly dangerous. He is determined to kill hundreds, maybe thousands of people without a whim. It is, in the end, all the same to him. And that, gentlemen, is what keeps me up at night. I do not know at this stage who Slatner really is, or where he is."

Mayerling stared into space, his thick glasses on and his face severe. "So, we don't have his real name yet. But we simply have to identify him if we're to make progress, any progress at all, period. Aside from that brutal fact, Kommissar, you describe a person who exhibits the usual criminal pathologies; the domination of ego, the rampant self-absorption, and concern only about himself; these are all symptoms of a disordered personality."

Braun nodded and turned to the doctor beside him, giving him a nudge. "You mean this guy's crazy, right?"

Mayerling shrugged and smiled. "Yes, he's crazy, to use a common term. He's clearly crazy as a loon. Kommissar, tell me, do you have any information on how old this Slatner is?"

Waldbaer fished a piece of crumpled paper from his pocket. "That's a good question, Dr. Mayerling. I have a copy of the contract for the slaughterhouse that Slatner rented. Slatner gave his age as thirty-two. Even though alias documents are fake, they can only slide the truth so far. I think we can safely say that Slatner is between thirty and thirty-five years of age. As for finding out Slatner's real name, that presents a different problem. I'm going to try to break the alias, and that is, I'm ashamed to say, all that I can really do at this stage, unless divine intervention comes to the rescue."

Mayerling nodded his assent. "Well, at least you know what you're looking for; the suspect is smart and enormously conceited. He only cares about himself. I would imagine that he is the product of a good education. He has access to significant amounts of money. He sneers at mankind, and is willing to kill indiscriminately. Those characteristics, at least, give you a good start."

Waldbaer laughed. "A good start, you say? Well, don't forget,

Dr. Mayerling, it is the finish that I am interested in. And there is one more conclusion that I have reached. You mentioned it earlier. This fellow that we know as Slatner is quite mad. There is no telling what he is going to do."

MUNICH, THE ENGLISH GARDEN

He was smiling as he walked through the English Garden in Munich at dusk, one hand grasping the shoulder strap of his olive backpack. He had seen the gathering of men underneath the bridge weeks before, and he hoped that it was their permanent hangout. There were five or six men, all of them indigents. "Homeless people, the poor indigent dears," he said to himself in English, and his sneer broadened into a smile. They were far too stupid to afford or keep a home. The collection of men were chronic alcoholics. They all looked the same: greasy hair and matted beards, fetid, shabby clothes that they slept in, and an appalling human stench.

He saw the bridge ahead of him, illuminated by the glow of a streetlamp through the branches of the trees. Shadows moved like specters against the concrete of the bridge abutments, and a raucous report of drunken laughter spilled through the air. Good, he thought, let's hope that there are lots of them.

As he approached he observed a tall, gaunt, white-haired man clutching a dirt-ensconced bottle and garbed in a stained raincoat and what appeared to be a woman's ochre shawl. The man was standing in front of six other men, huddled, sitting and laughing, and he gestured wildly and barked out a string of words, impossible to hear from a distance. The man took a long swig from the bottle and staggered again. The crowd that he was observing fell silent as they detected someone approach, and one man with shoulder-length matted hair pointed suspiciously at the backpacked intruder.

Go easy now; don't spook them. The man with the backpack

moved slowly toward the crackling fire and the collection of sullen, apprehensive faces.

What a gaggle of freaks, he said to himself, smiling at
the same time to convey that he meant no harm. He eased
the backpack off his shoulders. "Hello," he said, "Well, it certainly is cold tonight, and I suppose it will be getting colder.
At least you've got a good fire going." The figures remained
silent and suspicious, not reacting. Suddenly nervous, he decided to move quickly. "Look, I'm from the Caritas charity
center here in Munich and I've got some clothing items that
we want to distribute to those likely to need it." The men
continued to stare at him, but the individual holding the
backpack detected curiosity taking hold in their eyes. Like
dumb fish to bait.

Without a word, he unzipped the heavy olive backpack and
slipped a leather-gloved hand inside. He pulled out a lined, waist-
length jacket and tossed it to the swaying man with the bottle.
Taken by surprise, the man grabbed it, issued a grunt, and inspected the garment closely.

"That's a good jacket against this cold," the leather-gloved
man said. He grabbed another piece of clothing in his hand, a
thick woolen scarf, and gave it to a yellow-eyed man with gaping
holes in his mouth where teeth should have been. Seeing this, the
other indigents issued a guttural murmur and clawed the air, beg-
ging for a piece of clothing. He obliged, pulling gloves, a sweater,
and another jacket from his sack. "Don't thank me, thank Caritas.
They want you boys to be warm this winter," he lied with a grin,
repeating the name of the European charity to cover his seeming
altruism.

The pool of unwashed homeless and tubercular shapes became more frenzied, grabbing for the proffered garments. The
man who had distributed the coverings almost laughed out loud.
This grouping of the homeless and sick reminded him of something he had seen on a fishing boat off the Madagascar coast. Like
sharks to chum, he said to himself. Well, their carcasses will be

chum soon enough. The fleas hidden in the garb would do their lethal, ugly work over the next few days.

With the crowd of indigents now bickering loudly with each other and crudely pulling on the items of proffered clothing, the smiling man waved once, swung the backpack over his shoulder, snickered to himself, and walked into the night.

CHAPTER TWENTY-TWO

DORFRAM

Waldbaer sat with both hands placed on the solid oak table in front of him and a steaming porcelain cup of coffee, largely ignored, rested there as well. Wilhelma Beck, head waitress of the Adlerstube, sat, hands folded, across from him. Her hands, Waldbaer noted, were short-nailed and scrubbed.

It was fresh-faced Wilhelma Beck who did the talking. "So, Kommissar, do you have Andreas Pichler's killer yet? I don't mind telling you that the whole village is talking about it. At least, the residents who come into the Adlerstube are talking about it. And, whether it's fair or not, there's a lot of suspicion pointed at Count von Winterloch, mainly because people don't much like him. I know that talk is cheap, but that's what they're saying."

Waldbaer felt tired at this early hour of the morning and edged the cup of coffee closer and took a prolonged sip. "Gossip is as cheap as it is common, Frau Beck. I myself ignore gossip unless it is linked to fact. Facts interest me very much, as I'm sure they do you." He cast a weary smile across the table. The waitress smiled back and looked at the tabletop, a trace of blush coming to her cheeks. "Yes, Kommissar, people gossip out of boredom, that's certainly something I've learned over the years."

Waldbaer nodded, glad to get the preliminaries settled. He had come to converse with Wilhelma Beck about one question only. "Frau Beck, do you recollect if there were ever people at the Adlerstube who came from the castle? You've just said that the villagers drop in every now and then. What about the residents of the castle, do they ever come here for a beer or for a quiet dinner?" He picked up the cup of coffee again to give her a moment to respond.

The waitress flashed a smile and regarded Waldbaer. "The answer to that question is easy, Kommissar. Yes, we had people from Castle Winterloch as guests, at least occasionally. Frau Mayerhof was here a number of times, I recall, she had dinner with friends. I don't know when the last time was, maybe three months ago."

Waldbaer recalled that he had spoken to Frau Mayerhof as well, a correct, gray-haired cleaning woman at the castle. "And how do you know that the people she was with were her friends?"

Wilhelma smiled coyly, but in a manner that Waldbaer found endearing. "Kommissar, I am not gossiping at all, I am recounting a fact. I know the other women. Frau Mayerhof knows them as well, they all attend church together in the village and sing in the choir. I've seen them there. If you were to ask me what they were talking about during their dinner here, I would have to disappoint you. I really don't recall, although it seemed entirely social."

Waldbaer appreciated the admission of truth. "Thank you, Frau Beck. Tell me, aside from the Mayerhof woman, did you ever see anyone else from the castle here?"

Wilhelma's nod was vigorous. "Yes. I served Count von Winterloch at least twice here. He probably didn't think that anyone would know who he was, but he is well known to those who live in the area."

"Are you certain that the person you served was Count von Winterloch and not someone else?" Wilhelma had Waldbaer's attention now.

"Oh, yes, I'm quite certain. He's a tall man with thick white hair and a sort of ruddy face, and he wears traditional garb. He's also in very good shape for a man of his age; he doesn't have an inch of fat on him. He looks like a runner or a bicycle rider. He's not overweight like most people of his generation and he still has an excellent posture."

Waldbaer registered the inadvertent slight, but resolved not to take it personally. "Frau Beck, do you recall when the count was here?"

She nodded assent. "Yes. The first time was about four months ago, the last time I saw him in here was a bit over a month ago, I would think."

Waldbaer produced a ballpoint pen and a thin pad of paper from his jacket pocket. He scrawled a word or two on it before continuing.

"On the occasions when the count was here, did von Winterloch dine alone?"

"Well, when the count was here, he dined on both occasions with the same individual, I'm sure of that. I remember, because of the age difference between the two. The count, I imagine, is somewhat over seventy. He was dining with a young man who I'd say was about thirty or thirty-five at the oldest. He struck me as an earnest, good-looking young man. They were at that table over there." She pointed to a small wooden table placed against the opposite wall across from them which was unoccupied.

Waldbaer drew closer to the woman and directed his question in a low monotone. "Do you happen to know who this other person was?"

Wilhelma Beck bit her lip for a moment and swept a strand of blond hair from her forehead. "No, I'd never seen the young man before, and I've not seen him since. I've only set eyes on him when he was with the count. I don't think that he is from around here."

Waldbaer felt his heart sinking but allowed no trace of this to affect his features. "Think back, and take your time. Did the count, over dinner, ever call him by name?"

The waitress bit her lip with very white teeth and closed her eyes. Seconds later she opened them, as if in surprise. "Yes, I did hear a name. I didn't recall it until you asked. The count was talking to him as I delivered the dinner or a round of beer or something. He called him Tobias. And he used the 'du' form of address, so they must have known each other pretty well."

Waldbaer wetted his thumb and began flipping through the sheets on his pad of paper. "Tobias," he muttered. After a moment he stopped, and a smile flickered across the crevices of his face. "Yes, indeed. Tobias. That would be Tobias Steiner, I'd wager."

Wilhelma shrugged and offered an uncertain look. "I don't know, Kommissar. I don't recall the count using a last name."

Waldbaer rubbed his hands together. "Trust me, Frau Beck. The person dining with the count was Tobias Steiner."

MUNICH, THE ENGLISH GARDEN

The rat flea had no consciousness as to why it jumped from its temporary home in the fabric of the woolen scarf, but instinct instructed it to do so. Flexing its coxa and the three other parts of its tiny legs, the flea leapt two feet from its place on the neck, landing on a stray hair on the emaciated abdomen of its host. Moving its six legs in coordinated fashion, the rat flea wandered around the skin of the abdomen until it sensed that it was above a vein. The insect's head burrowed down until the mouth made direct contact with the human body, and it opened its maw and bit down.

The rat flea regurgitated saliva and bubonic plague just as it began to suck blood from its victim. The flea did not know that it was a vector of the plague, it did not know anything at all except that it had found blood, its necessary source of food. The flea's bloated body was eventually sated, and, finding a point of egress through the only partially buttoned shirt, it leaped again into the night, where it would slowly die from the cold.

Gunter Manstein took a long swig of schnapps and scratched absently at his abdomen. He adjusted the scarf more tightly about his neck and exhaled a breath in contentment. For Manstein, standing underneath the arch in the stone bridge in the English Garden, the evening was appreciably benign.

He raised the bottle again to his lips and let the schnapps trickle into his mouth, warming his entire body. Manstein looked around at the trees illuminated by a solitary streetlamp, and did not mind that he had no home, no apartment, and no address. He had no responsibilities either. Life and indecision and alcohol had left him content with that fate. Behind him, there was the cackle of gritty laughter from four or five mouths and the sound of breaking glass from a hurled beer bottle.

"Hey, Gunter, you crumb, why the hell don't you bring that bottle over here? Give me a slug and I promise I'll be your friend forever." More laughter erupted and cascaded across the cold surface of the arch, lit by a small fire of burning branches. Gunter Manstein nodded and shuffled toward the group of kneeling men huddled in their greatcoats. He scratched again at an annoying trace of discomfort on his abdomen.

Unknown to Manstein, other men in the desultory group were scratching too.

SCHLOSS WINTERLOCH

The sun was rapidly descending, as if forced to retreat by the resolute and implacable fabric of darkness which turned the broad lawn in front of the castle into a no man's land of morose gray. The chill air was making its presence felt as well, and Waldbaer buttoned up his loden jacket in a vain effort to stop its intrusion. Frau Mayerhof, protected by a full-length woolen coat, looked pensive and uncomfortable as she walked with the detective toward her two-door Opel sedan.

"It is like I have said, Kommissar, Tobias Steiner is apparently a friend of the count, and I have seen him, over the years, a number of times. I expect that the count could satisfy your curiosity better than I."

Waldbaer reminded himself that he was dealing with a lifelong employee of Count von Winterloch, and a woman of a certain age. She would try, as firmly as she could, not to meddle in what she believed to be the private life of von Winterloch. The count was a paragon of authority, and his individual virtue was best left alone by someone who relied on the coin of the Winterloch family to support her simple lifestyle. Waldbaer chose his words carefully.

"Yes, Frau Mayerhof, you are certainly correct in suggesting that the count is the person to whom I should speak. And I will be speaking to him shortly. But in a police investigation, we sometimes find that the words of a trusted employee or close acquaintance can be very helpful."

Waldbaer decided to coat his narrative with a little flattery. "You were, if I may say so, extraordinarily incisive during your first interview. The investigation would not have gotten to its present phase without your help. I am asking, Frau Mayerhof, for your help once again. No word of what you say will get back to the count, I assure you. I do hope I have made myself sufficiently clear. Frau Mayerhof, how long have you known about Tobias Steiner?"

The woman did not seem content but did seem to want to act responsibly. He waited.

"Tobias Steiner," the housekeeper measured her words, "has been an acquaintance of the count for, I would say, at least ten years. I do not recall ever seeing him before that."

"I see. Was he a friend of the family?"

Frau Mayerhof seemed even more uncomfortable and sank a degree into her winter coat like a turtle retreating into its shell. "No, I don't think you could say that. Tobias Steiner is an acquaintance of the count. There is no link, as far as I know, between the Steiner family and the von Winterlochs, if that is what you mean, Kommissar. Only the young man has been invited to visit the castle, his relatives never."

Waldbaer could not erase the distinctive feeling that Frau Mayerhof was holding back and was only providing the information reluctantly. He decided to take a different approach.

"Am I correct in assuming that the count has never married?"

The question seemed to take the woman off guard and Waldbaer noticed that she clenched her hands into fists, but she composed herself in a moment.

"The count never married," Frau Mayerhof said, her voice a subdued whisper. Waldbaer waited, saying nothing and biding his time. "He has had woman friends, of course, certainly when he was younger," Mayerhof added, her voice reluctant, "but he has never decided to marry. When he was a younger man— and please do not repeat this to the count or to anyone—it is rumored that he had a series of, well, girlfriends or lovers. The count is a lifelong bachelor. That is all that I know and all that I want to know. How we choose to live our lives is surely a private matter."

Waldbaer shrugged and distantly felt the cool trace of evening holding him in its uncomfortable embrace once again. "Yes, indeed, Frau Mayerhof, how we choose to live our lives is entirely a private matter. I can respect that. That the count never married is not my concern. But tell me, when he dies, will no one inherit the castle?"

Frau Mayerhof folded her hands in front of her. "I'm sure you'll understand, Kommissar, that I do not bother myself with matters of inheritance. But Count von Winterloch is the very last of the ancient von Winterloch line, we are told. Again, you would have to ask that question of him."

Their slow march to the Opel had concluded next to the door of the car. Waldbaer looked at the cleaning woman in the fading light. "Here is one question just for you, Frau Mayerhof. The count and Tobias Steiner were seen dining together a couple of times at the Adlerhof. Do you happen to know what they talked about or what they have in common?"

Frau Mayerhof drew her car key out of the pocket of her winter coat. "What they talked about? Oh my goodness, Kommissar, I wouldn't have the foggiest idea, no indeed. And what do they have in common?"

Waldbaer stared at her face, trying to discern any emotion that the rapid diminution of light might try to hide.

"Kommissar, the count has, it would seem to me, very little in common with Tobias Steiner, really. After all, the count is in his seventies. The young man, I would think, is in his thirties. They are both tall and thin and bright, I suppose, though, that doesn't mean anything."

Waldbaer tried to discern her meaning. "Tell me, Frau Mayerhof, I've never seen this Tobias Steiner. Could you tell me what he looks like?"

Darkness now covered the cleaning woman's features like a mask. "Tobias Steiner looks rather handsome, I would have to say. He has thick blond hair which he generally wears a bit long. And he has a bit of a red face, and sunburns rather badly in the summer."

Waldbaer stood in the darkness. He followed his first question with another. "It almost sounds as if you are describing the count as a young man. Tall, blond perhaps, and red-faced."

Frau Mayerhof inserted her key in the door of her car and opened it with a resounding click. Waldbaer could no longer make out her face as evening took hold of the terrain, but her stout form turned toward him. "Well, Kommissar, that is not a comparison that I intended. But now that you mention it, I suppose you could say that the count and the young man do bear a resemblance to one another. Like father and son, you might say, like father and son, yes? And with that said, Kommissar, I wish you a very pleasant evening." Her shape was enveloped by the car, the headlights flickered on and the engine purred as if the automobile were a gigantic feline. Slowly at first, and then unleashing more speed, the Opel left the parking apron and disappeared from view.

Waldbaer smiled wickedly and without humor. "Well, well, what do you know? Like father and son," he mumbled. He would call Hirter in Washington and relay the news. But first there was the little matter of the count to deal with, and he would handle that on his own.

* * *

Waldbaer sat at a small, ornately carved mahogany table, the four legs of which displayed taloned feet of silver. He shook his head, disapproving the pretense of it, and of the vanity of the nameless von Winterloch who had commissioned it over a hundred years ago. The light was dim and the air was cold in the Hall of Banners, where he had been placed to await the arrival of Rheinhold von Winterloch.

Count von Winterloch made his presence known through his footfall, which echoed through the hall as the owner of the castle made his way along the long corridor and then down the balustrade of the ceremonial staircase, done in stucco marble.

"To what do I owe the distinguished pleasure of your company at this unusual hour," growled the count, the familiar frown of displeasure the defining hallmark of his features.

Waldbaer was in no mood for verbal repartee and frowned as well. "Please have a seat," Waldbaer said with a wave of his hand. "I have a few questions that need to be answered."

Von Winterloch sighed as he fell into a chair, the legs scraping on the tiled stone floor. "Some questions, you say? But of course. Pray, what else could it possibly be? Perhaps, Kommissar, we can ask our questions quickly as it is evening, a little after normal business hours, although you may not have noticed. Perhaps some of your questions can wait until another day."

Waldbaer placed his hands underneath his chin and gave a casual nod of disapproval. "No, this is important and it can't wait. I suspect that you'll be able to answer them now. But don't worry, I will be as brief as possible."

The count grumped sullenly and crossed his legs.

Waldbaer continued, "You have been seen here and there with a younger gentleman named Tobias Steiner."

Winterloch smirked. "Yes. I told you before that Steiner is an acquaintance of mine. On occasion, we get together socially and share some time. What of it?"

"Wouldn't you say that calling Steiner an acquaintance is a mistruth; much more, a lie? Would you like to reformulate what Tobias Steiner is to you?"

Von Winterloch paled. He said nothing, his eyes fixed on Waldbaer's. The detective remained silent, quietly returning the count's stare.

Finally, von Winterloch, still pallid, mumbled a reply, his eyes studying the tabletop. "You are right, I suppose, Kommissar. I mischaracterized Steiner. He is a friend, and a relatively good friend at that. I misspoke."

"No, you're wrong again," Waldbaer said through an even smile. "Steiner is not just a friend, Count. Think of it this way. You and the body that we saw in the crypt, Count Heinrich von Winterloch, are tied together by blood. The same blood that ties you to Tobias Steiner, no? Blood and DNA."

Von Winterloch did not move an inch in his chair, but Waldbaer noted the panic in his eyes. "It is irrelevant, Kommissar. It is of no concern to me and it should be of absolutely no concern to you."

"It is hardly irrelevant, Count," Waldbaer said. "And it is of concern to you. Stop trying to protect a secret that has been discovered. Tobias Steiner is your son. That is a fact. A simple DNA test will prove that, and I can order that you take one, if need be. Steiner is, I imagine, the last name of the boy's mother, living or dead. Do you want to fill me in on the details, or will I have to uncover them on my own?"

The count put both hands over his eyes and then raised them to his mane of white hair. His voice was subdued, almost a whisper. His eyes searched the wall opposite him and did not meet Waldbaer's. "All right, you win. Here is the truth, God knows. Tobias Steiner is my son. His mother was a woman named Gertraud Steiner. I met her when I was forty, and she was thirty, and it was quite a different world then. We had a rather tempestuous love affair. For me it was purely physical, there was nothing more to it. When Gertraud announced one day that she was pregnant, I was, to be quite frank, not at all happy. I gave her a substantial amount of money to have an abortion and then I broke off the affair for good. But Gertraud deceived me; she never had the abortion. Gertraud lied to me. She went ahead and had the baby and pocketed the money I had given her. I did not know any of this at the time, I swear, and went on living my life as before. Sadly, Gertraud died of cancer ten years ago, in Berlin."

Go slowly, Waldbaer cautioned himself. "And when and how did you find out that Gertraud had a son?"

Winterloch sighed, rubbing his temples with both hands. "Ten years ago, a young Tobias Steiner knocked on the front door of the castle. He was a presentable young man. He announced who he was, and said that Gertraud, sick with cancer, had confessed to him that I was his father. I was stunned, of course. But Tobias was, if nothing else, insistent. And he was clearly bright, he had already been awarded a PhD. He said that he wanted me to legally accept him as my son, as an heir and as a von Winterloch, but this I declined."

"Why not accept him legally, if that's what he wanted? After all, he was your son," Waldbaer asked.

Von Winterloch's eyes grew distant. "Because it was difficult and because of who his mother was. Gertraud was, not to speak ill of the dead, a fairly wild girl, a party girl and a consort of all sorts of men. She drank heavily when I knew her and used liberal amounts of LSD and God knows what other drugs. If Gertraud was no stranger to virtue, virtue was perhaps a stranger to her. And, frankly, I was too old to accept a change of lifestyle. I was set in my ways and not about to change. Tobias, to his credit, accepted my situation. I would not acknowledge him formally or publicly as my son, but I would quietly support him financially. In fact, I promised to bankroll Tobias and his future studies and research. I promised to open doors for him, and I did, silently and behind the scenes."

"Open doors? Such as?"

Winterloch shrugged. "Tobias wanted to get a position in Madagascar to do research, and it was very competitive, there were several candidates. I was able to arrange that the position went to Tobias, through some influential friends I maintain in the Foreign Ministry. As far as Tobias' expenses for his research in Madagascar, I paid for them. But one thing you should know, Kommissar, is that most of the things Tobias wanted, he took care of on his own. I simply provided some assistance now and then when it was required."

Waldbaer collected his thoughts for a moment and splayed his hands on the polished tabletop. "What exactly is Tobias Steiner's profession? And what did he do in Madagascar?"

Von Winterloch's smile was weary. "Tobias is a professional microbiologist, one of the best in Europe. His true passion is research, and he has spent years laboring in laboratories like the Robert Koch Institute and the Chronic Disease Foundation, not to mention the Max Planck Laboratory in Berlin. Tobias has authored innumerable articles in journals; you can see these for yourself online. As for Madagascar, that was practical work in the field with communicable diseases. As I've said, Tobias is utterly focused and absolutely dedicated to his profession."

Waldbaer felt the chill of the hall and rubbed his hands together, wondering if he would develop arthritis. "So it would seem. Did you know, Count, that Tobias Steiner was working with the plague during his time in Madagascar?"

Winterloch blanched and leaned over the table, which reflected his image eerily in the heavy polish of the veneer. "No, I didn't know that, but I didn't ask. Does this have something to do with the plague from the crypt of Heinrich? And are you suggesting that Tobias has something to do with what the media is calling a public health warning?"

Waldbaer looked wearily at the count. "Let me rely on the facts. Tobias Steiner went to Madagascar for the express purpose of conducting research on the plague. The plague is very much alive there, and kills people every year. He most probably took illicit samples of the disease carried by the fleas back to Germany with him. I believe that he intended to keep working on the plague contagion secretly. It would appear that he choose the United States as a venue because it is big, has lots of medical devices, and is relatively anonymous. When he had successfully mutated Y. pestis in a laboratory there, he placed a host of fleas carrying it in the crypt. Do you happen to know anything at all about that?"

Winterloch's face flushed and he struggled to avert his eyes from Waldbaer's stern gaze. "Well, yes. The last time I saw Tobias I mentioned that I was worried about grave robbers, about someone breaking into the crypt. I told him that I had noticed headlights in the evening, and saw tire markings in the earth, not too far from here. I had the feeling that someone was watching me, or at least observing the castle. I told Tobias that there had been a feature on me and the castle in the *Münchner Merker* newspaper. It was Tobias who raised the crypt as the likely goal of someone committed to robbery. He said that I shouldn't worry as he was perfectly able to take care of it."

"Please do not take me for a fool, Count," Waldbaer said. "You can't expect me to believe that Tobias Steiner didn't say what he was intending to do. Did you show him the crypt?"

"Of course I showed him the crypt. He said he'd researched communicable diseases and could guarantee that any robber who invaded the crypt would soon be very ill indeed; deathly ill, in fact. Tobias said the thieves would have to check into a hospital and would be arrested by the police. As for the crypt, I took him to see it.

We entered through the chapel, where Heinrich's burial tablet is maintained in the stone floor. After we descended down the ladder, he asked for my assistance in moving the lid of the sarcophagus, and we did it together. Tobias did all of the work. He managed to place some material, I suppose it could have been the plague, into the stone coffin on his own. He said it would do the trick. We didn't have to punch through the wall surrounding the sarcophagus, of course, just took the ladder back up, the way we came. It all seemed so simple."

"By that stage, it probably was simple, compared to biologically reengineering the plague. Re-engineering the plague from samples taken in Madagascar must have been extremely difficult and exacting work, even for someone with as much knowledge and talent as Steiner had. Tell me, did Steiner ever mention a Russian doctor or professor, a former expert in biological warfare?"

Winterloch shook his head. "I don't recall Tobias ever mentioning a Russian. I don't know anything about that."

Waldbaer waved the matter aside. "It's not important, Steiner is important. Tell me, Count, what is Steiner like as a person? Describe him to me."

"Since the day I meet him, Tobias has hated small talk, it bores him enormously. He gets that from me, I suppose. Tobias is a serious man with serious pursuits and doesn't have much time for idle, stupid humor. He was always very fixed on his studies and later with his work." Winterloch paused and rubbed his head along the hairline. "I suppose that most people would consider Tobias a loner. I do not know if he even has friends. But I will tell you honestly, Kommissar, I can't see Tobias endangering innocent people, not for an instant. That he would defend himself and the von Winterloch estate against crass grave robbers, yes, but putting some bug in a crypt to get a thief is much like putting a watchdog in the living room."

Waldbaer spoke in a low tone. "Not bugs. They are fleas, rat fleas. They are the vector of the plague. And they're hardly the same as a watchdog. A watchdog bites, and sometimes bites a particular person ferociously. But the fleas with a mutation of the plague infect whoever they bite with a highly infectious disease. The disease the fleas spread is lethal. And the grave robbers were just the beginning. Innocent people have died from this plague, and I fear that we haven't seen the end of it. The evidence points to Tobias Steiner as at the heart of this crime, which is very rapidly becoming mass murder. Which brings me to a key question. Where is Steiner now?"

"I don't have a clue where Tobias is, or where he could be. He usually contacts me, he prefers it that way, and I don't interfere. But I do know that he keeps an apartment up in Garmisch, on the Maximilianstrasse."

"We will most assuredly visit it. Count, you are aware that I have sufficient grounds to arrest you, do you not? Those grounds would be concealing information on Tobias Steiner and conspiracy to deceive law enforcement. That would be more than enough to place you behind bars for the time being."

Winterloch glowered, crossing his arms protectively across his chest.

"At the moment, however," Waldbaer continued, "I will permit you to stay here at Schloss Winterloch. Here are the rules: you will go nowhere, absolutely nowhere, without first informing me. You will notify me immediately in the event that you are contacted by your son Tobias Steiner. Consider it house arrest if you'd like, that's up to you. You sought to protect your son from the police, and I suppose I've taken that into consideration. But I warn you, Count, do not test me further. And if any relevant fact about Tobias Steiner occurs to you, don't hesitate to call me. That is what I expect, nothing less. *Ist alles klar?*"

Winterloch regarded the detective with unspoken dislike. "*Ja, Alles klar, Kommissar,*" he mumbled at last and pulled himself from the antique table. He dispensed a brief, sullen bow and marched out. As his figure disappeared up the staircase, Waldbaer observed that the count, although perfectly postured, seemed much older than before.

CHAPTER TWENTY-THREE

MUNICH

Karl Schmidt, graying, unkempt beard streaked slick with vomit, pus, and blood, inhaled a final gout of air and was dead, eyes open and visionless. The spasm which coursed through him wracked his body at four in the morning, leaving him in a pool of urine and decaying flesh underneath the bridge in the English Garden of Munich. A female jogger would find his white-eyed corpse at seven and, in a fit of hysteria, report her find to the police.

Gunter Manstein collapsed at the entrance to Beck's department store on Saint Mary's Plaza in the center of Munich, not far from the statue of the Mother of Christ. The Red Cross first-aid team which had arrived minutes later in an ambulance nearly gagged at the stench issuing from the unconscious man and immediately noticed a massive bubo on his neck and another on his left arm. Manstein's eyes were dilated and a trickle of yellow saliva and thin blood stained the woolen shawl around his neck. In the ambulance, Manstein's breathing became labored and then highly erratic, and a paramedic applied an oxygen mask which instantly became coated in scarlet. Manstein was dead on arrival at the Schwabing hospital, and the first-aid men wheeled his covered form into the autopsy room on a gurney.

Four other homeless men in Munich between the ages of forty and sixty-seven died of the plague over the next few days, their lifeless forms found variously in abandoned buildings, near containers filled with discarded wine bottles, and washed up and bloated on the banks of the Isar River which flowed, cold and deep, through the city.

GAMSDORF POLICE STATION

Franz Waldbaer wielded a Magic Marker and added the six names of the indigents to his growing list taped on a sheet of paper to his office wall. The Munich papers and the radio and television channels had chosen the news as their lead stories. More than one of the news stories had carried the Stockholm ECDC's official commentary that the plague was far more virulent than originally thought, and was in its present form pneumonic, able to be spread through the air on a cough.

Munich and much of Bavaria, Waldbaer was certain, had incipient signs of panic. Hundreds of people who were as healthy as on any day of their lives were crowding the hospital and clinics, demanding to know whether they were infected. The six deaths, Waldbaer knew, could soon become six hundred, or for that matter, six thousand. And then the real panic would begin. Schools and universities would be shut, people would refuse to go to work, and the economy would begin to collapse. Waldbaer exhaled a long and heavy sigh and longed for the relaxation of a cigarette, but thought the better of wasting time. He had an appointment in Munich.

MUNICH

"This is death from the plague, Kommissar. Not to be morbidly sensational, but this is what we see when the bodies are brought in here, and this is what we believe we will see as long as this outbreak continues." Dr. Mayerling stood in his medical smock with hands folded and clasped in front of him. White tiles covered the walls and floor of the autopsy room. On a stainless steel table before him lay the remains of Gunter Manstein, the rampant beard severely trimmed away to reveal the abused face of an alcoholic with a network of visible veins running through his cheeks and nose. But there was something more. A black splotch the size of a quarter, oozing a trail of pus, lacerated Manstein's features. The ebony scar was located between the dead man's lower lip and chin.

Waldbaer stood beside Mayerling and surveyed the damaged body with dispassion, noting the surgical Y cut that left its stitch marks on Schmidt's upper body and stomach. Schmidt's eyes and mouth had been closed by the medical staff at the Munich police central headquarters. Visible upon Schmidt's utterly white body were three massive bubbles of skin, one on the groin, one on the armpit of the left arm, and a final one which erupted from the corpse's chest and covered most of the neck. Waldbaer could see that the accretions on the skin seemed full to the breaking point with blood and fluids.

"This is not a pretty picture, Doctor." Waldbaer said. "What exactly killed him?"

Mayerling shrugged. "The plague killed him. To be more specific, a flea carrying the plague bit the victim on the abdomen and the bacteria coursed through the lymphatic system. This man suffered pain in its most extreme form. Plague frequently causes a seizure as it certainly did in this case. Death was caused by he-matemesis; ultimately, the victim drowns in his own blood. Now, if you will, notice the hands, Kommissar."

Waldbaer stared at the hands of the corpse, the fingers curled inward. The tips of the fingers up to the first knuckle were completely blackened, as if they had been burned. "What exactly is it?" the detective asked.

"It's called necrosis. There are traces of it below the nose, as you can see, and on the forearms as well. It is frequently found on plague victims who have not been given any treatment. I would guess that the victim contracted the disease about four or five days ago. His blood-alcohol ratio, incidentally, indicated that he was intoxicated at the time he collapsed, but he was intoxicated for months and maybe years before that. He must have been con-fused and didn't know what hit him. We've seen necrosis on the bodies that have been autopsied here, and the medical authorities have reported the same effect on the corpses that they examined in Augsburg and Traunstein."

"And they all have blackened hands like this?"

Mayerling nodded. "Yes. In fact, the blackened hands are one reason that the plague was called the Black Death centuries ago, when it ran rampant on the continent."

Waldbaer was silent for a moment. "And you say this was caused by something as inconsequential as a flea bite?"

"Again, yes. There are tiny bite marks on the legs of the body, we've established that. We also found dead fleas in the material of the overcoat, which seems to have been an infested garment. The fleas have been sent to a health facility in Berlin for further analysis. We have a source, a friend of Schmidt's, who is also a displaced alcoholic, who says that Manstein was given this coat as a gift by an individual working for Caritas."

"I strongly doubt it, but we'll check it out. Is there anything else I should know, Doctor?"

"Yes, I'm afraid there is," Mayerling said. "As you search for a suspect who reengineered this bacteria you might want to consider that we examined Gunter Manstein's organs. The plague had in its final stages spread to his lungs. This means that Manstein could have spread the disease by sneezing or even coughing on another person. Or, for that matter, by passing around the bottle of schnapps that we took out of his overcoat pocket."

Waldbaer stared at Dr. Mayerling without answering for an instant, his silence communicating resignation. "So it begins, Doctor. Pneumonic plague, you call it? It is what I feared back when all of this started. It was my nightmare. But I confess, I do not know how this plays out. How this all ends is a mystery to me."

GARMISCH-PARTENKIRCHEN

Waldbaer stood back at the top of the staircase on Maximilianstrasse and let the Garmisch professionals do their work. A member of the Special Action Command, the Spezialeinsatzkommando, readied the jet black battering ram of tubed steel clutched in his gloved hands. Five other policemen, all of them clad in the black uniforms and helmets of the elite team, had pistols aimed at the center of the door in front of them. Waldbaer, his hands gripping a pistol underneath his jacket, tried not to intrude.

"Go," one of the helmeted men shouted and the officer with the battering ram crashed his device against the wooden door. On the second strike the door came off its hinges and exploded inwards. The six men stormed inside, weapons first. Waldbaer followed seconds later.

The inside of the apartment was as he had expected. It was unoccupied and unadorned, and Waldbaer had a sense that it had been empty for a while. The windows were stained and in need of washing. The police team entered a living room absent any personal touch, went down a short corridor, and entered a kitchen. Other than an abandoned Braun coffee machine and a ceramic cup, it too was empty. One member of the team banged open the remaining doors, but this revealed only a pantry and a tidy bathroom.

Waldbaer shouldered his firearm and walked back to the living room and surveyed it more carefully. A leather couch and chair were grouped around a flat screen television with a polished glass-and-aluminum coffee table in the middle, its surface clean except for a film of dust. Centered on the coffee table, in addition to the television remote control, was a sealed manila folder with an inscription in gothic letters. Waldbaer stepped past the couch, getting close enough to read the print. The letters were neatly arranged and spelled out: *TO THE MAN IN CHARGE* and were devoid of any other notation. Waldbaer called to one of the policemen and asked for a pair of plastic gloves. Examining the envelope for concealed wires, trace of fluids, or any hint that it could be a letter bomb, Waldbaer carefully separated the flap and removed the sheets of paper inside.

Mumbling a curse as the words would not come into focus, he drew a pair of glasses from his jacket and perched the glasses on his nose. The words instantly became intelligible forms and Waldbaer fell into the supple leather of the couch intent on reading the letter, carefully handwritten in block letters. *TO THE MAN IN CHARGE*, it said.

WELL, IT WOULD SEEM THAT YOU HAVE FOUND ME OUT. AT LEAST, TO HAVE GOTTEN TO THIS APARTMENT IS AN ACHIEVEMENT OF SORTS. I SALUTE YOU, THOUGH I DO NOT KNOW YOUR NAME. CONGRATULATIONS. AS YOU ARE DOUBTLESS CONCERNED ABOUT MY MOVEMENTS, OR MORE PROPERLY, WHERE I MIGHT BE AT PRESENT, I SURMISE THAT YOU ARE A POLICE OFFICIAL. SADLY, OR NOT SO SADLY, I AM UNABLE TO GREET YOU IN PERSON. A STAY IN PRISON JUST NOW WOULD FAIL TO AMUSE ME, AS I HAVE SOME RATHER FASCINATING SCIENTIFIC WORK TO CARRY OUT. I PRESUME THAT YOU HAVE DEDUCED THAT I AM RESPONSIBLE FOR THE DEATHS OF WHOEVER IT WAS THAT BROKE INTO THE TOMB OF COUNT HEINRICH VON WINTERLOCH. I DO NOT DENY THAT I AM THE AUTHOR OF THAT DEED, FAR FROM IT. IN FACT, I REGARD IT AS EXQUISITE IRONY THAT THE HUMAN DETRITUS THAT WOULD ROB A GRAVE SHOULD THEMSELVES FALL VICTIM TO ITS LIVING OCCUPANTS. I FIND THE IRONY OF THEIR DEATHS TRULY EXQUISITE.

I AM SURE THAT BY NOW YOU OR YOUR MEDICAL BETTERS HAVE DISCOVERED THAT WHAT KILLED THE THIEVES WAS YERSINIA PESTIS. I TOOK THE LIBERTY, YOU SEE, OF DEPOSITING SOME LIVING SAMPLES OF IT IN THE ARMORED UNIFORM OF THE NOBLE AND LONG-DEAD COUNT.

Waldbaer put the sheets of paper aside for a moment. Something in the letter was wrong, or at least odd, but what that was he could not clearly see. He held the missive in both hands and read further.

AS YOU ARE AWARE BY NOW, THE GRAVE ROBBERS WERE ONLY THE FIRST, HIGHLY DESERVING VICTIMS OF THE PLAGUE. SINCE THEIR DEMISE, I HAVE INFECTED OTHER WORTHIES WITH THE PLAGUE. HOMELESS PEOPLE, BELOVED BY THE MEDIA, HAVE BECOME A SPECIAL FOCUS OF MY EFFORTS. THESE PEOPLE OFFEND ME DEARLY. WHY SHOULD I NOT SPEAK THE TRUTH? THESE HALF-WITS ARE LIFE'S LOSERS; ALCOHOLICS, DRUG ADDICTS, AND THE GENETICALLY WEAK MINDED. HUMAN GARBAGE LIKE THE HOMELESS CANNOT BE EXPECTED TO ORGANIZE THEIR PERSONAL LIVES AND FINANCES ANY MORE THAN THEY CAN BE EXPECTED TO ORGANIZE THEIR CORRODED TEETH OR THEIR PERSONAL HYGIENE. I HAVE DETERMINED TO TREAT THEM SEVERELY FOR THEIR OAFISH STUPIDITY. IT IS MY UNSHAKABLE JUDGMENT THAT THE WORLD WILL BE BETTER OFF WITHOUT THEIR BRAIN-ADDLED PRESENCE.

I GROW WEARY OF WRITING AND, I MUST CONFESS, WEARY OF LIFE. WELL, MAN IN CHARGE, IT WILL NO DOUBT PROVE FRUSTRATING THAT YOU WILL BE UNABLE TO FIND ME, BUT THAT'S LIFE. AND WHO PLAYS THE ROLE OF AUGUSTIN, BELOVED AUGUSTIN IN THIS LITTLE AND PESTILENTIAL DRAMA? PERHAPS SOMEONE, PERHAPS ABSOLUTELY NO ONE. LET THE HIGH AND THE MIGHTY PERISH ALONG WITH THE TERMINAL MEDIOCRITIES AND THE IDIOTS. "OH AUGUSTIN, AUGUSTIN, YOUR GIRLFRIEND'S DEAD, EVERYONE'S DEAD." IF THERE IS A GOD, MAN IN CHARGE, IT MIGHT AS WELL BE ME. – STEINER.

The letter ended there. Waldbaer put it back atop the manila folder. He realized now what seemed out of place about the letter. It was the breathtakingly enormous ego of the author. The style of the letter revealed that the man who wrote it was quite mad, clinically insane beyond a shadow of a doubt.

Waldbaer glanced at the last paragraph of the missive again. The mention of Augustin was confusing and a bit bizarre. Augustin was, Waldbaer recalled, the protagonist in a children's tune from over a century ago, and he himself had learned to sing it as a child. He struggled a bit to remember the words, concealed for a moment in the mist of youthful memory. Then the lyrics came to him.

Oh, beloved Augustin,
Augustin, Augustin,
Oh, Beloved Augustin,
All are dead.
Money's gone, girlfriend's gone,
All is lost Augustin!
Oh, beloved Augustin,
All is lost!

Waldbaer stared at the letter. In legend, Augustin was a drunkard who survived the plague. Was the mention of Augustin simply the pointless raving of a madman? Troubled, he concluded that he did not know.

CHAPTER TWENTY-FOUR

Tobias Steiner stared in the bathroom mirror for a bundle of minutes, his hands resting on the stained porcelain sink. He was confronted by the face of a young man with full blond hair impeccably cut and combed into place. Two eyes, pale blue like an alpine lake in spring, regarded him through a pair of metal-framed glasses. The glasses were aviator style and gave him a bookish appearance. But the cleft chin was strong and square and a casual observer would have said that Steiner was handsome.

He stepped back a degree, regarded his toned body, and was satisfied. He was tanned and muscularly thin and wore a faded denim shirt over his jeans, cinched tight by a polished black leather Pierre Cardin belt. Satisfied with his inspection, conducted over several minutes every morning, he turned on his heels and confronted the day.

Steiner worried about keeping the fleas alive in the terrain trays. He walked over to the wooden dresser and regarded the clear plastic boxes placed on top of it. He carefully detached the air-holed lid from one and regarded the earth inside, shaking the container slightly. There was a trace of movement, exceedingly difficult to detect, of tiny black shapes traversing the brown soil. He was satisfied that his vectors were healthy at the moment, and that their larvae and pupae would continue to flourish, as they had to date. Steiner had carefully closed the windows of the apartment to preserve a modicum of humidity, which helped the fleas to thrive. He knew that many of them would find human hosts soon and infect them with Yersinia pestis.

Steiner moved to the small window of the room and took in the scene. The window, smudged with the accretions of dirt and time, looked out to the center of the city. The tall, solemn brick and onion-domed spires of the Munich cathedral dominated the urban scene. The cathedral was close, within walking distance, and so was Stiglmaierplatz, the underground U-Bahn stop that interested him. He decided that today was as good a time as any to make a test run. The feeling elevated him and gave him a fulfilling sense of purpose.

The cheap hotel with the imbecilic name of "Rhine"—the river did not even flow through Bavaria—gave him the necessary anonymity and he was able to use a second set of alias documentation that he had purchased in Florida to rent the diminutive suite. The slovenly staff regarded the customers with indifference, which well suited his needs. He glanced at the sky and saw its predominance of cobalt blue washed by the autumn sun. It was going to be a beautiful day.

GAMSDORF

Waldbaer had ordered a Franziskaner wheat beer from the waiter at the little bar down the street from the Gamsdorf police station. The bar was a small establishment which had, in the last few years, been a bakery, a Turkish fast-food restaurant, and a purveyor of chewing gum, cigarettes, and postcards. The owners of these businesses had come and gone, unable to make a profit because of the high rent. The current owner, a cheery and talkative Italian, had given the bar the name of Moby Dick, which made Waldbaer shudder. He detested maritime allusions. He doubted that the owner had ever read Melville's novel, even in the Italian translation. But the place belonged to the Italian, and he could name it whatever he liked. Perched at the bar waiting for his wheat beer, Waldbaer conceded that Moby Dick was no worse than myriad other names likely to appeal to the Latin heart: Roma, Firenze, Sicilia, Bella Italia, even Espresso, the list was surely endless.

Waldbaer's foaming, thin-walled glass of unfiltered Ayinger wheat beer arrived and was placed by the waiter atop a beer coaster at precisely the same time as the encrypted cell phone poured out a series of musical notes. Waldbaer frowned, took a quick sip of the tart beer first, savoring it through the foam, and then answered the phone.

"Good evening, Kommissar, Robert Hirter here, from Washington. Have I called you at a bad time?"

Waldbaer hunched his form over his glass of beer. "No, Hirter, there is no bad time for a man like me. Good to hear from you, and I hope that you have something for me. I could use some good news, something to cheer me up. And, by the way, we have six more dead from the plague in Munich, so I imagine the doctors at the ECDC in Stockholm and elsewhere are pretty damned scared, if they weren't already."

"The plague scares the hell out of me too, Kommissar, maybe even more than it does Dr. Nilsson. But that's not why I've called. I want to provide an update but with a little prelude. The Miami police department has covered a lot of ground looking into the Christian Slatner alias. That name was on two credit cards that he used extensively to purchase medical equipment, but that's secondary. He used one of the credit cards to pay for something else."

Waldbaer spoke into the phone with a sigh. "Hirter, don't tease me like an inveterate stripper. You doubtless received my message that the man we're after is named Tobias Steiner. I'm assembling additional information on him now. So, what did Steiner—or Slatner as he was known in the states—use his credit card for? You have my full attention."

There was a muffled laugh on the receiver. "Okay, get this. The police traced the credit card to a doctor's office in Coconut Grove. He paid for blood tests and a full physical examination with the credit card. To cut to the chase, Steiner—alias Slatner—

was told that he had pancreatic cancer. Severe. In addition to that, he was told by the medical specialists in Miami that the disease was far advanced because it had been undetected for some time."

"How far advanced?"

"For Steiner, pancreatic cancer is his death sentence; it's literally killing him. It's a terminal condition. The doctors say there is absolutely no chance of survival, none, period. What that means, Kommissar, is that we're chasing a dead man."

Waldbaer drew his hand into a tight fist across the bar. "No, it doesn't mean that at all, Hirter. What it means is that we're chasing a man who is soon going to be dead, and that's different. We can expect Steiner to behave like a wounded animal, like a bear that's taken a bullet but refuses to go down. If he knows he's dying, his enormous ego won't permit him to die quietly in a clinic or hospital. It will just convince him to complete his apocalyptic mission. I've seen a letter he wrote, Hirter. I suppose you could say that he wrote the letter to me, but that's another story. In my view, Tobias Steiner is very smart and—on the basis of the letter—he's also insane. Now I'm in need of some good news. Tell me, how long do you estimate that Steiner has to live?"

There was a pause on the line before Robert Hirter answered. "I asked that question of the doctors, and the best I could come up with from the medical experts is less than six months, maybe less than two or three. That's as good an estimate as the doctors can make. Remember, Steiner was already terminally ill when he was diagnosed, and from what I understand it's a rapidly progressing lethal disease. That's all the estimate that I have, I'm afraid."

"That's all right, Hirter. Thanks for the news update. I suppose it's good to know as much as we can about who we're chasing. I don't mind telling you that I've got a bad feeling about all this. I want to get inside Steiner's head, to figure out how he thinks, and I can't. Steiner is a cipher to me."

Hirter's voice sounded distant and was electronically warped by the encryption device. "Kommissar, if you want to get inside

Steiner's head, then maybe I can help. Let me see what I can do, and I'll get back with you as quickly as I can." And with that, Hirter signed off.

Waldbaer slipped the communication device back in his pocket and grasped his still cool glass of beer in both hands. The tune of "Augustin" played through his head repeatedly.

Augustin.

GAMSDORF POLICE STATION

The television news bulletins the next morning had all been grim. In Munich, a total of five people had died overnight, and an additional four had been admitted to hospitals. All had symptoms of the plague. Of the five dead, three had been indigents, but the other two had no relationship at all to the homeless; one was a successful banker and the other a third-year university student. As Waldbaer had anticipated, the disease was breaking out beyond the original target population.

Signs of growing panic were as infectious as the disease itself. The plague had become the lead news story throughout Germany in the papers, on websites, and on television. The Bundestag, or German parliament, had taken up the issue and the representatives of every political party were busily pointing fingers in a multitude of directions. Everything from global warming to federal budget reductions was to blame if you believed the politicians pontificating on the news shows. Waldbaer did not.

The detective had other items to occupy him. At the center of his desk was a file that the Gamsdorf police had assembled on Tobias Steiner from all available sources. Flipping it open, he extracted a single sheet of paper, put on his reading glasses, and read through the text. The police document presented a chronology of Steiner's studies since high school, or Gymnasium, in Berlin. It then listed Steiner's selection of courses at the Free University of Berlin; this Waldbaer found interesting. Steiner had been accepted as a federally subsidized student at the Institute for Biochemistry, which was not surprising given his excellent performance in high school. Waldbaer took a pencil and underlined the courses that Steiner had selected.

A course on communicable disease, taken in Steiner's freshman year, caught Waldbaer's attention. What appeared to be a similar offering, Avian Flu and Swine Flu and their Predecessors was taken by Steiner in his sophomore year. There was a general predominance of mandatory biochemistry studies: organic chemistry, experimental chemistry, advanced mathematics, and the like. Still, Waldbaer reflected, communicable diseases seemed to have fascinated the aspiring student. This fact became apparent during Steiner's doctoral work. The title of his doctoral thesis was revealing, The Plague as Communicable Disease, Contagion, and Contemporary Medicine.

Waldbaer found the name of Steiner's doctoral mentor interesting as well. The name was given as Dr. Aleksandr Akulov. Both the first and last names sounded distinctly Russian, Waldbaer thought. He would determine if that was in fact the case by making a phone call to the Berlin police.

Waldbaer put the paper aside and reached for another piece of paper, giving a summary of Steiner's travel conducted over the last several years. The trip to Madagascar stood out, partly subsidized by the German Ministry of Health. The reason for Steiner's six-month stay on the island was given as "research and experimentation into plague disease episodes and effective countermeasures." The subsequent travel to the United States was recorded as "private research" on the American visa form, and Steiner had secured authorization for a five-month stay. Waldbaer noted that the travel had been from Frankfurt to New York. Steiner had apparently traveled far south to Miami, Florida, by rental car or train to conceal his tracks and subsequently and illicitly purchased the alias Christian Slatner.

Waldbaer put this piece of paper down and reached for a glossy color photograph of Tobias Steiner. The photo was recent and likely had been obtained to accompany some official form or travel application. Waldbaer assessed the face, staring long at the image. Tobias Steiner, Waldbaer registered, had the same blue eyes of his father, and the same thick mane of light-colored hair. His manner, captured by the photographer, was solemn and unsmiling.

The face itself was young, the symmetry of features relatively handsome. But the unmistakable impression the photograph made on the detective was of a man consumed by resentment. Facts did not reveal this, but intuition did. Waldbaer traced his hand over the unsmiling image and felt certain of it. Intuition, Waldbaer knew, was often an affectation of a criminal investigator and, as often as not, masked an unspoken prejudice. Still, he had learned to give intuition its space.

Enormous ego, a letter written haughtily to the "Man in Charge," and a willingness to kill and kill again were at the epicenter of Steiner's being. Waldbaer hoped that Steiner would make a mistake, a small, seemingly insignificant flaw in his actions. As he returned the photograph to the file, it occurred to him that he had seen the face of the enemy. Waldbaer knew with unshakable certainty that he and Tobias Steiner were at war.

MUNICH

Tobias Steiner had equipped himself with a windbreaker to ward off the chill of the late November evening. He carried a backpack with him, infected with disease-laden fleas, nearly invisible to the human eye. Marching rapidly and with purpose, heels clicking against the uneven sidewalk on the street in front of his hotel, he turned a corner and made his way to the elegant Kaufingerstrasse, where crowds of Munich residents and tourists strolled every night of the week. He crossed through the crenellated expanse of Karls Gate, one of the remaining entrances in the old city walls, and merged with the boisterous crowds on their way to Munich's myriad and brightly lit shops and pubs. Dodging around a dawdling foursome of gesticulating tourists, Steiner moved with quick, certain steps toward his target. He felt contentment. He felt at peace, and his gait carried purpose.

His blind rage at being told he had terminal cancer had long ago subsided. The doctors in Florida did not quite know what to say. They had recommended an operation with no real purpose; it would perhaps extend Steiner's life for a few weeks. He had declined. The operation would have been futile. There was nothing to be done about the disease at all.

He felt pain, of course, as the cancer remorselessly ravaged his system. Still, he had tablets against such distress, and the pills kept the most severe spasms at bay. He had also learned to accommodate his increased yearning for sleep. Steiner routinely collapsed at eight each night and did not awaken until around ten in the morning. He awoke, invariably drenched in a pool of sweat, and after fortifying himself with a cold shower and strong coffee, was prepared to meet the day. He knew that the tolerable situation would not last. Steiner estimated that he had two months to live. Perhaps less.

But that was more than enough time to complete his self-appointed mission of infecting as many people as possible with the plague and having them precede him in death, foaming and coughing blood and gasping for air. The deaths of the plague victims would not be a pretty sight as it would entail a choking, trembling death struggle. He did not worry about becoming infected with the plague; he had taken an antidote he'd formulated for the pestilence that he had genetically modified. His own death, he imagined, would be more prosaic, the pancreatic cancer would slow him down bit by bit, numb him, and eventually, brutally stop his heart.

Steiner saw the venue that he had sought and it was fifty yards in front of him. The Augustiner beer hall and restaurant was an elaborate conceit of carved stone and large glass windows built in 1791. He cinched the backpack more tightly around his arms and entered the dark wooden reception door. The infected insects were contained in a Plexiglas tray inside the backpack, which Steiner intended to leave, flap opened, concealed beneath a dining table. He estimated that over the course of the evening the fleas would pass the plague on to twenty, perhaps thirty people.

The Augustiner restaurant was frenzied and crowded in the evening with a mob of people and a din of voices and laughter that merged into a dull roar, but that was how Steiner had known it would be. He made his way through the tumultuous mass of customers toward an unoccupied table with two seats against a paneled wall. Most of the other tables were occupied. He glanced around at the gregarious commotion and suddenly froze in his tracks.

Two policemen in black leather jackets and green, peaked service caps were making their way against the crowd, glancing left and right at the crush of seated, paying customers noisily raising glasses of beer. They were armed, their weapons holstered to their belts.

He had not expected to see members of the police force here and had never encountered them before in the Augustiner restaurant. He wondered, in a flash of panic, if the policemen had seen a photograph of his face and were hunting him. Perhaps the Man in Charge had acquired a photo somewhere and had shared it with the Bavarian police, this was something that he had not considered. As the two policemen haltingly bore down on him through the noisy, laughing mob of guests, Steiner decided that the risk of exposure was too great. He turned, keeping his head down, and doing his best to conceal his features, made his way toward the door he had entered just moments before.

Steiner pushed open the door to Kaufingerstrasse and felt the gritty pavement underfoot again. Relief at being outside the Augustiner restaurant washed over him as the cool autumn air entered his lungs, and he breathed deeply. He felt momentarily confused and uncertain. Clutching his backpack by the nylon straps, he headed down the street at a brisk pace, determined to reach the anonymity of his hotel room. There, at least, he could collapse and consider altering his appearance to provide protection against the authorities hunting him.

He needed to remain calm and in control. He did not know, after all, that the police were searching for him; their presence in the restaurant could just as easily be serendipity. But surely the police were on alert and were anxious to stop him by now. Anger again welled up in him, like a kettle of water on the boil. Time was the enemy, and it literally numbered his days. How long he had, he did not know, and this frustration bit into him just as profoundly as the pain in his cancer-wracked body. He needed a modicum of time to arrange the architecture of death to his satisfaction. Death by the plague still required the helping hand of his malign intervention. And then there remained the final, little matter of Augustin to bring to a close with a final flourish.

CHAPTER TWENTY-FIVE

GAMSDORF

Waldbaer had accomplished a few things on his own and felt cautiously, marginally in control of events. This was an illusion, he knew, as Tobias Steiner was still able to do as he pleased and remained as invisible to the police as a specter. But still, there were a few reasons for some modest satisfaction, and a likely reduction in Steiner's maneuverability.

For one thing, he now knew that he was after one man, a singleton, in police parlance, and that was a most welcome development. Secondly, Waldbaer and the police knew the identity of the man they sought, knew his true name as well as his professional strengths. Third, they had a very good, recent photograph of the killer. They knew what he looked like. All of these things were valuable cards, and it was up to Waldbaer to turn them into a winning hand.

The photo, at the very least, was valuable. Waldbaer had forwarded the image by a police fax machine across Germany and underlined that Tobias Steiner was wanted for multiple murders and had an arrest warrant issued against him in the state of Bavaria. Using his contacts in law enforcement, Waldbaer had urged the police to search for Steiner in public places such as concert halls and discos, public transportation, and major restaurants. Waldbaer was aware that this sudden police presence would not escape Steiner's attention. Perhaps it would cause Steiner to panic and make a mistake. The odds were set against this, but it was at least possible and Waldbaer ruled nothing out.

The plague stayed at the top of the news and had seized the headlines throughout the media. There were daily cases of hospitalizations for the deadly infection, and the death toll was climbing. The disease had claimed at least forty victims and there was no sign that it would stop. The plague had clearly become epidemic, and there were now instances in Ingolstadt, Bad Reichenhall, and Prien in addition to Munich and Augsburg. People who had been coughed or sneezed on by an infected person now also carried the deadly sickness. Normal medical countermeasures were having absolutely no effect.

It was as if Steiner had opened a malevolent Pandora's Box to the wind and the disease was blowing across the land unimpeded. Waldbaer thought back grimly to what he had read in the history books. Centuries ago the plague had wiped out a fourth of the human population in Europe. A fourth. Waldbaer wondered if it could happen again. He wondered if it was happening already.

CIA HEADQUARTERS, LANGLEY, VIRGINIA

Robert Hirter held his cardboard cup of coffee with a plastic top in one hand and tapped the five-digit code into the metal device affixed to the door of the vault and with his other hand, pushed it open. He strolled past a row of earth-toned office dividers, greeted a young and smiling CIA female secretary with long red hair, and entered his office which was cramped but mercifully had a window overlooking the Northern Virginia countryside. Take pleasure in the small things, Hirter thought to himself as he eased into his swivel chair and set his cup of coffee on his desk. Dressed in a patterned tweed jacket and burgundy tie, Hirter felt fit and alert, having jogged that morning through the streets of monotonous townhomes in his subdivision. He reached into his inbox for a bright yellow folder with a red sticker on which was stamped the word "Secret." The folder was from the psychiatric section of the Office of Medical Services. "Yes, indeed," he said with a smile, hoping that it was the analysis that he had ordered two days ago.

Opening the stiff paper file, Hirter noted the logo of Medical Services and focused on the words typed underneath it. The subject of the document was "Tobias Steiner, also known as Christian Slatner." A disclaimer cautioned that Steiner had never been subject to a psychiatric analysis in person and added that the findings in the two-page report were the impressions of two staff psychiatrists assigned to Langley. The team of psychiatrists had analyzed the documents available from the Miami Police Department, and "submissions on Steiner recently forwarded by a police inspector in Bavaria." The German policeman was Waldbaer, who had faxed his report on the conversation with von Winterloch, as well as a photograph of the young doctor.

Ignoring the rest of the bureaucratic boilerplate language, Hirter scanned down the page and began reading the text.

The subject, Tobias Steiner, is a successful medical researcher and specialist in biochemistry, and the author of numerous articles in peer-reviewed science journals on communicable diseases. He performed a period of field research in Madagascar which focused on Yersinia pestis, also known as the plague. Prior to his work on the plague, Steiner had been an "A" student in both high school and university, as well as an excellent student in graduate school.

According to the information we have received, Tobias Steiner was born to an unwed mother who engaged in an extramarital affair with Count Reinhold von Winterloch, a member of the German nobility and heir to an extensive family fortune. It is alleged that the mother of Tobias pocketed the generous funds that von Winterloch had given her for an abortion and raised the child on her own. Many years later, on her deathbed, Ms. Steiner told her son the identity of his father. Subsequent to his mother's death, Tobias Steiner confronted his biological father, Count von Winterloch, and asked to be formally and legally adopted according to state law. Winterloch reputedly declined this proposal for reasons of propriety. He did, however, as something of a compromise, agree to allow Tobias free access to the rural castle, which is the family seat, and offered as well to fund Tobias' studies and other pursuits, which doubtless involved a very considerable monetary expenditure.

How Tobias Steiner reacted to this arrangement can only be guessed at, and this document is a psychological assessment. His failure to obtain legal adoption was in all likelihood regarded by Tobias as unfair, and could have led to an unspoken and deep-seated sense of resentment. At some point, Tobias Steiner, flush with silent rage at being disowned, decided to use his knowledge of communicable diseases to reengineer the plague to make it resistant to antibiotics and thus more deadly as a mass casualty weapon. Subsequent to this development, Steiner was diagnosed with terminal cancer, assessed by medical authorities as incurable. We believe that receiving this diagnosis only intensified Steiner's feeling of "getting even" and extracting revenge for grievances large and small.

It must be emphasized that the current outbreak of the plague in Germany—and possibly elsewhere—was entirely the result of Tobias' practical work with the plague in Madagascar. We judge that this means that his decision to reengineer the plague disease must have at some point have occurred while he was still in Germany, well before his travel to Madagascar.

At this point, we will offer some psychiatric conclusions with which we are fairly confident. We assess Tobias Steiner as a highly educated and self-confident individual. Steiner has already secured his position as a top researcher in the field of communicable disease. Nonetheless, Steiner probably suffers from a severe and traumatic inferiority complex due to his perception of the illegitimacy of his birth and the presumed impoverished nature of his childhood. This sense of inferiority due to the conditions of his birth transformed with time into resentment and an active hatred toward society in general. We note that this societal hatred is general and indiscriminate in Steiner's case; it is not, repeat, not restricted to a loathing for German society. In terms of potential targets, we would caution that Steiner is likely to attack people on an international scale. If his movement is restricted to Germany, this could include large groups of Americans, many of whom would be tourists.

```
      In   our   view,   Tobias   Steiner   is   at
this  point  propelled  on  a  mission  with
intense  messianic  zeal.  What  may  appear
as  amoral  mass  murder  to  others  is  to
him  a  profoundly  moral  undertaking.  His
goal  is  likely  to  infect  thousands  if  not
hundreds  of  thousands  of  individuals  with
the  enhanced  plague  disease.  Conversations
with  Tobias  Steiner  on  his  actions  would,
in  our  analysis,  have  no  effect  at  all  in
convincing  him  to  give  up  this  mission.
In   our   view,   Steiner   is   committed   to
organizing  a  major  outbreak  of  the  plague,
quite  possibly  without  limits.  He  intends
to  accomplish  this  act  in  the  near  term
in  the  coming  days  and  weeks,  before
pancreatic  cancer  kills  him.
```

Hirter slipped the paper back in the file. He needed to get the document cleared for passage and send it on to Waldbaer. The language in the report about a possible attack on American citizens disturbed him. He thought of Munich, which was a magnet for thousands of tourists from all over the world. All of these tourists, at the conclusion of their vacation, flew back home to airports in New York, Chicago, Los Angeles, and elsewhere. He would voice his concerns to Waldbaer, darkly envisioning the ramifications of the plague run rampant and unrestrained on American soil.

MUNICH

The S-Bahn sped with efficient celerity to the Englschalking train stop, rapidly decreasing the velocity of its blue cars until it came to a stop in front of the concrete walkway braced by leafless trees where a dozen prospective passengers waited. The train's automated doors opened with a hiss and twelve men and women clambered in, seating themselves after securing their travel bags on the aluminum racks overhead. The S-Bahn, which had begun its journey in the center of Munich, slowly accelerated and proceeded with gathering speed toward Munich Airport, some fifteen miles away.

Tobias Steiner gazed out the rain-streaked window at the passing terrain. Across the landscape, gnarled trees held jealously onto the clutches of dead leaves that remained to them on a late November day. Occasional high-rise apartment buildings were seen in the half-light offered by the overcast and somber sky.

Absorbed by his own thoughts, Steiner mused that the depressing dreariness of the day whispered of death, his own death most of all. His pain had intensified despite the medication, but he bore its savage intercession without complaint. He noted that morning how the disease was slowly altering his features, his cheeks were severely sunken, and his eyes had begun to assume a hollow look. He had also declined to shave and his beard had changed his appearance. Having disguised his features successfully from police surveillance, he knew that there was much work still to be done.

The two passengers seated directly in front of Steiner, women in their twenties, were chattering and laughing in English. He nodded to himself; this was testimony to the wisdom of his targeting the light rail train servicing the airport. He overheard one of the women mention New York, and the other Washington. Glancing around the compartment, he saw that the car contained Turks, Asians, and Latin Americans, in addition to the granitic faces of bored Europeans. It was an exquisitely perfect laboratory selection.

Easing off his backpack, he placed it on the seat next to him and tugged open the covering. The trip to the airport was forty minutes, allowing plenty of time for the fleas to find a host. Steiner felt certain that the two babbling American girls would be among the first to be infected. Since the plague was pneumatic, many more people were likely to become victims in locations far beyond his physical reach. He recalled with mordant satisfaction the words from the Bible's Book of Revelation.

I looked, and behold, a pale horse; and he who sat on it had the name Death; and Hell was following with him. Authority was given to them over a fourth of the earth, to kill with sword and with famine and with pestilence and by the wild beasts of the earth.

Pestilence that covered a fourth of the Earth with its killing force struck Steiner as a highly desirable end. It was a task that he could try to accomplish before death consumed him as well. He would return to Munich using the same transport that had gotten him to the vicinity of the airport, the S-Bahn. And he would leave the backpack behind, like a calling card. His mouth felt intensely dry, but he still managed a smile.

CHAPTER TWENTY-SIX

Evening came early on the heels of the late autumn rainstorm, and the air grew suddenly cold and still, whispering of a winter fast approaching. Waldbaer stood in the grass of his back garden and looked at the spectral shapes of the pink roses that had died weeks ago with the first frost. We all have our time, every living thing, he thought to himself, as he huddled in his burgundy wool sweater, his hand still cradling a cell phone. The Berlin police department had just returned his call, with the information Waldbaer had requested on a non-German resident of that city, one Aleksandr Sergei Akulov.

Yes, the policeman with a chirpy voice in Berlin had pronounced, Akulov was indeed a Russian. The records gave his date of birth as November, 1951. He had been hired at the Free University of Berlin from an official position in Moscow. Residing in Berlin since 1990 but still retaining his Russian passport, Akulov had established a police record ten years later. He had been arrested for starting a brawl in a Berlin pub and hitting another customer over the head with a half-filled bottle of vodka.

Charges had been dropped, and Akulov got off with a warning. Two years later, however, Akulov had gotten into a shouting and shoving match with passerby on the Friedrichstrasse, during which he was knocked out and crashed through a display window at a Berlin department store. According to the police record the episode was also vodka induced and Akulov had been highly, hugely intoxicated at the time. Subsequent to his arrest, the university had quietly pensioned Akulov off, and he was now retired in the Spandau section of the German capitol.

Tomorrow morning Waldbaer would fly to Berlin, and the police would set up the interview with Akulov. He had insisted on speaking with the Russian scientist as an urgent matter. As evening settled and the mountain peaks were swept up in darkness, Waldbaer reluctantly declined to have a cigarette. He expected to learn something about Steiner from Akulov the next day. For the moment, at least, that would have to substitute for nicotine.

BERLIN

The one-hour up-and-down flight from Munich to Berlin Tegel Airport had been uneventful, even boring. A heavy fog held all of Germany in its moist grasp, and there was no view at all from the aircraft's windows except for a choking, swirling grayness. Waldbaer had refused the offering of a breakfast roll stuffed with preservatives and a slice of cheese wrapped in plastic.

He had been picked up by a police car at the Berlin airport, snappily saluted by the official police driver, and been brought a short way to the police station at Spandau. Constructed of dark-red brick and laced with the grime and soot of age, Waldbaer guessed that the turreted edifice had been home to the police for a hundred and fifty years or more. Inside, he was happy to see that the police interrogation chamber had an oddly cheery and modern look, comfortable chairs around a sleek teak table and soft, indirect lights reflecting off of crisp vanilla walls.

Dr. Aleksandr Akulov did not appear happy with the surroundings, or with anything else. Waldbaer regarded the other man as he entered and closed the door to the interrogation room, hearing the door click shut behind him. Akulov gazed at the detective, offering not a word of greeting. The Russian was dressed in academic style, Waldbaer noted, wearing a dark suit coat over a red-striped flannel shirt.

"*Grüss Gott,*" Waldbaer intoned and then remembered that

the distinctly Catholic greeting was not heard so fondly by all ears in the traditionally Protestant north. "Good morning, Dr. Akulov, thank you for agreeing to come here. I'm Kommissar Franz Waldbaer from Bavaria."

Akulov gave a formal, solemn nod of his head, maintaining his silence. His face was broad, in a Slavic way, and a thick mat of uniformly gray hair began at his forehead and was cut severely short. The eyes were deep brown and notably bloodshot, and Waldbaer entertained an educated guess that Akulov was hung over. Confirming this, Akulov's hands, clasped tightly before him, tremored slightly. Waldbaer took a seat and gazed across the smooth veneer of the table at a man who was no stranger to alcohol. No time like the present, Waldbaer decided, and eased into the interview.

"Dr. Akulov, you served for many years, as I understand it, as a teacher at the Free University of Berlin, isn't that right?"

Akulov looked at Waldbaer with partially hooded eyes, and spoke in a deep voice with a pronounced Russian accent, as if through a mouth full with gravel. "Why come to me with this question? The university human resources department could answer it just as well. But yes, if you want to know, I lectured students in communicable disease and transmittable illness for several years. I was a professor."

Waldbaer decided to ignore Akulov's hostility. "And what communicable diseases did you lecture on?"

"Several."

Waldbaer's smile became brittle. "Yes, of course. What diseases exactly, Doctor?"

Akulov sighed with resignation, as if he were conversing with a small child. "I said several. Swine flu, for one, and avian flu, for another. And anthrax, of course. I also discussed smallpox with my students, as well as tuberculosis and the Spanish flu of 1918. All of these are communicable diseases."

"I see. Tell me, did you ever discuss Yersinia pestis—the plague from the Middle Ages—as well?"

Akulov's eyes lost their lethargic look. "Well, yes. I suppose that I did lecture on it, or mentioned it in passing. I did mention the Plague of Justinian, and the more widely researched Black Death in the fourteenth century. What of it, is it illegal? Why are you asking me this question?"

Waldbaer nodded and pulled his chair closer to the table. "As I'm sure you'll recognize, Yersinia pestis is of considerable interest to me right now. You have certainly followed the outbreak of the plague in Bavaria, it's all over the news. It's the number-one story on radio and television at present, and it's taken in excess of forty lives, maybe more. It is a criminal matter. The medical experts have advised that a scientist, in effect, reengineered the plague or mutated it, making it effectively impervious to antibiotics. That's why I'm here, and that's why you're here."

Akulov's eyes regarded Waldbaer attentively, but he again fell into silence.

Waldbaer continued, "After much effort, we believe that we have identified a suspect who may have mutated the bacteria. And that, as it were, leads me to you. We believe that an individual named Tobias Steiner has a role in the acquisition of the plague disease, and in mutating it. Are you familiar with anyone named Tobias Steiner, Doctor?"

Akulov's face tensed, a tic appeared in his cheek, and he clenched his hands together. "Yes, I suppose I am." The words came out in a hiss.

"Good. What can you tell me about him?"

Akulov unclasped his hands and ran both of them with a slight tremor through his thick hair, saying nothing for a moment. "The Tobias Steiner I knew was a student at the Free University of Berlin. He was an extremely talented student, and he was preternaturally bright. I would have to say that he was one of the best students I ever had."

"I see. That is most impressive. What were his academic interests? Did he have any pursuit that stood out?"

Akulov hacked out a muffled dry cough before continuing.

"Yes. He had a fascination with the plague and the historical dev-astation the disease inflicted on European society in the Middle Ages. In fact, this fascination was reflected in his doctoral work."

"Yes, I know. He wrote The Plague, Contagion and Contemporary Medicine."

Akulov did nothing to conceal his surprise and arched his eyebrows. "You seem to know quite a bit about what Tobias wrote and what he accomplished. Congratulations. I say again, why do you ask me about these things?"

Waldbaer filed away the fact that the Russian referred to Steiner, in an unguarded moment, as Tobias. "I ask you, because I rather think that Steiner modeled himself on you, or at least, greatly respected the work that you had done. My interest in Tobias Steiner is driven by a criminal investigation. But you and Steiner shared an interest in disease and the medical countermeasures that can be employed to counter a disease, isn't that right? And that brings me to ask, Doctor, what precisely you contributed to biological studies. You were, at the time the Soviet Union collapsed, a Soviet official, if I'm not mistaken. Where from exactly?"

Akulov's eyes narrowed and his features took on a sullen look. "From Moscow. There's nothing secret about it. I worked for the Soviet military. I had done my studies at Moscow University, in medical science. After that, I was given a job by the science and research division of the Red Army of the Soviet Union. The German authorities are aware of all of this. I was eventually put in charge of a team of medical research specialists, and we were instructed to devise a way of making a communicable disease effective as a military weapon. There was nothing illegal about it, those were the times, and that was simply the world we lived in."

Waldbaer withheld judgment. "What disease did that involve?"

"You would call it swine flu, or perhaps pig influenza. Our task was to make this disease zoonotic, that is, able to be passed on to humans."

The detective eyed Akulov steadily. "And what were your results?"

Akulov shrugged and looked down at the table at his trembling hands. "I had a team of Soviet scientists working with me full time. We reengineered the swine flu to allow it to pass to humans, specifically to combatant soldiers. That, after all, was the intent; the soldiers would become infected with swine flu. It wouldn't necessarily kill them, but it would make them dysfunctional. They would develop severe headaches, which would make it difficult for a NATO soldier to pick up a rifle let alone fight, general weakness, a marked inability to follow orders, and gross disorientation. It would have been a highly effective weapon, make no mistake."

Waldbaer decided to forego a discussion of medical ethics. "Doctor, did you ever weaponize a strain of the plague?"

Akulov glowered at Waldbaer in disapproval. "*Nyet.* No, I never did. If it were weaponized, the plague would be lethal. I would have refused work on a lethal weapon of any sort. A mutated plague would be incredibly dangerous if used as a weapon; it could easily pass into the general population, regardless of the intention of those using it."

"That is exactly what I am worried about, Dr. Akulov. I am quite certain that Tobias Steiner has accomplished this."

Akulov stared at Waldbaer for a moment before responding with a subdued laugh. "That is none of my concern."

Waldbaer stared back. "No? A student of yours mutates the plague, based in part on his work with you, and it is of no concern? I cannot say that the authorities here will share your view. Especially if this plague becomes a pandemic, which is what keeps me up at night."

"I had nothing to do with this, absolutely nothing. The plague was Tobias' specialty, it was not mine. Why do you want to bring me into this, do you have something against Russians? I instructed him, it is true, in certain techniques that the Soviets used for the reengineering of communicable disease; some of the procedures are similar, whatever the disease. But that was years ago. I have not seen Tobias since the time he left Berlin."

"How well did you know him? Did you ever deal with him socially?"

Akulov looked drained, his eyes scarlet red and tired. "Socially? Yes, I suppose you could say that. We started by discussing his thesis, and one thing led to another. We went out a few times."

"For drinks, I presume?" Waldbaer asked.

Akulov's eyes suggested this was a hostile question. "Yes, we did go out for drinks, maybe for a few, maybe for more than a few, who doesn't now and then? Don't ask me where we went, I can't recall the locations. To some bars, beer halls and some pubs, and Berlin has hundreds of them."

Waldbaer took his time to consider his next question. Go slowly, he counseled himself, Akulov is already sullen. "On these occasions in beer halls or pubs, did you notice anything about Steiner's personality that you didn't notice before? Did you like him?"

A weary grin swept across Akulov's face, emphasizing the wrinkles that the steady abuse of alcohol had advanced. "Like I said, Tobias was very bright and inordinately intelligent. And he was witty, in a very cynical, acerbic way. He had, you might say, a high opinion of himself. I don't say this as a criticism, you understand, he was very talented in the practice of science, and he had an incisive mind and enormous self-confidence. But he did dearly love to hate."

"Hate? Whom exactly did he hate?"

"Everyone and no one, if you know what I mean. I didn't make much of it at the time, because it didn't concern me. It was just a distinct part of Tobias' rather odd personality."

"I see. Were there other parts of his personality that you did not see in the lecture hall?"

Akulov looked vastly tired as he summoned the appropriate words. "He had a few rather bad habits, you might say. Tobias had developed an obsessive taste for cocaine, crack cocaine to be exact. But I can tell you that it didn't affect his professional writing or any of his academic work. It was just a dark, secret side of Tobias. Some people drink, and other people prefer to take drugs."

Waldbaer raised his eyes in surprise. "Let me ask you, Doctor, would you expect that Tobias Steiner is still addicted to cocaine?"

Akulov placed his chin on his shaking, tremor-ridden hands. "Of course. It is an addiction, as you've just said, and it is not easily banished. Some of us prefer alcohol to wipe away our disappointments in life. Tobias is a cocaine addict, which is purely a matter of his choice. Whatever he has done with the plague, and perhaps that would shock us all, cocaine is his enduring pleasure."

"Is there anything else that you can tell me, anything I would want to know?"

Akulov's eyes took on a distant look. "You know, it's rather funny. As a student Tobias was always much focused, that was his nature. He studied the plague from every conceivable angle. But his discussions with me were always very precise, whether in a social setting or not. He wanted to know the ins and outs of reengineering a communicable disease; he wanted to know how the Soviets had accomplished it, how mutation worked. He was a good conversationalist and he had a fiercely nasty wit, but he was focused on one goal: how the plague could be, well, weaponized. It was an obsession with him, and you shouldn't forget that."

Akulov took on a reflective look. "Tobias is, you see, an extremely single-minded individual. He talked about the plague almost incessantly, about how it came close to wiping out mankind. He said many times that only the long dormancy of the plague and the discovery of antibiotics managed to keep it at bay. Tobias said that if it were immune to antibiotics, an outbreak of the plague today, in the modern world, would be like nothing in history. It would sweep through our carefully constructed societies root and branch like a fire; it would consume everything. There would only be the dead and those waiting to die. And on those occasions when he would make a comment like that, he would always end it with a quote from somewhere."

Waldbaer was puzzled. "A quotation? What do you mean exactly?"

Akulov shrugged and moved his head from side to side. "I'm sure it was a quotation, but I don't know the source of it, I confess. I am certain that the words are centuries old. Tobias would recite them. He would say 'Behold, I am death.'"

Waldbaer recognized the quotation with a start; it was emblazoned on the sword blade of Heinrich, the long-dead count. Waldbaer stared into the distance and repeated the quotation again, talking as if to himself.

"Behold, I am death."

CHAPTER TWENTY-SEVEN

DULLES AIRPORT, VIRGINIA

The plane landed on time at Dulles International Airport near Washington after an eight-hour journey from Munich. The passengers disembarked into the brightly lit, sterile air of the midfield terminal and with bored glances took in the sights at magazine stands, bookshops, and stores selling coffee and bright cotton t-shirts.

Over two hundred travelers felt tired, glad to have the long flight with its endless clouds behind them. Out of the mass of disembarkees, however, three men and two women were feeling out of sorts with a dull, pounding ache in their foreheads, and a persistent pain in their joints. A man and a woman from the flight each experienced a nosebleed inside of the terminal. Each of the five dismissed the signs of plague as the onset of a low-grade cold or the price of consuming disagreeable airline food. The plague, ten hours after it had been injected into their bloodstream by fleas released on board the Metro train to Munich Airport, was well on its way to silently and steadily building the architecture of its lethal malignancy.

GAMSDORF

Waldbaer was informed of the breakout of the plague in North America in a phone call from Dr. Nilsson from Stockholm. "The German and American authorities are at present unsure what to do about it," Nilsson had advised from his office in the ECDC.

"It might develop in the next couple of days that the Germans impose a travel ban on anyone leaving the country."

"What? That's not possible," Waldbaer had stuttered.

"Oh, but it is, Kommissar. Those desiring to leave Germany would first have to submit to a medical examination to ensure they do not carry the plague. Of course, you know as well as I do that this proposed solution, to say the least, is not optimal. Where would the doctors come from? Presumably the Red Cross, maybe the Bundeswehr, the armed forces. And if the sick are identified, where are they to be placed? Regular hospitals are not prepared to cope with this, not in Munich or anywhere else. And still not resolved is the question of what medical countermeasures to put in place. Keep in mind that it will take some time for laboratories to discover and produce new antibiotics that will be effective against the mutated strain."

"*Katastrophal,*" Waldbaer could only mutter.

"Catastrophic is exactly correct. As I say, the German authorities might ban travel; they have not done so yet, and you can imagine the consequences for the economy. I suppose that we will have to see how events move in the next few days, God knows. I do not want to be the source of unnecessary worries for you, Kommissar. You have a lot on your shoulders, I just wanted to provide some relevant information."

Waldbaer sighed mightily and rubbed the bridge of his nose. "The information you provided is all well and good, Doctor. But information has consequences. The press can't resist a sensationalist headline. The radio and television are already reporting that there is no available cure for this type of plague. We are not very far from a general panic in the population, and that is something that I don't want to see. To stop this new Black Death from spreading, I have to get my hands on the man who reengineered this mutated plague. Believe me, Doctor, I am trying."

There was momentary silence on the other end of the phone. "I wish you the best of luck, Kommissar," Dr. Nilsson said, his voice a half-whisper.

"Luck, you say? I will need that, but that is not why they pay me. Some damned good detective work is how I will solve this." Waldbaer rang off, not at all sure that detective work alone would stop Tobias Steiner.

FIVE AMERICAN PASSENGERS FROM MUNICH SICK WITH DEADLY PLAGUE, STRICT TRAVEL BAN CONSIDERED, was the headline in the *Süddeutsche Zeitung*, Munich's leading newspaper. Waldbaer glanced through the article with straining eyes, saw nothing new, and tossed the paper onto his desk.

He walked to an easel filled with butcher paper near the center of the room, picked up a marker in his fist, and wrote down a sentence in a series of slashes.

Where is Tobias Steiner?

Waldbaer stared at the sheet of paper a moment and then scribbled a few words.

Munich probably, a major city. Steiner wants anonymity. Able to launch plague attacks against throngs of people. Infection of international air passengers was almost certainly initiated in Munich U-Bahn. Backpack found on train had residual traces for presence of rat fleas.

Waldbaer continued writing.

Steiner has likely infected hundreds of people. He wants to infect thousands, even hundreds of thousands.

His writing was harsh, the lines uneven.

How does Steiner spread the plague? A colony of infected fleas from Madagascar. How does he keep them alive? Surmise: in a portable lab, something he devised and can easily carry.

Waldbaer paused, nodded to himself, and then continued.

Look for: backpack, shoulder bag or similar device for carrying the plague. A backpack is most likely, as it would blend extremely well into either an urban or a rural environment.

The detective rubbed a dull pain in the back of his neck and thought of Steiner underway with a backpack cinched on his shoulders. Again he placed the marker to the paper.

Steiner is dying and he knows it. He probably takes significant amounts of medication to moderate the effects. But Steiner must look sick, or he soon will. That gives us: a very sick man carrying a backpack. Steiner is certainly medicated; the medication could have been prescribed in Florida, or acquired in Europe.

Yes, Waldbaer said to himself, tossing down the felt-tipped pen on his desk. Steiner was not only trying to outrun the police, he was trying to outrun death itself, a race, in the end, that he could not win. That, at least, provided a hint of hope. It was, in fact, all he had.

WASHINGTON, D.C.

Derrick Alsop wheezed mightily and moaned, watery eyes not able to focus, his mouth dripping a steady stream of blood, before he barked out a ferocious cough as he entered Howard University Hospital in Washington. He was wearing a charcoal wool suit but his tieless white shirt was out, the tapered cotton ends of it stained with a slick viscous ooze of blood.

Two paramedics, chatting near the bright lights that braced the arrival desk, bolted toward Alsop to offer him assistance. He coughed explosively once more, covering them with invisible particles, while they forced his writhing open-mouthed form onto a nearby gurney and immediately set off down a corridor. Jenna, a tall black nurse, witnessing Alsop's collapse from behind the desk, saw with horror an unmistakable, massive bubo extending upward from his beltline to the folds of his blood-drenched shirt. The growth appeared purple in the surgically bright light of the hospital.

"Oh dear God, I know what that is," she said, grabbing the phone in front of her and pounding in an extension.

"Emergency room," came the impassive reply from a deep-voiced man on the other end of the line.

"This is Jenna. Heads up: we've got a patient on his way to you right now who is bleeding badly and has suffered a possible stroke. He has what appears to be a black lesion on his body. I think it is consistent with the plague disease that we're on alert for and that hit Washington the other day. And another thing, the patient coughed on the paramedics who are bringing him to you. You might want to detain them as well and submit them to an emergency medical checkup."

The voice on the other end was now focused, clipped and efficient. "Okay, got it, Jenna. We'll check all three of them. The paramedics are probably okay, but the patient is more problematic. Antibiotics are the usual treatment, but the ECDC has put out a warning that this plague strain has mutated. We'll see what we can do for him. Thanks."

Jenna hung up the phone, wondering if this was the only incident of the plague bacteria that she would see, or if it was only the first.

CHAPTER TWENTY-EIGHT

Steiner did not feel at all well, and had not for some months, but something was different this time. It was morning, and he had gotten a full night's sleep, but he still felt unaccountably exhausted. He had increased the amount of his pain medications, but the drugs now had a minimal effect on the relentless, irreversible progress of his disease.

He declined to look in the mirror because he feared what he would see. He felt the change within him, but he refused to see its ravages. His cheeks were sunken, and he traced his fingers over the crevices in his face. He knew that his eyes were sunken into his skull as well, and his skin was sallow. The pain, no longer responsive to medication, was gradually overwhelming him as the cancer metastized. He swept a hand though his hair and looked with silent reproach at the thick patch of blond locks in his palm. With a deep sigh and a surge of bitterness, he decided to shave his head and wear a hat on his excursions outside of the hotel.

But there were other, even more vexing markers of the disease. He had been unable to keep down any food for the past two days, vomiting after every attempt to ingest solid sustenance. Steiner knew that he had to digest a necessary quantity of vegetables and meat to keep up his energy level, but his physical system was now rebelling. He would try to force down a bland sandwich today, but if that did not work, he wondered what else he could do. Perhaps smoke an ever-increasing amount of crack cocaine, he decided; it seemed to deaden the incursion of the cancer, at least for a few hours.

But, Steiner knew his timeline for accomplishing the slaughter he wanted to wreak with the plague was fast diminishing. He had planned a few more forays, and he needed to translate these plans into action very soon. To accomplish his goals, Steiner had to resist the wall of pain. And then, of course, there remained the little matter of Augustin to sort out.

CIA HEADQUARTERS, LANGLEY

Robert Hirter adjusted his patterned blue silk tie, unbuttoned his dark-gray suit, and entered the conference room at CIA headquarters in Langley. The other attendees were already there, and a murmur of conversation filled the windowless chamber, decorated with copies of Monet paintings. With a glance around the room, he spotted a number of people wearing "guest" badges and knew they were representatives from the National Security Agency, the Center for Disease Control in Atlanta, and the FBI. Nodding to a female CIA acquaintance, Hirter slid into a vacant chair at the varnished table.

"Okay," a gravelly voice rang out above the cacophony of mumbled voices, "let's take our seats and get this conference started. We've got a lot to discuss this morning." The voice belonged to Dr. Milt Stennins, who had flown up from Georgia that morning. His hair stood above a mildly sunburned face like a thick patch of black-and-gray wire, and he wore a pair of horn-rimmed glasses on the end of a pudgy nose. "I'm Milt Stennins from the Center for Disease Control in Atlanta, and I've been asked to chair the conference, along with Robert Hirter from CIA." Hirter raised a hand, smiled, and gave a quick nod in reply. He preferred to let Stennins do the talking.

"I think we all know why we're here. To make it brief, a plane landed from Munich a few days ago and unloaded over two hundred passengers. Of those two hundred people, five were sick, in fact very sick, and did not know it. All of them subsequently checked into hospitals in Washington and Northern Virginia. To be frank, they all died there. The five passengers died from exposure to Yersinia pestis. It is a quick killer. All of the victims contracted the disease four days or so before expiring. That, ladies and gentlemen, is the reason we are here. Yersinia pestis, the plague, otherwise known as the Black Death. It is not a new disease. It is the same bacterium that infected people in the Middle Ages, and it was around before that, and since. You don't hear much of it these days, or didn't, because the plague has generally been responsive to modern antibiotics. But this strain of the disease is quite different. It appears that this version of the plague has been reengineered by a human being to resist antibiotics."

Stennins removed his glasses and placed them on the table in front of him. "Just so everyone knows, antibiotics were given to the five victims in the various hospitals, but to no effect. This mutation of the plague would seem to be impervious to streptomycin and chloramphenicol, among other established treatments. To be blunt, that is very bad news. All of us have been sent here by our prospective agencies to reach a consensus on what to do on the federal level. I have an opinion on what we should do—now—and will share it with you a bit later. But first, I want to give Mr. Hirter an opportunity to have his say and advise us on what has been going on where the outbreak of the plague first occurred, in Germany."

Hirter felt uncomfortable as he looked around at the forty or so animated faces. He did not like speaking to groups, but knew that the task was unavoidable. "Okay," he began, "I'll try to make this brief. Everyone here, I am advised, has a secret clearance. The plague comes from the state of Bavaria in Germany; that is the locus. The outbreak of the plague on the other side of the Atlantic started several days ago. I'm the CIA liaison officer in charge of monitoring this incident, and I'm in touch with a Bavarian police commissioner who is in charge on the German end. The key thing to note is that this outbreak of the plague is man made."

There was a murmur from the far end of the table, and a high-pitched voice rose above it. "What do you mean by saying the plague is man made? Dr. Stennins just said that it's been around for hundreds of years. You can't have it both ways. Which is it?"

Hirter's eyes picked out the individual who had asked the question, a man with wispy red hair and a moustache. "Dr. Stennins is right in saying the plague has been around for hundreds, if not thousands, of years. But two medical institutions working this, including the Center for Disease Control, have established that the plague has been reengineered to combat antibiotics. In that sense, the plague may be very old but this strain is man made."

Dr. Stennins looked up at the ceiling and exhaled a long breath. "Let me add a few facts. The plague exists today and is part of our world. There are cases of plague which have affected people in the United States. There are incidents of the plague in Africa and Asia. Madagascar is a country which has a persistent presence of the plague, and which has had hundreds of people die of the infection. Madagascar is the place where this plague is from, and that is beyond question. The European Center for Disease Control has established it. The current plague infecting Europe and the United States was apparently transported from Madagascar to Europe by a medical researcher. I'll let Mr. Hirter fill in the rest."

Hirter tugged at the knot of his tie as he continued.

"Right. We know that a medical specialist is responsible for the act of spreading the plague. We know his name, Tobias Steiner. He was trained in genetic engineering by a Russian scientist who had been a member of the old Soviet Union's weaponization program of communicable diseases. We know that Steiner is deliberately intending to infect as many people as he possibly can with this modern version of the Black Death. And we know something else. Steiner is dying of pancreatic cancer, and he knows it."

Another voice interrupted. "Well, that should solve the problem, shouldn't it? Steiner will drop dead soon and that's the end of it." A brief cackle of laughter followed the remark.

Hirter ignored the mirth. "Sorry, but that's just wrong. Steiner's dying will have little impact on the plague that has been released in Germany and the United States. If he were to drop dead right now, we'd still have a major problem on our hands trying to stop this disease from spreading."

Hirter glanced around the room and saw that all of the faces were somber. "We know some other things which I'll share with you. We asked for a psychological profile of Tobias Steiner. The report concludes that Steiner more than likely wants the plague to kill as many people as possible, maybe hundreds of thousands of people. That is what we're up against, a highly motivated, fanatical individual who has merged modern medical research with the ancient plague to achieve a goal of mass murder." Hirter decided he had spoken long enough to the people crammed into the conference room. "That's about it. Are there any questions?"

A gray-haired woman in a magenta suit raised her hand. "That's good background, Mr. Hirter, but what in the world are we supposed to do about it?"

"Let me respond to that," Dr. Stennins said. "Your question is very salient and here is the problem. The mutated plague originates in Germany, and that is where this Tobias Steiner is still on the loose. All of the Americans who became infected with the plague contracted the disease in Germany, in Bavaria, to be exact. Steiner is probably still spreading the disease. More Americans could be infected but do not yet know it. So, what do we recommend? Do we ban all travel from Germany to the states, effectively shut down the air transport system between the two countries? Consider for a moment the horrendous economic costs involved in that decision, and I think you would agree that is not the way to go, at least not yet."

"Well, what do we do, just let everybody in without restriction?" The bass voice came from the back of the room.

Stennins shook his head. "No, we don't do that, either. We have to look at this logically. To date, Bavaria is the only state in Germany experiencing an outbreak of the plague. There is not a single case in Northern Germany. Travel from Bavaria to the states basically comes from one place, Munich International Airport. I urge a quarantine of the Munich airport starting right now. We can advise the Germans that every passenger intending to fly to the United States will have to submit to rigorous medical attention. Please note that if a person has the plague, this can be determined through a simple blood test. Travelers to the states will not be allowed on a plane until the Red Cross has the results of a blood test. If it's determined that they are infected with plague, then they will be hospitalized immediately."

The man with thinning red hair and a moustache frowned. "It won't work because it can't work. People can travel by train or car out of Bavaria and out of Germany and catch a flight to the states from some other country in Europe. Quarantine simply doesn't give you the control over the situation that you need."

"No," Dr. Stennins acknowledged, "quarantine doesn't give you complete control, in fact, nothing under the sun does. Most passengers will be relieved to have a free checkup. They sure as hell don't want to die of this mutated disease. The blood test will hold up their travel for a day, maybe two days at the most. This is not a perfect solution, but it's something. What I am saying is that taking this step at least lets us get our hands around the problem. We've suffered five deaths, and I think this is an adequate, reasonable response at the moment. If deaths in the states attributable to the plague begin to spiral upward, we'll have to modify the response, and slapping a ban on all travel from Germany, even from Europe, is an option. Do I have agreement that starting quarantine procedure on flights from Munich to the United States should be adopted as an immediate course of action?"

There was a loud murmur of confused conversation, but a flurry of raised hands filled the air. Stennins turned to the CIA officer seated next to him. "All right. We will contact the Germans and urge them to start the quarantine tomorrow. Do you have anything to add, Mr. Hirter?"

"I was just wondering, Doctor, what will the other European countries choose to do? France, the Netherlands, Austria, and Poland, to name a few, are certainly aware of the potential for an outbreak of the plague, much as we are. What are they going to do about it? Do you know?"

"I suspect that they are waiting to see what this country does as their first course of action," Stennins said. "I think for the moment that they'll be grateful to follow our lead. I wouldn't be at all surprised to see the countries you've mentioned call for some sort of preflight quarantine as well. In the meantime, let's cross our fingers that the Bavarian police stop Steiner."

With that, the conference unceremoniously ended, and the participants drifted off to their respective agencies. Only Stennins and Hirter remained at the table. Stennins massaged his glasses with a handkerchief. "Tell me, Mr. Hirter, do the Bavarian police have a chance of catching Tobias Steiner?"

Hirter shrugged. "Everything is chance. Whether the Germans are lucky or not in getting Steiner is about as predictable as the outcome of a card game. The German police commissioner is a hound dog. That much I'm sure of, and I've seen him in action close-up before. The first deaths were reported at a Bavarian castle in the Alps, if you can believe it, and it's gotten crazier and crazier ever since."

Stennins subdued a laugh and unsuccessfully suppressed a smile. "This whole thing is completely crazy. The plague struck in the Middle Ages, now we're hit again. But, you know, it was just a matter of time. For years we've been warning the government about some insane person or a religious fanatic unleashing a communicable disease. The response? The government yawned and ignored us. And as a result, we have what we have. Steiner fits our stereotype of exactly the type of person that we would someday be up against. Your police commissioner must have his hands full."

"Well, that's one way to look at it, Doctor, but I'd say that Tobias Steiner also has his hands full and doesn't even know it."

WASHINGTON, D.C.

The isolation ward of Howard University Hospital had the look of a triage tent in wartime Afghanistan. The floors were doused with stringent ammonia that made the very act of breathing repellent. Still, Jenna knew that the combined odor of nitrogen and hydrogen was just one attempt of many to limit the plague. She had entered the isolation quarter moments ago and the automatic door had sealed tight behind her. Jenna breathed deeply, not liking the sour edge the air tank in her chemical protection suit dispensed.

As a nurse, she had been assigned the task of monitoring the patients every hour. In her darker moments, Jenna interpreted that as counting the living and counting the dead among the victims. A total of nine individuals had been delivered to the university hospital since Mr. Alsop had staggered in two days ago. The two paramedics who had delivered him to the emergency room had been examined and released, but Mr. Alsop had hemorrhaged and died.

Jenna looked into the first of six isolation rooms and was relieved to see that the nine-year-old girl inside seemed to be resting. Moving closer to the stainless steel hospital bed, the nurse studied the child in detail. There was no trace of blood visible from the nose or lips, and no evidence of a bubo. Upon admission, the child's heartbeat had been rapid, but had been brought back to a normal reading with medication. The nurse touched the girl's hands and feet and found no incipient traces of necrosis. "Thank God," Jenna said, murmuring the words into the polyester mask covering her face. The child, eyes closed in sleep, did not awaken, and Jenna stepped out of the room and moved to the second chamber.

Here the story was far different. The nurse was aware of the man's history. As she opened the door and moved past the threshold, she recalled snippets of the narrative. Duane Oldiak was a salesman who had returned from a week in Germany. He had been feeling unaccountably ill and had collapsed in his office and was rushed to the hospital by ambulance. He had been bleeding profusely from the mouth and had a large bubo on his left armpit which had been surgically drained. The medical intervention did not seem to help, however, as another bubo had formed overnight on his groin. Jenna observed him through her Plexiglas mask. Oldiak was awake and his eyes were deep red and he looked scared.

"Don't worry, we're doing everything we can. It's going to be okay, I'm certain," Jenna pronounced automatically, the words muffled by her protective suit.

"I don't feel very well," Oldiak said, his voice a rasp.

Jenna did not know what to say, and settled into silence. She inspected the man's hands and saw that the fingers of both of them were in an appalling state. Each finger was as black as if it had been dipped in tar up to the first knuckle, and all of the fingers were curved inward. The rest of Oldiak's body was pale, with a pallid green cast. If the past is any guide, Jenna thought, the patient would pass away sometime tonight. It had been that way with Alsop, the first plague victim; he was dead twelve hours after being admitted; he had hemorrhaged; nothing could stop the loss of blood.

Jenna left the second isolation room behind, stared down the corridor in front of her, and heard a loud groan issuing from the third room. She sighed and closed her eyes. The situation was depressing. Most of the patients were getting rapidly worse, not better, despite the hospital's robust treatment with a firewall of antibiotics. Jenna had seven more patients to monitor, four men and three women, and the prognosis for all of them was poor.

As she steeled herself to visit the remainder of isolation rooms, Jenna thought once again of the young girl she had seen just minutes ago. The nurse had a feeling, an intuition perhaps, that the girl would survive. What was it, Jenna wondered, that accounted for the girl's condition? In that particular medical case, was the will to survive stronger than the disease?

CHAPTER TWENTY-NINE

MUNICH

He moved slowly and achingly up the escalator which took him from the cavernous U-Bahn station underground to the very center of Munich at Marienplatz. A pair of yelling teenagers clambered up the stainless steel conveyor belt, jostling past him, and Steiner felt for a moment as if he would faint. The shouting teenagers disappeared into the sunlight that hovered above him like an apparition, and Steiner closed his eyes, knowing that the light would soon engulf him too. With eyes squeezed shut, he heard the low steady hum of the conveyance and felt the sudden burst of midday warmth. He gripped the rubber-coated handrail for support and released a quiet moan. As the mobile platform came to its destination, Steiner stepped off and forced his eyes to open and take in the scene that confronted him.

A marble pillar, thirty feet tall, served as a plinth for a statue of the Virgin Mary, a serene cipher adorned in golden ornaments. Behind the religious monument was the city hall, a rambling and noble gothic revival structure of limestone that was the centerpiece of the plaza, surrounded by busy commercial buildings and restaurants. Steiner fumbled in the pockets of his nylon vest and carefully removed a pair of sunglasses, to protect his eyes. He knew where he was going.

He forced his way through a group of Japanese tourists near the center of the square and continued past the arch of the Toy Museum and down the busy side street of Im Tal, crowded with a blur of business people enjoying their lunch hour. Steiner turned a corner, glad to be rid of the crowds, and moved haltingly to a street named Platzl. He came to a stop, breathing heavily and with his heart straining against his chest, and willed the enormity of pain from his system. Can't quit now, he encouraged himself, I'm almost there and there is work to be done. Forcing his legs to move forward once again, he shuffled toward the familiar shape of the Munich Hofbräuhaus.

Two policemen stood in front of the massive arched doors of the beer hall, hands in their pockets and seemingly bored with the world. With his shaved head concealed by a baseball cap, his sunglasses and vest and backpack, Steiner took a chance and walked by them smiling, partly concealed behind a trio of laughing Americans. To Steiner's relief, the policemen, looking vastly disinterested, ignored him. He moved past the tourist shop with its bright display of overpriced beer glasses and shirts and into the hall itself.

The hall was a cavernous affair of hundreds of heavy oak tables and benches, with the scent of spilled lager heavy in the air. The space was brightly lit, but Steiner removed and pocketed his sunglasses nonetheless, intent on fitting into his surroundings. A quick glance around the swirling, babbling crowd told him that no policemen were present inside the establishment. A Bavarian brass band, clad in dark lederhosen and consisting of trumpets and drums, was playing a melody of musical selections. Excellent.

He trudged ahead, though not steadily, occasionally grimacing and clutching a table for momentary support. The din of laughter from the crowd hurt his ears, boring in on him like bursts of thunder. Sliding the backpack from his shoulders, Steiner held it firmly by the cotton strap. He spotted an empty slot at a table, in between swaying guests holding aloft liter mugs filled with beer and foam. Making for the space and sucking in gulps of air, he collapsed onto the bench, causing a momentary frown from a teenage girl with whom he collided. Seconds later, a dour waitress in a red-and-green Trachten dress delivered another

round of beer in foaming liter mugs. To blend in, Steiner ordered
a beer, too.

Steiner now sat at the wooden bench, his backpack balanced
by his side. He felt a withering burst of exhaustion course through
him and placed his hands on the table as an anchor of stability.
He wanted to close his eyes but dared not do so, as the urge to
sleep was almost overpowering. He forced himself to breathe in
deeply, once, twice, and eased the backpack away from the others
crowded around the table.

Steiner unzipped the pack and inserted his hands into the
darkness within. He located the Plexiglas container by tactile familiarity, and removed the cover of the box containing a colony
of fleas. Quietly and nonchalantly, he placed the backpack unnoticed near the leg of the teenage girl he had bumped into. She
was drinking beer and shouting at another girl across the table
in a language that was not German. Steiner guessed that it was
Swedish.

The waitress appeared from the crowd and set Steiner's beer
on the table in front of him. The thought of drinking alcohol
made him nearly retch, but he placed his hands around the mug
with the blue-and-gold Hofbräu logo and feigned taking a sip.
The others at the table paid him no attention at all.

The teenage girl had braces on her teeth and long sheets of
blond hair. She giggled incessantly, which Steiner found irritat-
ing. The girl, her leg abutting the sack, would almost certainly
become infected, Steiner reasoned. Over the course of the next
half-hour it was likely that the others laughing and consuming alcohol at the table would be bitten by fleas as well, making
death by plague a virtual certainty. Steiner shrugged. It was all
the same to him.

That the victims were innocent of any crime was immaterial. Men and women, in his view, were no more than animated
pieces of beef. They had no moral worth, they were caricatures.
It was panic, and a screaming fear of death that was the point. He
knew, in fact it was his unshakable conviction, that he was infi-

nitely better than most men. Intellect was, in the end, the only
reality. Steiner gave the backpack a slight kick, nudging it more
firmly into place to infect the giggling girl and her friends. Soon
after, as the tumult of shouting and laughter at the Hofbräuhaus
rose, he left his spot at the bench behind and, in deference to the
grinding pain in his limbs and abdomen, slowly shuffled toward
the entrance.

* * *

At ten minutes after nine the next morning, a seventeen year old
girl named Hanna, with a pert nose and a cascade of blond hair,
fell into an empty seat in a second-class wagon of the Deutsche
Bahn at the Munich main train station. She was traveling with a
nineteen-year-old who had been with her yesterday amid the sing-
ing crowds at the Hofbräuhaus. They paid their fare at the ticketing office, and bought a paper bag of donuts, dripping grease, at a
nearby stand. Conversation was desultory as the two hauled their
duffel bags through the crowd of travelers, but Hanna supposed it
was due to the overindulgence in beer the day before. Ever since
she had woken up that morning, she had felt a pain in her head
and a slow, persistent complaint in her stomach.

The two young women took seats across from one another
and stared out the smudged window at the coming and going of
nearby trains, all of them done up in the red-and-silver colors of the
German rail. Hanna felt discomfort under her right arm, but tried
to ignore it. The pain would soon go away, she assured herself. Out
of boredom, she reached in the paper bag and plucked out a donut,
but after two half-hearted bites, she placed the remnant of donut in
the metal trash receptacle beneath the window. Hanna glanced over
at her friend and was surprised to see that she had fallen asleep, her
matted red hair hanging over her wool sweater.

There was a sudden burst of motion under her feet, and
Hanna looked out the window and saw that the train was slowly moving, picking up speed as it left first the train station and
then the city structures of Munich behind. Hanna yawned into

an open hand and then massaged her head, which felt as if it had been hit by a series of hammer blows. She would be very glad to reach her apartment in Stockholm, some twenty hours away.

* * *

Waldbaer stood at the entrance arch to the Hofbräuhaus under a sullen gray sky and shook his head. Dr. Mayerling was standing next to him, wrapped in a beige raincoat with the collar up and a cinched belt, a cigarette cupped in his hand.

"I never thought that I would see this, never," Mayerling remarked, shaking his head. The curved, stone arches leading to the main doors were crisscrossed with lengths of police tape with a placard announcing that the establishment was "closed until further notice due to health concerns."

Waldbaer watched enviously as Mayerling placed the cigarette to his lips, but willed himself not to smoke, and the packet of filtered tobacco stayed partly crumpled in the pocket of his jacket. "The city government owns the restaurant, and they're scared, Doctor. You know that much better than I do. Tobias Steiner wandered into the crowd and left a backpack full of plague contagion in there. Several people were infected, do you have the details?"

Mayerling took a prolonged puff on his cigarette, looked at it, and tossed it to the ground, grinding it into the wet concrete with the sole of his shoe. "Yes, I can tell you about it. From the reports we have, most of the victims were tourists, European tourists. There are two confirmed cases in Sweden, and one each from the Netherlands, France, and Luxembourg. A waitress from Munich is also affected."

"Are there any fatalities?"

"No, thank God, at least not yet. But all of the victims are hospitalized in critical condition. I don't want to sound cynical, but frankly there's damned little that the hospitals can do for them, other than limit their pain. We both know that the usual streptomycin and chloramphenicol antibiotics have no effect. In the past, if a person was given seven days of the antibiotic, they could be counted on to survive. Now they die. If you want to know my view, all of those tourists that Steiner infected received a death sentence."

Waldbaer felt a chill, and it was not from the temperature only. "What about an antidote of some kind? Isn't that a possible solution? Steiner is at the core of all this. Surely he's taken a chance on getting infected."

Mayerling slid both his hands into his raincoat. "Yes, an antidote is a distinct solution. I've been wondering much the same thing. Steiner is the scientist in all of this, and logically, he would have tested an antidote to the plague he was reengineering. If you're asking for my opinion, Kommissar, I would think that Steiner is immune to the disease. That way, even if he's bitten by a flea or contracts the disease through some other means, it will have no effect on him. If we had access to Steiner's antidote, we'd be well on the way to giving it to all of the infected victims, and maybe saving lives. The CDC in Atlanta is trying to develop an antidote now, based on the plague sample that was sent to them. But it could take months. The problem is, Kommissar, we need it now."

The detective swept a hand through his hair, wet with moisture from the spitting sky. "True, we don't have it. But it's something to think about. I think Steiner has it, and I think that Steiner is right here in Munich. He's in a third-rate hotel or a rundown apartment under an alias, but he's here. Maybe we'll get him. Or maybe death gets him first."

Mayerling nodded his head and looked at Waldbaer through his thick glasses, slick with rain. "I hate to say it, Kommissar, but my money is on death solving the Steiner problem. His cancer will kill him."

"Either way, Doctor, Steiner is doing what he set out to do. Look at this street."

Mayerling squinted through his glasses at the pedestrian walkway. The concrete and cobblestone passage separated the Hofbräuhaus from the adjoining buildings housing sushi bars, pretzel stands and the more traditional establishments selling Augustiner and Ayinger beer. Other than for two or three travelers, the route was empty. "Fewer people than usual."

"People are scared," Waldbaer said, "very scared. This place, Platzl, is usually a crowded scene no matter what the season. It's a tourist spot and popular with the locals as well. Only the fear of a communicable disease would empty it this effectively. Steiner can be quite content with the work he has done. If people continue to hide in their homes, and tourists in their hotels, this city's economy will sooner or later fall apart. The newspaper headlines and the radio reports are all the same: The plague, the Black Death, is in Munich, just as it was during the Middle Ages. And I suspect that Steiner is watching all of this on television somewhere in the city and laughing. And catching that son of a bitch is in our hands."

Mayerling said nothing for a moment. He removed his eyeglasses, rubbed them on his raincoat, and replaced them on his nose. "If there is a way of luring him out and catching him, Kommissar, I expect that you'll find it. You strike me as a man who likes to be in charge of events. You've probably got a plan already concealed in your head. That's what I think."

Waldbaer looked Mayerling in the eyes and smiled. "When I was a younger man, Doctor, I was a deer hunter. In the early morning hours, I would try to guess at where the deer would go, and why, and when. I learned to anticipate the deer's movement. You might say that I became the deer; I thought like him, I tried to reason like him. This is a trickier forest, though, and I see things only through fog and mist. The deer we are after is Tobias Steiner. And perhaps, just perhaps, I can set a trap for him."

STOCKHOLM

The room at Karolinska University Hospital in Stockholm was bathed in subdued autumnal light from the oversized window, the air warm and somnolent and piped in, ruled by a thermometer in the hermetically sealed space. The hospital cot at the center of the room had polished adjustable side rails, and a blue medical blanket covered most of the occupant. Magnus Nilsson stood straight and tall at the side of the bed, hands swathed in the pockets of his medical smock, and considered the girl lying in front of him.

"How long has she been this way?" he asked the balding, bearded man who wore a stethoscope around a thick neck and had a name tag attached to his unbuttoned smock that identified him as Dr. Burstrom.

The physician eased a hand over the pate where hair had once been. "That's the interesting thing. Miss Hanna Caris is the girl here, and she's seventeen years of age. She was taken ill and went to see a doctor two days ago, and he immediately called for an ambulance and had her brought here. When she was received into the hospital, Hanna had several symptoms that led us to conclude that she was the victim of Yersinia pestis, and had apparently contracted the disease when on vacation in Munich a few days ago. At the time she was brought to the hospital, she was much as you see her now. There was necrosis on the feet and hands, and, as you can see, under the nose. She had real trouble articulating, but managed to tell us that she was enormously exhausted and felt pain throughout her body. We tried to treat her with streptomycin, but it was clearly having no effect."

Nilsson went to the hospital bed and quietly took the girl's pulse with a plastic gloved hand, and sighed. "No. Antibiotics have been used dozens of times, here and in the United States, but this strain of the plague always overcomes the cure." Nilsson lowered his voice to a whisper. "Tell me, Dr. Burstrom, is it your opinion that the plague in this case will be fatal?"

Dr. Burstrom took time to stroke his beard before answering. "I cannot at the moment say that it will. She has no bubo anywhere on her body, not one. She seemed about to develop a bubo, but she did not. We placed her in an induced coma because, well, we didn't know what else we could do. But the induced coma seems to have stopped the progress of the plague, at least so far."

Nilsson looked at the girl's blond hair, efficiently taped back by a nurse. "I understand that there is another patient, a nineteen-year-old. She was brought here at about the same time that Hanna Caris entered the hospital. Both Hanna and she apparently traveled by train from Munich, where they'd gone together for a few days' recreation. Does she have the plague, too?"

Burstrom eyed the taller man. "We did have two patients, yes, and both had the plague. The other teenager died this morning, I'm afraid. We had her at first with a respiratory droplet, and then in an artificial coma as well, but she did not survive. She hemorrhaged, and there was nothing we could do. We were, in effect, helpless, entirely helpless."

Nilsson spoke in a low tone, as if to himself. "It's interesting, isn't it? Two teenage girls infected with Yersinia pestis in Munich. One is now dead, and the other lives. Both girls were severely infected and both showed signs of flea bites. Yet Hanna, the girl we see here, clings to her existence. She is fighting for her life."

Burstrom nodded agreement. "Yes, I know it's strange, but it's not new. Even in the Middle Ages and at other times throughout history when we've experienced a plague outbreak, there have been survivors. Some people were infected, apparently severely, and nonetheless recovered. This would seem to be a similar case. Maybe it has to do with the plague being reengineered. We lack the necessary information presently to make a judgment."

"Well, perhaps we can do something to give Hanna a fighting chance, whatever the odds. She is stable, which is exceptional under the circumstances. If you can give me just a bit of time to experiment with fluoroquinolones, we may have a course of action that might work, and might not. We are dealing with the world of the unknown here, Doctor."

"Have you ever seen a portrait of a plague doctor from the Middle Ages?" Burstrom asked. *Pest Meister* they were called, 'masters of the plague'. They were our predecessors in medicine.

The *Pest Meisters* covered their heads with outrageous and over-sized hats and wore goggles over their eyes and huge bronze beaks coated in perfume to protect their nostrils against infection from what was believed to be a disease that traveled on foul air. They spent their time dousing people who were victims of the plague with ointments. We can laugh about these plague doctors now. But, in fact, we are in the same position. When it comes to the plague, we know virtually nothing."

"You're right, Doctor," Nilsson said. "We fool ourselves occasionally, thinking that we've got superior knowledge, state-of-the-art medical machinery, and excellent medication. In a way we do, but we and the plague doctors have one thing in common. Just as they attempted, we are trying to save the innocent who have come into contact with the plague. In the end, I don't think that much more can be expected of us."

CHAPTER THIRTY

MUNICH

Munich International Airport had instituted quarantine procedures the previous day and, as Waldbaer had anticipated, all had not gone smoothly. Red Cross workers had pitched up white nylon tents in the main terminal to deal with passengers trying to return to New York, Miami, Washington, and Chicago. The lines for the mandatory blood test grew bloated as more and more travelers to the United States arrived at the terminal. Doctors and medical assistants explained that the results of the tests would not be ready for two days, at which time the traveler would have to return to the airport. The reaction was predictable; much shouting and shoving ensued and tempers snapped. Word about this situation at the Munich airport did nothing to lighten Waldbaer's mood as he sat in his office.

The picture throughout the rest of Bavaria was much the same. Work attendance was down; workers fearful that their places of employment were houses of contagion. The seasonal crowds of people at concerts, in pubs, and at public events had diminished markedly. A number of restaurants popular with tourists had closed their doors. Schools remained open, but parents were reluctant to bring their children, and many refused to do so. It was, thought Waldbaer, panic by degree, the slow death of functional civil society.

Television and radio, with clear taste for the sensational, reported the climbing number of people infected daily, and the hospitals were overwhelmed by the number of self check-ins. Hundreds of people were reputedly infected by the plague.

At least, Waldbaer reflected, the toll of victims was in the hundreds, and not, as well could have been the case, in the thousands. Still, the disastrous potential was present, and the disease could break out massively at any moment. It was, perhaps, only a matter of time.

He had telephoned the Munich police the evening before and proposed an action. The Munich police should aggressively check out every third-rate hotel and hostel in the city looking for Steiner. "It is at least disruptive, and should keep Steiner off balance," he said. "With luck, if he panics, we could arrest him. If not, we scare the hell out of him and maybe, just maybe, he makes a wrong move we can take advantage of." But that had been early last night and he had not heard back from his Munich colleagues, as he certainly would have had Steiner been arrested. He thought again of being a hunter, and Steiner the deer. He would flush the deer using beaters; people who banged drums and blew trumpets to scare the game into running through the forest. The Munich police would be efficient beaters. And he himself would be the hunter, with his weapon locked and loaded.

* * *

Tobias Steiner knew that in a normal world he would occupy a hospital bed and be on intravenous fluids and medications. But that was not the world he had made, nor the world that he wished for. It had taken him well over half an hour to rise from bed, his body greased in sweat. He cut himself shaving, the tremors in his hands now pulsed ceaselessly. With a flash of anger, he resolved not to shave again, not even every third day as he had taken to doing.

Uncharacteristically, Steiner was up before nine and squinted against the gray November light emanating from the window. The pane of dust-blemished glass was open, and Steiner shuffled over to it to slam it shut. As he gripped the rusting metal frame, he sighted movement on the street and stopped.

A green-and-white police car had pulled off the street into a parking space in front of the hotel, and two policemen had soon exited and were standing next to it. Their eyes seemed fixed on the small sign that said "Hotel Rhein." Zipping their leather jackets against the chilly morning air, the policemen sauntered into the entrance. "*Scheisse,*" Steiner groaned, supporting himself on the windowsill.

He had not expected to have to leave the hotel this quickly; it was his lair. There was no time to take his medication or to stuff his clothes into his remaining backpack. Hurriedly, he grasped the plastic-and-glass bio laboratory and sank it into the depths of the bag. He grabbed a cellophane bag of freebased crack cocaine as well, and zipped it into a compartment, and took four bottles of mineral water. He would have to move very quickly to escape the two policemen, Steiner knew, cinching the backpack onto his shoulders.

Steiner opened the door to his suite and pulled it shut behind him. The joints in his legs and ankles rocked with pain as he proceeded down the hall. Ignoring the elevator, he continued past it to the back stairs. He sensed that the policemen would be checking the hotel room by room, looking for him. Or, he thought, they might have a photograph, which was far more troubling.

Steiner approached the end of the hall and saw the stairs underneath a placard that announced "emergency exit"; the metal door was propped open with a worn rubber doorstop. Breathing sharply, he stepped forward and staggered down the concrete steps, lit from above by a bare light bulb.

The two policemen arrived at the door to Steiner's suite along with a reluctant and potbellied desk manager they had corralled in the lobby. The desk manager, a mat of slick hair pulled back in a ponytail, pointed at the door leading to Steiner's quarters, and whispered "If he's here, he's in there." The police signaled him to insert the master keycard into the door, drew their hand-guns, and crashed into the lifeless room.

Steiner reached the ground floor of the stairway and saw a faded sign that announced the lobby. Pausing for a moment, he considered the possibility that one policeman might still be stationed there. His head was aching as if it was being pressed in a vise, and he decided to take the chance. Leaning against the wall, he moved haltingly down the long corridor. When the reception desk came into view, Steiner rejoiced that it was empty.

A door opened automatically, dispatching Steiner onto the street, and he gratefully sucked in the cool autumn air. He started down the cracked sidewalk in front of the hotel, relieved to have gotten out undetected. Other pedestrians moved past him, bored and disinterested in his presence, and he paid them no mind. But Steiner's body was not functioning properly, and after progressing a few yards he was hit by a burst of pain from deep within. Groaning aloud, he began to fall but caught himself on the stone wall of a building, pulling himself to a standing position with both hands.

His body racked with labored breathing, Steiner took a moment to compose himself and allow the trembling to stop. Fumbling in his pockets with palsied hands he pulled out his sunglasses and shoved them onto his face. The pain continued to pulse within him, and Steiner looked around in an effort to orient himself. His glazed eyes caught sight of two towers of dark-red brick, capped with green bronze that formed onion-shaped cupolas. The domes, more than three hundred feet in height, were part of the Munich cathedral, located in the old quarter of the city. "Yes, I think I'll make a visit to the bloody church," Steiner hissed. He would head to the old city.

Even with many people staying at home for fear of contracting the plague, the heart of Munich was always bustling with life. He did not have long, he feared, and this excursion would likely be his last. He smiled through dry lips. "Behold, I am Death," he rasped before he wheezed out a dry, empty laugh.

STOCKHOLM

Dr. Magnus Nilsson sat on a stool in the isolation room of the Stockholm hospital. It was nine in the evening and the last tendril of sunlight had disappeared hours ago. A cold autumn night now reigned, and wind both persistent and frigid charged across the indigo landscape. There will be snow soon, Nilsson thought, and he dreaded the onset of a bitterly cold winter and of interminable months of snow.

He observed Hanna Caris, the patient sleeping silently before him. Although breathing through a clear plastic nasal tube, the girl's features appeared serene and peaceful. Her nose and mouth had stopped bleeding, and the monitors indicated that the condition of her organs was stable. Nilsson had ordered that Hanna be brought out slowly from the induced coma and had begun treatment with fluoroquinolones. He was guardedly content with what he saw and extremely content with what he didn't see.

Hanna had developed no buboes, for one thing. And the blackening of the hands, feet and nose had not advanced past the early stage; amputation would not be necessary. Since her arrival at the hospital, Hanna had been fed intravenously, and had not regurgitated. Although he could not be certain, Nilsson also suspected that her general pallor had reduced, her cheeks, at any rate, looked pink and healthy.

Nilsson watched as the girl turned her head slightly in her sleep. He realized that statistically, infected with a mutant plague that resisted medication, the girl slumbering comfortably before him should by all accounts be dead. And yet the plague had not taken her, due, it seemed, to the strength of her system. Hanna's girlfriend, infected along with her, had died in a mass of blood. Some unaccountably live, and some die, Nilsson conceded.

Something in the simple dichotomy of life and death gave Nilsson a start. How many victims of the plague had died in the last several weeks? More importantly, how many had lived? He knew that the disease was ferocious at its inception, and several people had become infected and suffered unenviable deaths. But what about the situation now?

Nilsson rose from his perch and walked to the corridor from the hospital room, deep in thought. He needed to collect all of the case histories from Europe and the United States. He reasoned that he should be able to chart statistically the lethality of the disease. Maybe there was something hidden there, some fact that they did not yet see or had ignored. He took his car key from his pocket, traced a finger over the Volvo logo, and hoped for a promising night at his office in the ECDC. The wind in the parking lot outside snapped at his legs and arms like an angry dog, but it did not matter. Nilsson did not even notice.

CHAPTER THIRTY-ONE

Tobias Steiner looked upward through a gray, spitting sky to where the massive brick domes of the cathedral disappeared into the mist. Closer to earth, the oversize, wooden doors in the arched nave swung open as a string of visitors and tourists entered, talking and gesturing. Steiner watched them for a moment, saw the door draw open again and decided to enter.

The interior of the cathedral was uncomfortably cool, and Steiner zipped up his jacket in response. He saw that at the far end of the cathedral expanse, close to the altar, several pews were taken up by visitors. A gray-haired figure in a green robe, presumably a priest, was occupied at the chancel, and Steiner guessed that he had stumbled upon a Mass in progress. He removed his baseball cap and stuffed it into a pocket of his jacket, and squinted at the wash of light flowing through the stained glass. The interior of the church was spare and devoid of the usual sculptures of saints that inhabited most religious buildings of the Renaissance.

Steiner felt a touch of dizziness seize him, and he made his way down the center aisle, grabbing the ends of pews in succession to balance him. He stopped for a second at an ornate monument of brown marble surrounded by life-size bronze likenesses of armored soldiers helmeted in the style of the late Middle Ages. It was the cenotaph of Emperor Louis IV, heir to the Holy Roman Empire, and a few tourists were gawking at it and taking pictures with their cell phones. Steiner paid them no mind. He was set on the much larger group of people occupying the pews toward the front of the cathedral. He moved forward cautiously, his progress marked by gnawing pain.

The litany of the Mass could be heard clearly now, a murmured few sentences from the priest serving as celebrant, and a louder, multi-voiced response from the gathered faithful. The priest was raising a glittering chalice high above his head. He watched as several of the attendees bowed their heads with closed eyes. With a sneer, Steiner pulled himself in to an empty pew immediately behind a group of ten or so people.

He sat, trying to regulate his breathing, as those in front of him knelt. Eyeing them more closely, Steiner saw that the group was Asian, in a collection of brightly colored windbreakers and various models of sport shoes. Their hair was uniformly a shimmering, shining black. Steiner guessed that they were from the Philippines. Excellent, he thought. If in the next few days these people were on their way to Manila, the plague might spread throughout Asia, too. It was a worthy selection. He undid his backpack, and hearing the absorbed, sibilant prayers of those attending the cathedral Mass, unlocked the Plexiglas cover of the box containing the writhing, infected fleas. He placed the box in a white plastic bag that he had also secreted in the voluminous backpack.

Steiner glanced furtively around to be sure no one was observing him. All eyes were focused on the priest. Satisfied, he placed the plastic bag on the floor and, with his foot, nudged the mass of plastic close to the kneeling legs of a woman in front of him. Steiner was confident that no one would see the plastic bag, or think anything of it if they did. It was, he reflected, the perfect crime. He had no doubt that he was engaged in murder, but that was of no consequence. With luck, the Catholics from the Philippines would become infected with the mutated plague. They would in time collapse, unaware of what was happening and spew blood and cough up their phlegm on others. It was, after all, what he wanted and had worked hard for. There was something exquisitely satisfying in sitting in an ancient Munich church and unleashing a scourge of pestilence upon the unknowing.

The priest reached the portion of the Mass when communion was served. Many of those who had gathered for the service rose to take part in the communal offering, hands clasped solemnly before them. Steiner rose as well, and took his backpack by the straps, tossing it over his shoulder. He felt unsteady again, his vision wavered, and he noticed he was sweating profusely. He felt a burst of pain from deep in his stomach and grimaced as hammer blows of unrelieved misery nearly made him groan aloud. Walking with the hesitant lurch of a drunkard, he shambled from the cathedral at a glacial pace, intent now on making one more connection before he died. He opened the cathedral door and breathed in the moist coolness of the air. As he did so, a song played in his head.

Oh, beloved Augustin,
All are dead.

STOCKHOLM

Dr. Magnus Nilsson was taken aback by the results on the lethality of the plague. He had asked the computer to crunch the numbers, and he looked at the results on the laptop screen, intrigued. He rolled his chair away from his desk and stared out the polished window of his office at the tangle of trees, nearly stripped of leaves, certain reminders of winter's approach.

The chronology of those patients in Europe and the United States who had contracted the plague was clear. There were over three hundred reported cases of the plague on both continents. The cases that had developed early on in Bavaria, in Prien, Munich, and Augsburg, had uniformly proven lethal. The same appeared to be true in the United States where five airplane passengers infected in Munich spread the disease by coughing or expelling liquid.

Although this initial phase was both ferocious and deadly,

something had changed, not all at once, but incrementally. Some of those infected with the plague unaccountably survived, including those who had coughed up blood and some who had buboes on various parts of their bodies. According to the reports, two paramedics from a Washington hospital were among the first survivors, and Hanna, the teenage girl occupying a bed in Stockholm, numbered among the most recent. As more reports of plague victims came in, however, Nilsson saw evidence of declining lethality in the disease. For every death by plague, two other victims survived. If one restricted the cases of infection to those reported in the last two weeks, three victims survived for every death.

Nilsson felt a burgeoning satisfaction at the statistics. The strain of the bacteria was attenuated, he judged. "This is not the Black Death, it's not the same thing by a long shot," he said out loud to the walls and to himself. The rate of death was in clear decline, and Nilsson suspected that he knew why.

The fleas released by Tobias Steiner carried his mutated Yersinia pestis. It stood to reason that some of the flees would have more of the inoculum, some less. Over time the bacterial load ejected by the fleas could even be diminishing. But more importantly, Nilsson conjectured, the genetic material of the bacteria had continued to mutate, resulting in decreased virulence. In other words, Steiner had failed to stabilize his experiment and mutations had continued such that in some cases antibiotics were starting to work. Steiner's mutated plague bacteria was no longer a mathematical certainty. The facts supported this.

The Yersinia pestis engineered by Steiner was indeed the same bacteria, the same genus and species, that caused the Black Death in the Middle Ages and the plague in Madagascar, but the strains were different. The Madagascar strain had mutated over the centuries with no human intervention, and Tobias Steiner's manipulated strain was now mutating further—most thankfully to a less virulent, more antibiotic sensitive form. It all fit, the strain of the bacteria was key to its lethality. Yersinia pestis from Madagascar appeared to be much less a killer strain of the plague than its ancient predecessor had been, explaining why the plague was not more of a problem in Madagascar.

Nilsson stood up and walked the few steps to the window where he watched the leaves driven down the road by a burst of wind. His thoughts turned to Tobias Steiner, who had reengineered and unleashed both the fleas and the plague. Steiner was an extraordinary medical specialist, perhaps a twisted genius, who combined book knowledge with practical field research. Steiner had been vastly clever in acquiring infected fleas from Madagascar and engineering the plague within to be resistant to antibiotics. But Steiner, despite his genius, was not infallible.

The 21st century plague that he had started was flawed. Steiner had doubtless thought that all of his laboratory fleas were virulently lethal, but that was an assumption. Steiner had no way of knowing that the Yersinia pestis carried by the flees would continue to mutate, that he had failed to control the mutation progress.

Nilsson cautioned himself that the danger of the plague had not disappeared, not by any means. Infection would still spell a death sentence in some cases. But it now appeared that getting to a hospital to seek treatment made considerable sense. Placed in isolation and treated with fluoroquinolones, about three out of four patients would respond positively to treatment. Maybe more in the future, but for now, there were still many patients who would have to be zipped into body bags.

Nilsson felt a surge of optimism run through him. He felt as if he had punched Steiner in the stomach. However guarded, there was reason for hope. Mindful of the different time zones, he would call Robert Hirter at CIA headquarters in Langley with the news, and then make a call to the perpetually frowning Franz Waldbaer himself.

DORFRAM

The rain clouds had skitted away during the night like a bad dream and dawn revealed a brilliant day as sunlight illuminated the alpine peaks and shimmered off of the yellow fir trees of autumn. A chill in the air warned that winter was taking up residence and persuaded Waldbaer to dress in a lined loden jacket suitable for the season.

He drove his Volkswagen down the road, working the stick shift with gloved hands, as he took in the terrain. The gently sloping hillside was taken up by tracts of farmers' fields, laced with a residue of dusty-beige cornstalks and yellow rapeseed. Turning slowly as the road curved, he saw a few stolid farmhouses of stone and aged wood and an array of rosebushes stripped of life for the season. The pavement gradually rose ahead of him and his forest-green car was surrounded by a tall and thick growth of trees on both sides of the road which seemed to stretch on for miles. Waldbaer spotted a patch of neglected ground up ahead and directed his car into the tumble of tall grass and dying weeds. He turned off the engine, reached for his cup of coffee in the beverage holder, and exited the vehicle.

He walked a few feet through the grass, felt his shoes pick up the dew, and squinted his eyes against the uncompromising, early morning sun. The crenellated silhouette of Schloss Winterloch was visible in the distance, as Waldbaer knew it would be, a windswept mass of ancient mortar and stone, crumbling slightly and discolored by age. He lifted the plastic lid off of the cup, saw it emit a rising twist of steam, and sipped a generous gulp of the warm liquid. He continued to stare at the castle, at the turreted towers and the keep. The castle keep, Waldbaer knew, was the tallest part of the fortress, meant to be a secure haven in times when the castle was under siege. With only a series of arrow slits substituting for windows, the edifice received little natural light. Within its walls, a series of lamps made up for the deficit.

It was to the castle that Steiner would return, Waldbaer reasoned. He did not know when, but it would have to be very soon. Steiner would have to return; he had spread the plague about as well as he could and he was dying, the young man's energy and enormous anger at life both winding down. The disease had thankfully not played out as Steiner wished; a telephone call from Magnus Nilsson in Stockholm confirmed that. Many of those infected were fighting back, something that Steiner could not have anticipated. Waldbaer also knew that Steiner would come to the castle at night, wrapped in the cocoon of protecting darkness. It was always so with those who were ruled by a malevolent mind. They expect to be shielded by the night.

Waldbaer again brought the cup of coffee to his lips and sipped deeply, savoring the gentle warmth that diffused through his body. He considered why Steiner was coming to the castle. Waldbaer closed his eyes for a moment of reflection. Steiner considers the castle to be his rightful home. It is an inheritance, after all, and Steiner believes it his right to claim the castle as his own. Steiner had lived a life of unbroken resentment. He would consider the castle a symbol of what was truly and rightly his.

The detective opened his eyes and took in again the outline of the castle, a massive and magnificent edifice against the mountain peaks behind it. There remained, he knew, what Steiner intended to do in the castle. There was only one possibility, given Steiner's demonstrated nature. The real reason for Steiner's return to the castle, quite simply, was to kill. How Steiner intended to kill, with dagger or pistol, bomb or arson, Waldbaer did not know.

The young man had unleashed a vast and lethal epidemic, killing at random those he did not know and could not know. Waldbaer had seen this indifference to death before; it was a warped moral order that perversely affected the criminal class of men. But in this final instance that the killer had saved until last, Steiner knew the person that he desired to kill, the person that Steiner avidly wished to precede him into the dark certainty of death.

But when would he come? Perhaps tonight in the hours when darkness draped around him like a concealing blanket. Or tomorrow night, or the night after that. But Steiner would come at last, that much was inevitable. Waldbaer smiled morosely; he would be there too on this evening, or on the following evenings. It was his opportunity to stop Steiner. And there was an obligation, he supposed, to save "Augustin" as well.

Waldbaer stretched, his bones giving a mild report of protest. It was the intrusion of advancing age, a note from nature that his best years were behind him and it did nothing to improve his mood. He pulled open the door of his Volkswagen sedan with a tug and lowered himself into the leather seat. The castle was ten minutes away at most by car, and he would put everything in its place, much as a hunter setting a trap for a wounded and crazed man-eating tiger.

THIRTY THOUSAND FEET ABOVE FRANKFURT

Robert Hirter cinched his seatbelt and locked it with an audible click as the Lufthansa Airbus passenger liner began the descent into Frankfurt. He had called Waldbaer on the encrypted phone and advised him that he was coming to Germany. "Avoid Munich airport, Hirter, it's an absolute shipwreck due to plague fears and the blood tests," was Waldbaer's terse warning. Hirter had decided to fly to Frankfurt, further north and several hours from Munich, and take a rental car to meet the detective in Bavaria.

The plane descended from thirty thousand feet, and Hirter felt a slight pressure take hold in his forehead. He wished he had brought aspirin. It was six-thirty in the morning and the sun illuminated a thick bank of gray cloud and, where the clouds ended, the flickering lights in villages below. Hirter looked for a glimpse of the River Main, but did not see it.

The businessman seated next to Hirter was studiously silent, but it had not always been so. For hours since the takeoff at Dulles, the man with thinning hair and a paunch had regaled his captive audience with details of his life and commercial dealings. Hirter had responded to the torrent of words with a smile or a nod, but Hirter's lack of communication merely signaled that the way was clear for a further verbal deluge. "You know, the plastic valves that we produce are damned good, first class, but the Germans don't want to admit it. We use plastic and resin and the Germans don't understand that it's as good as steel, maybe better." Hirter was thinking about the effects of the plague if the infection rate exploded, while his conversation partner was elaborating the benefits of plastic valves.

Midway over the Atlantic, the businessman, waving a glass of pilsner beer, had moved into an expansive soliloquy to his personal achievements. "I knew in high school that I had a career in management, and the teachers could see it too. So I took business courses in college, and, what do you know, I excelled. And my college experience, I can tell you, set me up for a career of damned successful sales." Hirter felt the tolerance draining from him. When the businessman asked his taciturn listener, "So, what do you do, anyway?" Hirter was ready.

"Me? Oh, if you mean what do I do that's interesting, I don't do that much really. I'm involved in espionage for the CIA, I'm a case officer. You know, spy versus spy, counterterrorism, weapons of mass destruction, covert action, that sort of thing. I played a bit of a role in stopping an al Qaeda terrorist at the Oktoberfest a while ago; in fact, I killed him. My current travel to Germany has to do with the Black Death, maybe you've heard of it. Boring as it is, after all, it's still a living." The wide-eyed businessman had been quiet since that time, and had sipped the remainder of his beer in silence.

The aircraft trimmed its wings and seemed to be moving more slowly now. With a glance out the window, Hirter saw the dark red rooftops of houses and commercial buildings come into view in the early morning sunlight. He felt a subdued, muffled shudder under his feet and knew that the landing gear had engaged. Moments later the jet skidded to a stop on the runway and turned toward the terminal. He had a five-hour car ride ahead of him, time enough to organize his thoughts. Hirter wondered how Waldbaer would react to his words.

SCHLOSS WINTERLOCH

The detective and the count walked at a leisurely pace through the Hall of Banners, both with their hands shoved into the pockets of their jackets. It was cold in the castle, which had no central heating, and Waldbaer had his loden tunic buttoned to the neck to ward off the chill. The two men walked through patches of darkness that paled gradually at the illumination provided by sconce lamps.

Count Winterloch frowned, his white hair falling in front of his forehead, eyes focused on the stone floor. "I am certainly not Augustin, Kommissar," he said. "It's so ridiculous, I could laugh. Tobias likes me, he respects me. To suggest that he would want to kill me is fully absurd. If anything, he desperately wants my counsel about confronting criminal allegations; he has asked my advice before."

Waldbaer grumbled a laugh. "Did Tobias ask your advice on unleashing the plague, on whether or not it was a good idea? No, he didn't. I'm convinced that he intends to kill you because it is the only thing that makes sense."

Winterloch stopped in his tracks and turned toward the detective. "Kill me! Kommissar, it's clear that you don't know Tobias."

"Oh, I think I do. To be honest, I think you've blinded yourself to his resentment. It simmers inside of him. In his note to the police, to me really, he mentions Augustin, from the old song that we all learned in school about the Black Death. The song libretto reads 'girlfriends gone' and that could be Gertrude Steiner, his mother. But the hatred, I suspect, is reserved for you."

Winterloch grinned. "Hatred? What hatred? If Tobias had wanted to kill me, he could have done it anytime."

Waldbaer shook his head. "No, he needed you. He needed your money most of all, and, by your own words, he helped himself to your largesse rather generously. I think that Tobias was entirely and utterly calculating in his relationship to you. What did you offer him? Frankly, nothing that he wanted. You did not offer him position. You did not offer him the respectability of the family name. To be blunt, money is about all that you offered him and so he needed you alive."

Winterloch glowered. "It most certainly was not."

"I am of a different opinion. You offered him the chance to finance his schooling and his specialized research, true. You funded the required travel to Madagascar and the onward trip to the United States. You paid for the laboratory equipment and perhaps, unwittingly for the alias identification as well. But, Count, you did not give him what he really wanted, what he intensely craved, and that was to be your successor and heir." Waldbaer waited for the explosion that he knew would come.

"What the hell do you know about Tobias, Kommissar Waldbaer? Nothing at all! I gave Tobias what most men do not have. Freedom and the ability to do what he wanted in life without worrying about the costs. He didn't have to worry about money to fund his pursuits; he had me to rely on. And he had this castle to come to anytime that he liked, for as long as it suited him; I granted him that. It's true that I don't know if Tobias very much likes me, we do not speak of these things, it's not our way. But he surely holds me in respect, I assure you. If he hated me as much as you seem to think, he could have done away with me a long time ago."

Waldbaer glanced up at the array of flags, bright splashes of color on silk that now accumulated dust. "We will disagree on my assessment of his motivation, Count, so be it. To my mind, Tobias Steiner wanted to be accepted into the family. He saw it as his right and his privilege. And he took the money you offered him, that is true enough. And he may, as you say, hold you in respect. But a man, if he is wise, often holds his enemies in respect, no? Like it or not, Steiner is your enemy. And like the Augustin in the old song, you have escaped the plague and are in good health. But make no mistake, Steiner is coming for you and he intends to settle accounts, by what means I do not know."

Winterloch, his face a mask of red, regarded Waldbaer with a hard stare. "We will disagree on that, Kommissar, but so be it. Tell me, do you intend to stay here through the night?"

Waldbaer swept a hand through his hair. "Yes. If you are in an upstairs bedroom, I'll locate myself down here on the main floor, somewhere with a view of the stone steps that Steiner will have to take to get to you."

"My personal habits are perhaps a bit unusual. I go to sleep very late as I have done for years. I have a collection of antique books and unpublished tracts that engage me, and I most often read until early morning. With a snifter of fine brandy, of course."

"Of course," agreed Waldbaer.

"I expect that I'll be over in the Great Hall tonight. You know where that is located. If you require anything, you can find me there. You may have a brandy if you wish."

"I won't disturb you, Count. And all that I require is Steiner. I will lodge here, in this mortuary of banners. And I'll be here all night, waiting to greet your son."

Winterloch looked steadily at the Kommissar, and his face did not betray emotion. "These banners are interesting, aren't they? They are the heralds of the German nobility, Bavarian, Saxon, and Prussian. Some of these flags are indeed dead relics, the families died out due to the attrition of war or for some other reason, and only the flag remains. Sooner or later, I will join their number. I am the last of the line, and I know it."

"You chose it, Count."

Winterloch smiled and dragged a tasseled loafer across the cold stone floor. "Yes, I suppose I did choose it, it was my decision. The bloodline goes to the grave with me. I am the last successor to Heinrich, the warrior knight. When I go, the long generational call of family ends forever. Like Heinrich, I will be buried in the chapel. With my passing, no harm can come to the family name."

Waldbaer studied the count. "*Après mois, le déluge.*" he said finally.

Winterloch raised his eyebrows. His gaze was distant. "Yes.

I suppose that sentiment is correct," and with that he nodded his head once and wandered off toward the Great Hall.

The deep, authoritative tone of the doorbell resonated through Schloss Winterloch bringing a domestic attendant in his sixties to the antique main door. Opening it, he was confronted by a man who was considerably younger, dressed in a brown bomber jacket. *"Grüss Gott, mein Herr.* My name is Robert Hirter. I was told by the police in Gamsdorf that I could find Kommissar Waldbaer here. I know that the hour is late."

The older man smiled but still maintained a degree of professional detachment. "It is late to be sure, sir, but I believe that the Kommissar is in the Hall of Banners. If you care to follow me, I'll try to find him, sir."

Winding a path that traversed several once impressive rooms decorated with oil paintings of past von Winterloch masters, the gray-haired servant came to a set of polished cherrywood arched doors and eased one of them open with a slight creak. He glanced inside, nodded, and turned to the visitor. "You will find the Kommissar in there, sir," he said before bowing and marching off to some other room of the castle.

Hirter proceeded down the five ceremonial steps, wondering at the array of silken rectangles high above his head.

"Well, well, do my eyes deceive me or is this Robert Hirter appearing, as usual, out of nowhere?" Waldbaer, arms crossed in front of his chest, faced the American across the room.

Hirter's features radiated into a smile. "It would be none other, Kommissar. I hoped to find you asleep at your post, and I'm a bit disappointed at my lack of success."

Waldbaer rumbled out a laugh. "I told you before, there is, alas, no rest for the weary or for police detectives. Now tell me, Hirter, how did you get here?"

"I called the always efficient Gamsdorf police to determine where you were, and then I used the GPS in my rental car. It was that simple."

Waldbaer took on a reflective look. "The modern world has every convenience, it seems. Perhaps this will be simple too, Hirter, if you don't mind my asking. Your unexpected appearance here means one of two things. Either you miss the intellectual illumination provided by my conversation, or you have some information for me. If it is the latter, the information is probably classified, no?"

Hirter returned the grin. "You exercise fine Jesuitical logic as usual, Kommissar. Bravo, in fact, you're right. I do have some information for you, and it is classified. But I do have the permission of my betters in Langley to brief you about it, orally. That is, if you're interested."

Waldbaer rocked on his heels and buried his hands deep in his pockets. "Ah, yes, the usual treatment, Hirter. Well, then, please have at it. I take it this has something to do with the Steiner investigation?"

"It does. You remember your trip to Berlin and your conversation there with Dr. Aleksandr Akulov? Well, it seems that Akulov may not have told you the complete unvarnished truth about his role in biological warfare research for the Soviet Union."

"I expected that he left a few details out," Waldbaer said with a thin smile. "But if your information is about Akulov's days in the Soviet Union, it is, I'm afraid, ancient history."

Hirter held out a cautionary hand. "Kommissar, I'll let you decide what's relevant, but it has to do with Akulov's past on the Soviet weaponization team."

"And what are your sources exactly?"

It was Hirter's turn to smile. "You know the rules, Kommissar, the Agency doesn't reveal the names of its sources. But I can tell you this. The information is from another Russian scientist who worked on Akulov's team. He was also a friend of Akulov, or more accurately, a drinking companion. According to this source, Akulov was very active in the Soviet weaponization of swine flu and avian flu, as well as anthrax. Not only that, but Akulov had also spent considerable research time on the plague. Then the Soviet Union collapsed, and Akulov headed west and eventually landed a job at the Free University of Berlin."

Waldbaer shook his head and shrugged. "He told me that he had not worked on the plague as a weapon. He said he would have refused the order, as the plague was a disease that could kill indiscriminately."

Hirter laughed, his mirth reverberating off the walls of the hall. "Frankly, Kommissar, all of the Soviet Union's biological weapons could kill indiscriminately."

Waldbaer nodded and stared up at the array of flags hanging above his head. "Yes, I am prepared to believe that. So Akulov lied. But no one is going to prosecute Akulov for his actions over twenty years ago due to the statute of limitations. More to the point, did your source say anything at all about Steiner and Akulov?"

"He did mention Steiner and Akulov, yes. According to the source, a few years ago Steiner offered to pay Akulov a substantial sum of cash to learn how to mutate the plague to make it resistant to medication. The offer was readily accepted. Steiner carefully reviewed the information that Akulov provided and was very happy. Akulov, by the way, is apparently an alcoholic and a gambler. He reportedly blew the money on drink, prostitutes, and casinos, in that order. And one other thing, before I forget. After his interview with you, Akulov must have felt he was on thin ice and might be picked up by the Berlin police. He vacated his Berlin apartment and headed east, probably back to Mother Russia."

Waldbaer sighed, and was not surprised to see his breath form like a specter in the darkened hall. "It was to be expected. I thought that Aleksandr Akulov might feel rather uncomfortable after my time with him. There's not much that I could have done to prevent his going to Russia. There is no police warrant on him nor is he wanted by Interpol. Akulov, as you say, is a chronic alcoholic and so his use for us would be limited, at best. Your source has told us all that we need to know, Hirter. Akulov was a man for sale; he was consumed by avarice. He gave Steiner the scientific details that Steiner wanted in return for money. Steiner used the information, and brought a mutated plague into being. That is the situation that we have and Steiner, and to a lesser degree, Akulov, are the guilty parties."

"We can forget Akulov, he's headed to Russia, and in a way he doesn't concern us any longer. Steiner is the man we want."

Waldbaer nodded in agreement. "That's why I am here, Hirter. Steiner has to come here; he has to come to this place. He wants to come here, it's part of his plan. He intends to kill Winterloch. And I intend to stop him, and put an end to this episode."

Hirter glanced about at the unmoving banners, gazing at one of brilliant blue which displayed a sword held in a yellow mailed fist. "I'd like the satisfaction of helping you, but I'm under strict orders to make this trip as quick as possible."

"We live in a hectic world, Hirter, perhaps one of our own making. Your CIA managers are anxiously braying for your return, the authorities in Berlin are screaming about the plague, and airport officials are moaning over the economic catastrophe caused by a quarantine of the Munich airport. But people will always find something to whine about, no?"

Hirter looked at the worn stone floor for a moment before answering. "You're right. Life is full of deadlines and demands. I've delivered the message that I was instructed to relate. Now I should get to Frankfurt and catch the next flight to D.C. But, as luck would have it, I've taken unaccountably ill. I'm sadly grounded for a day or two. And that means, by the way, that I'm at your disposal, Kommissar."

Waldbaer raised his eyebrows in mock surprise. "What? Lying to your superiors? How can you possibly live with yourself? Be that as it may, Hirter, I have a use for you. You can cover my back, I trust you. I have the police in Gamsdorf on call, but they're fifteen minutes away. Perhaps you could remain somewhat closer."

"My pleasure," Hirter said, "but tell me, what do you expect to happen? If Steiner is alive, he's got to be deathly ill."

Waldbaer's eyes were cast in shadows. "He's very much alive. He wants to finish what he started, and he's driven by his own approaching death. He intends to put an end to Winterloch, once and for all. That happens here, in this place. To Steiner, that is poetic justice. He may be sick, he may be weak or debilitated, but Steiner will make it into this castle, of that much I'm sure. He'll try to murder the count. In a demented way, he means to avenge his own death."

"Do you intend to kill Steiner?"

"I am a simple policeman, Herr Hirter. I am sworn to uphold the law, and that I will surely do. I intend to bring Steiner to justice, if the circumstances allow. If Steiner threatens my life, or that of Winterloch, I will kill him because I will have no choice. It's as simple as that. But speaking frankly, I do not think there is a breath of a chance that Steiner will surrender."

"If he makes it to this place then I don't think that Steiner will surrender, either. It's just not in the cards. But there is good news, and it has to do with the mutated disease. The plague seems to be getting less lethal than it was at first, and it is spreading less rapidly. Containing the disease is the main thing, and it appears that we're winning that battle."

Waldbaer began to walk across the Hall of Banners, thrusting his hands into the voluminous pockets of his trousers. "I see that Nilsson has informed you, just as he did me. Yes, it's good news. It means that Steiner, or Akulov, or both, rather made a mess of it. Thank God for that. It means that when Steiner finishes spreading the plague aggressively, the disease will, over time, die out on its own. If Steiner realizes that he's failed to unleash a pandemic, his ego is likely to implode. Maybe he'll hang himself. But I fear that because resentment is driving him, Steiner is going to be even more determined to finish things off with Winterloch."

Waldbaer opened a latticed wooden door that led from the hall to a long corridor sparsely lit and decoratively finished with an array of antique candle stands, benches and armoires. "As a policeman, I like to prowl about. This castle seems as endless as it does timeless. But this is a dusty museum, Hirter, not a home. There is no intimacy to it. No normal person in his right mind would want to live here."

Hirter threw out a laugh. "You mean the castle is not to your taste, Kommissar?"

Waldbaer growled a reply. "It should be to no one's taste. In ancient times it made an element of sense to live in a castle; it was secure and it could not be easily stormed. The world back then was a snarling, hostile place, and it was good to be protected by strong fortress walls and barred doors. But those days are long gone. Families lay claim to these heaps of stone without any reason, mindlessly. Having a castle is much like having a garage; it's a place to store unwanted furniture."

"You're forgetting suits of armor, Kommissar."

Waldaer nodded. "Exactly. And suits of armor, treasures from the past, are collected as if they're butterflies. The past is the past, Hirter, it is a game that is played out. The barons, and knights and counts that inhabit these crumbling castles did not slash and hack their way to the German nobility, their ancestors did, and the only thing the contemporary nobles do is pay to keep the castles up. It's the same with Schloss Winterloch. The count is independently wealthy but he invests a sizable fortune in keeping this place up. For what? Prestige or family honor? It's laughable; maintaining a castle celebrates the conceit of man."

"Well, Kommissar, I didn't realize that you held such passionate views on the nobility. It should teach me never to make assumptions. You know, I do believe your views rather reflect the thinking of Karl Marx."

Waldbaer glanced sternly at the CIA officer and narrowed his eyes. "I'm no intellectually effete Marxist. Those people know far less than anybody else. But now you know how I feel about the count and his precious castle. And it's relevant to the case. Steiner is Winterloch's son. Because his mother was not from the nobility, Winterloch would not marry her, don't forget that. Steiner went through life feeling disowned, as indeed he was. Winterloch in many ways is as guilty of hubris as his son is guilty of murder." Waldbaer stood silent, brushing a hand through his hair. "But, in the end, we have to protect him because this is a nation of law, not a nation of viewpoints, Hirter, of which, by the way, I have many."

"No problem," Hirter said with a smile. "Listen, Kommissar, you may be up all night, but I require a little sleep, especially after the plane trip. I'll find a chair or something, there's plenty of furniture around here."

Waldbaer swept one hand like a supplicant before him. "Foolish of me, I apologize. The Hall of Banners, where we just were, has some couches that might suit your needs. You doubtless have jet lag. But I imagine that you sleep like a cat, Hirter, and spring up alert with feline instinct at a moment's notice."

Hirter began the trek back toward the hall they had just departed. "I don't know about that. But I expect that I will sleep like the dead. If you find that you need me, just bellow at the top of your lungs."

Saying not a word, Waldbaer raised a hand above his head and walked toward the Great Hall.

STOCKHOLM

Magnus Nilsson watched the girl carefully, with the eyes of a professional observer. Hanna took a hesitant step from the hospital bed, her hand gripping the bedside table for support.

"I feel sort of dizzy," she whispered.

"Yes. You have been lying down for days on end, and your body has to get used to standing up. It's natural to feel a bit dizzy. Now, I want you to try to walk over to me." He crossed his arms over the white tunic.

The girl brushed strands of her long blond hair over her shoulder and took a step forward, and then, more confidently, another step, followed by another. After some halting movement, she found herself next to Dr. Nilsson and looked questionably at him. "How did I do?" she asked.

Nilsson flashed a smile. "You did perfectly. You're on the road to good health, that's clear. Tell me, Hanna, how do you feel?"

"I feel better, I don't have that constant pain inside of me, not any more. I remember that everything hurt, and I had absolutely no energy. I felt awful for a while, like I was going to die."

Nilsson's demeanor was objective, his voice soft. "If I may say so, you were in a very bad state when you were brought to us. You were bleeding internally, and we thought there was a good chance that your organs would shut down. But they didn't, and now you're recovering. You are a strong girl, Hanna, and you beat the disease."

Hanna cast a glance downward at the floor and spoke in a low voice. "But my friend didn't make it, she died."

Nilsson brushed a wisp of the girl's hair from her forehead and spoke gently. "No, she didn't make it, and we are all very sorry. We still don't know exactly why she died. You were both infected with Yersinia pestis, that much is certain, but you lived and your friend died. We imagine, but cannot yet prove, that the flea that bit you and transmitted the disease carried a weaker dose of the illness than the flea that bit your friend. And perhaps your body is more resistant to communicable disease than was the case with your friend. We will know what the answer is in time. Now the most important thing is to get you healthy again. I'm going to prescribe a little walk each day, and soon we'll have you walking throughout the whole hospital. In about a week you can go home and pick up your life as it's always been. We are tremendously glad, Hanna, that you proved stronger than this disease."

The girl looked at Nilsson, face still pallid, and, with a smile that hinted at embarrassment, she kissed him on the cheek.

Nilsson did not know quite what to say. "All right. Time to

rest, Hanna. I'll see you again tomorrow, now I must get back to my work."

He left the hospital isolation room behind him. There were many things that he did not choose to tell Hanna, he admitted, as he did not want to frighten her. Chief among them was the fact that all the doctors at Karolinska University hospital had been convinced that Hanna would die. She refused. A growing number of plague victims were showing resilience, both in Europe and in the United States. The plague seemed to have peaked in its lethality, and that alone was a godsend. Steiner had put much effort into mutating the disease, into making it resistant to normal antibiotics. But he had failed to make the plague more robust or the infection more deadly. In fact, human biology, hygiene, and resilience had made the plague less lethal than centuries before.

Nilsson stole a glance out of an oversized window at the funereal autumn scenery, gradually waning in the pale November light. He mused about Steiner's reaction to the news about the reduced mortality and morbidity of the plague; the media were already carrying items on it. He predicted that Steiner would at first be astounded by the news. He would doubtless be thrown into a paroxysm of rage and despair over his failed plans to replicate the Black Death of the Middle Ages as he had intended. He might attempt to reengineer the disease further, but death would take him away before that could happen. The Swedish doctor hoped that Steiner was dead already.

NYMPHENBERG, SUBURB OF MUNICH

He was shaking as if palsied, and it was not from the relentless disease alone. Steiner had just taken a newspaper from its distribution box near the park bench on which he was sitting and shook it open, anxious to read about the further spread of the plague. As he did so, he began to mutter "No, no, no, this can't be true." With a spiking heartbeat he tore the paper to shreds. Moments later, he willed himself to calm down and he sat on a worn bench in a tree-lined park in the Nymphenberg suburb of Munich, the crumpled and torn newspaper by his side. He had at first read the article on the plague with disbelief. "MORE PLAGUE VICTIMS REFUSE TO DIE," ran the headline.

It recounted the individual stories of those who had been infected by the plague in Munich and had boarded planes for the United States and for the Philippines. Invariably, the victims were sickened, some of them fatally. But by no means all of them. Many of the ill had not succumbed to death. The article cited a number of cases where those expected to die simply did not. The fluoroquinolone class of antibiotics was becoming effective. The number of survivors among victims of the plague, the article suggested, was increasing on a daily basis.

Steiner let out a moan, and his mouth felt enormously dry. He rummaged through his backpack until he located a plastic water bottle and he downed several gulps of alpine mineral water. Wiping his lips and looking about the park for any observers he regarded as suspicious, he saw no one and closed his eyes for a moment. He desperately wanted to sleep but steeled himself against the seductive blackness.

He had unleashed the plague hoping to replicate one of the worst outbreaks in history, matching the devastation of the Black Death which had killed one-fourth of the population in Europe. But Steiner now realized that repeating history was not to be. Perhaps, he reflected, it was the result of arrogance on his part, perhaps he should have tested the plague for genetic mutations. Still, he consoled himself, he had thrown Germany, if not the continent, into hysteria. Hundreds of people had died, and Munich airport had all but shut down, a sure sign of panic.

Steiner opened his eyes, squinting at the intrusion of sunlight. There was little more that he could do. It was too late now, he realized with self-reproach. His vectors of contamination—the infected rat fleas—had been abandoned in the hotel. He could have used the fleas to spread the plague further but, he concluded grimly, he no longer had the strength for it, and the energy he retained was ebbing fast. Steiner decided to take his pulse and lifted his wrist, placing a hand around it. He sighed in relief; his pulse was normal. But the normal pulse rate was not going to last long. Steiner now gave himself a few days of life at most, maybe a week, the relentless cancer was getting him. It was time to finish what he had planned.

With a grimace that did nothing to alleviate the pain, he lifted himself from the bench. He removed his baseball cap and ran a hand over his shaven head and down his cheeks, brittle with a few days' growth of beard. Even with a photograph, the police will not find him. He would take a train to Rosenheim, about an hour's ride from Munich, and there arrange for a taxi to take him to the vicinity of the castle. It would end as it should, Steiner assured himself with a burst of confidence. He lifted the backpack to his shoulders, let its weight settle against his shoulders and spine, and groaned though his teeth. There is not much time, he told himself, but there is enough, just enough. A smile etched itself on his face.

Oh, beloved Augustin, Augustin
Everyone's dead.

CHAPTER THIRTY-TWO

It had been an endless night, and entirely quiet. Waldbaer had, despite himself, dozed off, first propped against a paneled wall, and then, more permanently, in an unyielding chair. The count had eventually retired to his room on the second floor of the castle, and the policeman had found Hirter fast asleep with closed eyes and an open mouth, in the Hall of Banners. Gently, the detective roused his American guest.

Waldbaer and Hirter now stood on the sloping and thick-dewed lawn in front of the castle, having organized cups of black coffee with the kitchen help. The early morning mist still concealed the pine forest behind a wall of gray in the distance but was slowly lifting. Waldbaer shivered against the cold and took a long sip of coffee, feeling its welcome warmth course through him.

"Last night was not the night, alas. Steiner did not appear. Winterloch went to bed at three in the morning. Apparently, that time is not unusual for him. I imagine he is sleeping still."

Hirter moved a shoe through the wet grass, feeling the cool moisture. "Maybe Steiner is dead, maybe the cancer has killed him."

Waldbaer shook his head and looked out at the terrain. "No, Steiner is still alive, and he's out there somewhere. It's a feeling that I have, and I've learned over the years to trust my feelings. He will show up tonight, or the next night. He has to conclude things with a murder here. I have no reason to doubt it."

Hirter took a gulp of coffee and looked pensive. "And just for the sake of argument, what if he doesn't?"

"Steiner will come, rely on it. He manipulated the plague against the innocent to express in a physical way his rage against the entire world. And he intends to murder Winterloch for rejecting him and having abandoned his mother. Steiner now knows from the media that the plague did not work with the anticipated results. He has killed hundreds of people, upwards of a thousand could die before this is over, but he is not the grim reaper wielding the Black Death like a scythe. With Winterloch, Steiner does not intend to fail. He intends to see the lifeblood run out of the count before Steiner himself dies. But he doesn't realize that we'll be waiting for him."

Hirter was silent for a moment, and when he spoke, his words formed wisps of breath against the chill air. "I can't stay long, Kommissar. That would be pure disobedience. The German government doesn't even know that I'm here."

"Hirter, if it makes you feel better, feel free to consider me the German government in the flesh. But I do understand the sensitivity of your position. You are free to leave at any time; you have been of assistance."

Hirter nodded, holding the porcelain cup of steaming coffee in both hands. "I can swing one more night without being called home, Kommissar. I would dearly love to see this thing brought to closure and to report personally back to the CIA that Steiner has been arrested. The medical situation with the plague in the states is being handled by the NCDC, and if we can bring Steiner down, that would be a very fine end indeed."

Waldbaer finished his coffee in a long draw, swiping at his lips with the back of his hand. "That's marvelous, Hirter. The percentages are with us, I wager. Steiner cannot afford to wait long and he knows it, the clock is ticking within his own body. There is a crescent moon tonight, and Steiner may think that it will mask his approach. We will have the same drill as last night. Stay awake and alert and wait. Which reminds me, Hirter, do you have a firearm with you?"

"No, but I won't require one. Steiner has one foot in the grave. I'm sure that I can handle him."

Waldbaer looked directly at Hirter and raised an eyebrow in silent reproach. "You must know what you're doing, so suit yourself. I don't think that Steiner intends to become a police prisoner and he may be armed. Make of that what you will. I have a Glock, and that will have to do."

"I'll be okay without a firearm," Hirter said with a shrug of his shoulders. "I'm always obliged to rely on the impressive professionalism of the German police, Kommissar."

Waldbaer nodded and said nothing, feeling the comforting weight of the semi-automatic in his shoulder holster.

DORFRAM

The beige Mercedes taxi flicked on high-beam headlights as the driver shifted gears and the diesel-powered engine responded with a subdued growl. It was past midnight, and Steiner had hailed the taxi at the Rosenheim train station after traveling from Munich by rail. The thin wraith of a driver, about sixty years old with a diamond earring, chewed a stick of gum to ward off the boredom. The taxi rounded a curve and the headlights peered into the spectral growth of brush and pines in the tree line near the road. "We're almost there," the taxi driver said in a monotone, snapping his gum.

"Very good, pull over at the bus stop up the road," Steiner instructed.

Moments later the car pulled onto an asphalt parking apron, empty except for a round yellow sign designating it as a bus stop. The driver, seeing no one around to meet his passenger, seemed puzzled, but he punched a button that provided a digital fare. "That will be fifty-seven euros. Do you want a receipt?"

Steiner fondled the two-foot length of wire coiled in his

hands. Seated directly in back of the driver, he looped the garrote over the leather seat and yanked the wire tight around the driver's neck. The startled man wheezed loudly in a vain attempt to get oxygen into his lungs, and his hands pounded the roof of the car in a staccato frenzy. Steiner eased forward on the seat and pulled the wire tighter. "Now that you mention it, I don't think I'll be needing the receipt," he rasped. He could see the driver's wild brown eyes in the rearview mirror and he yanked the cord to the breaking point, severing the skin on the man's neck, unleashing a torrent of blood. In fifty seconds it was over. The driver's hands slowly descended to the sides of his body, and the eyes still remained open, motionless and unseeing.

Steiner let go of the garrote, letting it fall to the floor of the taxi. Opening the rear passenger door, he steadied himself before climbing out, cursing the pain that coursed through his body. The engine was purring loudly, causing him to open the driver's door and turn off the ignition, shutting off the lights as he did so. He shut the door but did not lock it. Someone would find the corpse in the morning, he anticipated, but that did not bother him in the least, in fact, it rather amused him.

His target was over a mile away, along a path through the forest. He pulled a flashlight from the pocket of his nylon jacket and clicked the metal cylinder on. He moved his arm and a spot of illumination cast the row of pine trees in a somber monochromatic light. Groaning, Steiner took two steps forward, steadied himself, and closed his eyes. Ignore the pain, and concentrate on what must be done, he ordered himself. There is just one thing left to do, one final thing. He breathed in the chill mountain air. Seeing where the path entered between the trees ahead, he trudged in that direction with the certainty of a sleepwalker.

SCHLOSS WINTERLOCH

Rheinhold von Winterloch wondered where all of the years had gone as he watched the flames consume a piece of oak that popped and hissed in reproach. His hair had been white, it seemed, for decades. He did not feel particularly old, or particularly weary, but then, the feelings of youth had quite evaded him. He had, he thought, always felt middle aged. He had ten good years ahead of him, perhaps even twenty, but death did not frighten him. He did not really believe in God, but then again, he did not understand theology, or, for that matter, the universe.

He raised the carved Czech crystal beaker to his lips and took a tentative sip of the brandy; the liquid felt warm and comforting. He gave a slow nod of deference to the portrait of Heinrich, gazing sternly down on him. Winterloch pushed aside the text he had been reading and closed the book cover gently. *Knights in the Time of Karl the Great*, it proclaimed and was emblazoned with the image of a helmeted, visored knight waving a great broadsword above his head. With a smile, the count realized that the knight could well have been Heinrich, his ancestor and the first of the Winterloch counts. He took another cautious sip of brandy, not wishing to be drunk, but enjoying the plateau between absolute sobriety and weak-minded besottedness. That was, he contemplated with a sigh, his standard evening ritual, and had been for a good two decades.

The Great Hall was the heart of the castle. Located at the very center of the fortress the hall was the first room to be completed in the sprawling vastness of stone. Its length and breadth were enormous and it could hold a hundred people or more. The room had been paneled and redone two centuries before and a veneer of once fresh redwood had long ago darkened to ebony. The presence of long, straight panels of aged wood gave the chamber a more intimate look, enhanced by the roaring flames in the oversized fireplace and the fleeting reflection of the blaze.

Winterloch rose from the long oaken desk and stood straight and tall in his russet leather hunting jacket and black shirt. He stared up at the wall where the portrait of Heinrich hung, looking balefully out at a suspicious world. Winterloch considered for a moment that it was the Black Death which had killed his predecessor, the choking pestilence having taken him away in a paroxysm of rotting flesh and a sea of his own putrid blood. Death in the Middle Ages, it seemed, was often less than kind.

Winterloch turned his thoughts to the present, and to Tobias. If what Kommissar Waldbaer said was true, then Tobias was a mass murderer, nothing less. But it seemed impossible, an insane fantasy, as Winterloch had never seen any evidence of Tobias' malevolent side. He reflected a degree further and was troubled. Tobias had, it was certain, made his professional reputation on the research of communicable diseases such as the plague. He had done practical work on the plague in Madagascar, and Winterloch had footed the bill. And then the boy had announced that he was traveling to Florida, though, come to think of it, the reasons given were a bit obscure. Winterloch had no reason to be concerned at the time, why should he? Kommissar Waldbaer darkly hinted that Winterloch should have known that something was wrong, but here the policeman went too far.

Winterloch leaned back on the oak table and held the snifter in his hands like a chalice, tilting the alcohol back and forth, watching the liquid run slowly down the sides of the glass. The truth was that Winterloch did not know what Tobias was doing in Florida, and he did not care to know. His relationship to his son had always been distant, it was his nature, he decided. Winterloch had assumed the Florida trip was work related because of the considerable checks he had been asked to write. "Medical research and related expenses" was all that Tobias had explained in an email. But that was Tobias' preference as well; he was parsimonious, even terse, with words.

Winterloch felt the chill in the air of the hall and took another sip of the amber liquor to warm his insides, closing his eyes for a moment. It occurred to the count that he did not really know his son, even after all of these years. He had opened his wallet, but not himself by any means. Tobias did not know it, and the topic was never raised in conversation with the boy, but, Winterloch reflected, his mother was a limited woman in many ways.

She had been pretty, and willing, and seductively attractive, it was true, but her familiarity with drugs and a long line of men was an addiction. Winterloch faulted himself for having fallen for her, even if the affair had been temporary and undisputedly physical. Gertraud had seemed new and refreshing, like an alpine shower in the summer, but this had been illusion. Gertraud had just been a small girl from a big city, and Winterloch had made his mark with her and gotten her pregnant. She took money from him, and then, without recrimination and without a word, she had drifted out of his life. Winterloch had not made too much of it, and, from that time on, had concentrated mightily on increasing the family fortune. He was more successful than he imagined he would be with making investments and quietly acquiring German businesses.

It was many years later that Tobias had appeared, young, fresh-faced and intense, at the castle gate. Winterloch had by that point decided, despite Tobias' pleas, that neither he nor the castle would have an heir. He, Rheinhold von Winterloch, would be the last to carry that ancient family name. He was the last of the clan.

Winterloch wondered if the Kommissar was right, if Tobias, through some process of reasoning that he could not understand, meant to kill him. It seemed absurd. Tobias had always been correct to him, even deferential. Even if the boy had perversely murdered others, it seemed quite impossible to think that Tobias contemplated patricide. It was a horrible thought, and it unnerved him. Draining his glass of the amber contents, Winterloch looked up at the portrait of Graf Heinrich staring down at him. I wonder what his advice would be, Winterloch thought. What would he say about Tobias? He ran a hand through his mane of white hair and decided to pour himself another drink.

THE DORFRAM FOREST

The mile along the uneven forest path had taken him forever and he had stumbled and fallen more than once over the protruding roots of trees. He had leaned against a damp, moss-covered boulder at one point, rudely discharging the meager contents of his stomach. He had paused only a minute to catch his breath after wretching; he dared not rest a second longer.

Steiner squinted through the darkness and saw the thick forest of pines begin to thin up ahead. Pointing the flashlight beam at the ground, he noted the terrain becoming more even as well, the footpath tramped deeply into the verdant earth. He stopped for a moment to get his bearings, and saw a short distance in front of him the wall that he had sought, twelve feet in height, made of boulders and chipped stones. The wall was an original work from the twelfth century and surrounded the castle captured within at roughly one hundred yards. Steiner had known of the wall for several years, and had discovered it, crumbling in parts and thickly lined with trees, in leisurely walks around the castle estate. It was to the wall that he now silently moved. Reaching it, he glanced upward at its looming height, looking for the telltale trace of a turreted tower. The wall seemed jet black against the dark-blue sky, and Steiner easily made out the form of the mortar-and-stone buttress, once intended for defense against Swedish raiders but abandoned centuries ago.

He stayed within reach of the wall, even touching its moist stone surface with his outstretched arm. When the tower rose directly above him, he let the flashlight play against the ground. His feet kicked at wet mounds of fetid leaves and grass, brushing them away in a dark heap. At first he did not see anything, save the dark earth and the writhing forms of sightless worms. Steiner gingerly dragged his foot against the loose, moist dirt, until it made unmistakable contact with an old and worm-eaten wooden rectangle below a few inches of earth.

Dropping painfully to his knees, Steiner smoothed away the sediment and the smattering of small stones until a door was visible. "Very good," he mumbled to himself, suppressing a cough deep in his lungs. The flashlight beam illuminated a rusting metal handle attached to the rotting wood, and Steiner yanked it toward him with force. The door groaned, and then yielded, and a cascade of pebbles fell into the threshold below with a subdued clatter. The flashlight beam revealed a primitive ladder leading to the corridor of dry earth some seven feet below.

Reaching for the door held above his head, Steiner's hands felt along the wood until coming into contact with a burlap bag, carefully taped into place by several firm strips of duct tape. Removing the earth-stained tape, he unwrapped the folds of burlap containing its concealed treasure.

The pistol contained in the burlap did not shine, its shape was burnished a dull metallic gray. The Luger P08 was considerably old, having been manufactured in 1911; its date of production was stamped on the metal of the weapon. Steiner knew that it was a durable and reliable piece of German machinery and contained an eight-round magazine of nine millimeter parabellum bullets. He had secreted the package here a year ago during a visit from Berlin. Steiner let a smile flash crookedly across his exhausted face. He would use one antique to kill another antique, there was justice in that. There was one more metal item in the burlap sack, and he pocketed that as well. Breathing deeply, he grabbed the ladder in both hands, balancing the flashlight, and entered the damp tunnel; he knew where it would take him.

SCHLOSS WINTERLOCH

Waldbaer was silent, his eyes on the ceremonial double door that served as the castle's main entrance. Hirter was there as well, careful to say nothing to challenge the policeman's assumption that tonight would likely be the night when Steiner would appear, intent on murdering his father. Still, Hirter had more than his share of doubts.

"What's the time," Hirter asked, feeling it courteous to engage in conversation.

Waldbaer regarded the CIA officer with a dark stare, and glanced at his Longines watch. "It is eleven o'clock. And it is much like last night, I dare to say. The count is in the Great Hall, fully at home among mountains of dusty books and doubtless buried in his thoughts and musings. I expect that at this moment he is drinking an expensive brandy, which professionalism sadly prohibits us from doing. But at any rate, I think I'll wander over to the hall just to be closer to the man that we're here to protect."

"Are you going to disturb his reading?" asked Hirter.

Waldbaer thought a moment and then shook his head. "No. Winterloch has the door shut, if past behavior is a guide. I won't disturb him unless I have a real need."

Hirter shrugged. "Then let me go over to the hall. If it's just a matter of having somebody stand guard outside of the Great Hall, I can play the sentry. If everything seems all right, I'll be back in twenty minutes or so. If Steiner shows up, I'll hurry back because I think that you'll want to greet him personally."

"Exactly, Hirter," Waldbaer said with a smile. "And if you need me, you can reach me on the cell phone."

With that, Hirter placed his hands in his pockets and wandered off down the corridor, his feet echoing on the ancient stone.

* * *

Steiner hunched forward and moved with careful steps, his Docker shoes scraping on the stone floor of the tunnel. The tunnel was not broad and gave him only the clearance of an inch or two on either side. The walls of the passageway and its ceiling were raw, pounded earth, occasionally laced with the roots of centuries-old trees located above. The air was cold and damp and choking, and Steiner subdued an inclination to gag. Still, he had been here before and knew that the tunnel was nearly a kilometer long and would bring him to the interior of the castle, far from the outer walls. He had come across mention of the unused passage in an old architectural tract and had trudged about the fortress wall until he had found the tunnel entrance and its door buried in the ground, still intact after centuries. He had told no one and devised a way of his own to use the covert entrance to the castle keep.

Steiner's flashlight beam reflected on the subterranean out-croppings of brown earth and the rude stone floor and told him that no one else had violated the passageway in the interim. There was much about the castle spaces that was unexplored and un-known to the residents, and to anyone else. Even Andreas Pichler, the murdered handyman who knew much about the castle, had not known of the tunnel, Steiner was sure of it. It reconfirmed his judgment on the gross stupidity of men.

The passage was now rising slightly, and Steiner estimated that he would be at the other end in ten minutes' time. He felt the Luger, cold and unyielding, tight against his belt. He felt poorly but forced himself to put one foot in front of the other. His unan-ticipated appearance, he had reason to believe, would prove most dismaying to his victim.

* * *

Waldbaer leaned back against the wall and took in the dramatic scene of the oil painting opposite him. It was an old representa-tion of a battle between a Christian army of armored knights and a ferocious Muslim force, the colors darkened by age.

In the painting, the Christians were clearly winning. Swords drawn in unison, their visors down, the knights on horseback gestured heroically toward the enemy in panicked flight. For their part, the turbaned Muslims and their chargers were overcome with fear of the attackers and they abandoned their scimitars and spears along with all hope. At the head of the advancing column of knights, banners unfurled above them, a lone figure rode his horse, the mailed fingers of one hand curled around a broadsword. He wore no helmet, and his blond hair fell around the shining black armor at his shoulders. The knight pointed an iron-gloved hand to the sky, where, in the distance, the sun was rising over the scene of a just victory.

But was it really so, Waldbaer wondered. Were not the as-sembled battle-hardened Arabs a worthy enemy, little related to the caricatures painted on the piece of canvas? He wondered about the swarthy, panicked faces of the Muslims as they fled the battle scene in their billowing robes and curled slippers. And curiously, given the hacking and slashing hand-to-hand combat, there was no blood at all captured in oil. It is artistic license, Waldbaer concluded. He stared at the helmetless knight again and wondered if it was meant to be Count Heinrich, the lord of slaughter. For all of his battles, lost and won, the well-preserved Heinrich was now in his grave beneath the castle chapel. Waldbaer recalled that during the Crusades not only Muslims but ostensibly Christian men and women had often been cut down and eviscerated or raped by bands of knights and mercenaries who often resembled hordes of murderous bandits out to loot and pillage. The Middle Ages was by no means a time of chivalry and gentleness. Nor, for that matter, was the present.

With a low sigh, Waldbaer tugged the Glock from his shoulder holster and gave it a quick check. A round was in the chamber, and the safety lock was engaged. Tonight Steiner will come, he will come, Waldbaer insisted to himself; he willed it.

* * *

The tunnel came to an abrupt end, and Steiner let out a sigh of relief. A thick slab of wood covered the threshold of the passageway and blocked every sliver of light from escaping the room within. Beyond the slab of wood which, in fact, formed an entranceway, lay the Great Hall of the Winterloch castle. Using his flashlight, Steiner located the heavy door handle, an arched semicircle of partially decayed metal. He pressed his ear closely to the wood and listened. For a moment, he thought that he heard the distinct clinking of a glass decanter, but he could not be certain. He forced himself to breathe deeply of the dank air. "No time like the present, so let's get on with the show," he whispered to himself. Then he placed both hands around the piece of metal and rolled the door open to the light.

CHAPTER THIRTY-THREE

Count Winterloch's ear caught the sound of slight resistance as the door to the passageway hissed open, stirring a layer of dust to brief, swirling life. He turned on his leather heels to see a rectangle of gaping darkness where a moment before an expanse of polished wood had been. From the murky hole of darkness there was a display of movement as a man shuffled forward, taking tenuous, uneven steps. In a moment the man was in the room, staring directly at the count.

Winterloch was struck nearly speechless, less by the man's presence than by the gaunt and wasted look on an otherwise familiar face. "My dear God! Can it be Tobias?" he cried, his voice disintegrating into a moan.

The pallid face was covered in sweat, and the vision swayed unsteadily. A smile much like a rictus crossed the face of Steiner. "It's me. The one and only."

The count moved forward to steady him. Steiner held out a hand and muttered, "Don't try it." Something in the voice made Winterloch stop.

"Tobias, what in God's name is this? What is this door and where does it go? I've been thinking about you. Come here and sit down." Winterloch grabbed for a chair, pulling it away from the oak table.

"I will stand. And the concealed door that even you didn't know about? Why, I discovered it over a year ago, and apparently no one else has found it. You remember last year, when I was here for two weeks, don't you? I told you then that a truly energetic man must never be idle. Well, I wasn't idle at all. You burrowed through those useless histories, and I read more practical tracts in your collection. All castles dating to the Middle Ages had a hidden tunnel or two, didn't you know that? I found a notation about where I could find the passageway, hidden for all those years, and find it I did. The tunnel is burrowed under the earth from the outer walls to the Great Hall. But no matter, you were absorbed in history, reading words about the distant and boring and very dead past, and I read about how I could gain covert entrance to this place." He wheezed out a chuckle.

Winterloch stared at his son as if he were an apparition. "Tobias, I must tell you that the police are here. There is a Kommissar, and he's looking for you. He said you'd show up, and I frankly didn't believe him."

Steiner flashed cavernous eyes at Winterloch. "A Kommissar? How impressive. You know, I wrote a letter to the police and left it in my apartment in Garmisch. I addressed it to the Man in Charge. Perhaps this is him in the flesh. I'll certainly see him soon. But first and foremost, I have an item of business to conclude."

Confused, Winterloch wondered about the cold, acidic tone and indifference of Tobias' words. He was talking like a stranger.

Winterloch collected his thoughts. "The Kommissar is heading the investigation into the plague, yes. Tobias, you are severely unwell, I can see it. You should rest a bit, compose yourself, and then give yourself up to the police. Let me pour you a drink."

"No," said Steiner, the loud invective startling Winterloch. "I don't want a damned drink. You see, Count, I'd immediately vomit it up. That's what this wretched cancer does to the system, it eats everything away; it's devouring me. And just so you know, I will by no means be surrendering to the police or to the Kommissar. I have one final act to complete." He issued a skeletal smile that made Winterloch grow cold.

"Tobias, nothing on God's earth can ease my pain. Let me call the Kommissar. He'll have an ambulance here in twenty minutes, maybe less. We'll get you to a hospital."

Steiner grasped the Luger at his belt and pulled it free, pointing it at the count. He planted his feet apart, in an effort to minimize his constant swaying. "No damned Kommissar and no ambulance."

"Tobias, what's wrong?" It was all the count could think of to say.

Steiner started to laugh, but it quickly broke into a gagging retch. A gush of earth-toned fluid cascaded from his mouth, staining his shirt, jeans, and shoes. He breathed in deeply for a few moments and swiped a hand, moist with sweat, across his lips.

"What's wrong? Do you mean what's wrong with me? I fear I'm repeating myself: I have terminal cancer, a corrosive growth in my guts. It's eating my organs and will kill me soon enough. Do those harsh words perhaps upset my father? But then, you don't particularly like my calling you *father*, do you?"

Winterloch reasoned that it was best to be solicitous. Tobias had never seemed so hostile before. "It doesn't matter, Tobias, you are my son, that is our shared bond. Not on paper, but in blood."

"There will be considerable blood before this is over," Steiner said.

"I'm the last of the line, Tobias. No one knew you would get this terrible cancer, no one could know. But we're in this together now."

Steiner's features turned angry. "Oh, please, Father, cut the crap. My having cancer doesn't change anything. I didn't measure up to your obsessive, self-absorbed inclination of what a Winterloch should be, and neither did my long-dead mother. You made that entirely clear all those years ago when we first met, and you've never strayed from that position. You tried to buy me off by writing a flurry of checks. You figured money is the solution to every problem. It's not, and it was never a solution to me." He lifted the pistol with effort until it afforded a clear shot at Winterloch's abdomen.

Winterloch registered the movement of the Luger directed at

him with sudden horror. "Tobias, what do you mean to do with that handgun?"

Tobias responded matter of factly. "I intend to shoot and kill you, Father. The magazine has eight bullets. That's more than enough to finish you off, don't you think?"

Stunned, it took Winterloch a moment to respond. "Tobias, why in God's name would you want to shoot me? I've been enormously generous to you, and we've never had an argument, not once. You want to shoot me here, murder me, in the castle hall?"

Steiner again hacked out a laugh. "I expect to shoot you here, yes. The Kommissar will hear the report and come running, and I'll shoot him, too. As for my murdering you, well, that's only fair, isn't it? It's retribution. After all, you murdered me."

Winterloch could not comprehend the spindly, sweating wraith before him. "I don't understand, Tobias, I simply don't understand," he said, his voice a whisper.

Steiner regarded the count as if he were an untutored schoolboy. "My God, you're nothing but a study in narcissism. You murdered me, that's clear enough, isn't it? The day I showed up to claim what was rightly mine, you rejected me utterly. The grounds you gave for not taking me as your heir were laughable. Propriety, you said, and your so-called standing in the community of nobles. You meant that you were ashamed of the liaison with my mother, that she somehow wasn't worthy of you and deserved only a tryst, that she wasn't good enough to be taken seriously. She wasn't of noble birth, and according to your logic, I wouldn't be either. So you did what you've always done. You offered me money, take it or leave it, as if I were a cheap prostitute. Well, I decided to take it and cut my losses. After all, it put me through school and got me a doctorate. But from the very day I took your money, I had you in my mind and in my sights. Now you will pay the price of having denied me my name, and the castle, and society. I am a von Winterloch, as much as you."

Winterloch had his eyes trained on the pistol as he spoke.

"Surely, Tobias, you know that's not true, it's a fantasy. The reason I didn't legally adopt you wasn't propriety, it was time. I was set in my ways and too old to change, and I didn't want the assorted problems of signing endless documents and legal depositions and God knows what else. And I admit, I'm a comfortable bachelor; I guess that's what I've always been. I thought that I gave you access to what matters most in this world, money. You always had expenses, it's true, but I don't recall that you ever asked where the money came from. I can tell you now that it came from the investments made by my father and grandfather, and all of the various Winterlochs who preceded them."

"What of it? Do you think I could possibly care where the money came from?" Steiner growled.

The count pushed a hand through his layered mane of hair. "Tobias, we Winterlochs own stocks in industrial firms throughout Europe. I gave you very sizeable amounts of money because I felt you would use it constructively, and wisely, to build your life. There are not many who know it, but the Winterloch name owns and silently controls substantial businesses internationally, and you profited from them." Winterloch paused and his mouth felt dry. The gun was still aimed at him. "It was my decision to allow you access to the funds accumulated by the Winterlochs' initial investment. It was, in a sense, your inheritance. Perhaps I made a gross mistake considering what has come to pass. But I must ask you a question, Tobias, and it's more important than money. Did you unleash the plague? I've refused to believe it so far, because it makes no sense. I know you planted the plague in Heinrich's grave, but that was against those scum that rob the dead."

Steiner moved with unsteady gait toward the paneled wall and leaned heavily on it, wiping a glistening sheen of sweat from his face. "I'm delighted you asked that question, Father. Of course I started the plague, who else could do it if not me? The plague has always fascinated me, even obsessed me, ever since high school. Look at how the disease progressed and the chaos that resulted. It very nearly wiped out humanity in Europe at a single

stroke, and no one was immune. If you think about it, you'll realize that most people in the world both then and now are mental defectives anyway; the great mass of men, the majority in fact,
are no better than idiots. So you might say that I engaged in a
cleansing operation. When you mentioned that you were afraid
of thieves invading the crypt, it occurred to me that would be a
marvelous way to begin to migrate the plague from Madagascar to
Europe. Don't you find my creative impulse absolutely delicious,
Father? Anyway, the trash that robbed the grave were just the first
victims. Since then, many more people have succumbed, and on
three continents at last count. I take pride in that. It was a simple
matter of bringing infected fleas together with the public. So to
answer your question, yes, the plague is my creation. The victims
of the plague are my victims."

Winterloch's features had grown florid, and he was aware
that his heartbeat had accelerated. "But you don't even know
those people who died of the plague. They were innocent men
and women. Tobias, something isn't right with you."

Steiner showed his teeth and a trail of mucous dripped
unnoticed from a nostril. "These people are of no account, Father. I
don't expect you to see that. Forget about morality, it's just an illusion.
And your caring about these so-called victims is gross hypocrisy. You
care only about yourself and this precious castle and the family name."

Rheinhold von Winterloch's face hardened and he set his
jaw. "You are lost to me, Tobias, utterly lost. I cannot understand
or sympathize with the wrong you have done. You are, as the
Kommissar said, a murderer."

Steiner's eyes narrowed. "Spare me your further stupid com-
ments. Here's a little something for you." He lowered the gun and
pulled the trigger. The air exploded and resonated in the Great
Hall as the round caught the count in the upper leg and sent him
crashing to the floor.

"My God," bellowed Winterloch, seizing his leg with his
hand, immediately aware of warm, pulsing blood covering his
trousers.

"Please don't pass out. I want you to see the coup de grace. I've thought about this for years and prepared it especially for you, Father." Steiner eased a dagger from his pocket, weighing its heft in his hand.

Through frantic eyes, Winterloch saw a golden grip embossed with jewels that formed an amber cross, glittering in the hall's indirect light. The braided and glittering pommel ended at a black cross-hilt, and beneath it extended a six-inch, double-edged blade, sharp as a razor. "What are you doing?" he gasped.

Steiner wielded the pistol in one hand and gripped the dagger in the other. "I found this here, hidden among the books and parchments. The texts that describe this dagger claim that it belonged to Heinrich. It is a ceremonial piece, but he could have used it in fighting his various wars. I thought of you when I discovered it. What better way to meet one's end than to be stabbed by the blade of an ancestor? After all, you avoided the plague, the new Black Death, just like Augustin did. I've christened you Augustin, Father. You remember *Augustin*, don't you? As the old song goes, 'oh, beloved Augustin, everyone's dead'. Well, you won't avoid the blade of your noble predecessor. The past crashes against the present. You might say that it's a collision of centuries."

"You've gone entirely mad," groaned Winterloch as he attempted to staunch the flow of blood from his leg.

"That may be. We'll enjoy the world of the dead together, if you believe in an afterlife, Father. Call it heaven, or call it hell."

* * *

The report of the Luger resounded throughout the castle. It stopped Robert Hirter in his tracks along a seemingly endless arched corridor, on his way to the Great Hall. He raced toward the direction of the sound. Underneath a sconce lamp he noticed a plaque with a rusting medieval mace on the wall. He stopped and tore the weapon from its placard with a screech of wood and was gratified that the implement did not disintegrate in his hands. It was old and heavy, but it was still a weapon. Without time to formulate a plan, he continued to run down the corridor toward the distant hall.

* * *

Waldbaer was jolted by the blast of the Luger and pitched upright from his position leaning against a wall. He recognized the sound. An intruder was in the castle. Heaving himself out of the Hall of Banners, he unholstered his own handgun hidden beneath his loden jacket and flicked the safety off.

How in the hell did he get in here? He knew that Steiner must be inside the castle. Waldbaer pulled a cell phone from his pocket and called the Gamsdorf police station for immediate backup. "Get every available policemen up to Schloss Winterloch immediately. Shots fired!"

Waldbaer had another worry. Where was Hirter?

* * *

"No. Please don't do it, Tobias," Winterloch pleaded.

Steiner was whispering a song. "Oh, beloved Augustin, Augustin, everyone's dead." His voice lilted and turned, barely loud enough to be heard as he clutched the dagger in his fist.

The door to the Great Hall burst open, exploding with a mass of hard flesh and muscle against wood as Hirter crashed in. He saw the two figures in a split second, one lying on the floor and the other hovering above him, a pallid ghost in light and shadow standing over him with a gun and knife. Hirter saw that the prostrate man was bleeding. He decided in a split second to charge and hunched his frame to offer Steiner less of a target, as the bald man raised the pistol unsteadily.

Hirter lunged toward Steiner like a football player going for a goal. He heard the loud crack of another round, this time fired at him. The round slammed into the wall behind him, but Hirter's leg connected with the table, and he pitched forward. Aware that he was falling, Hirter aimed and pitched the battle mace full force at Steiner. The mace flew through the air led by the spiked flange and followed by its solid iron chain. The ball of heavy iron with its inch-long spikes slammed into Steiner's shoulder with force, causing him to crash to his knees with a loud cry, flinging the dagger away.

As Hirter tried to pick himself up from the floor, Steiner raised the Luger and fired. He aimed for the center of Hirter's chest, and the pistol kicked in his hand as the round found its target.

Hirter jerked back with a gurgled moan. He lay flat on his back with one leg bent at the knee and a pool of blood gathering on his chest, staining his shirt bright red. His body went numb and he wondered whether he was dying.

Steiner groaned loudly. The mace was embedded in his flesh, having torn through his shirt at the shoulder. Lifting a palsied hand, he felt the metal ball and its rows of serrated blades. Holding his breath, he yanked the device from his flesh and collapsed on the floor from the immediate and brutal surge of pain. Breathing in deep gulps, his eyes focused on the dagger, now located several feet away. He turned his head toward Winterloch and saw the look of horror with which the count regarded Steiner. A smile made its way through the cracked lips across his face.

Oh, beloved Augustin, Augustin,
Everyone's dead.

* * *

The second report of the Luger caught Waldbaer by surprise. He realized that the shot could have been the end of Winterloch, and for that matter, of Hirter as well. "*Scheisse*," he murmured as he ran toward the hall where the half-lit corridor led into a spacious anteroom. Moving through the chamber, firearm pointed in front of him, Waldbaer surveyed the scene. The room was unscathed by any trace of violence, and an archway revealed an open door to the Great Hall. Breathing hard, Waldbaer proceeded, his handgun in the lead.

He stayed back from the open door, not wishing to make a target, holding the Glock in both hands. He listened for sounds from the hall to determine his course of action.

* * *

Steiner found the gold-pommeled dagger with effort and struggled to his feet. He held the Luger loosely in his other hand and in a shuffling gait struggled to Winterloch.

The count was lying still, unable to move without excessive pain. His hands were slick with blood from his leg wound. He watched transfixed as Steiner staggered toward him. "Please don't kill me, Tobias," he groaned in a dry whisper, "I've done nothing, absolutely nothing, to you. For as long as I've known you, I've always given you whatever you have wanted."

Steiner looked at him with glazed eyes. "You've done rather enough, Father. You'll have to excuse the interruption, but I took care of the Kommissar."

Winterloch glanced at Hirter's form and did not correct his son's error, hoping that the real Waldbaer was near. "Perhaps I'll show you how a von Winterloch dies, Tobias. I'm sorry it has come to this, but I'll be damned if I don't die proudly and with honor."

Steiner spit out his reply. "Nobility is just another quaint illusion for the weak minded, Father. You will feel pain and terror before all of this ends, unfortunately just not as much pain as I am suffering. Quite aside from the cancer, it was you who destroyed me. Unleashing the plague gave me great pleasure. And putting an end to you will be exquisite."

* * *

Waldbaer heard the words as a murmur, but guessed that Steiner was the originator. He could make out Winterloch's voice as well, signaling that the count was alive, but the strain in his tone made it evident that he was wounded. The detective could see no trace of Hirter, nor hear him inside of the hall. But he must have heard the shots and rushed into the great room, possibly connecting with a bullet. Waldbaer felt a mixture of fury and guilt at the situation. He greatly admired this American and he did not want him to die, not here.

Cautious not to make a sound, Waldbaer maneuvered toward the wall of the hall to reach the door. He held the Glock above his head in a hand that was shaking slightly. He judged that he would have to barge into the room, fall to his knees, and fire. His actions needed to be instantaneous.

* * *

Steiner flexed his hand around the pommel of the dagger, feeling the pattern of gold caress his flesh. He felt his strength waning, as if it were being drained out of him. Now is the time to finish this!

* * *

Winterloch considered what to do about his son's approach. There were very few options. He drew his arm over his chest, hoping to protect his heart from the first strike of the blade. He struggled to remain conscious, but his loss of blood was severe. Perhaps I should just prepare to die, he thought, and then angrily dismissed the reflection as cowardice. He would fight his demise and would not go passively like a sheep.

"Move your damned arm," Steiner rasped, drooling.

"You'll have to do that for yourself, I'm afraid," replied Winterloch.

"Then die anyway, you old bastard," Steiner shouted, lunging down and driving the sharpened blade into the count's forearm, beneath the elbow.

Winterloch screamed and used his final burst of strength to slam Steiner in the knee with his uninjured leg.

Steiner yelped in pain, and pitched forward. He landed on his thigh, hitting the floor heavily as he moaned, "You miserable son of a bitch!"

* * *

Waldbaer heard the chaotic struggle from inside the Great Hall. Placing the Glock in front of his frame, he bolted into the room.

* * *

Out of the corner of his eye, Steiner saw a burst of motion, a shock of dark hair and what appeared to be a form in a leather jacket. "No you don't!" he screamed as a pistol came into his line of vision. Frantically, from where he was kneeling, Steiner managed to pull the long oaken table down in front of him. The table provided cover, and he huddled behind it. Dropping the dagger, Steiner held the Luger now in both hands. His breathing was heavy and erratic.

* * *

Waldbaer had gotten a fleeting look at Tobias Steiner, a deathly gaunt vision with cavernous eyes, as he had pulled the table to the floor as cover. Glancing around, he saw the prostate form of Robert Hirter, sprawled out on the floor with a pool of blood emanating from his chest and puddling by his side. The CIA officer was motionless. He wanted to call out to Hirter, but first he needed to stop the man who had shot the American.

"Steiner, you're under arrest. It ends here. Throw down the gun and then come out slowly with both of your hands raised."

The room was filled by a wheezing cackle which was transformed into a prolonged hacking cough. Waldbaer held his pistol with both hands steadily in front of him. The muzzle of the weapon was aimed at the center of the overturned tabletop.

"Well, well, you must be the Man in Charge," Steiner spit out. "You will forgive me, but I thought that I had already killed you. I was mistaken. But the other fellow must be a policeman. He came barging in, and I shot him dead."

Waldbaer realized he must mean Hirter, and that Steiner thought him a subordinate to the detective. Waldbaer prayed that Steiner was mistaken and that Hirter remained alive.

"But I'm glad to see the real Man in Charge. You're here to rescue my father, but I'm afraid that you're a little late for that patrician act. And as for surrendering, why don't you just come over here and ask me politely."

Waldbaer played for time and advantage. It was clear to him that either Steiner would be killed, or he would. He estimated the thickness of the overturned table from his kneeling position, yards away. The table appeared old and solidly built. A bullet from his Glock was unlikely to penetrate it. He would have to think of something else; buying a few seconds time was the only course available.

"Steiner, you're smart enough to know it's over. Throw your gun over the table. You know you're sick, and you know that the cancer is terminal, just look at yourself. You've only got a couple of weeks at most. Give yourself at least the opportunity to die with some dignity."

Waldbaer hoped that mention of Steiner's disease would shock the gunman. He waited for the reply.

Steiner emitted a guttural sound, clotted thick with rage. "You pompous bastard. I hate to disappoint you, but I'm still very much alive at present. Come over here and see for yourself, I dare you."

Waldbaer decided to take another tack. "It's not worth it, Steiner. Nothing is working out the way that you intended, is it? Your work with the plague was flawed; there's no pandemic now, and there won't be a pandemic. For whatever reason, the plague is no Black Death anymore. You've killed lots of people, it's true, but not nearly a fraction as many as you anticipated. Your attempt to bioengineer the pestilence clearly failed. In my estimation, that means you, yourself, are a failure. Like all criminals, you are, in the end, a loser. As for killing your father, you may be able to do that. But then I'll take you down, I swear it."

Steiner yelled in rage and flung an arm holding the Luger over the table and fired. Waldbaer pitched forward as one bullet impacted the floor, and a second round also went wild. Waldbaer fired once into the tabletop, but saw that his bullet was stopped by the thick wood. He concluded that even in his foaming fury, Steiner was keeping his body safe and secure behind the table.

A long moan filled the expanse of the room. Winterloch's voice, Waldbaer knew, meaning that the count was alive, but for how long, he could not calculate. He needed to find a way to take Steiner down quickly, or both the count and Hirter would bleed to death.

* * *

Hirter had lost consciousness but found himself stirred awake and suddenly awash in pain. He drew in a shallow breath and opened his eyes, recognizing the whitewashed, high vaulted ceiling of the Great Hall. He remembered that Tobias Steiner had fired at him, that the bullet had knocked him down, that he was bleeding. He must have a round buried in his chest. When he tried to turn his head a degree, he felt pain, a dull, oppressive ache. Without further moving his head, his eyes took in the scene around him.

In his peripheral vision, he saw the count, unmoving but visibly breathing. Immediately behind him lay an overturned table with a bullet round in the polished veneer. He estimated that the table provided cover for Steiner. There was a rustling sound from somewhere behind Hirter's head, and he knew it had to be Waldbaer, who would certainly be cradling a pistol.

"Steiner, your aim is no damned good, no good at all, in fact it's pitifully bad. It's no better than your efforts to mutate the plague. It embarrasses me to say it, but you shoot like a child, or even worse, an amateur." He listened as Waldbaer attempted to goad Steiner into making an ill-considered move.

Hirter believed he could assist the situation and tried to move his right arm, feeling it twitch in a wave of torment. With intense effort, his hand found and entered the pocket of his trousers, inch by inch.

* * *

Steiner had to kill the count, that alone mattered. He would use his gun and dispense with the dagger. It was too late for death to be delivered with the planned elegance. Winterloch was in front of the table, and Steiner knew his approximate location. He reasoned that if he fired from the tabletop in the direction where the count lay, his chances of scoring a hit would be good. He checked the safety lock of the semi-automatic and grasped the butt of the weapon.

* * *

Hirter had found the cluster of coins in his pocket and his fingers closed around them. He felt some U.S. quarter dollars, the largest coins in his possession. He felt a one euro coin and other round shapes as well, and realized they were a mix of American and European currency. Hirter knew that he would have to act quickly, or risk unconsciousness again overtaking him. He tried to judge the distance to the overturned table.

* * *

Steiner pressed his frame to the wood of the table and held his pistol at the ready. He would shoot the count, that was certain, and then he would aim for the Kommissar. If he were killed in the process, he reasoned, so be it. Although he did not welcome death, neither did he fear it. To take a bullet was brutal, but it would be a release and far better than wasting away of cancer. He placed both feet firmly on the floor, ready to spring.

* * *

Hirter had the coins wrapped in his fist and pulled his arm slowly from the pocket of his trousers. He felt their heft and wondered if his scheme would work. If not, he would just draw fire and that could well be fatal. He forced that thought aside. He hoped that Waldbaer could react instantaneously as everything depended on it. Inhaling and exhaling deliberately, Hirter felt a flash of pain in his arm as he flung the handful of coins into the air, glittering in the light and flying in an arc toward the table.

* * *

The coins were half-seen shapes that reflected the light and engaged Steiner's side vision. Tense and reactive and full of adrenaline, he thought for a split second that Waldbaer was rushing to attack him. He rose up from the cover of the table firing the Luger, as if at a clay pigeon in a game of skeet. As the coins fell to the floor with a thin metallic resonance, he was confused.

* * *

Waldbaer did not see the coins but heard them cling and roll as they fell to earth and tumbled around the floor. He saw Steiner's head and shoulders rise up suddenly over the protective tabletop. Waldbaer locked on the target and fired three rounds in rapid succession. One round went wild, but the next two hit Steiner in the chest and knocked him backward with a massive jolt, leaving him swaying like a drunken man.

Steiner looked strangely perplexed, and blood poured from his open mouth, but he still managed to aim the Luger at Winterloch's crumpled form.

Waldbaer fired two more shots, felt the pistol kick in his hand, and saw Steiner spin like a dervish and go down, arms flailing above his head, the gun flying from his hand. He stood still for a second, showing his back to Waldbaer, took a step, then crashed to the ground.

Waldbaer's hands were shaking and he drew his arms to his side in an effort to steady them. Rising to a standing position and aiming his weapon at his target, he inched forward. Tobias Steiner was in front of him, the young man had collapsed on his knees, his torso facing the ceiling. The face was an uneven mask of blood from the nostrils and mouth. Waldbaer sprang up, closed the remaining space and, still staring down the barrel of his gun, saw that Steiner's eyes were open, like many who die violently. Rest in peace, you narcissistic bastard, he thought, and then shook the sentiment from his head as unworthy.

A prolonged groan brought Waldbaer to Hirter's side. He noted that his CIA colleague's eyes were open, but with relief, saw that the American was blinking them, and his focus seemed intact. Blood covered Hirter's chest, and Waldbaer grabbed a pocket handkerchief from his jacket to help staunch the flow.

"I'll be okay, Kommissar, the bullet's lodged in my chest, I think," Hirter said in a low whisper, "but you had better check the count. He went down before I did."

This Waldbaer did, finding Winterloch pale and unconscious. One of his arms twitched spasmodically. Waldbaer located the leg wound and took off his belt to make a tourniquet, cinching it tightly.

A burst of rapid footsteps caused Waldbaer to raise his Glock again and to aim it toward the open door. But the gangly form of Braun and three other policemen appeared at the threshold, all of them brandishing handguns. "You're a bit late to the dance, gentlemen. The show is over, boys," Waldbaer called out. "We need two ambulances for the wounded. The third fellow over here is dead, so there's no hurry with him." Waldbaer gave a concerned glance to Hirter again and saw that he was smiling.

CHAPTER THIRTY-FOUR

The plague in Europe and the United States remained front-page news until the number of survivors grew exponentially. Gradually, the news of death by communicable disease was replaced by other stories, serious and mundane. Reports of political improprieties and celebrity scandals took over the pages of newspapers until the reemergence of Yersinia pestis was quite forgotten.

Waldbaer visited Hirter at the Munich Emergency Hospital in the suburb of Schwabing every other day, bringing chocolates and magazines and, on this occasion, concealed half-liter bottles of lager beer.

"You know, Kommissar, I'm not sure that I will be allowed to take this with me when they fly me out of Landstuhl," Hirter said, gazing at the bottle of Augustiner.

Waldbaer nodded. "You're quite right, Hirter. Better to drink it here; you never know."

Hirter laughed and placed the beer bottle, smiling monk on the label, on his bedside table. "I've been wondering about Steiner and what he did. Did he almost replicate the Black Death? He was certainly trying to do so. He could have screwed up the mutation process and made the plague less virulent without knowing it. Dr. Nilsson in Sweden and other experts tell me that people today are more robust and resilient than they were centuries ago, but still I wonder."

Waldbear nodded. "I'm not a doctor, Hirter, why ask me? But I am a natural skeptic. What I think happened is this. Steiner was far too sure of himself and too contemptuous of others. I suspect that Steiner made mistakes. For one thing, he took the advice of a Russian weapons scientist on how to reengineer the plague. But the Russian scientist was a world-class drunkard, hardly a paragon of superior knowledge. And Steiner acquired his fleas with the disease in their guts through his so-called research in Madagascar. If you really think about it, the Madagascar plague is nasty and it's deadly, but it isn't, for whatever reason, bad enough to cause a pandemic. Madagascar has cases of the plague every year, but never an epidemic. If you want my view, we've been lucky, very lucky. If another country with the entire resources of a nation at its disposal had weaponized the plague, I suspect this story might have a different, and not particularly pleasant, ending. But I suppose we'll never know. I suspect we don't want to know. We don't even want to think about it."

SCHLOSS WINTERLOCH

Waldbaer's dealings with Rheinhold von Winterloch were more complex. The count's wound had severed a nerve and caused him to walk permanently with the assistance of a cane. Waldbaer noticed with irritation that Winterloch had a new cane made especially for him by the local silversmith. It was of polished mahogany, and the hand rest was burnished silver. It bore the facsimile of a lion rampant, taloned legs improbably outstretched. Waldbaer withheld comment on the childishness of grown men.

"I received the artifacts that had been looted from the grave a few days ago, courtesy of the Munich police. They were placed in the crypt with the remains of Heinrich, and I hope that his sleep will never be disturbed again. I had the entire crypt sealed to prevent any further intrusion. That provides a sense of closure to this entire horrid episode."

Winterloch had more to say, and the police detective silently waited.

"I believe I owe you a word of thanks, Kommissar. No word of Tobias being my biological son has reached the press. The media has only reported that Tobias Steiner was responsible for re-engineering the plague and the reporters say nothing of his lineage. The von Winterloch name, at least, has not been dragged through the mud, at least I am spared that. You played a part in not going to the press with what was, in fact, the truth. I am humbled, Kommissar, and I am grateful."

Waldbaer responded with a slight inclination of his head. "The information on Tobias' parentage is not relevant to the public, Count. It alters nothing. I cannot guarantee that an enterprising investigative reporter doesn't pry around in the future, of course, but as far as I'm concerned, Tobias Steiner carried out this crime entirely on his own, and his actions should be the focus of attention."

Von Winterloch looked down at the sodden earth and hid his eyes from the policeman. "I will never understand, Kommissar, what happened to Tobias, and I suppose I never will. Perhaps I had something to do with it, after all. And I owe you an apology, and enormous thanks for having saved my life. You were right. Tobias tried to kill me out of resentment and hatred." The count shook his head in remorseful self-reproach. They stood outside the moss-stained walls of Schloss Winterloch on the broad expanse of lawn reaching to the tangle of solemn trees that comprised the forest. Winterloch looked old, the familiar red face worn and haggard, the thick mane of white hair hanging limply in place.

As the two men strolled toward the distant trees, Waldbaer chose his next words cautiously. "What happened to Tobias Steiner happened long ago, it seems. He felt severely wronged and in his warped view he saw you as the one to blame. But you were not to blame—I mean that, and you should reach the same conclusion. After all, Steiner had enough common sense to know what was right and what was wrong. I learned that in my grammar school catechism class. It was odious and wrong to kill hundreds of innocents with the plague. It was wrong to attempt to kill you. He knew it, and you should know it as well."

Winterloch stopped and leaned forward on his cane, closing his eyes for a moment. "I do know now that Tobias behaved criminally. He wanted a place in the von Winterloch family, which I could not give him."

Waldbaer gazed at the pines in the distance and offered nothing, neither solace nor reproach.

Count von Winterloch turned back to the castle and gestured. "He wanted Schloss Winterloch, you know, and he didn't understand what a terrible burden it is. Now Tobias is dead and gone forever, and after I die, the castle will go too."

Waldbaer watched the count looking at the structure with a certain wonder, as if for the first time.

"What will become of the castle?" he asked.

Winterloch shrugged. "It will have no individual inheritor. I am the last Winterloch, and I have no heirs. It is in my will that the castle ownership will go to the state of Bavaria just as the castles of King Ludwig did. The Bavarian government can do with the estate as they wish, the politicians can decide. I would personally like to think that they will use the castle as a museum, as a monument to the noble past, going all the way back to Heinrich."

Waldbaer wondered if the castle wasn't really a museum already. Because Winterloch had lived all his life within the cold stone walls, he failed to see it. In fact, living in the decaying fortress was very much like living in a tomb, thought the detective, but he said nothing.

Winterloch raised his head in the air, as if sniffing the breeze. "The workers will be taken care of. All of the staff, Frau Mayerhof and the others, will receive their full pension when I die," he continued. "They have, each and every one, served me well throughout the years. I'm an old man, or soon will be, Kommissar, and I have no one who will come after me."

The detective nodded but did not address the words.

Winterloch is self-absorbed, but doesn't even realize it, he mused. Waldbaer wanted suddenly to leave, and return to the world of the living.

"My police work is done here, as I'm sure you'll agree, Count. I came to uncover a murderer, and I did. The castle, by the way, well captures what it meant to live in the Middle Ages. The epoch was, after all, a testament to the times; a rapacious, brutal minority preyed upon a largely defenseless and desperately poor majority. For every knight and nobleman who dined on fine game at a table, a hundred peasants chewed toothlessly on roots in a hut, or under a tree. Museums are a doorway to the past. Things have changed today, so it's probably a good thing to remind our citizens what the past was like."

"I suspect that your sense of history is more than a bit one sided, Kommissar, but turning the castle into a museum when I'm gone is, perhaps, a good idea. People can determine if the nobility of this country conducted themselves with honor, or its opposite."

Waldbaer decided to let the count have the last word, and he said his farewells and shook hands. They would never agree. The space between them was too great, the space between their generations even greater. He looked again at the castle as he made his way to his car on the parking apron.

The brooding and stolid collection of gray, black, and green stone seemed determined to jealously hide its list of secrets, which were as long as its past. Waldbaer was glad to be rid of it. Something about the castle and those who lived there did not sit well with him. It was as if he was allergic to the stone structure and he was happy not to see it. He saw again the sally port that opened onto the Hall of Banners and its collection of must-ridden, dusty silk; a memorial to the distant, forgotten past. Why had Winterloch endeavored to maintain the castle as his home in the twenty-first century, through what folly, he wondered?

Waldbaer sighed and willed his ruminating contemplations

of ancient nobles and knights, peasants and paupers, to go far away. It was more than time to get back to the police station and his familiar office in Gamsdorf. He thought as well of driving to Innsbruck and strolling along the banks of the River Inn with Sabine Reiner. The world of the living, of the beneficent good and the malignly wicked, beckoned.

AFTERWORD

There is, of course, no plague epidemic loose in the world today, and Germany and other Central European countries have not suffered hundreds or thousands of victims in eight hundred years to the insidious disease. As stated in the novel, Yersinia pestis, the plague bacteria, resulted in the Black Death of 1348, which killed between one-fourth and one-third of Europe's population. As a footnote to that ruthlessly fatal disease from the past, contemporary construction projects often unearth the bones of victims of the Black Death who were hurriedly tossed into mass graves during the Middle Ages.

The Oriental rat flea, Xenopsylla cheopis, is widely regarded as a primary culprit of the plague epidemic and is responsible for the spread of the disease today on the island of Madagascar, where the plague constitutes a true health hazard. The number of lethal cases there, thankfully, has not risen markedly in modern times. Still, where sanitation and hygiene are atrociously poor, the fleas, vectors of the disease, will flourish. Medical specialists warn, perhaps Cassandra-like, that it is purely a matter of time before some epidemic—the plague, MERS, Ebola, or another yet unnamed disease—infects some region of the world and spreads internationally with the speed of a brush fire.

The medical specialists who survey this theoretical problem voice an additional caution. They warn that in an age where hospital-acquired infections are keeping pace with medical technology, we may not be prepared to effectively fight the disease, as was the case with the plague doctors wearing their thick glasses, black, foppish hats, and long bronze beaks in the distant, almost forgotten, Middle Ages.

ABOUT THE AUTHOR

John J. Le Beau served in the Clandestine Service of the Central Intelligence Agency (CIA) for twenty-five years and was active in countries experiencing insurgency, warfare, and terrorism. Dr. Le Beau was also Professor of National Security Studies at the George C. Marshall European Center for Security Studies in Garmisch, Germany, teaching students from the Middle East, Europe, and the United States. He is Chairman Emeritus of the Partnership for Peace Consortium's Combating Terrorism Working Group.

Collision of Evil, Le Beau's debut thriller introducing Franz Waldbaer, deals with international terrorism and was nominated Best First Novel by International Thriller Writers. The second in the Waldbaer series, *Collision of Lies*, is a contemporary tale of weapons of mass destruction. *Collision of Centuries*, the third in the series, focuses on the riveting and relevant theme of international bioterrorism. These three novels form a trifecta of realistic fiction that feature Bavarian Detective Franz Waldbaer as he takes readers to breathtaking locations around the world.

As a former CIA officer, everything that John J. Le Beau writes is submitted to the CIA for clearance; this is as true for works of fiction as it is for nonfiction. *Collision of Centuries* has been cleared by the CIA as well as its predecessor works to prevent the release of classified information.

CPSIA information can be obtained at www.ICGtesting.com
Printed in the USA
LVOW07s0856140815

449685LV00004B/4/P

9 781608 091621